To Owen, Rosalie, Calvin, and
Benjamin, and to anyone who
dreams of remarkable futures.

The science and designs in this story are real. Mostly.

CONTENTS

First Ascent

Book One in the Ascending Carbon Series

Douglas Phillips

First published 2025
ISBN 9 798316 552047
Proton Books LLC
522 W Riverside Ave Ste N
Spokane, WA 99201 USA

http://douglasphillipsbooks.com

A NOTE TO READERS

This story features a wide range of measures. It's also set in the future, so let's pretend that all nations have finally agreed that base ten is super cool and everyone speaks using the metric system. (I'm pretty sure you'd tire if I kept switching between two systems of measure, so let's not go there.) For those not used to metric in their daily life, this table may be helpful:

Metric:	Equivalent to:	Imperial:
1 micrometer	Spider silk	0.000039 inches
1 centimeter	The width of a pen	0.39 inches
1 meter	Elbows splayed with fingertips touching	3.28 feet
1 kilometer	A 15-minute city walk (42nd St to 30th St in Manhattan)	0.62 miles
1,000 kilometers	A flight from Dallas to Denver or Baltimore to Chicago	621 miles

Carbon, the sixth element in the periodic table, is also important to the story. Carbon is a rather promiscuous atom, willing to hook up with almost anything. Carbon monoxide (CO) and carbon dioxide (CO_2) are the most familiar forms, but we often use chemical names without realizing they are carbon-based: methane (CH_4), propane (C_3H_8), ethanol (C_2H_6O), and glucose ($C_6H_{12}O_6$) are just a few. My all-time favorite carbon-based molecule is a ridiculously complex protein found in human muscle tissues called titin ($C_{169,719}H_{270,466}N_{45,688}O_{52,238}S_{911}$).

With those details out of the way, the story can begin.

1. PLATFORM

GUNNERY SERGEANT BENITO ALVAREZ rolled the helicopter's side door open, ushering in a torrent of tropical air along with the rhythmic thumps of rotor blades overhead. Scraps of paper blew around the cabin. His uniform flapped wildly. He leaned outside, straining against his seat harness. A scant hundred meters below, blue ocean rushed by.

The helicopter shot past a lazy flock of pelicans making their way toward the Galapagos Islands marked by clouds on the horizon. Behind, the coastline of Ecuador thinned to a strip of sandy lowlands backed by green mountains. Solitary white peaks stood above as if to prove that snow could exist even at the equator for anything willing to reach high enough into the sky.

Alvarez unclipped tie-downs and slid a twenty-millimeter single-barrel autocannon from its stowed position, locking the big gun to a swivel mount embedded in the cabin floor. He checked its ammunition feed and flipped its safety switch off.

Lieutenant Ortiz, their mission commander, sat in the rear-facing jump seat behind the pilots. Head down, Ortiz studied documents secured in the rushing airstream by a clipboard and a firm hand. Red letters were stamped across its first page: *NO AUTORIZADO*. Somewhere ahead they would find an offshore oil rig that had appeared overnight. It wasn't supposed to be there.

It might be a mix-up. The tugboats assigned to tow the deep-water platform into place could have arrived earlier than expected. Perhaps an oil company clerk had forgotten to check the proper box on government paperwork. It might be nothing more than an Ecuadoran official who hadn't been properly notified. Or paid.

They'd find out soon enough. The pilots would touch down on the platform's helipad, rotors still turning. Alvarez would casually drape one arm across the autocannon pointing out the door, and Lieutenant Ortiz would demand to speak to whomever was in charge. Phone calls would be made. Large amounts of money would be transferred between banks, and that would be that.

But this time might be different. The lieutenant's terse preflight briefing had cautioned all hands to be ready for anything. Apparently, no one had seen the platform being towed; it had simply appeared overnight. That fact alone suggested something illegal. The Colombian drug cartel might be involved. For that matter, the oil rig might be Peruvian, and those *Pelu-anos* were always up to something.

"*Allá*," one of the pilots yelled over the wind's roar, pointing ahead through the forward windshield.

The helicopter banked left, providing a better view out the open side door. A dark shape loomed ahead. Its flat deck was charcoal in color, supported on four dull gray pontoons rising at least two hundred meters above the sea. No shine, no glints of sunlight, as if hiding in broad daylight had been its goal all along.

Above the center of its deck, a smoothly sloping superstructure rose high into the sky like someone had inserted a tentpole beneath a coating of tar and pushed it straight up. Scattered buildings formed a perimeter along one edge, but the usual collection of cranes, pipes, and cables found on every other oil rig was missing.

The lieutenant unbuckled and squatted near the doorway's edge, looking up to the curving black cone that reached hundreds of meters into the sky. "*Dios mío!*"

He yelled to the pilots, repeatedly jabbing a finger down. They began their descent for landing.

Alvarez peered through his telescopic gunsight. No one walked the barren deck below or climbed its superstructure. But as he scanned for opponents, a sparkling mist began to form along the platform's edge. The mist roiled, growing rapidly in width and height. Pixelated, it glittered with multiple colors like holographic sequins.

Alvarez looked up from the gunsight, puzzled. With sunny skies above, fog was unlikely—sparkling fog even less so. The phantom mist now encircled the platform, stretching across their path like frost on a windowpane. The platform was still visible, but what had been a solid structure now wavered.

Straight lines crystalized within the fog, quickly joining into a six-sided geometric shape as big as the helicopter. The enormous hexagon extruded forward from its misty wall, hovering in the air like an ancient stone ghost blocking their path.

Lieutenant Ortiz saw it too. His brow furrowed. He jabbed his hand forward and shouted. A second later, the helicopter pierced the heart of the floating specter.

Just as quickly, lights began flashing across the pilots' control panel. A loud chime clanged repeatedly. Displays winked out. Mechanical dials spun. The rotor blades whined with an ever-increasing pitch. One pilot yelled, suddenly desperate to wrangle his control cyclic with both hands.

Thick mist enveloped the helicopter, blotting out the last trace of sunlight and sending jolts of turbulence through the cabin. Damp air pouring through the open door suddenly felt electric, as if a lightning bolt could strike at any second.

With one hand, Alvarez braced against the autocannon's mount. His other hand fingered the inflation pull tab for the life preserver strapped around his body. His heart pounded. Adrenaline spiked.

Ahead, a dark hole opened where platform, pontoons, and sea had once been. The hole yawned ever wider, becoming a chasm filled with the roiling mist but without any discernible boundaries. Alvarez clasped both hands together in prayer.

The helicopter pitched violently onto its side, plunged into the swirling mist… and vanished.

2. SHOWTIME

SAHALIE SPARK HURRIED DOWN the television studio hallway, ten minutes behind schedule. Manageable. Video was complete, voiceovers too. Next up was the final script run-through with her producer, Paul Reddick. It would all come together by the time the audience was seated. It always did.

An *enthusiastic* audience. Now in its second season, Sahalie's weekly streaming show, *Don't Believe It!*, was widely popular with a growing viewership. Nothing worthwhile was ever easy, but a show that debunked misinformation had its own challenges. For one, the opposition was often better funded.

Framed photographs lined the studio hallway, almost all featuring Halie (as friends called her) standing alongside people from every walk of life, some famous, others who should be. The show often drew attention to unsung heroes while exposing purveyors of misinformation and conspiracy theories. The bad guys never made it on the wall—a studio rule.

More images of Halie's smiling face could be found on billboards, at bus stops, and along metro escalators around the world—often the same photo, her arms crossed, dark hair pulled back into a neat ponytail, a side glance into the camera with a smile beginning to curl that whispered, "I know something. Want to hear?" Some called her a superstar.

The hallway opened to a small studio, its stage already lit. Self-guided cameras floated across a polished floor like electronic phantoms. At center stage, Halie's anchor desk was flanked by oversized monitors and a green screen for virtual backgrounds. Offstage right, theater seating for up to thirty guests gave the show its live—and often lively—audience, one of the reasons they'd been successful.

A few guests were already filing in.

Halie opened the door to her all-glass office overlooking the stage. Floor-to-ceiling windows along the room's opposite side looked out to Sunset Boulevard, Los Angeles. Brown hills in the distance contrasted with the white dome of the Griffith Park Observatory perched on top. Lean hard enough, and you could even see part of the Hollywood sign.

"Transparency," Paul had said when he'd first guided her into the immodest goldfish bowl. She'd taken his offhand comment to heart. A show founded in science could be nothing less.

Let everyone see what we do.

It had taken Halie sixteen years at Kolby News Service to get here. From day one, she had carved out a singular role, seeking relatable stories in science and technology while providing sensible explanations any adult could understand. She'd done dozens of three-minute reports on everything from vaccine efficacy to earthquake prediction. She'd also blazed the trail for longer spots using a catchy title: *Your Six-Minute Science Sizzle.* The format had given her time to explore deeper questions about life or the universe. *Sizzle* had earned her three Emmys—the trophies still proudly displayed on her office shelf.

Halie took a seat at a circular conference table and tapped a tablet computer to bring up this week's script: CyberBees. A tech company had created the world's first artificial bee, indistinguishable from a real bee and programmed to pollinate crops—or so they claimed. But since their funding came from the pesticide industry, the prime suspect for declining bee populations, opponents lamented that use of artificial bees would only increase the use of pesticides. Real bees would suffer.

Topics for the show typically varied between nutty and deadly serious, with CyberBees a mix of both. The claims of effective pollination were dubious, but there were suggestive hints that electronic bees could communicate with real bees via the bee waggle dance. Halie had a feeling today's audience would be all over that revelation.

Paul would be happy too. He regularly pushed for an entertaining show—funny, even. Halie was often resistant. Though Paul's format was unquestionably a hit, the show shouldn't be about poking fun at anti-science lunacy. As Halie saw it, their job was to dismantle misinformation down in the trenches. Hand-to-hand combat. Flat earthers could be laughed away, but the multibillion-dollar wellness industry or gun lobbyists armed with falsified data were another matter. Health and lives were at stake.

Unquestionably, the never-ending stream of misinformation had become fatigue-inducing. Who wouldn't get tired of yet another "proof" that the moon landings were faked? Halie's days of reporting on cool science discoveries were long gone. Now her thoughts were consumed by fraud and lies, twenty-four-seven. She was beginning to think Paul might be right; a little fun now and then might soothe the psyche.

But only a little.

A minute later, Paul walked in.

"The intro script looks fine," he said without any greeting. They'd both been in the studio for hours but tended to text each other to keep interruptions to a minimum.

"Tone okay?" Halie asked. She'd written the draft, but in this studio, collaboration mattered.

Paul pulled up a chair next to Halie and took off the reading glasses normally perched at the end of his nose. "Tone is good. We just need to avoid science snobbery at the transition."

Halie studied the text. "You're right, maybe one too many *science tells us* and *experts disagree*. I can adjust."

Transitions pulled viewers from claim to conclusion by peeling away logical fallacies and exposing the heart of a proponent's claim to scientific scrutiny. With the studio audience sworn in as jury, claims were ranked from Highly Likely to No Way in Hell. Many fell into the bottom category, hence the show's name, *Don't Believe It!* But sometimes even the wackiest of ideas had merit. Electronic bees might be one of them.

"The rest isn't elitist at all," Halie offered. "That entomology professor from UC Davis was totally into bees—just from a different perspective. His pitch for why bees make hexagonal honeycombs was brilliant. Who knew that Charles Darwin himself once weighed in on the topic?"

Paul leaned closer to survey Halie's tablet. "The clips from their CyberBee training lab are great too. All that butt waggling is kind of sexy in an odd way." He wasn't referring to bee bums. CyberBees were trained in the bee waggle dance by human instructors with wireless accelerometers taped to their backsides.

"People *are* into weird." Halie laughed.

They reviewed the remainder of the script with only minor edits, then Paul excused himself to greet incoming VIP guests. A few minutes later, Halie posted the final script to the control room director, who would add technical notes, then load the teleprompter.

A rap on the office door was followed by a studio intern peering in. He spoke with a meekness that matched the apology on his face. "Sorry, Ms. Spark... uh, Sahalie. You have a visitor? Kind of a pushy guy. Asian. His name is Kong, but I might have that name wrong, because, you know..."

"King Kong," Halie finished for him. "I don't know anybody with that name, so just thank him for stopping by and point him to the web page."

"Sorry... but he left this card. He said you'd be interested." The intern hurried over and handed Halie the card. She stared at the name in disbelief.

윤지호 동화그룹 대한민국 서울	**Yoon Ji-ho, CEO** **Dongwha Group** **Seoul, Korea**

"Yoon Ji-ho?" Halie read. "He's in the lobby?"

She would certainly recognize him. The man wasn't shy when it came to pitching his latest products. A South Korean billionaire, Yoon commanded a manufacturing consortium that built cars, aircraft, consumer electronics, and more. Halie had even done a segment on one of his inventions a few years back: Buoyant brand car seats that made the driver feel weightless. Surprisingly, the comfy seats did exactly that.

"Uh... no. Just Mr. Kong. He says he represents Yoon. The guy won't sit. He's making Jen nervous." Their receptionist wasn't the type to get nervous over nothing.

Halie stood, glancing out the office window to the studio floor. The stage manager had finished seating the audience and was giving them instructions prior to Halie's entrance. "I'm on in five minutes, and I'm doing a VIP dinner after the show. Get the man's phone number. I'll call him when I can."

Halie knew the game. When corporate types came calling it meant they were looking for a promotional partner. Halie's three million social media followers could create an instant buzz for a new product. It might also be a ploy to get ahead of negative publicity for an existing flaw. Whatever it was, Halie wasn't biting—even for a billionaire.

"If Mr. Kong gives you any trouble or keeps bothering Jen, call security. They'll take care of it."

"Yes, ma'am, I can do that." The intern left with renewed confidence. A new hire, young, but he seemed bright. A small confrontation might be good experience for him.

Halie stepped in front of a full-length mirror, took a deep breath, and cleared her mind. She brushed away stray lint from her blue suit, then added a striped scarf at the neck. Shoulder-length dark brown hair framed her face with a few loose strands to keep things interesting. Off camera, she normally kept makeup to a hint of blush or lip gloss, but on camera was a different matter; she'd let the makeup pros work their magic during the audience warm-up.

"Showtime," she said to her reflection.

Halie dropped down the half flight of stairs into the studio and caught the eye of the stage manager who waved her in. She strode on stage to enthusiastic applause from the audience along with a boisterous cheer from one guy in the back wearing a *Don't Believe It!* t-shirt.

Stopping at the stage's edge, she calmed the crowd with open hands. "Thanks, everyone, and welcome. I'm Sahalie Spark…" More applause. "Very kind, thank you. We'll get the show underway in a few minutes, and, as I'm sure you know… *you* are part of it. We'll present the case, you listen to the evidence, then decide what's real and what's not. You don't need to be a scientist, but you will need to summon two talents I know you have. One is your common sense, which, for example, should tell you things like… oh, I don't know… that the US Department of the Interior isn't part of a global conspiracy preventing us from learning the Earth is hollow?"

The audience laughed. The guy in the back yelled out, "Hear, hear!"

"The other talent you'll need is *reasonable* skepticism. Don't be a denier, but pretend you're from Missouri, the Show Me state. Look for evidence. If it's not there…" She raised her hands like an orchestra conductor, and the audience chanted in unison, "DON'T BELIEVE IT!"

Halie smiled. "I see we have talented people here today."

The makeup woman brought out a chair and Halie sat. "While she tones down the reflective glow on my forehead, I'm happy to answer a few questions."

Hands shot up, and she picked several people, including one child who asked about the cameras circling around the stage. Halie explained they were basically intelligent robots that had learned the script plus cues entered by the control room director. The cameras would zoom in or draw back as Halie spoke or would point to the audience at appropriate moments. They could even single out who was speaking. When the kid replied, "That's dope!" one camera swiveled toward him.

"See, it found you!" Halie said.

Makeup and audience prep complete, Halie took her chair behind the anchor desk. The stage manager advised the crowd to get comfortable—react, but don't interrupt—then took his position in the shadows backstage. Lights were adjusted. Cameras drifted into position. A disembodied director's voice came over the intercom. "When you're ready, Halie."

She looked to the nearest camera, flashed a genuine smile, then read from the teleprompter below. "Good evening and welcome. I'm Sahalie Spark, and you're watching *Don't Believe It!*"

She kept her tone cheery and informal, with pauses in the right places to create a casual warmth. Some might call it a performance, but her on-air persona wasn't just for the studio audience or the millions more on the other side of the camera lens. Her fans were simply good friends she hadn't yet met.

Halie turned to the camera at her right. "Tonight, we dive deep into a topic that's sure to leave you with a buzz. I hinted at it last week." She briefly closed her eyes, nodding. "Yup. CyberBees."

A side monitor displayed a video clip of a man who didn't seem to mind as hundreds of bees crawled across his neck and face. When he picked one off, the camera zoomed in. Callouts popped up to identify parts of the artificial bee: mechanized wings, embedded microchips, and a Bluetooth receiver.

Halie delivered the voiceover, "They look and act like bees, but they're actually tiny robots in disguise. CyberBees Incorporated claims these fuzzy drones can shoulder the job of crop pollination as bee populations decline. Handy for farmers—but only if it works, and there are troubling undertones to this story. For one, development money comes from the primary killers of bees, the hundred-billion-dollar pesticide industry. But CyberBees Inc. counters by explaining they're doing everything they can to support real bees. In fact, they claim their electronic bees can teach real bees to *take the day off* when farmers spray their fields with pesticides. How does this advance warning happen, you ask? Via the waggle dance that bees use to communicate with each other."

The video switched to a woman with yellow plastic boxes stuck to her hips. Each box featured a small antenna. LEDs flashed as she swung her lower body left and right. An inset showed a bee making similar moves using its black and yellow striped abdomen.

With titters coming from the audience, Sahalie lifted her eyebrows. One camera pulled in tight. "Join me as we search for the truth, figure out who's just flapping their wings, and determine exactly how sticky you'll need to get to waggle like a bee."

She tipped her head and shrugged with the casual air of a girlfriend getting together with her besties in a cozy coffee shop. "Hey, I like to dance. Hang tight, my friends, keep an open mind, and we'll be right back."

3. UNINVITED VISITOR

THE JURY'S VERDICT turned out to be No Way in Hell, based on evidence that CyberBees were inept at pollinating and because real bees could easily tell the difference between their mates and an imposter. One video clip showed the hive stinging a CyberBee to death.

But the audience agreed that the waggle dance might ultimately become a communications path from humans to bees. By the end, several audience members attempted the bee dance moves themselves with Halie joining in for an impromptu bee conga line. She closed the show posing for selfies, and Paul handed out bee pins.

All good fun, but their next show would be far more serious. Even in the late 2030s, climate change still divided people along political lines, though the debate had become more nuanced as killer summer heat waves made outright denial a tough sell. Halie had long been curious about climate computer modeling which had, so far, been spot-on for its predictions. A deep dive into the subject might help dispel the never-ending conspiracy theory that climate scientists were only gaming the flow of government grants.

While conclusions based on evidence ought to be enough to settle any argument, Halie wasn't naive enough to believe the world worked that way. The human mind often chose sides based on emotion, not evidence. Halie's own father, once proud of her television career, had more recently turned a cold shoulder.

She could lament her role in a divided family and a divided world, but she wouldn't let up. Fans of the show reminded her of that commitment every day. Stay in the trenches, they'd say in reviews and emails, fight misinformation and phony claims. People will come around.

A modern renaissance might be too much to expect, but the show had had successes along the way. They'd covered alternative medicine, psychic readings, even some mind-blowing magic tricks that Halie still couldn't figure out even though she'd been standing right there. The list of unexplained weirdness and evidence-free pseudoscience was apparently endless. The secret to publicly exposing which portions were misinformation had turned out to be a careful balance between investigative journalism, science, and good humor.

With this week's show wrapped, Halie joined Paul for a schmoozing dinner with representatives from their newest advertiser. The insurance company reps had praise for the show—and deposited a large sum into a KNS bank account—but spent most of the dinner talking about an unexplained helicopter crash in South America, hoping Halie would cover it.

"It fell out of an interdimensional hole," one rep claimed. "There were eyewitnesses!" Halie kept her response as polite as she could manage. She hadn't seen the news report herself. She promised to follow up.

Now back at her studio office, Halie flicked a finger across her tablet to keep her word. Paul sauntered in, apparently curious too. As it turned out, the insurance guys were right, even if the report itself was as preposterous as they came.

Illegal offshore oil platform bends space-time, the headline read.

"Really?" Halie asked, wondering what oil production had to do with advanced astrophysics. Breaking news reports were often unreliable, especially with such a sensational headline. This one was probably just clickbait.

The report said a military mission off the coast of Ecuador had gone terribly wrong, resulting in a helicopter crash with injuries. Nothing metaphysical about that, but the crew claimed their helicopter had been sent through a portal and slung three hundred kilometers back to base in an instant.

Paul circled around the conference table and peered over Halie's shoulder. She clicked on a video with a date tag of April 21—yesterday. A reporter thrust a microphone into the face of a man in uniform.

Halie's Spanish was only good enough to pick out the most familiar words: *"Turbulencias intensas!"* Heavy turbulence. *"Negro como la noche!"* Black as night. Text scrolling across the bottom was in English. *Gunnery Sergeant Benito Alvarez: "A wall of mist pulled us into a dark hole. But then I saw the runway at Guayaquil below. Only the devil could have such power!"*

The soldier kept talking, but the image changed to a live shot taken from a ship. A black platform floated in the ocean on four enormous pontoons. Above its deck, an inverted funnel reached into the sky.

Paul put on reading glasses and leaned in close. "Hell of a story."

Halie shrugged. "The pilots probably miscalculated their landing approach or didn't spot a thunderstorm. In my experience, space-time portals are rare. Aviation interference from devils even rarer."

Paul tugged one side of his face into a half smile. It was hard to get much more of a reaction out of him. He pointed to text beneath the video. "Apparently, the Ecuadoran Army has GPS location data showing an instantaneous *discontinuity*. That sounds intriguing."

"*Unreleased* data," Halie cautioned.

"Point taken. So, maybe there's a story there, maybe not. I guess it doesn't matter. Sending you and a camera team to South America isn't in the budget."

The budget was in better shape than Paul would ever admit, especially after tonight's contribution from the insurance guys. But Paul was a worrier at heart. Halie let his reasoning lie. She wasn't about to push her way into a story that logically belonged to one of the international reporters for Kolby News Service.

She shut off the tablet. "Are we done? Mash still needs me for some last-minute video edits before we post. Oh… and there's that guy I still need to call. King Kong."

"Good luck," Paul said raising his brow. "Sounds like you'll need it. I'm only here long enough to verify the bank transfer from our insurance guys."

They headed down the hall, with Paul peeling away to his own office, and Halie continuing deeper into the technical regions of the studio. She turned down a side hallway and opened an unmarked door. The tiny room was packed floor to ceiling with video equipment and a dozen playback screens. *The Closet*, as the staff had nicknamed it, only had room for a single chair—already occupied by Halie's longtime videographer and friend, Mashup.

Halie had first teamed with Mashup (no last name) at Kolby News Service, Halie in front of the camera as science correspondent, Mashup behind. Behind the camera was normally where producers put androgynous people with spiked purple hair (pink on Thursdays), prominent multicolor tattoos (cartoon characters included), and piercings decorated with jewels or mini chains depending on their mood.

"Bugger!" Mashup pointed a rainbow-painted fingernail to a playback screen embedded in a wall of electronic equipment. She replayed the clip faster than Halie could absorb its content. "See that?" In one frame, a man's head loomed from behind Halie's shoulder. "Makes you look like you've got two heads. Which you don't."

Mash, as Halie called her friend, picked up a wireless pen and outlined the offending spot, then hit a key on her controller. The second head disappeared.

"Tell me again why you needed me here?" Halie asked.

"Emotional support."

"Snipping out background junk is emotionally disturbing for you?"

"Everyone has their quirks—you too."

Mash had a point. Cuts to the script were sometimes painful. But after eight years as colleagues, Halie still wasn't sure she understood the complexities going on inside this one's head. Ten years younger, Mash often seemed to have been born on a different planet. Gender dysphoria had something to do with it.

Mash used female pronouns. "It's easier that way," she once told Halie, explaining that she detested those online forms that included an "other" checkbox. "Nobody cares if your gender is trans, queer, or Mr. Roboto without a ding-dong. Which, by the way, is the official description on my California driver's license."

The occasional peek into what made Mash tick helped bring them closer, both inside and outside of work. Rollerblading at Venice Beach was the most common crossover event in their otherwise dissimilar lifestyles.

Noise erupted from the hallway outside—a woman shouting. Halie looked up, and the door swung open. An Asian man barged into the small room, followed closely behind by an agitated receptionist with two hands clamped onto the man's shoulder. "Sir! You can't come in here!"

Halie stood up, reflexively taking a defensive posture, fists clenched. These days you never knew when an assault by some nutcase with a grudge might happen. He wasn't armed; good news there. Bonus: he wore a finely tailored suit.

With the receptionist still hanging on, the man bowed deeply. He held out a business card with both hands: Yoon Ji-ho's card, the same card she'd been given before the show. "Please," he said. "Miss Spark. For you."

Halie made eye contact with the agitated receptionist still grasping the man. "It's okay, Jen. I've got it. Just let Paul know that our visitor has returned."

The receptionist finally let go; the man hadn't seemed to notice her anyway. Built like an Olympic wrestler, he could have walked down the street carrying Jen plus three more on his back. Paul would be here soon, most likely with security right behind. Until then, Halie would humor their uninvited guest. He'd been polite so far.

The man released his bow and spoke in accented English. "Mr. Yoon wishes to speak with you."

"Yeah… I think we already established that."

The man held up a phone. "Directly."

Pushy. But in this business, she'd seen every type. "Look, Mr. Kong was it? We need to set some rules—"

Paul shoved his way through the door, face flushed, eyes wide. With four people now crammed inside the closet, it was starting to look like a Marx Brothers movie. Mash glanced between Halie and the Asian body-builder-in-a-suit as if she were placing a bet on how this encounter might play out.

Halie quickly explained to Paul, "Apparently Yoon Ji-ho wants to speak with me. Directly."

Paul twisted the whole left side of his face into a confused grimace. "The Korean billionaire?"

Halie nodded. "Second time today. I guess I wasn't convincing enough in my first thank-you-but-no."

The intruder offered a business card to Paul, who stared at it, mouth open. "Who turns away the world's leading techno-oligarch?"

"I do." Halie stood firm. "At the time, I had a live audience waiting." The Asian man still held out his phone. He even started dialing.

Paul shrugged. "Well, the show's over. It couldn't hurt to see what he wants. Maybe there's a feel-good story on whatever futuristic tech he's dreamed up?"

Last season, they'd turned the show's normal format on its head. Instead of debunking yet another junk theory, they'd devoted a segment to something astonishing but true. Paul's idea. He had colorfully declared (on more than one occasion) that a show that wallows in sewage begins to stink. So why not showcase the amazing, the mind-blowing, the magical? With evidence of its veracity, of course.

At first, Halie had been resistant. The show was named *Don't Believe It!* for a reason. Their job was to expose the fakes and grifters. In a world where dumb ideas and downright lies seemed to be winning, Halie felt a duty to speak the truth. But the ratings had been through the roof, and another feel-good format followed.

"Paul, I like the format. I really do. But we can't be a promotional agency for every CEO who comes along."

Paul waved his hands. "Fair. But this is Yoon Ji-ho we're talking about. Hypersonic subways? Kung-fu movies injected directly into your brain? That guy. Assuming, of course, that our large friend here is legit."

The brainwave movies were taekwondo, not kung-fu, but Halie wasn't going to quibble. She'd find out soon enough if the eccentric billionaire really wanted to speak with her.

The phone connected. Halie peered into its screen.

A middle-aged Korean man stared back, Yoon Ji-ho himself. He looked like his press photographs. Rounded face, balding. Fifty-five, with a wife half that age if the gossip magazines were correct. He relaxed in a tall leather chair, dressed casually in a knit golf shirt, logo cap, and slacks.

"Miss Sahalie Spark," Yoon said with a broad smile. "Thank you for taking my call. I apologize for not coming in person, but time is short, and I have much to attend to."

Halie was pleasantly surprised that the intruder had turned out to be legitimate and somewhat humbled to be in a business where she could gain instant access to one of the more intriguing entrepreneurs in the world. Yoon was the type to hold his tongue behind a tight smile before unveiling a surprise, and Halie was pretty good at reading the room. Something big was up.

"Nice to meet you, Mr. Yoon. My producer, Paul Reddick, is also here. An unusual introduction, but what can we do for you?"

"I hope Quong inflicted no damage. I know he can be insistent."

Halie smiled, tentative. "No harm done."

Yoon's eyes sparkled. "A moment of your time, then. A quick taste of my current project. I can promise you exclusive access to some very private information."

Exclusive. An arrangement that hinted of preferential treatment or quid pro quo, never a good look for an investigative science show.

Halie stood her ground. "Honestly, Mr. Yoon, I'm surprised and flattered to receive your call, but I have to tell you that we're trying to limit the corporate whiz-bang tech stories we do. There are no charlatans to expose, and frankly not enough mystery."

Paul gave a thumbs-up.

Yoon nodded slowly, as if Halie had just revealed wisdom to be passed down through the ages. "You need mystery... yes, I understand. Perhaps I can help." He spoke several words in Korean.

Their intruder, Quong not Kong, reached into his jacket pocket and produced a thin wire about ten centimeters long. He held the wire vertically in the air for a few seconds, then let it go.

It didn't fall. The wire hung in midair. Seconds passed. Paul stared, eyes wide. Halie cocked her head and leaned to one side, looking for the hidden threads holding it aloft. Nothing.

The wire began to spread horizontally, dissolving into a sparkling rectangle hanging in the air. Misty. Translucent. Like a frosted pane of glass. Halie could see Quong's amused face behind it.

"Whoa," Mash said, standing up to take a better look.

At the rectangle's center, sparkling frost resolved into six angled lines forming a hexagon. Halie thought of bees and their honeycombs.

Quong took a half step back and held out one hand, palm up. "Touch, please."

"Touch the hexagon?" Halie asked. It did resemble a button, though far more illusory than anything on a keyboard or touchscreen.

Quong nodded politely. Halie reached out and gently poked the misty phantom. It felt like nothing at all.

The hexagon disappeared, and the floating mist reformed into a three-dimensional structure that extruded from the foggy plate like a page in a pop-up book. Its edges sharpened to reveal a flat platform resting on four cylinders with an inverted funnel-shaped chimney rising above. Miniature animated waves broke around the cylinders.

Halie stared, mesmerized by the specter and the amazing technology that had produced it. She immediately recognized the shape, but not remotely within the context of a billionaire's offer of information. Now it took on new meaning.

She spoke softly. "It's that platform... the one in South America."

Yoon gently nodded. "Enough mystery for you?"

Halie looked at Paul, openmouthed. If it were anyone else, she'd blow it off as a high-tech ruse. But Yoon Ji-ho was not your average nutcase. Paul's blank expression made it clear he was a few steps behind. She'd explain later, but right now, she had a deal to make.

Halie pointed to the floating apparition. "You're offering exclusive access? Just me?"

Yoon nodded once more. "You are the only person who could properly tell this story. My plane will be departing for South America within the hour. Please join me. I'm sure you understand that time is of the essence."

Halie felt her pulse rise. It wasn't hard to put it together: Yoon's advanced technology that often approached the level of magic, the familiar shape formed from mist, and the news story out of Ecuador. She had dismissed it as nonsense. Now she knew better.

Halie stared once more at the misty platform hanging in the air.

That's no offshore oil rig.

4. STRATOSPHERE

HALIE AND PAUL MET PRIVATELY while Yoon's beefy assistant, Quong, waited in a limousine parked in front of the building, ready to take Halie to the airport.

She rapidly flicked a finger across her tablet, searching for an engineering diagram that was at least five years old. Paul waited, clueless.

"Hang on, it's here somewhere," Halie mumbled. Her finger stopped on an image. "Gotcha!" A smile spread across her face. She swiveled the tablet so Paul could see. "Yoon's design from four years ago."

An artist's sketch showed a platform floating in the ocean on four pontoons. An inverted funnel stood above like a narrow umbrella protecting the deck from rain. Two thin wires exited from the funnel's peak and continued straight up.

"It's not an oil platform," Halie said. An icy shiver began in her legs and tickled up to her neck. "It's a space elevator."

"A cable to orbit? That kind of space elevator?"

"Yup."

"And you think Yoon actually built one?"

"It's clearly his design. You saw the video from Ecuador. There's no way that platform has anything to do with oil."

"But how could Yoon build a space elevator? How could anyone? There were a dozen companies working on designs and prototypes, but every one of them abandoned their plans four years ago. Yoon too."

Paul was right. They had.

"Look, I have no idea how he managed it, but you have to admit Yoon has the money and the high tech to pull it off. You saw his little magic wire thingy. Who does stuff like that?"

Paul shrugged. "He wants you, which makes sense. As I remember, you used to cover these stories."

"I was immersed in them. I studied every technical detail. Trips to Japan, Germany, and China. I met the experts. But Yoon jumped out in front with a prototype. I remember a phone interview with his materials science guy—Adam somebody-or-other—from a university in Peru. The guy made it clear that the technical issues to make a ridiculously long tether had been solved. Manufacturing was already underway, and spool deployment was close behind."

"Too bad they had to shut it down."

Halie sighed, recalling those dark days. "Yeah, too bad. But what if Yoon has the Kill Zone figured out?"

Emotions surfaced from the past. Feelings of adventure, discovery, and pride that she'd almost forgotten. Four years ago, Halie was covering new technology that screamed of a bright future for humankind. Space elevators were a prime example.

The Kill Zone ended everyone's dreams.

"Go," Paul said with conviction. "CyberBees will run this week, and our time slot for next week is already taken by that KNS special report on Arctic shipping routes. That leaves us until next Tuesday to figure out what Yoon has up his sleeve. Truth or a lie, we'll get a show out of it either way."

The gears were turning, though Halie still harbored misgivings. Jetting off to South America in a billionaire's private plane felt like abandoning her post as the world's sentry against misinformation. Could she do this? Should she?

Halie ventured a tentative step. "What if Mash comes with me? Maybe broadcast a few live shots, on location?"

"Absolutely. Old man Kolby eats that stuff up. I'll talk to him. Grab Mash and anybody else you need. Yoon's paying for the flight, so budget doesn't matter. Go."

Halie stood, warming to the idea. "I admit it's amazing stuff. An elevator into space, are you kidding me? Plus, there's that Ecuador helicopter that hyperjumped back to base before crashing. What's going on there? This story is jam-packed with juicy bits."

Paul gave her a gentle push. "Hurry. That guy parked at the curb won't wait forever, and you still need to stop by security." He pointed to the inside of his elbow. Halie's own arm had what looked like a tattoo there but wasn't.

Halie opened a cabinet and grabbed her go-bag, a necessity for any journalist needing a quick getaway. If she'd pegged Yoon correctly, Ecuador would be the biggest science story of the year. She couldn't let that slip away. "Okay. Let's do it."

She was halfway down the hall when Paul yelled after her, "Make sure Mash gets shots of people in white lab coats. This is a science show!"

Halie laughed. *As if I don't live that every waking minute.* The show sometimes ventured into lighter topics—bees were one—but that didn't mean it was fluff. It wasn't, never had been, and wouldn't be if Halie had anything to say about it.

She picked up Mash, who proffered no questions and voiced no complaints. "Riviera Chic Gig," Mash drummed out in her signature four-beat-two-beat cadence. Mash often used a language all her own, sometimes including a singsong patter that substituted for the swear words so common in the modern world. In this case, her made-up phrase probably translated as something like, *I'm cool with a mystery job in a faraway place.*

Mash crammed multiple cameras into a shoulder bag. A stabilizing harness, transmission equipment, and extra batteries filled another. She slipped a toothbrush and a spray bottle of StayFresh instant clothes cleaner into a zippered pocket. "Good enough," she said, slinging both bags over her toothpick-skinny frame.

On the ground floor, Halie stopped by the security office, signed out for an international assignment, and downloaded legal documents guaranteed to put even a cocaine addict to sleep. She wouldn't bother to read them. She had something better.

Halie rolled up her sleeve, and the security guy waved a wand over the bull's-eye tattoo on the inside of her arm. "The signal's strong," he said. "You're good to go."

A thin microchip embedded beneath the skin reported her geolocation every five minutes. A predefined finger tap code would alert security from anywhere in the world: *immediate assistance required.* As long as she remained clear of a short list of hostile countries, they'd have an extraction team at her side within an hour.

Halie walked out to the curb, thankful to find Yoon's limo still waiting. She took the seat next to the minibar while Mash piled her camera bags on a rear-facing seat, then clipped a seat belt around them. Mash had always been protective of her gear, Halie being the only other person on Earth allowed to touch it.

Yoon's assistant, Quong, sat up front and never said a word all the way to Van Nuys Airport, the usual port for those lucky few who owned private jets. But when the limo pulled up next to a gleaming blue-and-white aircraft, Halie wondered if she had ever understood luxury travel.

It wasn't the latest Gulfstream. This sleek machine looked like a cross between an advanced military fighter and the supersonic Concorde from the 1980s. Its needlelike nose widened only slightly to a narrow fuselage perched above tall landing gear. An elegant delta wing incorporated two cylindrical bulges that ran parallel on either side and flared to engine exhaust ports jutting out from the trailing edge. Two stubby ducts beneath the bulges hung straight down.

Mash leaned over and whispered, "Even the guy's plane has balls."

Halie half-glared, half-smiled at her sometimes-tactless young friend. Unless Yoon's plane was undergoing major maintenance, the hanging ducts were more likely some kind of vertical thrust.

Halie stepped out to a light breeze and the medicinal scent of JCOL-40, an alcohol-based jet fuel that had taken the world by storm—a rare win in the ongoing fight against global warming.

Quong ushered Halie, Mash, and her gear bags up an airstair. At the top, Halie peered into a narrow but well-appointed cabin.

Two pilots, a man and a woman, both Asian, were busy behind a partially closed cockpit door. Oversized lounge chairs formed a first-class cabin. A flight attendant opened a curtain and glided up the aisle. She wore a full-length flowered silk dress. Filipino, Halie judged, unquestionably some of the most beautiful people on the planet, and this stunning woman proved the point.

"Ms. Sahalie Spark," the flight attendant sang in sweet lilts. She bent sculpted eyebrows together into a quizzical look. "Please forgive me, but we were not expecting your associate."

"My videographer," Halie replied, hoping Mash's ragged purple hair, Bloody Heart band t-shirt, and prominent lip piercings wouldn't become fashion liabilities for this upper-crust flight. "Mr. Yoon offered exclusive access. This is what access looks like. She goes where I go."

"I see. One moment, please," the woman said, then glided back down the aisle. When she returned, her gentle smile and oh-so-soft voice hadn't changed. "Mr. Yoon understands your needs. This way, please."

Mash kept close behind Halie. "Kind of highbrow around here. Maybe I shouldn't ask him about the plane's balls?"

Halie couldn't suppress a giggle that turned into a cough. "Good call. Think... best manners. Pretend you're visiting royalty."

Mash scowled. "I don't do curtsies. Gotta draw the line somewhere." She pulled out a slim video camera from one bag and switched it on. "We're rolling."

For now, the shot might be the back of Halie's head, but Mash stuck to every photographer's mantra: capture everything from every angle, then edit out the junk later.

The flight attendant pushed aside the curtain, leading Halie into the plane's inner sanctum. Two more swiveling lounge chairs faced a fine desk with an elegantly curving edge.

Yoon looked up from behind the desk. He had changed out of his golf shirt into a long-sleeved white robe with a bright blue silk sash at the waist. He stood and bowed slightly. "Ms. Spark. I am so glad you could join us."

"*Annyeong haseyo*," Halie replied, returning the bow. She hoped the Korean greeting was right.

Yoon's eyes widened. "Well done, Ms. Spark. Foreigners often neglect the honorifics of our language."

"Put *yo* at the end of everything?" Halie asked with a smile. "Americans can grasp the simplest rules of foreign languages, but most of us don't get much further than hello, goodbye, and thank you."

Halie introduced Mashup, who waved from behind the camera. Quong pushed through the curtain while the flight attendant continued further down the aisle into a galley.

Yoon nodded toward Quong. "Like you, my assistant Quong goes where I go. We shall make a good foursome. Do you play golf, Ms. Spark?"

Halie shook her head. "Tried it once. The little white balls didn't go where I told them to go. And, please, call me Halie."

"Halie. A modern version of Sahalie—a Native American name, I believe?"

Halie was pleasantly surprised since few people made the connection. He'd surely looked it up online, but his effort still spoke of a personal kindness. "Sahalie was the name of my great-grandmother, a member of the Chinook tribe of western Washington and Oregon."

"How wonderful. A woman with history in her name. And Halie, since you mention the suffix *yo*, you may also understand that in Korea we use seven levels of honorifics depending on a person's relationship, age, and gender. Luckily for all of us, when in America I am simply Yoon." He smiled and offered a chair.

Halie sat. Mash roamed, capturing the introductions from various angles, then finally sat when the plane's engines started. The flight attendant asked everyone to buckle up, and soon they were taxiing.

With the story sitting right in front of her, and Mash recording every word, Halie's tone shifted slightly, becoming Sahalie Spark, host of the world's number one science program. "Yoon Ji-ho. International business tycoon. A household name when it comes to futuristic transportation or high-tech consumer electronics. A man full of mystery and a few surprises now and then. I sense we'll soon be learning about another one. Something very special is happening down in South America. Something... I think... the whole world will be watching."

"You honor me with your praise." Yoon was clearly aware of the camera, but he made no request to shut it off.

"The oil platform near Ecuador is yours, isn't it?" Halie asked, already knowing the answer.

Yoon tilted his head to one side and pinched his lips.

Halie continued. "But it's not an oil platform, is it?"

"No, it is not."

"It's a space elevator."

Yoon grinned. "Well done. But then, you are the famous Sahalie Spark. Destroyer of myths and misinformation. A household name when it comes to the scientific method. A woman of mystery who broadcasts surprises now and then."

He'd turned the tables on her. Yoon leaned closer to Mash, looking straight into the camera. "Ms. Sahalie Spark quickly puts two and two together, as Americans say. She is quite aware of my earlier attempts at space elevator technology. Failed attempts. But, as she has guessed, this time our hard work has succeeded."

Halie leaned back in her seat as her suspicions were confirmed. "Wow. An elevator into space. No rockets. No dramatic acceleration to reach orbit. Just climb a tether and you're there."

"A space elevator is never that simple," Yoon cautioned.

Halie snapped out of her dreamy aside. "No, of course it isn't. The tether material has to be stronger and lighter than anything humans have ever produced. For the physics to work, the tether has to reach beyond geostationary orbit—thirty-six thousand kilometers, ten percent of the distance to the moon. And to stay taut, it has to be anchored to the ground and to a counterweight slinging in a circle as Earth rotates. The challenges don't end there. You need continuous power all the way up, lightweight machines that climb, you have to engineer for loads, avoid stretching the tether, and dampen oscillations."

She could have gone on. She'd read almost everything available about the dream of space elevators. It wasn't a new idea, but the means to build such a technical marvel had remained out of reach until a few years ago. She shook her head like she was arguing with herself. "But the engineering issues don't matter, do they?"

Halie stared at Yoon, imagining him a genius or a fool and not yet sure which. She continued, "The fatal flaw with a space elevator is the same problem that every country on Earth has faced since the onset of the Kessler Syndrome four years ago. You can't build a space elevator for the same reason you can't launch a rocket anymore—at least, not if you expect it to reach its destination in one piece. Nothing gets through the Kill Zone."

Yoon sat quietly without acknowledging the issue but not denying it either. The largest space disaster in history had created high-velocity wreckage that now circled the Earth, destroying everything in its path. A Kill Zone they called it, starting somewhere near the top of the atmosphere and reaching a thousand kilometers up. No more space launches. No rocket could survive the barrage of a trillion bullets, each with enough energy to rip a solid oak door off its hinges and turn it into an explosion of wood chips.

Halie put the pressure on. "The Kill Zone is what ended your last elevator project, right?"

Yoon paused, then spoke with the firmness of a tech leader. "Yes, the so-called Kill Zone is a debris field of grave danger. For now, low Earth orbits have been rendered unusable, but we must also understand that this is not a permanent condition. Through diligent work we may improve the situation."

"They've tried lasers, magnetic induction, they've launched capture bots, but none of it—"

Yoon held up two hands to interrupt. He signaled Mash to turn the camera off, which she did—reluctantly.

Yoon spoke barely above a whisper. "Please, Ms. Spark. Halie. Do not prejudge what you have not yet seen. As I recall, you provide similar advice on your own television show."

Halie shrugged. "Got me there. So, you're saying I should just wait and see? Normally, I'd be fine with that, but South America is a long way away."

Yoon leaned back in his chair. "Ten hours by commercial flight. My plane can do it in seven. We will take a somewhat longer route over the ocean, but even with the three-hour time change, we will arrive in Ecuador before the sun rises."

Engines roared. The plane barreled down the runway and lifted off far quicker than a commercial flight. Halie glanced up to a digital wall clock—nine p.m. The flight would be a red-eye, but something told her the accommodations would be better than a coach seat next to the lavatory. She was anxious about what lay ahead, but sleep would be important. Tomorrow was shaping up to be a busy day.

Stow the aggressive reporter persona for now.

"Thank you, Yoon. I'll... be patient. But if you've managed to... well, you're going to be a very popular guy with a bunch of managers of grounded space programs."

"And your reporting will help us get there," Yoon said.

That was probably true, but only if he delivered the goods. If this story turned out to be a sham, she would expose it. She'd have to.

A pilot announced they could unbuckle. A minute later, the flight attendant returned, offering a tray with several glasses of juice. Halie and Mash each took one.

"I'll prepare the forward cabin," the flight attendant said. "Please retire whenever you wish." She left through the curtain.

"This flight will be both quick and comfortable," Yoon said, pointing a thumb aft. "I have my own accommodations. Quong will take the security office, and Jaya overnights up front with the pilots. The forward cabin is all yours. Please make yourselves at home."

Yoon shut off his computer and stood. Halie took the hint and stood too. "*Gamsa hamnida.* For taking us with you."

"You are most welcome," Yoon said with a slight bow. "An adventure has begun. We shall explore it together." He bowed once more, then left through the galley corridor.

Mash stuffed her camera in the gear bag. "Bonzo bananas! Adventure plus a fancy plane all to ourselves."

Halie peered out through a large oval window. The city lights of southern California were already disappearing behind. Ahead was nothing but the black indifference of an ocean that stretched to the horizon and beyond. Their climb was longer than normal, but the pilot came over the intercom once the plane leveled. "Welcome aboard. We're at twenty-two thousand meters, cruising at Mach one point nine. That's twice the speed the airlines fly. This high in the stratosphere there's never any turbulence, so no need for seat belts. Relax. Enjoy the flight. If you need anything overnight, press the call button and Jaya will be there."

Halie and Mash returned to the forward cabin, where two seats had already been refashioned into reclining beds, complete with sheets and blankets. A bottle of water and a box filled with assorted snacks completed their first-class service.

Mash fiddled with camera gear while Halie tapped the in-flight map on a tablet hinged to the seat arm. An airplane icon was already halfway down the length of Baja. Somewhere below, a sonic boom was rocking the decks of Mexican fishing boats.

Amazing plane. You have to admire the guy. Yoon was in a class of his own. A touch of humility helped.

Not ready to sleep, Halie raised her seatback and stared out the dark window. Above, stars were visible on a moonless night. At more than twenty kilometers, they were as high as any airplane could manage. Going higher required a rocket. At least, it used to. Far to the south they would find out if Yoon had created a new way of climbing to the edge of space and beyond.

He would be hailed as a hero if he'd figured it out. The past four years had been catastrophic for space flight and business that depended on low Earth orbit, LEO. Collectively, the world had lost more than a hundred thousand working machines: communications satellites, spy satellites, Earth mapping satellites, plus every crewed orbital laboratory—and the people who worked there.

The International Space Station had deorbited in 2031, but its intentional destruction only proved to be a harbinger of what would come. With countries and corporations crowding ever more satellites into a fixed amount of space, near misses became more common. Space tracking systems were losing control, and every government knew it.

The first collision came in June of 2035. A polar orbiting spy satellite slammed into a commercial telephone satellite that had been incorrectly marked in databases as *deorbited*. The explosion sent a million chunks of high-speed metal and plastic in directions no one had planned for or could reasonably track. Unlike historical mishaps, a second satellite went down within hours. Then another. The cascading chain of debris, explosions, and more debris closely matched a doomsday scenario called the Kessler Syndrome, predicted since the late twentieth century.

The first two weeks were cataclysmic. In two months, every satellite orbiting between 300 and 1,000 kilometers had been destroyed. Thirty-four astronauts working in six commercial and government space stations were killed. Only one station managed to evacuate in time.

But the tragedy didn't end there. The debris field surrounding the planet—now labeled the Kill Zone—made launches impossible.

Even rockets with reinforced shielding were blasted like a paper target in front of a shotgun.

With no way to reach the US and Indian moon bases at the moon's south pole, the temporary residents living there couldn't be resupplied or rescued. Seventeen more people suffered a slow death.

One was only a child, Halie recalled. *Who thinks that bringing a teenager to the moon is a good idea?*

Only the higher orbits survived. Midlevel satellites at 20,000 kilometers were still operational, including global navigation satellite arrays like GPS, GLONASS, and Galileo. Geostationary satellites at 36,000 kilometers survived too: weather and science satellites, television broadcast relays, and communication satellites with higher latency.

Crippled but not beaten, space technologists soldiered on. The remaining satellites would need to last until the debris could be cleared, a task that turned out to be more difficult than anyone imagined. Overnight, a debris capture and deorbit industry sprung into existence, but after four years, they had eliminated only one percent of the problem. Every day, chunks large and small spiraled into the atmosphere and burned up, but with billions more still orbiting, experts envisioned a future where humans might not return to space for a century.

Fingers pointed. It was greed from the billionaires, many said. They had launched tens of thousands of corporate satellites with little or no oversight—the Wild West free-for-all of the 2020s. Others reasoned that the problem was the lack of international cooperation. Earth orbits were like any other limited resource—certainly not inexhaustible. Orbits were just as precious as gold or titanium, they argued. Shouldn't they be regulated, with high price tags attached to their consumption?

Halie had often asked these questions when interviewing a member of Congress while covering the disaster for Kolby News Service. She hadn't gotten many answers.

Science reporting has its downsides. Halie shifted uncomfortably in her seat.

Yoon had been one of those arguing for better regulation of space resources, using his own space elevator design as an example. If the construction of a permanent space elevator required permission from multiple governments of the world—and it did—then why not require the same level of scrutiny for satellite launches?

After the Kessler event, he used a different argument: if a space elevator's tether could be shielded from high-speed debris, it could serve as a method to declutter LEO. His company proposed several designs that included enormous nets made from elastic gel that stretched but did not break when struck by debris.

Unfortunately, every space elevator project began with a tether unreeled from a spool parked in geostationary orbit. Tethers hung down, they didn't reach up. It was the only way to tap into Earth's rotational force. But no one had yet figured out how to haul the spool through the Kill Zone without turning it into useless confetti.

Halie closed the window shade and settled into her seat. Had Yoon finally solved the problem?

Tomorrow, I just might find out.

5. TEMERARIO

ADAM ESTRADA CLIMBED THE gangway to the guided missile frigate, *Mario Vargas Llosa*. The flag of Peru waved in a light breeze under low marine clouds. Sunbreaks produced glitters across blue-green Pacific waters that stretched to the horizon.

Peruvian sailors wrangled multiple crates up the ramp. A younger Adam would have winced at each bump and scrape of precious lab equipment, but after four years in Peru, he'd learned to ignore crumpled car bumpers and cracked kitchen windows. As the locals colorfully said, anyone still standing has no reason to cry.

Of course, he'd need to run calibration tests on every scientific tool he'd carefully packed in those crates, but there would be plenty of time once the ship got underway. The border with Ecuador wasn't far by air, but a ship would need several hours to get there.

Their destination was a floating platform in coastal waters claimed by both Peru and Ecuador. Adam had little interest in their conflict. He was far more curious about what they'd find at their destination.

The phone message had been terse: "Your skills are needed. Bring a portable lab, if possible." It wasn't much to go on, but the sender was Yoon Ji-ho, and that made all the difference.

"*Lo siento, Profesor Temerario!*" one sailor called out after banging the large crate he was carrying against a bulkhead.

"*Vivimos, morimos, a veces estrellamos,*" Adam answered. We live, we die, and sometimes we crash along the way. It wasn't a bad guiding principle for life. Adam had crashed several times while piloting various motorized machines—and walked away. The ten-thousand-dollar microscope inside that particular crate simply needed to come to terms with its fate.

Adam had. Though only forty-two, he imagined his date of death was already carved on a stone somewhere and somewhen. He could either lament that fact or live his time on Earth to its fullest.

He chuckled at the sailor's label, Professor *Temerario*, which had nothing to do with his name or position. A *temerario* was a reckless lunatic who stared death in the face and spit. Along with scientific equipment, Adam had brought a personal jet pack onboard. The sailors had stored it in a locker on the ship's flight deck, ready for use. The turbine-powered, strap-on flying machine could be airborne in less than a minute. He could reach altitudes of several thousand meters and speeds a racecar driver could only dream of. The jet pack was a thing of beauty, and Adam fully intended to use it on this voyage.

The sailors wrestled the crates through a tight passageway, down a steep metal ladder, and finally into a cubbyhole mostly filled by one desk and a chair—Adam's onboard lab, he presumed. Small, but it included an adjoining cubby. He'd set up the microscope there.

Yoon Ji-ho could have only one reason for Adam's expert services: to examine a tether. And not just any wire, rope, or cable. The tether Yoon had in mind would be a ribbon no thicker than cellophane yet strong enough to lift a frigate out of the water without snapping. Ten frigates for that matter. A material capable of such a feat would be considered unholy by some, miraculous by others. But for a materials scientist like Adam, a tether forming the backbone of a space elevator would be the crowning achievement of a lifetime.

Has Yoon really deployed his space elevator?

Adam had his doubts, though none were related to materials. The tether unquestionably existed. He'd examined it himself, years ago. Watched, as it was spooled onto a roll that nearly reached to the factory ceiling.

Humans were capable of great achievements. And of great folly. These sailors had no idea what they were getting themselves into. They talked of a poisonous mist surrounding a mysterious floating platform. They worried their ship would be sucked into a "portal to nowhere." More likely, they were heading into armed conflict.

Their officers seemed to understand. Ecuador was unfriendly territory and had been since a nasty border dispute in the 1990s. Even now, nearly fifty years later, the two countries hadn't fully reconciled. This new apparition floating in the Pacific could easily spark a fight for control.

But only if it really is a space elevator.

Adam's phone beeped; another message from Yoon. He smiled as he read. "What the hell, Ji-ho? Flexing your rich-guy muscles?"

No doubt about it, Yoon had social leverage. The man could waltz into any boardroom, private club, or movie star's mansion and walk out with someone powerful or famous by his side. But this time, he'd outdone himself.

"You're bringing Sahalie Spark with you?"

6. ARRIVAL

HALIE OPENED HER EYES to that special experience of waking at high altitude. Jet engines hummed in a coordinated symphony of twin turbines slicing through the stratosphere one blade at a time.

The cabin air felt cool on her face. A blanket tucked up to her chin kept the rest warm. The scent of coffee drifted though. She lifted the window shade a crack, revealing an orange glow camped on the horizon.

A multipronged streak of white briefly brightened the dark sky, then fizzled—more space junk burning up in the atmosphere, an event so common these days most people didn't bother to look up.

Shuffling sounds pulled Halie's attention from the view outside. Jaya lowered a tray with a steaming cup of coffee in its center. "Colombian coffee," she tempted. "A good day for it since we're flying close to its source."

Halie brought her seatback to an upright position and reached for the cup. "You are an angel, thank you."

"Care for breakfast? We'll be starting our descent soon, but there's still time to eat."

Halie nodded vigorously as she took a sip of the rich blend. "Whatever you have is fine."

Jaya left. Across the aisle, Mash was still buried under a blanket. Halie switched on the seat-side tablet. Its moving map updated, sliding the plane icon from Baja to a point west of Colombia. Ecuador lay directly ahead.

Halie sipped her coffee and searched out the window for a coastline but found nothing except the oranges of a hazy dawn. Jaya returned with a breakfast tray any first-class traveler would relish. A toasted bagel and scrambled eggs were served on a gold-rimmed plate. An embroidered linen napkin featured Yoon's company logo.

She started on the eggs. "Best flight in a long time," she told Jaya.

Jaya tipped her head. "Then you'll have to join us again."

"Hey, there's always the flight back—which, come to think of it, will probably end up being commercial. My boss only gave me a few days." Paul wasn't literally her boss, but the description was convenient when making conversation.

Jaya squatted next to Halie's seat. "From what I hear, you'll be busy."

"Did Mr. Yoon tell you where we're going?"

"Oh yes. A skyway to the stars."

"Well… maybe a slight exaggeration."

Jaya's crescent-shaped eyes sparkled above a movie-star smile. "You might be surprised. Mr. Yoon is well known for delivering at a higher level than his promise."

"You know something I don't know?"

Jaya shook her head. "I don't think so. But I know Mr. Yoon. He's a humble man with an optimistic vision."

"So, you like him?"

She stood. "I could not imagine a better boss."

Halie nodded, and Jaya left. Their thirty-second exchange had provided more information about Yoon than any corporate C-suite web page. Halie hadn't pegged Yoon as humble, but every famous person wore a public mask that disguised a more private personality. They were minutes away from finding out if his vision had legs.

The drone of engines reduced to idle, and the plane settled into a descent somewhat steeper than a commercial flight.

"Galapagos," Mash called out. She was still under a blanket but had raised her seatback upright. Halie set her unfinished meal aside and hopped up to look out the right-side window. Several flat brown islands peeked out from beneath low cumulus clouds.

"I doubt we're landing there," Halie said. A second later, the plane banked left, confirming their destination would be Ecuador.

"You are correct." It was Yoon, now dressed in what could only be described as Indiana Jones casual—all khaki, with a darker brown trim on the sleeves and collar. A broad-brimmed hat provided flair. He looked ruggedly handsome.

He tossed the hat on an empty seat. "The hat may or may not join me. We will see how windy it is upon landing."

Mash climbed out of her seat, fully clothed. Halie inspected her own clothes. A few wrinkles, but it wouldn't matter. Hair and face were more important when the camera started rolling. She'd spend a few minutes in front of the lavatory mirror to spruce up.

"Where are we landing anyway?" she asked Yoon. There was still no view of the Ecuador coastline.

"It depends," Yoon said. "The pilots tell me we have more than enough fuel to reach Quito, Guayaquil, or Lima. But first we shall make an inspection."

He reached into his pants pocket and pulled out a slim phone, speaking to it in Korean while observing the screen. "Closer than I thought. We may soon catch a glimpse out the left side."

They each picked a window and peered out. The sun was now lifting above the horizon, casting long shadows beneath scattered clouds.

"There!" Yoon pointed ahead. The plane banked slightly, keeping a tiny black square in front of its delta wing. From this height it didn't look like much.

The female copilot spoke over the intercom, "Radar is picking up a vertical obstruction. We will circle as close as possible." Mash pulled out a small camera and started recording.

As the plane turned, a vertical line flashed in the sky, then disappeared. "Was that it?" Halie asked.

"Possible," Yoon said, his eyes still peeled out the window.

The plane turned in a circle, keeping their target on the left. When they finished a full loop, the flash appeared again—a vertical glint rising from the black square on the ocean to their altitude. A second glint flashed, disappearing as quickly as a lightning bolt.

"Two in parallel?"

"Standard design," Yoon acknowledged without elaborating. He excused himself to speak with the pilots.

Halie thought about the designs she'd seen in video simulations that were popular before the debris catastrophe. Two tethers—one for going up and another for coming down—provided higher capacity for carrying both people and satellites.

Mash paused her camera and whispered to Halie. "That's all we get?"

"What do you mean?" Halie asked.

"Well, a sun glint isn't much to look at. Where's the gigantic tower of titanium? Isn't a space elevator supposed to be like a skyscraper to the moon?"

"Ah, gotcha." Halie nodded. "You've seen too many movies. A real space elevator uses a stiff tether, either a cable or a ribbon. They attach a climber that grabs on—either with opposing wheels or maglev technology—and up it goes. So, don't expect a skyscraper or some ridiculously tall cell tower. It's likely to be more like an aerial tram, but straight up."

Mash shrugged and switched her camera back on.

Halie returned her gaze to the window, wondering what would happen if an airplane hit a tether anchored in space by a ten-thousand-ton counterweight. Would the tether break? Or would the airplane be ripped in half? Either scenario seemed plausible.

Each loop in their descent produced the same double glint, but only when the plane reached a critical angle to the sun. It suggested they were circling something thin and flat, noticeable only when sunlight reflected off its surface and otherwise invisible.

Definitely a ribbon, not a cable.

Halie had never considered herself an expert on the subject, only informed. Now that she was facing a real tether into space, her own mental images might need to be refined.

After several more spirals, they finally reached the cloud tops. Gaps between cotton balls revealed whitecaps on the sea and a patch of fog surrounding a black square platform. A ship was docked at one side, providing a better indication of the platform's scale—as big as a city block.

Details on its surface were now visible too. A central cone, skinny and with the same sheer black color, rose from the center straight up to the clouds. It appeared to be a protective sheath like a scabbard for a sword.

"Looks like one of those Cirque du Soleil tents," Mash said of the sheath. "You know, stretched so pointy it might pop."

Rectangular shapes gave additional relief to the otherwise flat deck. Building-sized, they might be workshops or storage units. Some formed a perimeter along one edge.

A loud roar filled the cabin. Halie jerked her head in time to see the spinning blades of a military helicopter flashing past. Yoon rushed up the aisle and opened the cockpit door, giving Halie a direct view inside. One pilot gripped a control wheel, the other furiously flipped overhead switches and adjusted dials.

A stern voice blared from a speaker on the panel. "Attention fixed-wing jet, tail number Victor Hotel 422. Respond on 121.5."

Yoon's pilot spoke into a headset microphone. Halie couldn't quite make out what he said. The speaker blared once more. "Victor Hotel 422, this is a restricted area. Preauthorization is required. Return to Guayaquil and contact the tower, 122.8."

The helicopter slipped alongside them, easily keeping up with Yoon's jet. On its door was a United States flag with CVN-81 written beneath. A large insignia of an eagle flying above an aircraft carrier included the ship's name, USS *Doris Miller*.

Halie lifted eyebrows to Mash without saying a word. Together they crept closer to the open cockpit door. Halie leaned against a storage locker. Mash crouched, pointing the camera on her shoulder straight into the action.

"I repeat," Yoon's pilot barked, his voice now on the speaker too. Yoon stood behind the pilot's seat, holding on to a hand grip. "Authorization is already approved. The platform's owner is on board. Mr. Yoon Ji-ho. Look it up."

Nothing like a little air-to-air conflict. Halie hoped they weren't in trouble, but privately she was jazzed the stakes had just leaped to dodgy.

There was a pause. "Stand by, 422." The radio went silent.

Yoon pointed down, and the pilot steepened their descent. A few minutes later, they leveled out not far above the black deck and still circling. The fog they'd noticed higher up seemed thicker now, though Halie could see through to the deck and pontoons. The bigger question was why a bank of fog had formed at all. The rest of the ocean was perfectly clear.

Can't be a coincidence.

Halie recalled a *wall of mist* mentioned in the news report of the lost Ecuadoran helicopter. She'd seen a smaller scale version in Yoon's magic wire. Could this be the same unexplained phenomenon?

Yoon's pilots aimed for one corner of the deck, where a painted white circle indicated a helicopter landing pad. Yoon handed a thin wire to the copilot, which Halie recognized immediately: the intriguing high-tech device Quong had used so effectively to convince Halie something unusual was in store.

The copilot lifted the wire to a position above the control panel, then let go. It floated vertically in place, exactly as it had done in the studio.

"Are you getting all this?" Halie whispered to Mash.

Mash gave a thumbs-up, her eye never leaving the camera viewfinder. "Mystical apparition captured."

The wire expanded widthwise, as before, becoming a misty rectangle floating in the air. A hexagon shape formed at its center, but this time, no one touched it. In this new context, the translucent display almost looked like a secondary instrument for the pilots, with the hexagon acting as a targeting sight.

Yoon twisted to Halie and Mash. "Please take a seat. We will be landing."

"We're landing?" Halie asked, incredulous the plane's owner could make such a decision, especially after a US military official had just told them to scram. She'd sit if absolutely necessary, but there were too many questions to acquiesce just yet. "Your plane has helicopter blades that pop out?"

Yoon shook his head. "My design is better." He stopped and began again. "My *engineers'* design. I do nothing but watch as the amazing people who work for me turn my childish visions into reality. This a STOVL aircraft. Short takeoff, vertical landing. We could have departed Los Angeles from the street outside the airport and been off the ground before the first traffic light. Landings are even easier."

He pointed through the cockpit windshield to the landing pad ahead. "More than enough room."

"But didn't Ecuador have difficulties landing on this platform?" Halie continued. "Something about the fog?" According to the original news reports, a spacetime portal had thrown an Ecuadoran helicopter hundreds of kilometers back to base. The more likely explanation was that its crew needed an excuse for their unapproved landing at a beachside bar. Still, the idea of repeating a potentially dangerous maneuver made Halie quiver.

"The rumors are nonsense, and the fog is of no concern," Yoon scoffed. "The platform simply has security features, and these military cowboys lack the key."

"Your magic floating wire?" Halie asked.

"In this case, the wire will function as a test. To tell you the truth, I am not sure what will happen. Or what your country's navy will do." He gave a broad smile and leaned against the cockpit doorway as if provoking a fight with the world's largest military inside a restricted area was an everyday thing.

She could argue, but the pilots seemed focused on the landing pad looming close ahead. The engines' pitch changed dramatically, becoming an unmistakable roar that felt closer—directly beneath them. She imagined the ducts they'd noticed at the airport were now redirecting thrust straight down.

Nervous, but unable to do more than observe, Halie returned to her seat and buckled in. Mash did the same. If they were about to be violently tossed back to Los Angeles—and survived—that alone would make a great story to tell.

Yoon never buckled up, never even left the cockpit doorway—a prerogative of the airplane's owner? Rules didn't seem to apply.

The radio speaker blared once more. "Do not attempt to land."

"We already have landing authorization," the pilot challenged.

The Navy helicopter reappeared above and to their left. "Other aircraft have tried and failed due to an electronic interference of unknown type. Break off your approach. If you guys keep going, we'll be fishing you out of the sea."

The fog loomed ahead with the platform's edge visible beyond. Enormous pontoons supported it from beneath with ocean waves crashing against them several hundred meters below. The ship they'd seen earlier—from Ecuador, judging by the flag it was flying—was attached to one pontoon by mooring lines.

Yoon's pilots paid no attention to the continuing demands on the radio, focusing purely on their instruments and the wire's floating rectangle above their control panel.

As they approached, the fog began to glitter in multiple colors. Halie had never seen a natural fog bank do that. Her heart raced. She gripped the seat armrests.

A large hexagon coalesced in the sparkling fog as if fine droplets of water could collectively understand how to draw such a geometric shape. An alarm went off inside the cockpit, startling Halie. Mash nearly dropped her camera.

Halie wasn't sure what actions the military might take beyond yelling at them, but she wasn't anxious to find out. The curtain of colorful, sparking fog was an entirely different matter. Were the rumors true? Would a portal open up and swallow them?

The plane's forward speed reduced to a hover and the pilots finally quieted the alarm, though the roar of redirected engine thrust only increased. The pointy nose of the plane pierced the fog, slicing directly through the center of its misty hexagon.

"The wire is a navigation device?" Halie asked aloud. She didn't expect an answer and didn't get one. She had never seen or read about anything remotely like this landing experience. Pilots had instruments on their panel to guide them. Heads-up displays were common, but a physical fog with matching hexagons outside and inside the cockpit? It felt oddly coordinated, as if the miniature hex in the cockpit was synchronizing with its big brother outside.

"Is it a security system?" Halie asked again. Yoon had suggested his wire was the key.

The hovering jet transitioned through the fog and lowered to the black deck. Puddles from a recent rainfall sprayed away as jet blast reached the surface. Descending the last few meters, they touched down inside the white circle. The roar of engines vanished, replaced by the whine of turbines spinning down. The radio went silent— apparently the military warnings had been a bluff.

The engines finally shut down, leaving only the distant thumps of a retreating Navy helicopter.

Quiet at last. Halie breathed a sigh of relief.

"Welcome to Alpha Base," the pilot announced with a hint of celebration in his voice.

Mash shut off her camera and locked eyes with Halie. "Did we really do that?"

Halie couldn't help a laugh. "Wow! I wasn't expecting that kind of arrival." She unbuckled and went straight to Yoon, who was still standing at the cockpit door, peering through the forward windshield to a broad expanse of a flat deck as big as a soccer field and black as coal.

"I had no idea you were such a rebel." She grinned at Yoon. "Is rich privilege built into those billionaire bones, or did you know they weren't going to do anything?"

Yoon hung his head, smiling. "A game can only be won by those willing to risk loss." He lifted his eyes. "Did I scare you?"

"A bit, yes." Her heart was only beginning to calm.

Yoon locked eyes with her. "My sincerest apologies, my new friend. Perhaps I should mention that our mission may have more surprises ahead."

"I'm glad you're forthright about it," Halie replied. "And perhaps I should mention that I'm still one hundred percent on board."

He reached for her hands, and she gave them. "Good for you, Sahalie Spark. You are brave. Perhaps not quite fearless, but the inconveniences that lie ahead will be worth your while, I assure you."

He waved up Jaya, who unlatched the airplane door and swung it outward. A warm breeze blew in; sea air, carrying tropical scents and high humidity.

"Exactly on the equator," Yoon said. "Shall we explore?"

7. EQUATOR

"I HAVE LIVED IN THE GREEN FOREST between the white mountains and the blue sea my whole life," Léelk'w Sahalie is rumored to have said at the age of seventy-five from her seaside home near Astoria, Oregon. "Before I die, I would like to see the red desert."

Halie had never known her namesake. Léelk'w—the Tlingit word for grandmother and borrowed by the Chinook—had died not long after Halie's birth. Halie had learned about her through Chinook family stories, all clever, none written. Accuracy was another matter.

Had Léelk'w Sahalie gotten her wish? That part of the story was never told, probably because describing a long car trip to Utah wasn't as dramatic as the old lady's final wish itself.

What would she think of me now?

Halie stepped off the airstair from Yoon's plane and filled her lungs with tropical air, moist and salty. A breeze blew across a barren deck that stretched at least a hundred meters in two directions from the corner where they'd landed. Tumbling wisps of fog hung in the air in every direction, with sunlit blue sea further out. In the deck's center, an enormous sloping cone—as black as the platform—rose hyperbolically into the sky. Puffy clouds floated near its peak.

Mash dropped her camera bags next to Halie and stared up. "Monkey Donkey King Kong." Mash's often indecipherable four-beat-two-beat patter somehow captured the scene. They could have been transported into a video game, or to a black-and-white 1930s movie set on a cloud-capped mountain island.

Mash stomped a foot on the black surface. "Feels softer than asphalt. It's supposed to be a giant weight, right?"

"Pretty much," Halie replied, recalling at least a dozen designs she'd reviewed in her science reporting days. Tethers into space needed a firm attachment point since tension was a key design element. The tether's own weight kept it dangling down from space, but things got tricky within the atmosphere. "They don't want the tether to sway, especially if a storm blows through. Fixing it to a floating platform takes care of that."

Halie glanced right. Yoon and his assistant, Quong, had been the first out the door and were already at the platform's edge. While Mash captured the scene, Halie decided to get a feel for the place. They'd coordinate later with Paul for a live shot. She pulled out her satellite phone—good service, since it was linked to one of the geostationary Comsats far above the Kill Zone. Phone services dependent on low Earth orbiting satellites had all gone out of business in the debris catastrophe. Many blamed the unchecked proliferation of those satellites as the primary *cause* of the disaster.

Halie headed toward Yoon, who stood with his toes literally on the platform's corner, speaking with his assistant in Korean. Beyond them, the mysterious wall of mist seemed no more threatening than coastal fog rolling in over Santa Monica Beach.

But this fog couldn't possibly be natural; it seemed more of a security system. *Overly dramatic high-tech*, Halie surmised. Yoon's magic wire had somehow provided the key to let them pass.

With no railing—an obvious safety oversight—Halie approached as close as she dared and peered to the ocean. Several hundred meters below, the ship they'd seen from the air was tied up with a rope wrapped around one of the giant pylons. No dock, no cleats, and no ramp to ascend to the deck. More design oversights. The whole reason to put a space elevator in the ocean was to provide for easy shipping of heavy equipment destined for space.

A gust of wind blew Halie's hair straight up. "A little dangerous on the edge, don't you think?" she said to Yoon and took a step back.

Yoon nodded without reply. He'd left his hat in the plane but still looked enough of an action figure to lead this adventure. He spoke a few more Korean words to Quong, then turned and walked briskly back to the airplane. Halie hurried to keep up.

"Are they Ecuadorans?" she asked of the ship's crew below.

"Soldiers," Yoon said. "They are attempting to reach the deck using grappling hooks and ropes. Quite medieval. If only we had pots of boiling oil."

"So, you don't want them here?"

Yoon turned toward the towering circus tent at the center of the platform. His pace remained energetic; he had something in mind. Mash hooked a camera into the stabilizing shoulder harness she often wore and jumped out in front. Halie was thankful to have a partner who rarely needed direction.

Even with a camera pointed at him, Yoon answered without breaking stride. "We have much to do on our own without soldiers and governments interfering."

"You do realize that just minutes ago you ignored a direct command from the US Navy." Being blunt might provoke more complete answers. She had a hundred more questions lined up for this sometimes evasive billionaire, and they'd only just arrived.

Yoon laughed. "We are in international waters. The United States has no authority here. Neither does Ecuador. It does not matter that we are inside an exclusive economic zone. That law applies to fishing and mineral rights. It has no application to a space elevator."

"So, besides adding a safety railing around the edge, you have other construction tasks still to complete?"

Yoon nodded. The huge cone that dominated the center of the platform was directly ahead. From the deck, it looked less like a tent and more like the sloping roof of a circular building. Its bottom edge left a gap above the deck tall enough to drive a truck through. Dark shadows made it difficult to see what was beneath.

Halie threw out her first burning question. "How did we get through the mist? The Navy seemed to think we were about to take a nosedive into the ocean, and I got the feeling we wouldn't be the first. Maybe that's what happened to the Ecuadoran helicopter?"

Yoon smiled. "Secrets." He kept walking. The towering structure ahead grew ever larger.

"You said your antigravity wire thingy is a key. Does the smaller hexagon fit into the bigger hexagon, allowing us to land but no one else?"

Yoon's smile grew, but he didn't answer.

"Exclusive access," Halie reminded. "Questions are supposed to have answers."

"Give me one moment," Yoon said.

"I'll give you two moments," Halie snapped back. "But the camera is rolling, and it'll stay that way until we've captured your very thorough explanation." She motioned to Mash, who trotted in an orbit around them.

They stopped at the edge of the circus tent roof and looked up. Even from the ground, it looked like a sheath. Its steep pitch probably had something to do with wind flow around the tether. Deep snow—if such a meteorological event were possible at sea level on the equator—would have little chance to linger.

Yoon walked on and Halie kept up at his side. The tent's dark interior mimicked its exterior. It felt like standing under the bell of a trombone. A collection of low buildings—sheds, really—created a maze of structures separated by narrow passageways. A larger main pathway brought them straight to the tent's center, where steps led up to a semicircular elevated platform surrounding two vertical ribbons spaced ten meters apart.

Halie followed Yoon up the steps. They stopped only an arm's length away from one of the ribbons. A silvery mirrored surface gave it the look of a sheet of aluminum foil stretched as tight as a bandsaw blade.

About a meter in width and thin as a kitchen knife, the ribbon dropped through a slot in the deck to an unseen attachment point somewhere beneath. Overhead, it soared straight up until its slender profile was entirely lost in the shadows. A pinprick of sunlight far above exposed its final exit point—the same opening in the sheath they'd observed while circling for landing.

Halie felt a twinge of excitement being so close to the heart of the space elevator system. She struggled to imagine its extraordinary length. This ribbon rose higher than the tallest building, taller than every skyscraper in the world stacked on top of each other.

"It's so thin," she whispered. She reached out, her hand pulled toward this object of exquisite beauty just as an unthinking tourist reaches out to touch a Greek statue. Quickly, she withdrew, overcome by an odd feeling that a creation of such scale must remain unsullied.

While its flat surface looked like polished metal, Halie knew it couldn't be aluminum, steel, or even titanium. No matter how strong, a metal ribbon would be useless. The problem was something the engineers called *tensile strength*: the weight borne by a given material. A wound steel cable snapped under its own weight once the length exceeded a calculated threshold.

"Graphene or nanotubes?" Halie asked, aware she was showing off, but only because she needed a more transparent conversation with Yoon. She had read a dozen engineering summaries, and single-crystal graphene had been the choice of designers since the 2020s. Under a microscope, the material looked like hexagonal chicken wire. In nature, tiny bits of it glommed together to form ordinary graphite used in pencils. But when produced as a uniform crystal, graphene provided enough tensile strength to span thousands of kilometers without breaking. It had made space elevators possible.

Yoon answered her question obliquely. "Multilayered graphene is the preferred material. Carbon nanotubes are essentially rolled-up sheets of graphene, but they're hard to manufacture at the lengths needed for a tether."

He reached out and lightly stroked the ribbon.

"Shouldn't you be wearing a glove?" Halie asked.

Yoon huffed. "It's a working tether, not an antiquity." He placed his palm on the ribbon and pushed. The rigid material didn't flex any more than an iron plate at the base of the Eiffel Tower. "Try it yourself."

Halie tensed, not sure if Yoon's offer came from a place of generosity or was part of an experiment. She'd read somewhere that carbon nanostructures weren't just strong, they were also good conductors of electricity. Could a tether long enough to wrap around the world build up a static charge? And what would happen if a lightning bolt struck it?

She cautiously reached out, at first glancing a single finger off the shiny surface, then two. Finally, she pressed her whole palm against its width.

It felt solid. Cold, like touching a windowpane on a winter day.

Mash brought the camera in close. Halie held her hand very still, sensing something in her fingertips. "It trembles. Just a tiny bit, but noticeable. Do you feel it?"

Yoon nodded. "Far above us, the tether is taking hits."

Halie's eyes widened. She pulled her hand back. "The Kill Zone?" The trembles were no more than microflexes, but she could imagine shocking violence somewhere above as each bit of high-speed debris slammed into this ribbon and produced a vibration down its length.

"Will it survive?"

Yoon gave a crisp nod without a hint of doubt. "It will."

Halie glanced around and saw nothing that looked remotely like a device that might latch onto the ribbon. "So, how do you climb it?"

With eyes closed and his jaw tightened, he looked a little disappointed at the question. "To be determined."

Halie decided not to press. Yoon already seemed unsatisfied with his new creation; maybe he'd unveiled it too quickly. The twin tethers and the base platform were significant accomplishments, but his crew hadn't even installed handrails around the deck perimeter, or at this elevated platform. They might need months before this marvel of engineering would become operational.

Disappointing, but Halie still had exclusive access to a story that would eventually dazzle. Even the simple fact that a tether into space was surviving regular hits from the Kill Zone was noteworthy.

I can adjust. It's a good first step.

Even if it only survived a year, Yoon's creation could be a pathway to replace aging geostationary satellites. And if a big hit took one ribbon down, there was still a backup.

She'd work with Paul to broadcast a live shot, then organize enough material for a show to be aired at a future date. Maybe she and Mash would return when Yoon was ready to make his first ascent. A small delay. No big deal.

They retraced their steps back to the parked airplane. Both Yoon and Halie pulled out phones. Yoon spoke in Korean, probably to someone in Seoul. Halie gave him some distance and called Paul.

"*Saludos* from sunny Ecuador," she said when Paul picked up. It was predawn in California, but the sounds of sipping coffee made it clear she hadn't woken him.

"Is it totally amazing? What does it look like?" Paul asked with the enthusiasm of a parent whose child was on a field trip.

"Well, it's big. It's mostly black. It's got a huge spire going up into the sky. Mash is getting everything. She probably has a terabyte of background video already. Good news, the tether is real. I touched it, Paul. I felt that thing quivering against my hand. It's very sturdy. Yoon says it's being hit by debris, but it's holding up to the punishment. I don't know how, but that alone would make a great topic for the show. The only bad news is this place is still under construction. Yoon's not ready to climb it. He's on the phone to his people right now. Doesn't sound happy either, so I'm guessing there are a few kinks to work out."

"But he's still keeping this exclusive, right?"

"Yup. In fact, we're the only people here. Yoon has some kind of futuristic landing control system built into this place. Both the Ecuadorans and the US military are on-site, but they can't land on the platform. Yoon has the only key."

"That's good, I guess. I'll get a time slot for your live shot from the network and call you back. But, Halie, give me something good. Not just a talking head with the platform in the background. Go back to that tether. Put your hand on it again and describe what you feel. That's pure gold."

"I'm on it."

When she hung up, Yoon was standing next to her. "No live broadcasts. Not yet."

Halie spun around, instantly infuriated, mouth open. "What? You promised."

Yoon held up his hands defensively. "I know. I did. And I want you to tell the world. Your reports will be to my advantage. Just... not yet."

Halie felt her blood pressure spiking. "We had a deal."

"We still do... within boundaries. I have the electronics to block your videographer's satellite uplink, but I would rather not create a confrontation. You and I are on the same team, but before the public sees this creation for what it is, there are a few issues I must work out."

"Such as?" Halie took a deep breath and exhaled hard. It didn't do much to release her frustration.

"Ecuador, for one. They are claiming the platform as their own. Even now their soldiers are attempting to climb it. If they succeed, I expect they will confine me to my airplane and confiscate your cameras. Not good for either of us."

"Maybe so, but that was my producer. He's lining up a live slot as we speak. I promised him I would deliver, and I don't go back on my promises. If it's South American politics that worries you, I can limit what I say, but I still need access. News stories don't wait. For all we know, there's an embedded journalist with the Ecuador military who wants this story too. And they'll tell the story from Ecuador's perspective. Probably not good for you."

Yoon lowered his head, sighing. "I expect you are right, but you don't understand the full picture."

"Then explain it to me."

"A ship from Lima will be arriving soon." Yoon spoke barely above a whisper, though no one else was near. Mash was off gathering more background video, currently pointing her camera at Quong, who was playing with the magic floating wire.

"Peru is involved now?"

Yoon nodded. "I expect their arrival within two hours. On board is equipment and a specialist from the university in Lima... an associate of mine. I need his help. If you delay your live broadcast until after the ship arrives, I can promise you a story far better than simply touching the tether. I will include you on our first ride up."

Halie's jaw dropped. A ride up Yoon's space elevator? Who turns that down? So far, she'd seen no means to accomplish an ascent, but maybe that was about to change.

"Two hours?" Halie repeated. It was certainly better than coming back next month, and a short delay wouldn't make much difference for the live shot as long as Ecuadoran soldiers didn't start swarming across the deck to confiscate cameras. For that matter, the US Navy helicopter must have come from an aircraft carrier steaming this way. The platform might soon be crawling with multiple militaries, which was exactly Yoon's concern. Their goals were aligned, as long as Halie set her journalistic intensity aside.

"Like you, I keep my promises," Yoon said. "All I need is your cooperation."

"And we can continue recording in the meantime?"

"Please do."

Halie calmed, shrugging. "My producer may not like it, but I'll tell him what you told me."

In reality, Paul wouldn't be that difficult. Live shots were notoriously fluid, often delayed depending on circumstances at the location. It wouldn't be a deal breaker, particularly since she could imagine an ultimate shot that would knock the socks off KNS execs—not to mention every viewer on the planet.

I'm going for a ride on a space elevator.

Even if it was a short test and they stopped below the Kill Zone, it would be an experience like no other. Halie had been to the top of New York skyscrapers, but those were lowly ground dwellers compared to the view she'd get at the top of the atmosphere. Even Yoon's high-flying jet had barely reached twenty percent of that height. With Mash capturing the action and Halie narrating, they could do a lot.

She held out a hand to Yoon, "It's a deal." This time they shook on it. He'd better keep his promise.

They split up again. Yoon spoke with Quong while Halie walked to several low-rise buildings near the platform's east edge and called Paul. He didn't explode. On the contrary, he said the network wanted to wait anyway. A noon Eastern time slot would be better for the live shot. More eyeballs on the television.

Back on track, Halie scanned the deck, searching for Mash. The American helicopter flew by once more. It made no threatening moves and issued no gravely worded warnings over a loudspeaker. Perhaps they'd resumed their police role, guarding an important site in international waters even while tacitly allowing the owner to inspect his property. There wasn't much they could do about it anyway. Yoon had the key—they didn't.

Grappling hooks from the Ecuadoran soldiers were another matter. Halie had a hard time believing Yoon's ring of fog could keep a determined climber out. Likewise, if an aircraft carrier was on the way, its conning tower might be tall enough to reach the platform's edge. Shoot a few rope lines and they could run one of those bosun's chairs across.

She'd worry about that later. For now, she'd make sure Mash had captured enough background video.

Mash was nowhere to be seen, but it was a big place, and Halie hadn't explored anything beyond the tent that surrounded the ribbons. She wandered, calling out Mash's name and finding more of the low-rise buildings, particularly along the platform's perimeter. Given that none of them had doors or windows, they might only be housings for machinery, perhaps equipment that helped manage the tension on the ribbon.

Halie passed beneath the central tent and walked around the twin tethers and out the other side. She spotted Mash down a corridor between two buildings and yelled, catching her attention.

"Dazed and amazed," Mash said, running up. She still had her primary video camera attached to the stabilizing harness, but she had added one more piece of equipment: a small tablet computer wired directly into the camera. "This place is freaking me out."

"In a good way?"

"In a freaky way. Look at this." Mash located a video clip she'd previously recorded and played it back to the tablet.

In the recording, Quong held the same magical wire he'd shown them back in LA. He lifted it in the air and let it go. The wire spread out to the same fuzzy rectangle they'd seen before, but this time a very different image formed in the mist. It looked like a board game with hexagonal game pieces.

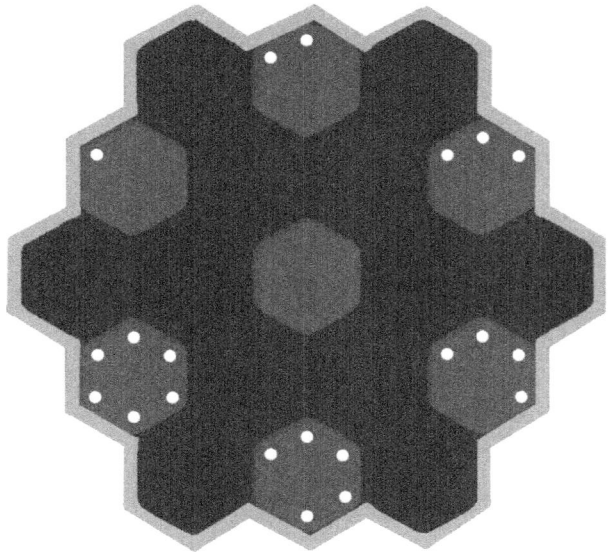

The game pieces—dark gray hexagons—were set inside a larger container outlined in light gray. One piece was unlabeled, but six were numbered with white dots similar to the way dice are printed, one through six.

As Halie watched Mash's video clip, the image changed. It now displayed the same board game but with the pieces in a different configuration.

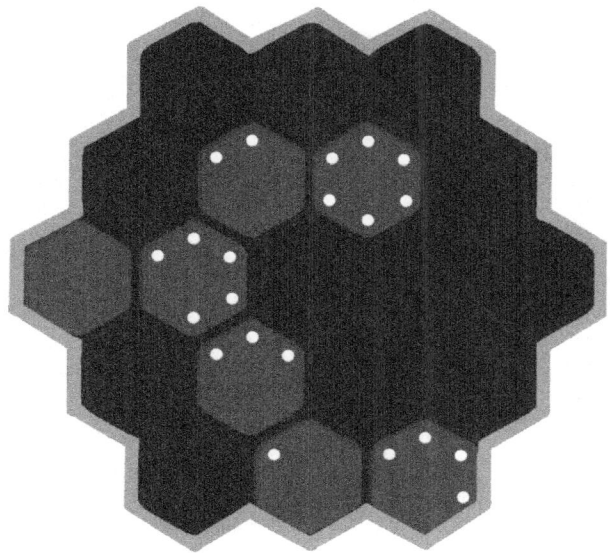

"Quong was playing a game with his fancy floating wire?" Halie thought her guess unlikely. Quong seemed to be one of those stoic types with a sense of fun close to zero.

"Definitely not a game. It wasn't interactive. More of before-and-after pictures. But you tell me. You're seeing exactly what I saw."

The misty image switched between the two versions, back and forth. When Quong finally touched the floating screen, it collapsed down to a thin wire, which he plucked out of the air and put in his pocket.

"It's a puzzle?" Halie asked, staring at Mash.

Mash shut off the playback and stared. "That's what I think. Solve it, and something happens. Of course you have to find it first. I swear to God, Quong was looking all over the place."

"Wait. Why would Yoon's assistant be searching for a puzzle here? Didn't Yoon build this platform?"

"All I know is the moment Quong shut off that wire, he was on the hunt."

"So, did he find it?"

A fiendish grin spread across Mash's face. "I saved the best part for last."

"You mean…?"

"Indeed, I do. Quong never found it. But I did."

8. PUZZLE

HALIE FOLLOWED MASH TO a cluster of low-rise sheds beneath the tent roof. Narrow pathways between them became a maze without exits. It might be why Quong hadn't searched this dead end for the hexagonal puzzle Mash said she'd found.

The boxy buildings with no windows and no doors came in varying sizes, some with tops head-high, others that reached halfway to the bell-shaped roof. Somehow, Mash navigated the intersections that led deeper into the maze. She turned down one particularly dark corridor. "Kind of creepy here," she said.

Halie agreed. It felt like negotiating the back alleys of a lifeless city.

The path ended at a blank wall several meters wide and at least forty meters tall. Mash examined one side, then waved her hand in the air. A small light flicked on, dimly illuminating a hexagon shape embedded in the wall.

"There you go," she said.

"Nice!" Halie moved closer to inspect the physical version of the misty shape. It looked like a hexagonal boardgame chiseled into the wall. Its edges were sharp—light gray with a black interior. Seven smaller hexagons extruded a centimeter above its background—the gameboard's playing pieces. Six of them were numbered with white dots at the hexagon corners. The game piece in the center had no markings at all.

"Definitely a puzzle," Halie said. She slid the unnumbered center piece to the right, pushing it up against pieces marked with three and four dots. The piece moved easily, possibly hooked into a track in the game board, though in the dim light she saw nothing but a black surface.

With the center piece now up against two other pieces, there was nowhere else to slide it but back to its original position. With six corners, the hex shapes proved to be a greater challenge than the sliding puzzles commonly sold in toy stores.

"Okay, a little trickier than I thought," Halie said, "but it can't be that hard to solve since we already have the answer."

Mash patted the tablet on her camera harness. "Got it on a freeze frame. But are you sure you want to mess with it? I figured touching something Yoon's bodyguard was looking for might be a bad idea."

Halie scrunched her nose. "Why is Quong searching at all? If Yoon built this platform, then he's also the guy who put the puzzle in the wall. Am I missing something?"

"Yoon's the CEO. Not a hands-on guy. Maybe he knows it's supposed to be here somewhere, but he doesn't have the blueprints."

Lost in thought, Halie didn't answer.

"Yeah, dumb idea," Mash said.

Halie waved. "No, not dumb. It's just that it raises more questions that hadn't occurred to me until just now. Nobody builds a structure as complicated as a space elevator without a big team. Designers, manufacturing people, installation crews... so where are they? Sure, Yoon has a thousand workers in some big factory in Korea, but wouldn't there at least be a few project managers here? A contingent of security people? Other than Yoon's flight crew, we seem to be alone."

Mash pointed a finger at Halie. "You don't trust him."

"Not really. Do you?"

Mash shrugged "I don't trust anyone, so nothing new there. But you're the girl scout here, not me... and I mean that in a good way."

"You actually don't."

"Okay, I don't. So, I'll reclassify you as a skeptic who happens to be super nice."

"I'll take that."

"Whereas I'm an unruly subversive with a twisted mind who knows her way around a camera. It's my devious nature that tells me Yoon is lying."

"Lying about what?"

"Either this is a Tallahassee Steam Roll and that ribbon into the sky is nothing but smoke and mirrors... or somebody else built it, and Yoon's trying to take control."

Halie put a hand to her lips, thinking through those possibilities. The whole thing could be an elaborate hoax, as Mash's made-up phrase implied. Halie had busted a few in her career. But Yoon didn't fit the type. He might be confused, even pissed off at someone on his team, but there wasn't enough reason to think he would concoct a blatantly false narrative in front of live television cameras.

Unfortunately, Mash's other alternative might be worse. "Okay, I'll admit that it's possible that a competitor built this platform, and Yoon is trying to steal it."

"He stole the floating wire," Mash offered without proof. "You said yourself, it's the key. Maybe our story angle should change. Maybe this is industrial espionage." Mash tilted her eyebrows, clearly ready to expose a vast network of spies.

"Look at it another way." Halie often argued with herself as a way to reach the right answer. "If this platform belongs to someone else, then where is *their* security team? Where are *their* project managers?"

"Yoon bumped them off."

"So now he's a corporate mob boss?"

"Could be."

Halie shook her head. "I don't know. Evil mastermind just doesn't match his style."

Everything Halie knew about the man painted a picture of a stable, thoughtful businessman—the opposite of the previous batch of self-aggrandizing yahoos who'd dragged the world into the Kessler Syndrome mess. Yoon had long been one of the biggest cheerleaders for space elevators. He had stood at many lecterns preaching the advantages of an electric lift versus rockets well before the debris catastrophe hit.

Halie also had a fair understanding of how space elevators were supposed to work, having covered the story for nearly a decade. As a KNS science journalist, she'd watched the promos and attended the regular news conferences hosted by the International Space Elevator Consortium.

Every competing design had been sea-based and included a platform with helicopter landing pads and docks for ships. Each design used tethers made from carbon, and they all placed a high-mass anchor above geostationary height. From there, the designs diverged. Providing reliable power to climbers—or ascenders—that would carry people or hardware into space had turned out to be complicated. A few designs featured observation decks. One had a space hotel. Others were more utilitarian, focusing on launching satellites at one-tenth the price of rockets.

But a key fact stood out in Halie's mind: the various designs had enough similarities to one another that the CEO of one company could stand on a competitor's platform and know roughly how it worked.

As long as they had the keys to the car.

Yoon did. His magic wire had given them entry and was still keeping multiple navies at bay. But did the key belong to him? Or had he stolen it? There might be a way to find out. The wire had already provided clues.

Halie pointed to Mash's tablet computer. "Bring up the answer. Let's solve this puzzle and see what happens. At the very least, it keeps us one step ahead of Yoon."

"But what if he finds out? He'll be pissed. Might bump us off too."

Halie loved her friend's active imagination and valued her creativity. But Mash could be paranoid at times. Then again, maybe Mash's fears were justified. The world could feel like a hard place when you didn't fit into one of the regular slots that society fashioned for people. Halie had once listened intently as Mashup had described her rebellious teenage years; she'd stood out from "normal" in almost every way.

"How about this—I'll solve the puzzle while you live stream it back to the studio. The video gets safely stored on our server in LA and becomes our ace in the hole. Then we confront Yoon and show him what we found. No matter what the puzzle unlocks, Yoon will almost certainly be happy—he's searching for it too. But if he's pissed, we'll still have our ace to play. Nobody's going to get bumped off when the secret has already been leaked."

Mash raised a tight fist. "Cowabunga High Ride," she hammered out in her singsong cadence. In this case it probably didn't mean anything more than *fuck yeah*, but Mash's linguistic alternatives to casual swearing were always welcome.

They bumped fists.

Mash set up the shot, fiddling with a satellite datalink on her harness. Halie was only vaguely aware of how it all worked, but she knew much of the process was automated. Once configured, the camera would feed directly to their studio, where the video would be stored. And Halie would stay true to her word not to broadcast without Yoon's approval.

While Mash worked, Halie studied the dual images on Mash's tablet, comparing the puzzle's initial configuration to its solution. When Mash hoisted her camera, Halie began sliding the movable pieces around.

She quickly realized the winning strategy was to create empty space in the middle by temporarily moving pieces to the outer rim. She could then move each piece a little closer to its destination until they were all approximately where they needed to be. In one final sweep, she clicked each piece into place.

"Now what?" she asked. Mash moved the camera in close.

"Try pushing it," Mash said. "Like it's a mist button."

Halie did. The light above the puzzle clicked off. Air hissed, and a door-sized panel slid open, revealing a dark chamber large enough to produce echoes.

Halie rolled her eyes. "Always with the secret doors. These billionaire geeks and their toys."

Not feeling quite as fearless as her flippant remark suggested, she peered into a cavernous space. Something very large was inside. She swallowed hard and took a step through the open doorway.

As her foot crossed the threshold, half of the wall on the far side of the chamber slid open, ushering in daylight and instantly illuminating the interior.

Halie froze with Mash right behind.

They stood inside a spacious hangar with a high ceiling. A fantastic vehicle of metal and glass stood upright in its center like a futuristic rocket plane ready for launch. Its fuselage was mostly cylindrical, divided into an upper passenger compartment enclosed by wraparound glass and a lower open bay like the bed of a pickup truck. Swept-back wings jutted out on one side, but unlike a jet or space shuttle, the wings were folded inward to form a V shape. Wings and body smoothly tapered to a rounded point at the top, giving it the sleek lines of a bullet train—standing vertically.

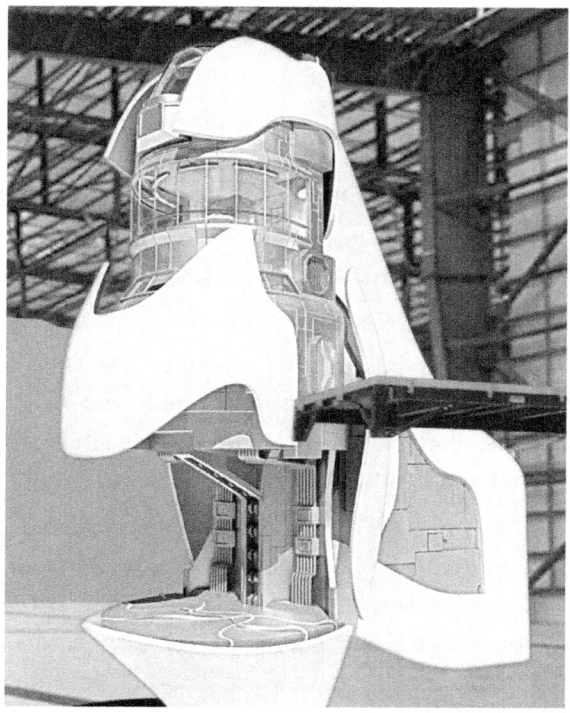

"It's an ascender," Halie said with certainty.

Upper-level glass provided a clear view into the passenger compartment, also divided into two levels, a lower entryway and a ladder that climbed to a seating area. The ship's entry door was at least ten meters off the hangar floor, but a mezzanine level jutted out from the hangar wall providing access via stairs.

Halie remained on the hangar floor for now. She circled the vehicle, trying to absorb the details of such a magnificent machine. Mash followed, capturing everything. The open cargo bay was currently empty but seemed capable of carrying a large load. Straps hung from eyelets positioned around its curving back wall. At the ship's backside, wings extended outward as if a dolphin was attempting to clap pectoral fins. They joined the fuselage at a thin slot that split the vehicle's cylindrical shape from top to bottom like a hot dog sliced down the middle. The slot was no more than three or four centimeters across and a half meter deep.

Perfectly sized to attach to a ribbon?

Halie didn't need an engineering drawing to know that vertically spaced magnets would be embedded on both sides of the slot, a design that would propel the ship upward via magnetic levitation. It also explained the V-wings. They had nothing to do with flying. The design kept the center of gravity over the tether centerline, which eliminated ribbon distortion as it climbed. She remembered a similar Japanese design from years ago.

Halie finished her circuit of the glistening spacecraft, arriving at the far side of the hangar where shelves stocked a variety of spare parts— magnets, coils, electrical wire, and switches—all neatly arranged but without inventory labels.

Further along, the large hangar doorway that had slid open on its own provided an unobstructed opening at least thirty meters high. When she stepped across its threshold, she found herself back in familiar territory. To the left, a wide stretch of open deck ended at Yoon's airplane parked at the platform's corner. Jaya and the pilots casually strolled the deck like sightseers at a tourist site. They were too far away to spot Halie or the newly opened hangar door.

To the right, the twin ribbons stood waiting—almost beckoning for the ascender to join them. She hadn't noticed before, but a slot in the deck led directly from the hangar to the twin ribbons. Halie crouched, peering under the ascender to confirm that the machine perched atop a metal frame dropping into the slot.

A broad smile spread across her face. Halie climbed the mezzanine stairs and stood next to the ascender at its midpoint. Now far above the hangar floor, the machine felt even larger. She stepped through its open door without hesitation.

Down on the hangar floor, Mash lowered her camera. "Careful in there. Don't push any buttons."

"Exactly what I'm looking for," Halie replied.

The lower passenger level was plain, almost utilitarian. Shelves on one side seemed ready for luggage. Two lavatories looked similar to those found on airlines. Halie opened one, finding the expected toilet. No light switches. No mechanism to close the entryway hatch, which stood open on hinges much like the door on an airplane.

"Up we go, then," Halie said.

Sturdy rungs where the wings came together in a V-notch made the climb to the second floor easy, leaving her standing in a semicircular passenger seating area. A C-shaped couch followed the curve of floor-to-ceiling windows around the ship's front side, leaving a narrow aisle along the window. At its backside, the interior between V-wings provided standing room with more windows facing out and in.

Seating for twenty people easy. Thirty, including standing room. But where do the pilots sit?

Overhead, the compartment narrowed to the ship's bullet-train nose with enough glass to allow a clear view straight up. No cockpit. This ship was no airplane.

Returning to the ladder, she finally spotted what she'd been looking for. A rectangular metal plate was embedded into the wall at eye level.

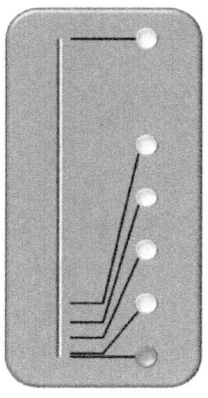

It was copper colored with a vertical line etched into its left side. Six circular indentations were unevenly spaced down the right side. Callout lines connected the circles to positions on the vertical line. Every few seconds, the circle at the bottom blinked green.

"It's an elevator diagram," Halie whispered to herself.

For a brief moment, she hovered a finger over the second circle from the bottom, then withdrew. If the panel was merely an indicator of current position, her touch might do nothing at all. But if this ascender was controlled like any building elevator, a simple touch might suddenly send her into space. The blinking light was a sure sign this ship already had power.

She shook off the overly simplistic thoughts. It couldn't be that easy. More likely, there were defined procedures to position the ascender on the tether, secure its slot magnets over the ribbon, balance its load against weight and torque limits, and test its braking and pressurized air systems. Only when a panel of lights lit up green at some launch command center located in one of the many sheds scattered around the platform would anyone dare to begin an ascent to space.

She would need Yoon's full attention. For that matter, a launch might require Yoon's magic wire. It had been the key to landing at the platform and the key to unlocking the hangar. The advanced technology built into this device was still unexplained, and lack of answers had never sat well with Halie.

Time to find out.

She rejoined Mash on the hangar floor. "It looks ready to fly," Mash said. Halie nodded her agreement.

Yoon would have the answers, and if he didn't, he'd call one of his engineers in Korea. The launch command center might even be there, with all ascents handled remotely. But before anyone went anywhere, Halie needed the answer to a very different question: was Yoon the man he claimed to be? Was he the owner of this technology, or not?

They exited through the smaller door they'd first entered. Halie repositioned several of the puzzle pieces and pushed the hexagon once more. Both hangar doors closed, leaving no trace of a seam.

"Let's find Yoon," she said. "That guy has some explaining to do."

9. FIRST ASCENT

HALIE PAUSED AT THE PLATFORM'S center. Overhead, an unrelenting sun was a reminder of their equatorial location. "Let's ditch the camera for now," Halie told Mash. They would need straight talk from Yoon, and a journalist's assurance of being off the record had a way of loosening lips.

Mash grunted. "I'd rather tear my eyeballs out. We're onsite, so I'm always rolling. Always."

Halie had to admit that newsworthy events had a way of popping up when least expected. "Fine, but switch from the shoulder cam to something less… conspicuous?"

"How's this?" Mash reached into a zippered pocket on her gear bag and withdrew a hair clip accessory. She jammed it into the tangle on her head, sending one disheveled lock sideways and another straight up. In an odd way, the disguise worked. "This thing's great for raiding illegal Mahjong parlors and back-alley drug deals," Mash assured.

Camera camouflage settled, they continued across the open platform against a breeze carrying complex scents of salt and seaweed. Yoon stood at the very edge near his supersonic jet—still the only aircraft to manage a landing, though several were circling. Quong was on hands and knees, leaning over the platform's edge to the sea below.

Halie marched straight to Yoon with Mash lagging behind. While she understood Mash's reluctance to raise sensitive issues, Halie still believed the story had little to do with corporate espionage. The platform and its tether to space represented an answer to the debris problem. *That* was the story the world needed to hear, and one way or another, Yoon would be the path.

"Found you," Halie said, interrupting an intense exchange in Korean that included several shouts from Quong to someone below.

Yoon swiveled. "Our friends from Ecuador seem to have a very different perspective about this patch of ocean. I don't speak Spanish, but I believe they plan to force our surrender."

Halie leaned over the unprotected edge far enough to see several uniformed soldiers in climbing harnesses swinging from a rope. She couldn't see where the rope had been attached, but the soldiers weren't more than twenty meters below the deck. Their attempt to scale the platform wasn't the only worrisome development. A second ship had moored where the pontoons met the sea, with at least forty soldiers on its deck. Armed.

"I see what you mean," Halie said.

The man highest up the rope yelled something in Spanish. Halie didn't recognize any of the words, but his tone was unmistakably hostile. Quong yelled back in Korean, making a counterpoint if only for his personal satisfaction. Quong probably had enough muscle to prevent the soldiers from crawling over the deck's edge, but any physical confrontation risked gunfire from below. This argument would be better served by a Spanish to Korean translator.

A US helicopter roared past, low enough to blast the deck with the downwash from thumping rotor blades.

Yoon stood his ground, though the gray hair on both sides of his head was blown out of place. "The American aircraft carrier will be here soon. They will bring electronic countermeasures capable of defeating jamming. And I should point out that if either of these militaries take control of the platform, your access to cover this story will surely end. My humble apologies—a development I did not expect."

Halie pursed her lips, feeling the truth of Yoon's statement. "Don't apologize just yet. There's something I need to show you, but we'll need to hurry."

She waved him away from the edge, then led toward the platform's center at a trot. For his age, he kept up well. Mash joined them, her camera packed away as Halie had requested. With the military closing in, they wouldn't have much time, but Halie was determined not to lose her access.

They returned to the maze of dark passageways under the circus tent and located the blank wall with the embedded puzzle. Halie waved her hand just as Mash had done, and a light flickered on.

Yoon drew close, staring intently at the mostly completed puzzle. "You found it."

"We did. Mash did. Were you looking for it too?"

"It… it was misplaced," he said, clearly still hiding behind a cover story with a bigger truth waiting in the wings.

Halie bristled but bit her lip. Once this door opened, Yoon would have to spill the beans. She pushed the two out-of-place puzzle pieces into their proper locations and commanded, "Push it."

He did. The panel to their left slid open once more. Halie stepped through, which triggered the hangar door on the far side to slide open. The magnificent ascender stood tall in the center. Yoon stared up, speechless as he wandered around it.

"The V-pod," he finally whispered.

"The what?"

He brushed a hand against its smooth surface. "It is a V-pod, a tether climber. V for vertical, ascent or descent, but also because of the V-slot in back where it attaches to the ribbon. The shape leaves room for station attachment cables to fan out from the ribbon's outside edge. Unmistakably my design… yet subtly different." He studied the ship's surface like he'd never seen glass before.

"Is it yours or not?" Halie demanded, arms crossed.

"I… I," he stuttered, then started up the mezzanine stairs to the ship's open door. "I must be sure."

Yoon marched directly into the ascender with Halie right behind. He wasted no time at the lower passenger level, quickly climbing the rungs embedded at the ship's V-notch. He seemed to know where the controls would be.

At the second level, Yoon stopped in front of the copper-colored panel with its six circles. He nodded vigorously and spoke with excitement, his hands hovering over the circles. "Yes! Exactly! The full tether, marked with six levels. The flashing light, quite clearly showing our current location at Level 1. Level 6 would of course be at 35,786 kilometers above us at geostationary height." A smile spread across his face.

She'd given him enough rope to hang himself, so the morbid expression went. Yoon unquestionably was discovering the features of this ascender as he described them. Not exactly the behavior of the man who had recently finished construction.

"So, who made it?" she asked, keeping her voice as pleasant as she could manage.

Yoon looked up from the panel. "It is"—he bowed his head—"a long story. One that I promise to share." He looked up once more. "But not now. I must accomplish a critical task, and I fear my time is running out."

"The Ecuadoran soldiers?" Halie asked.

Yoon nodded. "And the American Navy too. We must hurry. We shall ascend at once."

"Ascend?" Halie asked, incredulous at how fast things were moving now that a simple puzzle had been solved. "Right now?"

"We have not a moment to lose." Yoon hurried down the ladder, with Halie taking two rungs at a time to keep up. The corporate confession she'd been expecting had suddenly become a journey into space. Today. This instant.

"I'm going too?" Halie jumped off the bottom rung as Yoon hurried out the ship's doorway.

"You and your videographer. I will need photographic evidence beamed to the world. It is, in fact, the whole reason I asked you to come."

He launched down the mezzanine steps, past the equipment shelves and out the large hangar door. Halie and Mash dashed after him.

"Better get ready to shoot," Halie yelled to Mash as they ran across the deck toward Yoon's airplane. "We're heading up."

"Up?" Mash asked.

Halie grinned. "Outer space, baby. This game is on!"

Cameras and shoulder bags swung around Mash as she ran. "Uh... just to clarify... we're going into space led by the man who is confused about the structure he claims to have created?"

"True, we still need answers, not the least of which is why everything is a hexagon around here... but I have a feeling we're about to get them."

Halie skidded to a halt at the bottom of the airstair leading into Yoon's plane. Yoon was already inside, but Quong blocked its doorway. A minute later, Yoon returned with an armload of gear. Quong and Jaya helped him carry it to the deck.

Yoon unrolled a bodysuit, similar to the neoprene suits divers wore. He held it up to Halie. "It should fit. Put it on."

Halie took the suit, feeling its slick texture and sturdy fabric. "Over my clothes?"

Yoon bent over the other gear. "Take off your clothes if you wish or leave them on. Either way, the suit will keep you safe..." He looked up. "A precaution only. The V-pod should be fully pressurized."

Mash accepted her own suit from Yoon, speaking to Halie. "*Should* be pressurized, he says. But for some reason we still need spacesuits."

"Put it on," Halie said under her breath. "Doesn't matter if God himself built it, we still need to be careful. This is a first ascent."

Halie could almost hear a more critical version of herself screaming to hit the brakes on this impromptu plan. The man guiding them was hiding something. The machine—though strikingly beautiful—was untested. And space was deadly even on a good day.

You came here to get the story, she told herself. *Cold feet are for penguins.*

She slipped the bodysuit over her shoes and pants which turned out to be easier than expected. The interior material was less like neoprene and more like nylon, essentially a full-body snow ski bib that zipped up the front and included zip-on gloves that dangled at the end of each arm.

With Jaya's help, all three were suited up quickly. Yoon handed out helmets. Lightweight, they were considerably slimmer than a motorcyclist might wear and provided a wide glass front that covered the full face. He hooked his own helmet under his arm, explaining they wouldn't need to wear them just yet.

He slipped one more item into a pocket at the side of each bodysuit, a red metal cylinder about the size of a water bottle. "Supplemental oxygen. Just in case."

Mash nodded to Halie with a mocking expression. "Just in case."

Jaya handed out three small backpacks to complete their gear. "Food and water for your trip. I prepared the spring rolls myself. I hope you like them."

"Thank you," Halie said, wondering exactly when Jaya had known that an ascent into space had been the plan all along. How long would they be up there? The pack wasn't heavy. If it held more than a lunch and dinner, Halie would be surprised.

Quong inspected the suit his boss wore, then checked Halie and Mash. He spoke with Yoon in Korean, nodded, then returned to his post at the platform's edge.

"Quong will keep the soldiers at bay for as long as he can—within reason. We don't wish to start a war, but we do need to be the first up the tether."

"Why?"

"For the same reason that the first climber atop Mount Everest is the only name we remember. Sir Edmund Hillary."

"You want to be remembered."

"I need to establish ownership."

"Rightful ownership?"

"Is there any other kind?"

In fact, there was. History was replete with stolen ideas, hostile takeovers, and plagiarism. Hillary was a prime example since his Nepalese guide was likely the first to summit Everest. For now, Halie was willing to follow through with the ill-defined story she'd signed up for. They'd soon find out if the space elevator worked. They could sort out ownership later.

With Quong still yelling unseemly Korean phrases at Ecuadoran soldiers and an American helicopter buzzing overhead, they hurried across the deck to the open hangar door. Their gleaming spaceship stood inside, ready for its first flight.

"Um... how much testing did you do?" Halie asked. She acknowledged a level of comfort in Yoon's willingness to take the first ride, but Mash's points were well taken. Halie herself maintained a sensible fear of heights, or more accurately the fear of falling. It was nothing crippling, but like anyone peering over a sheer cliff after being told a mule would soon carry her down its steeply switchbacked trail, Halie grasped the issue. Climbing up was easy. But coming down? The mind was adept at imagining every fatal result of a slip.

Yoon happily answered. "We once floated a test tether beneath a cluster of helium balloons and successfully climbed to twenty-three kilometers. A world record."

"But twenty-three kilometers isn't into space."

Yoon laughed. "Officially, space begins at one hundred kilometers, a height that has been inaccessible for the past four years. It is time we changed that, don't you think?"

"I completely agree, I'm just wondering what I'm getting myself into."

"An adventure!"

"But, a reasonably safe adventure, right? You billionaire types don't exactly have the best stats on first launches."

Yoon smiled.

Halie took a deep breath, then followed Yoon into the rocket ship that wouldn't require a rocket to launch. At least electricity and magnets weren't flammable. They left packs and camera gear on the lower-level storage shelves. Yoon gave a slight tug on the open door, and it sank into its frame with an airy whoomph.

Mash pulled out a midsized camera and hoisted it to her shoulder. "We're on," she said with a distinctly raised voice. "Live streaming to our studio manager in LA. I figured I should add that little fact so that you don't decide to bump us off once we're in space."

"Bump off?" Yoon asked. He didn't seem to be familiar with the American idiom, and Halie wasn't about to spell it out for him.

"Mash has her funny phrases," she said instead. "Nobody really understands them. So, Mr. Yoon... maybe you can show us how the V-pod works?"

Yoon nodded, waving them up to the second level. At the top of the ladder, they gathered around the copper control panel. "Automation is a key element in any space elevator design," he explained. "It ensures that there can be no operator error. As we boarded, I could tell by the sound of the door seal that the pod is fully pressurized. The panel's blinking light demonstrates that power is available, but also that each subsystem is online with no error codes. If we were carrying a satellite strapped into the equipment bay on this V-pod, its security would also be tested."

He turned to Halie. "This single blinking light is all the assurance we need. We are safe to fly."

Halie put a hand on his arm. "Thank you, Yoon. That's helpful… truly it is." She took a step back. "Now stay right where you are, Mash and I have a job to do."

She turned toward the camera, cleared her throat, and spoke. "I'm standing inside what is called a V-pod, a very specialized and highly automated spacecraft that is designed to grip a thin ribbon located just a few paces from this hangar. The V-pod works a lot like any elevator, though there's more going on behind the scenes. We're in the final countdown to launch now." She swiveled to Yoon. "What do you think, Mr. Yoon? Are we ready for the first trip into space in four years?"

Yoon nodded thoughtfully, then waved toward the panel. "For our first trip, we will climb only to Level 2. Then return."

"And how high is Level 2?"

"Notice the horizontal marks. They are proportionally spaced. Level 2 will be approximately 300 kilometers overhead. Quite high and well into space, but still less than one percent of the total distance to the tether's apex."

"Isn't 300 kilometers where the Kill Zone starts?"

"Slightly below. Low enough to keep us safe."

Regardless of the secrets Yoon was still harboring, Halie was reasonably satisfied with his answers. The impromptu interview would be streaming to a storage medium somewhere in California right now. Paul might even see it.

Without fanfare, Yoon reached out and pressed the circle next to Level 2. From somewhere beneath came a clank and a whir. The V-pod began to move. Sideways.

The winged glass spacecraft lumbered through the hangar doorway and out onto the black deck, feeling a little like an airplane bumping along a taxiway. It followed a curving path that caused the ship to pivot and back its V-shaped wings into one of the ribbons.

Yoon slipped on his helmet and locked a ring to the pressure suit neck. It made a satisfying click. Halie and Mash did the same. The task wasn't hard, no more difficult than a motorcycle helmet.

They took seats on the circular couch facing wraparound glass. There were no seat belts, but so far Yoon's V-pod felt less like space transportation and more like a comfy window seat at a trendy bar. Halie knew better. They'd soon be riding a high-speed mag-lev train, straight up, and their space suits might become more than a precaution.

The ascender rolled into a position between the two ribbons. The steps they'd climbed to touch the ribbon now formed a launch gantry, its height exactly matching the ship's mid-level entryway. A pivot turned them to face one ribbon, but the ascender moved backwards to the other ribbon, only partly visible through smaller windows on the wings.

This is really happening.

Nerves tingling and a tight smile growing, Halie glanced at Mash. Her camera held steady, but tight lips revealed a nervousness. Halie reassured her with a thumbs-up and a tight fist.

Just go with it. We'll be fine. She imagined a countdown in her head: ten, nine, eight.

Clicks and whirs coming from behind the ascender's wings probably meant the V-pod was hooking onto its ribbon, leaving the barest of gaps for electromagnetism to do its thing. A routine procedure for the mag-lev trains found in China and parts of Europe, but it had Halie's heart racing.

Yoon grinned like a kid at Disneyland. Mash trained her camera on Halie and zoomed in for a close-up. She'd done it a thousand times before, and Halie provided a big smile for the camera, this time through the glass of an astronaut's helmet. "Off we go!" she mouthed.

Muffled sounds of an electric motor spinning up didn't match the drama of rocket ignition, but a mag-lev tether ascender was designed for efficiency, not thrills. With the barest tremor, this most modern of spaceships lifted from its launchpad and rose smoothly into the air.

"Success!" Yoon shouted, his voice coming through an intercom though Halie could hear it nearly as well coming from outside the helmet.

Halie leaned toward the wraparound glass and peered down. The steps quickly receded. Overhead, the ascender's glass top provided a splendid view of both ribbons converging toward the pinhole of light at the shroud's exit point.

A noticeable acceleration kicked in, pushing Halie into the padded couch. Not uncomfortably. More than a skyscraper's elevator, but less than a roller coaster. Rushing air created a whistle that increased in pitch as they rose.

Yoon pulled out his phone and texted, probably to Quong. Strangely, phone reception would probably improve as they climbed higher toward the geosynchronous satellites that provided service.

The pinprick of light above widened to a round hole. Seconds later, they shot through into sunlight. The airship soared through a layer of scattered clouds—essentially a jet on a vertical climb but with a steadier feeling. Horizontal seats and an attachment to a solid tether might forever relegate stomach-churning turbulence to airplanes.

They shot higher into a deep blue sky. Wind outside roared past. The morning sun was now well above the eastern horizon. In the distance, a shoreline was now visible—Ecuador. They'd had the same view from Yoon's plane, but Halie suspected they'd be blasting through that altitude any second.

Yoon pulled out a small device from a pocket. "The pressure vessel is holding as designed." He removed his helmet and took a deep breath. "Keep your helmet on or remove it if you prefer. With practice, it can be quickly sealed to the suit in the unlikely case of decompression."

Halie practiced as Yoon had suggested and decided the helmet could stay off as long as it was nearby. Mash paused her recording and did the same, this time without snark. Halie made eye contact with her friend, enough to say, "Are you okay?" Mash only shrugged. She'd manage, once acclimated; Halie would make sure of it.

Feeling reasonably safe, Halie stood. Her legs wobbled from the acceleration, but the effort wasn't any worse than squats with twenty-kilo weights in each hand. She placed one foot in front of the other, reaching out to the glass. It wasn't anything like walking down the aisle of an airplane in flight. It felt steadier, as if the spacecraft was bolted into granite, which was not far from the truth given the tether's rigidity and strength.

Mash switched on her camera and Halie responded. "This is fun! We're already higher than planes can go." It was an educated guess, confirmed when Yoon glanced at his handheld device and called out fifty kilometers. Even weather balloons didn't rise that high. "The crazy part is we're still accelerating. We're going straight up, but at jet speeds."

Yoon nodded his agreement.

Halie narrated for a future audience. The words poured out effortlessly. "That's the coastline of South America. Ecuador, Peru. The Andes Mountain range. When I was eighteen, I went to Machu Picchu for my college gap year and I remember our guide pointing out two of the highest peaks in the range, Salcantay and Sahuasiray. See those two snowcapped peaks? I'm sure that's them. Totally mind-boggling that we can see that far."

She fell silent, letting the stunning view speak for itself. Their perch felt impossibly high—overwhelming but not terrifying. The curving glass surrounded her, insulating her from what was surely subzero cold outside. A firm floor eliminated any fear of falling. The enclosure created a calm feeling of being wrapped inside a cocoon, freeing her emotions to soar along with the ride.

Earth's spectacular beauty could never be overstated, but the planet always shined brightest from altitude—a cliff overlooking a Norwegian fjord, a rooftop in Manhattan, the slopes of a Cascade volcano. The location didn't matter. Simply climb, and Earth would reveal its treasures. But in all of her life, Halie had never been this high. The smile on her lips wouldn't leave for days.

And still the V-pod accelerated, ever upward.

The sun stood brilliant in the east, but a few stars were now visible in the cobalt-blue sky. The horizon hinted at curvature.

"This is real," Halie said, choking up but not afraid to show the emotion in her voice. "We're riding an elevator into space."

Enchanting, astonishing, breathtaking. Anything Halie could say was still insufficient. Pictures were a key part of this story, and Mash already had enough for a program that would blow away every previous show.

But why wait? Halie pulled out her satellite phone. Five bars. Connections didn't get any better than that.

10. GOING LIVE

HALIE FACED YOON, HANDS ON HIPS. "My producer scheduled a live spot. I've got five minutes to prepare before the network interrupts their regular schedule. Ten million eyeballs live. A hundred million more, post broadcast. I'm not missing that opportunity."

The V-pod had finally reached its cruise velocity. With the heaviness of acceleration gone, sitting and standing felt normal. Wind noise was gone. Only a subtle vibration gave away their speed—380 meters per second according to Yoon, straight up.

Yoon faced the glass in the cubby formed by one of the ship's vertical wings, enjoying the view from above the atmosphere as much as anyone. Maybe more. Without looking back, he simply nodded.

She'd take that as permission to broadcast. Even if he had objected, she would have found a way. The first ascent on a space elevator was not just technically amazing and jaw-droppingly beautiful, it was historic.

Mash flipped switches on her satellite link and strapped the camera stabilizing harness over her flight suit. She looked wicked cool.

"Helmet off?" Halie asked, inserting a wireless bud into her ear.

"Definitely off," Mash said, "but keep it in your hand so people get the sense that you might need to whip it back on. The audience loves danger. And we'll need dangerous numbers too. Speed, height, that kind of thing."

"On it." She conferred with Yoon, who seemed to have every observational detail anyone could ask for on his palm-sized device.

"Two minutes," Mash called out, clipping a small camera to her harness and hoisting a larger camera to her shoulder. "We have a connection." She pointed a finger at Halie. "You're on with the KNS news director."

Sahalie Spark, television host and former science journalist, came alive. Her pulse quickened. It did every time. "Hi, Tom. Can you hear me?"

A voice came over the earbud. "Sahalie. Where the hell are you?"

"Oh... nearly two hundred kilometers above the equatorial Pacific. You know, the usual on-location stuff."

"Jesus Christ, Sahalie, this is going to kill. I'm getting the feed coming in now. Can you have your camera operator point out the window?"

Mash was receiving the same voice in her own earbud. Keeping the shoulder camera pointed at Halie, Mash adjusted the harnessed camera. Once set, it would auto-swivel to keep the glorious view centered no matter how Mash moved.

"You should be getting a dual feed now." Halie straightened the collar of her flight suit. They'd be live within a minute. The director would give them a countdown.

"Hell of a shot! We're thirty seconds out. Just do your thing. I trust you. Be ready for some questions from Fedora, but we're keeping this to three minutes. Cool?"

"We're ready when you are."

Technically ready, but Halie had never been so nervous. She shook it off and stared straight into the camera. Tom started a countdown, going silent for the last two numbers.

A new voice came into Halie's ear. Female. Halie had sat across the lunch table from Fedora just last week.

"We'll get back to the vice president's comments in a just a minute, but something amazing is happening right now that we need to show you. Sahalie Spark, host of *Don't Believe It!* is joining us live... and friends, you're definitely *not* going to believe it, but Sahalie is *in space*. I know... people are not supposed to be there anymore, but something remarkable has just happened. Sahalie, are you there?"

Halie smiled. The director would have already switched to Mash's camera feed. A banner would now be scrolling across the bottom of ten million television sets, tablets, and phones noting that Kolby News Service was interrupting with breaking news.

Halie looked straight into the camera. "Hi, Fedora. Something remarkable indeed. I'm standing inside what is called a V-pod attached to a space elevator tether. That's a ribbon stretching from the ground straight into space. We're two hundred kilometers above the ocean near South America and climbing fast. Picture a military jet flying straight up, full throttle, at more than a thousand kilometers per hour."

With a dual feed, the news director could easily switch to the view outside, leaving Halie's face in a corner inset.

"Oh my, Sahalie, that's really gorgeous," Fedora said.

They were already above the hazy blue-white layer of air protecting all life on Earth from the cold vacuum of space. In the distance, a few cumulonimbus clouds were building over the Andes, giving a good sense of the V-pod's tremendous height. The clouds were nothing but cauliflower florets.

"Fedora, your viewers might remember a story about an illegal offshore oil rig that appeared overnight?"

"Right, with a helicopter that was sent through a portal?" Fedora asked.

"I can't vouch for the portal rumors, but it turns out the mysterious platform wasn't an oil rig at all. It's a space elevator. Fully operational too. I'm proof. The ribbon we're climbing is proof." Mash pointed her camera up. The tether glinted in the sunlight, though the background was now black. "We have our host to thank for this wonderful technology, the one and only Mr. Yoon Ji-ho."

Mash panned to Yoon standing alone. He bowed his head.

"A space elevator? But what about the Kill Zone? I thought all those plans were shelved."

"They were. Mr. Yoon and his engineers figured out a way around it. He's guiding us up to what he calls Level 2, a waystation located just below the Kill Zone." She held up her helmet. "Don't worry, we're fully protected. We don't plan to climb any higher, even though the ribbon goes all the way to Level 6 at geostationary height, where weather satellites are located. I'm told the ribbon *is* being hit by debris, but it's holding up to the punishment like a champ."

"That is truly remarkable," Fedora said. "Does this make you an astronaut?"

Halie laughed. "I suppose it does. Doesn't matter how you get to space, right? What's strange is that I'm not weightless. Space doesn't cause weightlessness; it's the free fall that makes astronauts float. Their spacecraft flies in an orbit, and it's moving so fast it's falling around the curve of the Earth. That's not the case with a space elevator. It's fixed to the ground like a giant ladder. At the other end is a big rock that's being slung around as the Earth turns to create tension on the ribbon. Of course our V-pod accelerated during the climb, which pushed us into our seats, but every elevator does that. I expect we'll be decelerating soon too, but right now, I'm standing on a floor no different than at the studio."

"You're not *at* the studio, are you? I sure hope this isn't a green screen."

Halie laughed again. "Nope, perfectly real." She suddenly felt her feet go light. "Hang on… we just started decelerating, and my stomach jumped into my throat." She reached out to Mash, who had braced herself against the glass wall. "You see, V-pods are completely automated with no announcements… apparently. While we're decelerating, how about we do a quick experiment?"

Halie lifted her helmet over her head and let go. It fell in slow motion. "There you go. I'm not weightless, but I'm also not immune to the upward force of deceleration, which is acting against gravity and slowing my helmet's fall. I couldn't pull off a stunt like that in the studio."

"Bless your heart, Sahalie, you're such a science expert."

"Hopefully there's a lot more science coming," Halie said, lifting her eyebrows.

"I can't wait," Fedora said. "Keep us informed, will you?"

"Will do. For now, this is Sahalie Spark signing off from…" She glanced out the window. "Closer to 250 kilometers up."

She held a smile, waiting for the all clear, which came from the director a few seconds later.

"Really nice spot, Sahalie," he said in the earbud. "Coordinate with Paul if you get more. I'd love to do another live shot when you reach that station. Maybe a lead-in to the five p.m. Eastern slot?"

"I'll see what I can do, Tom. Thanks for greenlighting on such short notice."

"Jesus, Sahalie, how could I not? You've got the biggest space story in four years. How the—?"

"I got lucky. Yoon's the man you'll need to hear from next. I'll try to arrange something."

They shut down the feed and Halie checked her phone. A congratulatory text from Paul ended with a string of exclamation points.

"We did good?" Mash asked, putting away her camera.

"We did great." Halie hugged her friend. "This is going to be breaking news around the world."

"And you're going to be a busy girl. CNN, BBC, Al Jazeera. They'll be all over you for some Hoity Toity Pig Slop. The wallflower becomes the homecoming queen."

A shy wallflower suddenly thrust into the spotlight was a standard euphemism for when a journalist *becomes the story*. Halie wasn't sure about the rest of Mash's banter. "Hey, KNS signs my paycheck. If anyone else tries to cut in on this story, Paul will handle it. But yeah… the news directors at KNS are going to want a lot more."

With the strong deceleration, Halie needed to sit down. She hadn't noticed before, but the couch did have seat belts of a sort. A thin strap the same color as the couch was tucked into its seam. Once extracted, the strap wrapped around her waist and clipped to itself. It wouldn't do much in a collision, but its purpose seemed to be different: preventing the occupant from floating away, which might be an issue for higher levels where gravity would be lower.

Halie glanced up and noticed something new above: a disc, off-white in color. It stood out against the black backdrop of space with the twin ribbons pointing straight to its center. The ribbons even provided a feeling of distance in the same way a divided highway merges to a single line when the driver can see far enough down the road.

Halie pointed, asking Yoon, "Is that the waystation?"

"It should be." He consulted his device. "We're passing 280 kilometers, moving at 190 meters per second and slowing. We should prepare." He put his helmet back on. Halie and Mash did too.

Halie checked the red bottle mounted on her hip. Its tube ran up a slot in her flight suit to the helmet. A switch atop the bottle had on and off positions. Simple enough. Maybe too simple since there was no indicator of how much oxygen was left.

Same as emergency masks on an airplane, she reasoned.

The disc over their heads grew as they approached, revealing its structure. A hole in the center allowed the tether to pass through on its way higher, giving an impression of a giant donut hanging in space. A much thinner second ring surrounded the donut leaving a narrow gap. Altogether, the structure was larger and more complex than Halie expected. Even Yoon seemed surprised.

He didn't build it. It was the only answer that made sense. She'd already challenged him but didn't relish the coming confrontation. He was, after all, the sponsor of the trip and the holder of a key that had opened the door.

With their velocity down to highway speeds, the tether's silver texture became noticeable once more. The V-pod crept the last hundred meters much like an aerial tram approaching its station.

A shadow fell over them as the disc eclipsed the sun and brought a distinct chill to the air. House sized, the station had a flat bottom. Halie peered through the donut hole and noticed cables dropping down to the station's roof—its support system, as Yoon had described. The V-pod was attached to the inside edge of the ribbon, leaving the outside edge for structural ties. The V-notch on the ascender's backside would slide right past the cables.

They slipped into the hole and slowed to a stop inside a white cylinder that enclosed both ribbons. Halie watched in amazement as a horizontal membrane stretched inward and snapped around the ascender's girth like an elastic wrist band on a coat sleeve. It formed a floor at the same height as the ascender's door. Overhead, a similar membrane formed a ceiling, snapping tight to each ribbon.

Got to be an airlock.

A minute later, a slight whooshing sound provided evidence. She glanced down the ladder leading to the ascender's lower level. The V-pod's glass door on the lower level was standing open. If this had been a commercial flight, they'd already be pulling luggage from the overhead bins.

Yoon stood, grinning. "Shall we explore?"

"Can't wait!" Halie said through the helmet intercom. Though the station clearly had an elaborate airlock system, she felt more comfortable leaving her helmet on. Yoon still had some explaining to do, including how this station had air.

Halie followed Yoon down the ladder and out the open door with Mash right behind, camera rolling. Though plain, the cylindrical airlock felt a little like a train station with two vertical tracks. Today, it hosted only one V-pod, but Halie could imagine two parked side by side if Yoon's ultimate plan included large numbers of visitors transported both up and down.

The airlock's tightly curving white wall was interrupted by a single door, which also stood open. Halie followed Yoon across the newly-snapped-into-place floor, which felt surprisingly solid. An elastic material that hardened within seconds? Still more explanations were needed.

Yoon stepped through the doorway. Halie followed into an open floor space bounded by a curving outer wall. She pirouetted in place. Windows looked out to every direction. The station seemed to be an observation deck but on a small scale; more of a cozy, donut-shaped lookout. Yoon was already standing at one window.

Halie rushed to join him. An overhanging roof screened out the sun, providing a view that was even better than their ride up. Halie immediately recognized the coastline of Colombia as it angled northwest to meet the thinnest strip of land in the world, Panama. Beyond the isthmus, a sun glint shimmered across the Caribbean Sea. Still further north, the greens of Costa Rica, Nicaragua, and Central America peeked from beneath broken clouds, finally disappearing into a haze on the horizon.

Halie pressed the faceplate of her helmet against the glass. "Nice!" She could be standing atop a skyscraper; ridiculously higher, of course. She glided around the curving windows, never once concerned about her footing or the sturdiness of the structure. Yoon even took his helmet off. Eventually Halie did the same. The air was fine.

At the west side, the Galapagos Islands now felt closer, given a broader view across the Pacific. She kept walking, eager to feast on views that seemed better now that she wasn't moving. To the south, the backbone of the Andes and the browns of coastal Peru, Bolivia, and possibly Chile. Finally, the dark green expanse of the Amazon rainforest to the east. She'd never seen anything like it. Not from a mountaintop, not from any airplane window seat. Earth—a good portion of it, at least—lay at her feet.

"You could sell tickets to this place," Halie gushed, hanging on Yoon's arm. His eyes were lined deeply by crow's-feet. He seemed equally delighted with the lookout, and nearly as surprised to find it.

"Public access was in some of our designs, a smart strategy now that I see the view for myself. Space should never be restricted to the business of satellites or scientific experiments. Space tourism provides a legitimate value to society. Every astronaut returns to Earth with a new sense of our fragile planet. Now that I'm here, I see why."

Halie patted his hand. "It's stunning. The land, the sea. And with no sign of borders. Even cities are hard to spot. You have to look carefully." She pointed to a patch of gray nestled within green mountains. It was probably the city of Quito, though without a map it was hard to be sure. Green spread beyond it—the Amazon River basin, no doubt. There would be towns and villages out there, but from this height they were invisible.

Yoon withdrew a thin wire from his coat pocket—the same floating wire Quong had used. He held it in the air for a few seconds, then released it. Once more, the wire inexplicably fixed itself in place, vertically.

"How does it work?" Halie asked in earnest. She had no guesses except that magic tricks were always grounded in reality even if the truth was well hidden.

"I'm not sure," Yoon said.

It wasn't the answer she expected. Yoon's comments were becoming increasingly unpredictable. She hadn't caught him in any lies, and he wasn't trying to conceal anything. He seemed more bewildered.

The wire expanded to a misty rectangle floating in the air, this time forming the shape of the copper-colored control panel they'd used to bring the V-pod to this Level 2 station. The image had the same vertical line, the same horizontal marks denoting each of six levels and the same buttons.

"What does it mean?" Halie asked. This time, she expected a proper answer. They'd come too far for platitudes.

"Nothing," Yoon answered without a pause. "At least, nothing new. It is the same image Quong observed after you opened the lock to gain access to the V-pod. It seems to be telling us how to use the controls to climb the tether, something we already understand."

Frustrated, Halie snatched the apparition out of the air, instantly shutting off its misty image. Now just a stiff wire, she waved it in front of Yoon's face like a teacher scolding a student who had been distracted by a toy. "Mr. Yoon, you and I have an exclusive access deal. We shook on it. I've done my part. I've followed your rules. But honestly, you've deferred, delayed, and obfuscated since we left LA. It's time to fess up. You have some explaining to do."

Yoon took the wire and pocketed it. Halie crossed her arms and stared lasers at him, waiting.

His whole body slumped. "You're right, I have delayed. I had hoped the wire's image would be different at this level. It seems to be sensitive to both place and time. On the golf course in Los Angeles, it portrayed the platform and the tether. Of course, I knew at once what the image represented, but I did not know where to go until I heard the story of the Ecuador oil rig."

Halie's mind raced, piecing together her own account of the last twenty-four hours. She'd read about the oil rig first, a story easy to ignore. Only later, when Quong had arrived at the studio and revealed the platform's image, had she put it together. She'd come to the same conclusion, but in the opposite order.

A shudder rippled across the station floor.

Mash yelled from the opposite side of the donut. "Did you feel that?"

Halie would have discounted it as a bump in the road, but they weren't moving anymore. "A hit on the tether above us?"

Yoon nodded somberly. "Most likely. We are near the Kill Zone now. But that hit was more than a lost screw."

With years of news reports on the Kill Zone, Halie practically had the statistics memorized. Trillions of pieces of debris orbiting Earth had been measured and remeasured. Their distribution fell into a skewed bell curve based on mass. The bulk of the junk was under five grams: small chunks of shredded aluminum, plastic, bits of glass. Further along the curve were the bolts, tools, and bigger chunks of what used to be panels, hatches, and solar arrays on satellites or space stations—now obliterated. At the top of the scale were the structural spars, electrical motors, and engine shrouds that might be mangled but were still in one piece.

And all of this junk was zipping by at orbital speeds: eight kilometers per second. Far faster than any bullet. If a bigger chunk hit, you'd have less than a microsecond to notice your spacecraft— and your body—exploding into a million pieces. But even something as innocuous as a paint chip could puncture a toothpick-sized hole straight through reinforced aluminum, leaving only minutes to patch it before the air was sucked out.

Halie glowered at Yoon. "You said we'd be safe. You said the ribbon would hold. Will it, or are you just making things up as you go?"

Yoon turned away, lowering his head. "The tether *should* hold, but I admit I cannot be sure. It is why I have asked for help. Dr. Adam Estrada, a materials scientist, will be on the ship from Peru. Perhaps he has already arrived."

Halie stared at Yoon, unrelenting. "Fess. Up."

With a slight bow, Yoon acknowledged his need to comply. "The truth is, I do not know who built this structure. At first, I had thought it was a breakaway team. There were so many similarities to my designs. A few of my top engineers were angry when the project was canceled four years ago. I thought it might be them. My plan was to arrive and take control of what was rightfully mine. Of course, I would have given them credit for their initiative, but this..."

He looked around the donut-shaped observatory. "It is more than I expected. And the roof you see outside is a debris shield. Thick. Heavy. Very likely designed to deflect orbiting debris beginning reentry. None of my designs had such a feature. None was this elaborate. The expense would have been too great. The extra weight placed on the tether would have forced significant improvements in tether materials."

He wandered in a circle as he talked. "This is not mine. It can't be. It belongs to whoever created the key." He pulled the wire from his pocket, staring at it like a foreign object retrieved from a dimension beyond reality. "Our journey began with this curious wire, but I honestly cannot tell you where it will end."

11. SCIENTIST

HALIE HAD HER SCOOP, an exclusive too, but not the story she thought she'd be telling. Yoon hadn't built the platform or its tether. She'd guessed that much, and he'd now confirmed it, though portions of his designs may have been stolen by a competitor.

But the story might not be corporate espionage either. Yoon had been given an activation key—the magic wire. He explained he'd been playing golf in LA with business associates and noticed what he'd thought was a twig stuck to the windshield of the golf cart. One thing led to another, and the first clue appeared in floating mist: an image of the platform.

He had jumped to conclusions about former employees that he now admitted were wrong. Which left the burning question: who had built the space elevator, and why hadn't they come forward to bask in the adoration of the world?

That was the story Halie needed to cover.

She stood close to Yoon in the center of the Level 2 observation deck. "I won't expose you," she offered.

"Nonsense," he answered. "Tell the world. It is your job. But for our mutual benefit, please wait until Dr. Estrada—my friend from Peru—has analyzed the tether. His results will offer clues, I assure you. I would give you an update on his arrival time, but Quong is not answering his phone—likely busy keeping the Ecuadoran army at bay."

Halie nodded, agreeing to hold off on another live broadcast until she knew more about whoever built this space elevator. She could imagine a criminal mastermind holed up in a mountaintop lair, plotting how to dominate space telecommunications when every other player was grounded. Perhaps Yoon had been intentionally lured into the scheme to provide the cover of legitimacy.

Or not. There was a weirdness to this place. Undeniably glorious, but still weird, especially now that Yoon had admitted that he'd had no part in creating it.

Halie put a hand on Yoon's arm, needing to voice one more concern but not sure she wanted to hear his answer. "Yoon... if you didn't build it, how do we know the station's shield will protect us? Or that the tether will hold?" There'd been tremors across the floor as they'd talked. There would certainly be more.

He nodded thoughtfully. "We should descend."

They returned to the V-pod. A blinking green light on its control panel highlighted the second button from the bottom. With four more levels above there was much to explore, but Halie pressed the bottom button. Best to descend, then figure out the next steps.

Automation kicked in. The pod detached from one ribbon and rotated one hundred eighty degrees to reattach on the opposite ribbon. The airlock's lower membrane opened to reveal an unobstructed drop to an ocean ridiculously far below. Every muscle in Halie's body tensed.

Like a roller coaster at its summit, the bottom fell out.

Halie slapped one hand over her open mouth. "Oh, my..." The instant plunge lifted her from the seat. She begged for working brakes.

Future tourists to this observation deck would be advised not to eat a full meal before departure. Mash had her eyes closed tight. Even Yoon clutched the cushion. "We may need some adjustments," he said unhelpfully.

Halie lifted her helmet and let it drop to the seat, proving the plunge wasn't quite a free fall. Mag-lev brakes were functioning, if only with the lightest touch. Eventually, the plunge stabilized to a steady velocity and frayed nerves calmed. They rode down without speaking.

Mash finally broke the awkward silence. "Universidad Nacional Mayor in Lima, Peru."

"Huh?" Halie asked.

Mash examined her phone. "That's where this guy is from. Dr. Adam Estrada, the materials guy. Well, actually he's on temporary loan from MIT in Boston. I guess they move big shot scientists around like chess pieces."

"Ah, yeah. One of my interview targets back in the day," Halie replied. "Technically, I've met him, but only over the phone." She swiveled to Yoon, who was standing at the window near to the V-pod ladder. "Dr. Estrada is widely known?"

"The best in his field," Yoon answered. "A man who enjoys his work with insights that have been invaluable to me over many years. Adam will help us find the answers."

"Convenient that he's so close." Halie wasn't trying to accuse Yoon of further deceit, but she'd rather not have unexplained loose ends when the story was already getting away from her.

"Adam speaks Spanish. He helped Peru with their own space elevator plans. In fact, Peru was a leader, behind only Japan and Singapore."

"Helps to be near the equator?" All space elevator designs were on or near the equator, where the centrifugal force from Earth's spin was highest.

"Location is a factor," Yoon said. "And Peru's university is top-rated, another factor."

Halie nodded. She pictured Professor Estrada as a white-haired septuagenarian who wrote incomprehensible equations across a chalkboard, but the photo on Mash's phone was of a much younger man. Would he have answers?

Yoon left, climbing down the ladder to its built-in lavatory. Halie cozied close to Mash and whispered, "Your best guess on where we stand?"

Mash's volume was normally set to outrageous, but she could be quiet when she wanted to. "Well... our Korean big shot didn't exactly lie, but he withheld."

"Agreed. His designs may have been copied, but he doesn't even recognize some of this stuff—like the magic wire."

"But somebody wanted him to have it."

"Right. So, who creates tech like that?"

"Aliens." Mash clearly shared Halie's own uneasy feeling; she was just more imaginative.

Halie gave Mash's way-out theory the same serious consideration she would for any *Don't Believe It!* topic. "It did appear overnight, I'll grant you that. And tethers do drop down from space. Plus, it's hard to imagine how Yoon or anyone else could deploy a spooled tether without anyone noticing the rocket launch. But…"

Occam's razor, she reminded herself. *Unless evidence suggests otherwise, the simplest explanation is the most likely answer.*

Halie continued. "Do you remember the floating billboard story we covered last year that turned out to be a swarm of microdrones? This could be another case of ordinary physics hiding beneath the limits of our vision. What do you think?"

Mash accepted Halie's explanation with a shrug. Without enough information to solve the mystery, they fell silent again. The remainder of the ride down lacked the excitement of the ride up, though the view was just as spectacular. They were soon back in the atmosphere, with the silence of space replaced by the roar of air rushing past. Yoon took off his flight suit. Halie and Mash followed his lead. They stacked the suits and helmets in a corner, ready for the next ascent—if there was one.

Halie finally spotted the platform partly hidden beneath clouds building in the morning sun. Their trip had been remarkable, accomplished in only an hour. Getting feet back on a solid surface would feel good.

A braking system kicked in—again with no announcement. Deceleration pressed them into the couch, not uncomfortably, but anyone standing at the window with a drink in their hand would regret being too casual.

The ship pierced a cloud, then dropped through the hole in the circus tent shroud. Their speed reduced to a crawl.

"Uh-oh." Mash pointed down. Halie craned her neck to see below. Armed soldiers were pouring into the covered area. They quickly formed a circle around the twin ribbons.

"Ecuadoran soldiers," Yoon said. "We knew it might end this way."

The glass ship lowered the last few meters and stopped at the elevated gantry. Soldiers climbed its steps, pointing their rifles. When the V-pod's door automatically opened, their leader yelled, "*Todas ustedes salgan ahora!* Out now!" He gave a firm wave of his hand.

Yoon sighed. "I suggest we do what they say." He led down the ladder and out the V-pod's door. Halie helped Mash gather her camera gear and followed.

A fresh tropical breeze blew through the gap between the shroud and the deck. Stern faces and high-powered weapons told a less pleasant story. The Ecuadoran squad leader pulled Yoon aside. Two more soldiers shoved Halie and Mash toward the gantry stairs and continued to push them out to the deck. Halie grabbed Mash's arm and pulled her close. They'd stick together, whatever happened.

Yoon's plane was still at the deck's corner, but now two military helicopters were parked nearby. Beyond them, bright sunshine sparkled across a blue ocean.

Where's the fog?

The misty ring that had surrounded the platform was gone, along with the exclusive protection it had provided. Halie wondered what had become of Yoon's flight crew. No doubt Quong would have put up a fight, but gentle Jaya may have been subject to rough treatment—or worse.

Ahead, a large military group gathered. Halie had never believed people were inherently evil, but she worried that anyone inclined to blindly follow could be nudged into depravity. All it took was a sociopathic leader. She hoped this wouldn't be a test of that theory.

Hope came when she spotted two khaki uniforms among the camouflage worn by the Ecuadorans. Americans? While no military was free of brutes, a shared nationality would be in their favor.

Ignoring their escorts, Halie began a trot, pulling Mash with her, and didn't stop until they reached the two officers, a white man and a Hispanic woman. Silver and gold leaves adorned their hats and the lapels of their short-sleeved khaki shirts.

"I'm Sahalie Spark," she said breathlessly. "I'm an American journalist here on assignment with my videographer, also American."

The man gave her the I-know-who-you-are look that Halie had grown used to as her fame increased. The woman smiled with the same recognition.

"We were expecting you, Ms. Spark. I'm Commander Stevens, USS *Doris Miller*." He offered a hand. "This is Lieutenant Commander Gutierrez."

Halie shook their hands, breathing deeply and never in her life more relieved. They were only two in a group of forty or fifty soldiers, but their presence would be enough. Antennas and communication dishes of an aircraft carrier's island tower poked above the platform's edge. The US Navy had arrived in full force.

All around, arguments in Spanish were accompanied by hand gestures and finger pointing. Guns were everywhere but were either holstered or held at rest. "Seems we have an ownership dispute?" Halie asked as politely as she could muster.

Commander Stevens nodded. "Let's call it an international negotiation. The United States is acting as an intermediary. And while we're happy to see you safely on the ground, Ms. Spark, your assignment may need to change. Once we're done here, we'll let you know if you'll be invited to stay or asked to leave."

He flicked a finger to one side. "In the meantime, we must ask you to keep your distance. The parties involved are entitled to privacy—away from the press."

Staying away from angry men with guns was fine with Halie, but now that she and Mash weren't to be thrown overboard, some intel might increase her chance of successful journalism. "Who exactly are the parties involved? It's always helpful not to piss anyone off."

Stevens chuckled. "The number seems to be increasing by the minute." He counted on his fingers. "Ecuador is allied with Brazil—though we haven't seen a Brazilian representative yet. On the other side is your friend Mr. Yoon, his private security team, and a contingent from Peru."

"The Peruvian ship arrived?"

"Yes, indeed. The same time we did. The dark green uniforms are Peru. Yoon's team is in white. On top of that there's some guy zipping around in a personal jet pack"." Stevens searched the sky, but only a few pelicans flew by. "Nobody knows who he is, but the Peruvians cheer every time he passes overhead, so we asked CIC not to target him with surface-to-air missiles."

"As you can see, it's a fluid situation," Lieutenant Commander Gutierrez advised with a smile. "More so, now that Mr. Yoon has returned. By the way, how was it up there?"

"Amazing," Halie answered. "A functional space elevator is worth arguing over. I only hope the ownership question is settled peacefully." She withheld Yoon's confession, which might only make matters worse. Yoon would need to deal with that himself.

"I speak Spanish," Gutierrez said. "So far, lots of swearing and name calling. Ecuador and Peru aren't especially good neighbors. If it escalates beyond words, we'll sound a general alarm. I guarantee you'll hear it no matter where you are on the deck."

Behind Halie, more Spanish swearing erupted. Several Ecuadoran soldiers ran from beneath the tether's shroud. The V-pod was on the move once more, sliding along its slot back to the hangar. Agitated soldiers banged on its side, but the pod disappeared, and the hangar door closed.

"Automation," Mash said.

"You're right," Halie said, then explained to the naval officers, "According to Yoon, everything here is highly automated. With no passengers inside, the V-pod probably knows to return to its hangar."

"How do you call it up again?" Commander Stevens asked.

Before Halie could answer, Mash replied, "Haven't got a clue."

Halie smiled weakly. With Mash poking her in the ribs, she thanked the officers and excused herself. She and Mash headed toward Yoon's plane, logically the safest territory on the platform.

"What was that about?" Halie asked Mash when they were out of earshot.

"Never give away your advantage," Mash replied. "If that hex locking puzzle is re-scrambled, these gun luggers will never figure it out."

"Advantage to Team Yoon?" Halie had little interest in the ownership squabble except that a win by Ecuador might end her participation. A story worth covering still waited. Who had built the space elevator? Would its tether survive the pummeling from space debris? Yoon himself wasn't sure, but could anyone be? Their brief ascent to Level 2 might be the first and last trip up.

A high-pitched whine overhead sounded like a leaf blower set to tornado mode. Halie looked up. A man in a jet pack hovered fifty meters overhead. Predictably, cheers came from the contingent of Peruvian soldiers—their Rocketman had arrived.

He maneuvered over Yoon's jet, then came straight toward them. Halie and Mash backed up.

Jets strapped to each arm produced a downdraft that rearranged hair and blew dust across the platform. The flying man lowered to the surface, then turned off the noisy jets, leaving only the sound of the ocean wind and a few lingering cheers.

He withdrew each arm from an assembly of compact turbine blades in a tube connected by fuel lines and who knew what else, then pulled off a helmet. Thick strands of dark hair pointed in an infinite variety of angles.

With a tap of his finger, a wraparound cyclops visor became instantly transparent, revealing dark eyes and long lashes. He approached Halie with an extended hand.

"Ms. Spark, you have no idea how much I love your show."

Halie tentatively shook his hand.

The stupid grin on his face matched his fanboy enthusiasm. "I'm Adam Estrada." He sounded American and probably was. His bio said he was originally from the Boston area. There'd been no mention the man was also a part-time maniac.

"Actually, we've met. By phone, at least," Halie said.

A sheepish grin spread across his face. "I know. I just didn't think *you'd* remember. Being a celebrity and all that."

Halie felt strangely off-kilter. This wasn't supposed to be an autograph moment. Regardless, he was Yoon's colleague and the materials science expert they'd been waiting for.

"Sahalie, please—or Halie. It's what my friends call me. Um... do you always fly to your appointments?"

He laughed, revealing straight white teeth. "I try to. Parasail, hang glider, wingsuit. I have one of each. This one's my favorite." He unstrapped the large backpack and laid it on the deck, now looking less like Rocketman and more like the rugged alter ego behind every male superhero. The cyclops visor remained perched on his nose, likely giving him an augmented reality view.

"Funny, I thought you'd be a bit more... professorial."

"Oh, I can do the professor gig pretty well too, but you know... it's a nice day... I'm out in the Pacific with a famous woman to impress." He grinned again, this time with the confidence of a well-mannered rogue.

Halie blinked. She'd be swooning pretty soon if she didn't watch out. Mash poked her in the side, and Halie responded. "Sorry, my videographer, Mashup."

Adam enthusiastically shook Mash's hand, practically yelling, "Rama Lama Ding Dong!"

Mash twisted her brow into a contortion. "You know about…?"

"I looked you up. Had lots of free time on the ship that brought me here. Rhythmic onomatopoeia is fascinating stuff." He turned to Halie. "Mashup is almost as famous as you."

Mash shook her head in a vigorous no. "Only among a select group of people. Like… minuscule."

"Dingers," Adam answered.

Halie was only vaguely aware of this part of Mash's life. The four beat-two-beat cadenced expressions Mash regularly injected into her speech were a thing among adherents who called themselves Dingers. Their cultish expressions were inspired by a 1950s song, "Rama Lama Ding Dong," and blossomed from there.

"We'll talk," Adam said to Mash. "But right now the three of us have important business."

"Besides avoiding rough soldiers?" Halie asked.

He nodded rapidly. "Here's the deal. Peru and Ecuador both claim ownership because this platform is located in a disputed part of their offshore economic zones. Everyone saw your broadcast. Trust me, these guys grasp the revenue potential. Whoever controls the gateway to space can charge a hefty fee for every spacecraft deployed and every space tourist who wants a view. But there's one caveat, and it's a big one: Will space debris break the tether? Not much of a revenue stream if it only lasts a few days, right?"

Halie and Mash both nodded.

Adam continued. "So, all parties want an answer, and they've authorized me to find out. Yoon wants you involved as an unbiased witness. Game?"

"I'm in," Halie said. "But maybe you need Mash and her cameras more than me?"

"I'll need a tether sample, so Mashup can record that. But the rest is lab work, and a science correspondent makes a good witness. I didn't just bring my jet pack, I have a portable lab back on the ship. Electron and atomic force microscopes, multiwavelength spectrometer, micro tweezers, cantilevers, scribes, needle probes, you name it."

"Ooh, a lab," Halie quipped. "You definitely know how to impress. Plus… the jet pack thing."

"All part of the mystique." Adam grinned. He picked up his gear. "Shall we?"

From across the platform, Yoon strode toward them with his team at his side. Halie was relieved the soldiers hadn't detained Quong or hurt Jaya.

Yoon enthusiastically grabbed Adam by the shoulders and hugged him. "Good to see you, my friend. Thank you for coming. Once again, we have work to do."

"I'll try to be of help," Adam told him. He stared up to the tether's shroud soaring into clouds overhead. "It's the real deal, isn't it? What we'd always dreamed about."

"It is," Yoon answered. "You should see the Level 2 station."

"I'd like to. But first, we need to figure out who built it." He placed a hand on Yoon's shoulder. "I wish it was yours, Ji-ho, but I think we can agree it is not."

Halie was surprised to hear such a firm conclusion so quickly. Adam had only been here for a few minutes. Yoon had said his materials guy was good, but did he also have the deductive powers of Sherlock Holmes?

"You'll do a thorough examination?" Yoon asked.

Adam nodded. "If it came from the competition, we'll know soon."

Yoon's arms hung at his sides like deflated balloons. He'd lost the childlike zeal he'd had when they'd first arrived. "I want to know."

"I know you do," Adam said.

"Do it now. The situation can only get worse. Brazil's representative will be arriving soon—Marco."

"The footballer?" Adam asked. "How the hell does Brazil pick a lunatic as their rep?"

Halie was equally surprised to hear the name. Marco might be the best soccer player Brazil had ever known, but since retiring he'd become a vendor of wellness products clouded by questionable benefits. He traveled the world, filling whole stadiums with adoring fans eager to hear his unique pitch blending a healthy lifestyle with traditional values. Technology, pharmaceuticals, and modernism were Marco's idea of villains. His all-natural product line and themes of overt masculine leadership were the solutions.

Halie had highlighted one of his products on her show, a cream used to treat prostate cancer. Its ingredients had turned out to be saw palmetto, with results no better than a placebo, and sodium bentonite, a water-absorbing clay commonly used in cat litter. The audience had unanimously judged No Way in Hell.

Marco could be dismissed as just another pitchman, but he had lent his oversized voice to a variety of conspiracy theories too, including some of the craziest stuff Halie had ever heard. "The guy thinks pediatricians should be arrested for implanting radio frequency identification chips into infants and toddlers. I am not making this up."

"Doesn't matter," Yoon said. "Marco commands attention, and Brazil knows it. His presence will create a media blitz. Peru's claim—and our access—may not hold up, especially when I tell them…"

Yoon glanced at Halie. She raised eyebrows back at him.

"No, I haven't yet," Yoon responded. "The timing for *fessing up*, as you called it, is not good. Marco will bring trouble. His latest post tied me to Amazon river dolphins known to be shapeshifters who can appear in human form."

Halie laughed. "I'm surprised to hear you're a cetacean, Yoon." She studied his rugged adventure clothing. "You're well disguised."

"Ha! Unfortunately, Ms. Spark, as a representative for what Marco calls *scientific radicalism*, you're even worse."

"He referenced me in his post?"

Yoon nodded. "By name. I am sorry to bring this upon you."

Halie sighed. "It comes with the territory. Always has."

12. MICROSCOPIC SCALES

Halie led Adam to the towering black shroud always in view from anywhere on the platform. Mash followed behind, her camera rolling. A squad of Ecuadoran soldiers blocked their access to the tether, pointing accusing fingers at Halie. Adam spoke in perfect Spanish that included a reference to Los Angeles. Whatever he'd said, the soldiers parted without argument.

"My Spanish is spotty," Halie told Adam. "What does *enviará* mean?"

"*She will send.* As in, if you guys are nice, she will send you tickets to her television show in Los Angeles."

"Ah. Clever. I can absolutely do that, but what made you think of it?"

"I was hoping to snag a ticket for myself."

Halie snorted a laugh. "It'll be waiting for you at will-call under the name Impish Rogue."

Adam pumped his fist, then started up the gantry steps. He dropped his duffel bag at the base of the ribbon and studied the shiny surface with hands on hips. He could easily be mistaken for a tourist admiring a mirrored art display in a public space.

Halie stood next to him. Their reflections in the mirrored surface hinted of a texture different than glass. "You can tell who made it just by looking?" she asked.

Adam unzipped his duffel and searched inside. "Remember the guy in that tornado movie who could tell when the storms were coming just by spilling a handful of dust?"

"Yeah."

"That's *not* how it works."

"Didn't think so. You said you had a microscope?"

"Two microscopes, plus a spectral analyzer. We'll figure it out."

He pulled out a roll of clear tape, a small pair of scissors, and a thick pen labeled with a yellow warning triangle. "Hold these. Careful with the laser." The slender pen was no lecture hall pointer. Halie cupped it warily in her palm.

From a duffel side pocket, he produced a red marker and a flashlight. He drew three horizontal lines on the tether spaced about ten centimeters apart, then flicked on the light. It produced a violet glow, which he ran across the tether between the two upper marks, leaving the lower band untouched.

He held out his hand like a surgeon. "Laser, please." Halie handed it to him. He rested his wrist against the ribbon, tapped a button, and drew a tiny circle with the laser, then repeated the same surgery on the lower section.

"Ultraviolet," he explained. "Powerful enough to burn a hole through your hand in half a second, but the cut depth on the tether will be negligible. A minor scratch, enough to break a few covalent bonds. Tape, please."

Fascinated, Halie didn't mind playing the role of assistant. Adam peeled a long strip and held it up for her to snip with the scissors.

"Okay, let's see what we've got." He laid the clear tape across the ribbon, spanning both bands. "The upper part has now been cleansed of any dust, spores, pollen, and most of the bacteria. The lower part is the control sample." When he pulled the tape away, two mottled silver-gray smudges stuck to it.

"What's the silvery stuff?" Halie asked.

Adam lifted his eyebrows. "That's what we're going to find out. Graphene? Carbon nanotubes? Both are allotropes, which are—"

"Crystalline structures formed from carbon. I get it. I've studied space elevators enough to know how a tether is made."

"Sorry, I didn't mean to mansplain. After all, you are the fabulous Sahalie Spark."

"Well... any scientific fabulousness is because I'm inquisitive. I have a science education, but I'm not in the same league as the brainiacs out in the field—which apparently includes you."

"Nanomaterials and atomic chemistry, that's my thing," he said while searching again in the duffel. "But you're boundless. I've seen you explain complex stuff in physics, chemistry, robotics, pharmaceuticals. You have a wide range."

He was definitely a fan if he knew about her previous work in science journalism. "I ask questions. If I don't understand the answers, I ask for comparisons. I tease it out of them. The people you see on the show are the smart ones, but sometimes they need to be coached on how to speak like the rest of us."

"Ah, here it is," Adam said, holding up a small plastic device about the size of a computer mouse. "Do you know about chirality?"

Halie squinted, her way of hedging. "Sounds familiar, but give me an example."

"Aha! The Sahalie Spark method in action. Before this day is done I'm going to need a selfie to show the guys back home who I met today."

He clipped the mouselike device onto the ribbon's outer edge and pressed a tiny button on its side, lighting an LED. "A general purpose monitor," he explained. "Records stuff. Alerts me if there's anything unusual... you know, like if the tension suddenly drops because the tether snapped five hundred kilometers above us."

Halie hoped his example was no more than a what-if.

When he was done with his work, they made their way back to Yoon's jet. He talked as they walked. "So, chirality. Kind of important. You probably already know that carbon loves hexagonal and tetrahedral shapes. Graphene, graphite, and nanotubes are hexagonal allotropes. Diamonds, another allotrope of carbon, are tetrahedral. Carbon makes these patterns because each atom has four valence electrons that are free to connect to other atoms. Carbon either forms a flat join—the chicken wire hexagons—or a pyramid-shaped join."

"The editor in me condenses that down to 'a carbon lattice can come in multiple geometries.' Am I right?"

"Exactly right. I guess that's why you're on TV and I'm not." Adam tipped his head. "So, chirality is a measure of how those carbon hexagons line up when a lattice curls into a nanotube—either along the tube's length, along its width, or some angle in between. Dial in the chiral angle and you can vary the nanotube's strength and electrical conductivity. Make it a superconductor, semiconductor, insulator... whatever you want."

"I get it, but why do you care?"

"Different labs have different capabilities. If there are nanotubes in this sample, once I check the chirality, diameters, and whether they're single- or multiwalled, I'll have a pretty good idea who made it."

Halie nodded. "Ahh, the light turns on."

Back at Yoon's plane, Adam dropped his duffel and strapped on the jet pack he'd left. With a tap, his super-cool cyclops visor went into sunglasses mode. He handed a nylon web harness to Halie. "Ready to go?"

Halie stared, not entirely sure what he was asking and doubtful she was going to like the answer.

He slipped his helmet on. "There's enough power to lift two people. I've done it before."

Halie held up a hand and wrinkled her nose. "Death-defying stunts are not really my thing."

"Well, the only other option is a rope ladder hanging off the platform's edge. Frankly, the jet pack is safer. I've logged more than three hundred flights and not a single mishap. Well... once my shoe fell off because I didn't have it laced."

"But carrying a second person? I'd get in the way."

"Not at all. Just don't grab my arms—that's where all the control comes from. It's really quite intuitive, like balancing on a skateboard. And think of the great shot Mashup could get."

Mash walked up, having lingered midplatform. "You're going with him?"

"Wasn't planning on it," Halie said.

"He's right, it would make a great shot."

Halie rolled her eyes, then bored a hole through Adam with her stare. "You're sure it's safe?"

"It's just up and down. Thirty seconds and you're there. You really do need to see my lab."

Halie rolled her eyes and held out a hand, palm up. Adam gave her the web harness, then helped her cinch it around both legs and arms. Mash started filming, narrating the scene as she circled.

Halie stood straight. "So, what do I do?"

Adam spun her around, her back toward him. "Just hold still for a sec while we get cozy." He scooted in close behind, their bodies touching. Two clicks connected them together like a first-time skydiver and her instructor.

His mouth touched the back of her ear. "Want to be my navigator?"

"Not really, no."

Her answer didn't seem to matter. He slipped his wraparound visor over her eyes and tucked it into her hair. It fit like ordinary sunglasses but did far more than shade the sun. Suddenly, Halie had a digital dashboard hovering in front of her. A compass bearing changed as she rotated her head. A digital strip on one side showed her altitude steady at 125 meters. Other markers and indicators would require a pilot to interpret.

Adam slipped his hands into the jet sleeves, then wrapped his arms around her so she could see the results. "Cross your arms over your chest and keep them there. Whatever you do, don't get in the way of the jet blast."

"This is great!" Mash zoomed in on one of the twin engines that had replaced Adam's hands.

"Great? For whom?" With the mention of jet blast, Halie's heart was suddenly racing like a snare drum. How did she get herself into these things?

"Okay, we're cleared for takeoff. You ready?" he asked.

She lifted one arm and gave him a tentative thumbs-up.

"Remember, keep those arms crossed." She obeyed.

A whine started up on the left side, then another on the right. Mash backed away, with her camera pointed straight at Halie. Halie did her best to smile, but it would probably turn out more of a grimace with teeth.

The whine became a roar. The harness dug into her legs and underarms. Halie suddenly felt light on her feet. Their bodies wobbled in unison, and they were off the ground, rising fast.

Mash's purple hair tangled in the blast, but she kept the camera on them as they rose. Adam said something Halie couldn't hear. He angled his right arm outward, and they twisted to face the ocean. The visor's heading indicator spun. Its altitude readout soared past 300 meters. Below, the huge US aircraft carrier stretched the full length of the platform. They flew across it middeck, then out over the ocean.

Halie dared to look straight down.

A fall from this height would kill. She squeezed her fists together remembering to keep her arms crossed. Crazy stuff, but so far the impromptu flight was no more threatening than a carnival ride and probably less stressful than a bungee jump—something she'd never done and never would.

Fun? That might be a stretch. Exhilarating, though.

The roar slackened, and they began to descend. Halie quickly remembered why she should have stuck with her gut reaction to Adam's insane proposal. Going up was fine, but now they were heading down. The technical term was basophobia, a doctor had once explained, the fear of falling. Forty percent of people had it to some degree, and for good reasons. Halie imagined the myriad ways their landing could end badly.

At first, Adam seemed to be heading straight into the sea, but after more maneuvers, a smaller ship came into view. A minuscule deck at its stern was the only possible landing area. Aiming for such a small target would require talent, luck, or both.

They dropped further. Sailors came out to the ship's railings to watch. Adam's arms twitched rapidly as he directed the thrust. Just like skateboarding, he'd said. She'd never done that either, but she'd seen plenty of teens sliding off railings and crashing onto hard pavement.

And I'm not even wearing a helmet.

Jet blast blew across the ship's superstructure. Somehow Adam pointed their feet to the center of the flat spot. He hadn't told her what to do for the landing, so she pulled her feet up against his thighs. His shoes hit the deck, and the jets powered down almost as quickly.

"You can stand up now," he said, removing the augmented reality visor from her head.

Halie lowered her legs, glad to be on solid ground but proud of herself for taking on the challenge and not complaining. "Thanks for the ride," she said as he unclipped her from his harness. "To be perfectly honest, I don't normally do things like that."

He flipped up the visor on his helmet. "But you're glad you did?"

"I am. Because now I get to see your chemistry lab. And that's the stuff I live for."

Peruvian sailors helped Adam stow his flight gear in a locker, then he led down a steep ladder and through an oval hatch. Out of the tropical sun, the ship's interior was dark and smelled of oil and paint.

Another man in uniform joined them along a walkway crowded with fire control equipment and overhead pipes. Adam spoke to him in Spanish. Halie managed to grasp a few words. *Vuelo*, flight. *Volver*, return. And *mujer*, woman. She could piece the rest of it together, especially given the hearty laugh by the sailor at the end.

Further down the walkway, Adam stopped at another hatch and opened his hand for Halie to step in first. "My apologies for the crude comments by my shipmate. He assumed you don't speak Spanish."

"I don't, at least not like you do," Halie said, entering the small compartment made even smaller by stacks of boxes. "Do they think I'm your captured woman?"

"Not quite that bad. He used the verb *salir*, which in this context means *to date*."

Halie couldn't suppress a snicker. "Okay, that is funny. Do you regularly fly your dates to events?"

"First time." Adam didn't linger on the slightly awkward exchange. Instead, he picked up a cube the size of a toaster. "Ever seen one of these?"

Halie shook her head. With a polished white surface, it looked scientific. It was even inscribed with a chemistry-sounding logo: LabSource.

"It's a microtome, basically a fancy meat slicer. We stick our sample in here and thin slices come out the other side—one micrometer thin. For comparison, cellophane is forty micrometers."

He pulled the sample from his pocket. Two black smudges marred the transparent tape. He plucked medical gloves from a dispenser and used a scalpel to slice the smudged tape into five tiny pieces, then pushed one piece into each of five small holes drilled through a resin disc the size of a penny.

He fed the coin into the microtome, set dials, and pressed a button. Buzzing and whirring sounds spoke to the precise slicing process going on inside. A minute later, a nearly invisible circle dropped into a tray. Adam lifted the wispy disc with tweezers and held it up to the light—an ultra-thin slice of the original resin coin as flimsy as tissue paper. Having approved of its quality, he placed the slice into a circular cutout on a tray that could have been the drawer of a jewelry box. Two miniature clips held the slice in place.

"Okay, your turn." He handed the tray to Halie. She held one hand over her nose and mouth for fear of blowing the delicate sample away.

Adam led her into a second room, where a vertical white cylinder stood atop a desk. Complex components were attached along its length. Wires ran from the machine's base to a laptop computer.

"Meet TEM Junior," Adam said. "His big brother is in Lima, but this portable microscope is perfect for a mobile lab. Only twenty kilos and better than one-nanometer resolution." He pointed to a slot on its side. "The sample tray goes in there."

Adam pulled up two chairs and typed on the laptop while Halie fitted the miniature drawer into its slot. "I've never seen an electron microscope before." She took a seat next to him.

"*Transmission* electron microscope," he corrected. "One of two types. A scanning electron microscope bounces electrons off the sample, getting an image of its surface. A transmission electron microscope sends the beam straight through the sample where the electrons hit a collector plate on the other side. It gives us a 3-D view. Rotatable too."

"Can you see individual atoms?"

"Pretty close. A carbon atom is only a tenth of a nanometer—below the resolution. So, it's hard to make out individual atoms but easy to see their patterns."

Halie was already intrigued by the setup process. A view into the world of atoms might rival the dramatic view from Level 2.

Adam pressed a key, and the machine made a noise like a hair dryer. "Sucking the air out," Adam explained. "We don't want our electrons to deflect off anything but the sample."

"The ship's rocking won't affect it?" The waves weren't big, but she could feel a surge every few seconds.

"Honestly, the sonic vibrations from our voices have a greater impact—a thousand hertz versus two hertz. But it's all negligible. The electrons are accelerated to such high speeds, their travel time from source to target is a few picoseconds. The microscopic world isn't just orders of magnitude smaller, it's faster too. From an electron's perspective, you and I are standing still."

He reached for a set of knobs and twisted one marked Magnification. An image resolved on his computer screen—a mesh of squares, black lines with white interiors. As he twisted, the image zoomed in on one square. Adjustments with a scrolling ball placed the square in the center of the screen.

"You probably didn't notice, but each of the one-millimeter holes drilled in the sample disc has a 200 by 200 copper wire mesh. We're now looking at one square in that mesh." An indicator on the screen showed a magnification of 6000x. "We don't care about the copper, it's the stringy stuff in the middle we're going after."

A grayish-black smudge in the square's center didn't look like much. Adam dialed up the magnification, and the image smoothly zoomed in. The smudge became a million micro striations oriented from left to right. Some lines were regularly spaced—grid-like—with a three-dimensional depth that suggested stacks of flattened cardboard boxes as seen from the side. Other lines wandered as if someone had unrolled a million skeins of yarn across the cardboard. Magnification now showed 150,000x.

"Wild," Adam said. His eyes never left the screen. "The layered stacks are a laminate of single-crystal graphene. Standard material for any tether. But I'm not sure about the yarn. Tangled-up nanotubes? This I have to see."

Adam picked out a single thread and zoomed in. A remarkably animated picture filled the screen.

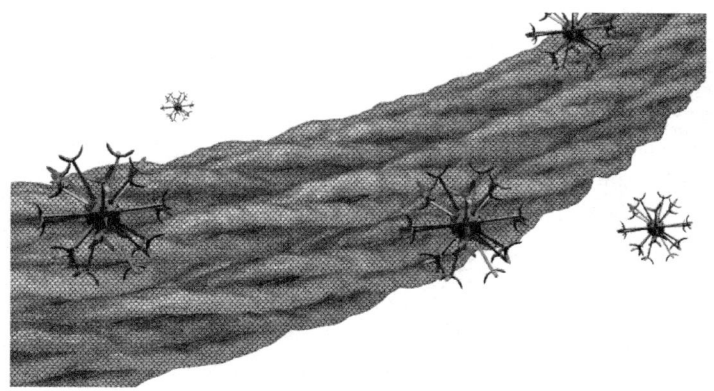

"Ooh!" Halie scooted her chair closer to the screen.

"Yikes!" Adam said.

What had been a tiny thread resolved to a multistranded cable. Spiky balls zipped along its length in a rolling-bouncing motion, pausing in places, then continuing on at high speed.

"What are they?" Halie asked, her eyes transfixed on the active scene. The miniature creatures almost looked like they knew where they were going.

"Too big and too perfect to be viruses," Adam answered. "Nanobots, most likely. Different than I've seen before, but it's a developing field, so anything is possible."

One of the spiky balls fell off the thread. Adam zoomed in even closer on it. Claws at the ends of multiple poles pinched together, grasping at nothing. "This one looks lost," Halie said.

"Yeah, nanobots aren't particularly smart. They're usually designed for a single function, executed repeatedly. This one's about 600 nanometers across, normal for a bot." He scrolled to another strand of yarn devoid of nanobots, keeping the magnification high.

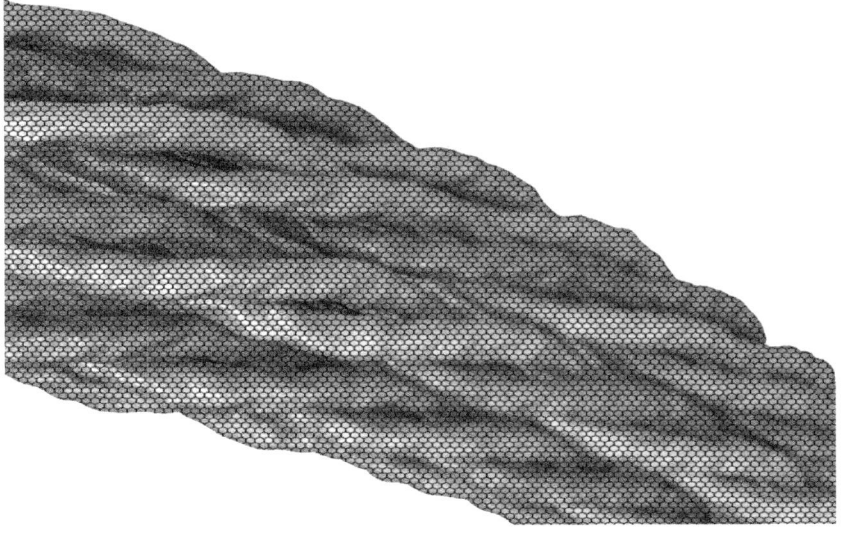

"Killer structure," Adam said with excitement. "Three nanotubes twisted into a triple helix. Check out the graphene lattice—the chicken wire. Each hex is six carbon atoms."

"It's so…" Halie struggled to find the words. Atoms felt familiar in name but utterly foreign once observed. That nature allowed for such complexity at minuscule scales left her feeling awed—and wanting more. "I see what you mean about being able to see the structure but not the atoms themselves. Six per hex? There must be a million carbon atoms in this single picture. And this is only one thread out of a thousand you could have zoomed in on."

"And it's only a small sample. The tether probably has many millions of these threads across its width." He looked up from the screen and stared blankly at Halie. "I expected to find the graphene—every tether needs a strong backbone. But the rest? I'm really not sure how to characterize it—it's not like any material I've seen."

Halie pulled out her phone. "I need to capture this."

He pushed her hand aside. "I can do better. The microscope is recording everything we see." He clicked a button and a QR code pattern popped up on his laptop. "Just scan that to transfer."

Halie scanned, then watched as several video clips appeared on her phone. Adam returned his stare to the thread, propping his chin on one hand.

"I'm tempted to call it a new allotrope—not that that's a big deal. Materials scientists come up with one or two every decade. Odd-shaped buckyballs, nanotubes with different properties, that kind of thing. But this one is unique. It's going to be hard to pin down its source. A deep-cover Chinese lab? One of Yoon's more clandestine competitors? Little green men from Planet X? I don't know."

Halie's ears perked up at the mention of an alien origin. "Mash was wondering the same thing. I can't blame her. When a complex space tether and a major sea platform appear overnight, something strange is going on."

Adam shrugged. "And think about the platform itself. It has no flag flying, no markings of any country, no corporate logos. The helicopter landing pad and the stairs leading up to the ribbon are evidence it was made *for* humans, but that doesn't mean it was made *by* humans."

"This place is weird," Halie said, using that word for the second time. "But I've covered stories like this before. It helps to keep asking questions. Like, if aliens built it, then where are they?"

Adam pointed up. "You only made it to the lowest station."

"Fair point. Three *hundred* kilometers out of thirty-six *thousand*. A lot left to explore. Plus, you haven't seen Yoon's wire. It hangs misty images in the air—pretty amazing stuff—and he doesn't know where it came from. The wire's last image was a V-pod control panel, with each of its buttons lit up, one through six. Maybe it's telling us to climb?"

"Want some company?" Adam stretched a smile. "You and Mashup have cameras, but I've got tools. Major league stuff that I haven't even shown you."

Halie smiled back. Could they go up again? Ecuadoran soldiers controlled the platform now, not Yoon. Although Adam's expertise made him more of a neutral party, Halie and Mash had already been ordered out of the V-pod at gunpoint. She couldn't imagine they'd be allowed back in, and so far, Yoon and Peru seemed to be losing the ownership struggle.

A knock pulled their attention to a Peruvian sailor at the hatchway. He held a single sheet of paper in his hand.

"*Qué pasa?*" Adam asked him.

"*Uno mas,*" the man said, handing him the paper.

Adam stood and read the single paragraph quickly. His eyes widened. "It's a newswire report. A cargo ship eighty kilometers southwest of Telukdalam, Indonesia, spotted another platform exactly like this one."

Halie held a hand to her mouth, finding herself scrambling to process the shifting events of this story. "Wait... there are two space elevators?"

13. EXPONENTIAL GROWTH

HALIE FURIOUSLY SCROLLED Google Earth from Ecuador to Indonesia using Adam's commandeered laptop. Once an idea had lodged in her head, it quickly became a tickle that had to be scratched.

Her location, as reported by her phone's GPS, was latitude zero—exactly on the equator—and longitude 82° 37' 12" west. She'd stuck a map pin at that position—460 kilometers due west of Quito.

From Adam's shipboard lab, Halie began a search to the other side of the world for a town named Telukdalam. She found it on Nias Island west of Sumatra. Using the app's line tool, she marked a yellow line southwest from Telukdalam, 80 kilometers long, and dropped a second pin. The tool dutifully reported the pin's latitude and longitude.

The numbers turned out to be exceedingly close to those she had already computed in her head: latitude 0°, longitude 97° 22' 48" east. "Exactly one-hundred-eighty degrees around the Earth," she said, looking up. "It's the antipode." Drill into the sea floor beneath their feet, continue straight through the Earth's core, and the hole would surface at an antipode on the opposite side of the planet.

Halie locked eyes with Adam. "It can't be a coincidence."

He nodded his agreement. "It adds an element of geographic design."

"But it raises even more questions. Why two platforms? Are they both tethers into space? Why duplicate such a colossal effort? Is one a backup in case the other breaks? Who is doing this, and why haven't they shown themselves?"

"All good questions."

Halie quickly realized one question stood above the rest. "Why does Yoon have a key? His floating wire. Without it we couldn't have landed before the military. Mash and I wouldn't have found the ascender. Somebody wanted Yoon to climb the tether first. Why?"

"You asked him?"

"I did. He doesn't know either. And at this point he seems more focused on retaining control than where the platform came from. It's like he wants to be sure he's not going to miss out on tourist revenue."

"Everyone has their priorities. What are yours?"

Halie gave him a crooked smile. "Getting answers. Not for my show—we already have plenty of material. But this tether into space is hiding mysteries. I can't walk away... I have to know."

She shivered, recognizing an intensely personal feeling. A big-picture, far-from-this-reality feeling that surfaced from time to time. Awe and curiosity—but tangled up with an anxiety that not a moment could be wasted. Given the chance to learn something fundamental about life, or people, or this world, or the next world— Halie *had to know.*

"You have the Marie Curie bug," Adam declared.

Halie leaned back in her chair, allowing a broad smile to cross her face as the truth of his statement dawned on her. "That's it. It comes from her famous quote..."

"Nothing in life is to be feared," Adam started.

They finished the quote together: "It is only to be understood."

Halie filled in the deeply personal part. "I have to understand things as they really are. If I fall short... I won't exist."

"I completely get it." Adam scooted his chair close and lowered his voice. "When I was ten, my family lived in an old house in Maine close to the Canadian border. Lots of house noises because something was always in need of repair. The water heater rumbled, the steps creaked. But one year there were these weird scratching sounds—scraping, like something being dragged. Spooked us all. My mom can be superstitious, and she said it was ghosts. My dad thought rats were more likely and called for an exterminator. We decided to move to a hotel for a few days, and while my parents were packing I had an idea. My upstairs bedroom had an entry into a crawl space. Too narrow for my dad to get through, so I gave it a shot. You know what I found up there?"

Halie didn't dare a guess.

"A wild lynx. A kit. Couldn't have been more than a few weeks old. We never saw the mother—maybe she abandoned the kit, or maybe a hunter got her. The Fish and Game people came by, pulled the kit out and nursed it back to health. Poor thing was half starved. Had been trying to scratch its way out."

"What a story."

"When my dad asked me why I did it... I mean, that's pretty scary stuff for a ten-year-old kid to be crawling into a musty old attic filled with ghosts... I told him I had to know."

Halie stared into his face. An honest face, well worn around the eyes from the lines that time and frequent smiles had etched. He was a man born of the same spirit to seek out the unexplained and find answers. She could use a partner like that.

She reached for his hand. "It's wonderful to meet you, Adam... *really* meet you."

His eyes creased into the smile that had caused the lines in the first place. "I was pretty sure I knew you after three episodes."

Halie laughed. "Does the real person disappoint?"

He squeezed her hand. "The real person is exponentially better."

"That much?" Halie couldn't suppress a hoot. "I probably shouldn't ask how high the exponent goes. I wouldn't want to ruin the moment. Besides, you and I have work to do."

"You want to find a way back up the tether, don't you?"

"It might not be that hard." Halie stood, wandering around the lab. "There's only one V-pod, currently locked inside its hangar. Only four people know how to unlock the hangar's hex puzzle: Yoon, Quong, Mash, and me. Trial and error would take days to solve it. We have an advantage."

Adam leaned against the opposite wall. "I buy that. But those soldiers have guns." He winced. "And to be honest… they don't like you."

"So, giving away tickets to my show only gets me so far?"

He nodded. "Not as far as that hangar door."

Halie shrugged, thinking through her options. Admit defeat and go home? Not likely. The biggest story of her life waited, tantalizingly close. She'd already discovered an incredible lookout that lacked any explanation for how it got there. And four more buttons waited to be pressed. What other wonders would they find higher up?

"Actually, there are two hangar doors, and one of them is hidden in a maze, so stealth could be an option. There *are* places to hide."

"But one way or another, the V-pod has to attach to the ribbon. Right in front of them… and they still have guns."

Ocean waves gently rocked the ship as Halie pondered. Another thought came quickly. "Their bullets would be useless."

His eyebrows furrowed. "How so?"

"Think about it. The V-pod is designed to carry people up a tether that passes through the Kill Zone. We're talking micro-debris hits every minute at eight kilometers per second. The glass is bulletproof. It would have to be—otherwise Level 3 would be out of reach."

Adam stroked fingers across his chin. "You're right, but it can't be glass. Even bulletproof glass wouldn't survive orbital debris speeds. It has to be an aramid."

"A what?"

"Aramids are molecular chains of benzene rings—a carbon hex fringed by six hydrogen atoms. They bond with neighboring chains to form threadlike fibers. You've heard of Kevlar, right?"

"Sure. Police vests."

"Kevlar is a brand name, but it's a type of aramid—basically, woven fibers that stretch but don't break. Of course, an aramid strong enough to survive space debris would take some effort to make. And transparent? I don't know, I might be wrong. But if you can get us to the V-pod, I have an infrared spectral analyzer in my duffel."

"There's our plan," Halie said with confidence. "I'll unlock the hangar and off we go, stopping at Level 2 so you can do your test before we go any higher. The only hard part is getting to that hangar door. If we're caught we could trigger an international incident."

"Even if we succeed."

"True. But who says Ecuador owns this place? Or Peru for that matter. Nobody even knows where it came from. Yoon has just as much right as anyone, and as his materials guy, you have every right to examine it."

"Still... guns."

"Yeah." Halie thought about her hasty proposal. "Wait until dark?"

Adam shrugged. "I'm game. Waiting until dark also gives me time to run one more test on the tether sample. It's a need-to-know thing."

She waved to the scientific equipment piled up around them. "Have at it."

Adam went to the outer office to prep another sample. While he was gone, Halie texted Mash to give her a heads-up that stealth might be in their future. She'd be all over that.

Adam returned and started fiddling with another instrument. Halie looked over his shoulder. "Another cool toy to play with?"

He pointed to a small screen where a Cartesian graph displayed an animated orange line. At the left side of the graph, the line wiggled with negligible amplitude, but on the right side it spiked to the top.

Adam explained. "I inserted a nanoprobe into both ends of the triple-helix thread. Nanotube number one shows no electrical conductivity at all. Expected because of its zigzag morphology—

high-strength, electrical insulator. But nanotube number two is a superconductor—no electrical resistance even at room temperature. It's probably where the V-pod is drawing its power."

He turned a switch on the device and a far more complicated graph appeared with animated spikes left and right across the x-axis. "This is the third nanotube. Multiwalled. Likely a semiconductor inside with an insulation wrap around its outside. Could be a data line, but semiconductors have lots of uses."

He swiveled to his laptop, still connected to the mondo microscope. "And check this out."

The microscopic view now showed the tip of one of the triple-helix threads. Dozens of spiky ball nanobots gathered at its broken end, probably where his scalpel had snipped the sample.

Halie moved closer to the screen, not sure what she was seeing. "Are they making it longer?"

Adam nodded enthusiastically. "Most of the bots are building new structure at the thread's tip. Who knows where they're getting the carbon. Pulling atoms out of the air? But look at this guy."

He pointed to one of the bots further along the thread. "He's making a copy of himself."

Halie bent over and had to squint to see the tiny creature busily assembling spikes onto a central core. "A clone?"

"Exactly. Nanoengineers design it into a bot's instruction code. Tell certain bots that their job is to create more bots, which gives you exponential growth. You see what that implies?"

Halie put it together quickly. With exponential growth, a starting count that doubled every minute would produce astronomical numbers in less than an hour. If half of these bots had been assigned to build more bots and the other half built structure, the whole tether could have formed quickly. "An army of workers, resizable to the task. It might explain why these structures are appearing overnight."

"Exponential math is trippy stuff." He pointed back to the screen. "Notice what our cloned bot is doing?"

The newly created creature hadn't yet moved even though it appeared to be fully assembled. "Nothing. Is it defective?"

"Uninitialized is more likely. We disconnected this sample from wherever they're getting their instructions. With no connection, the new bots are nothing but spikes and claws. They don't know what to do."

The discovery of self-replicating bots was both intriguing and worrisome. She'd come here to reveal a space elevator to the world, but the story was quickly getting more complex. Creepier too. "We should tell someone," Halie said.

"About inactive bots?"

"About *self-cloning* bots capable of exponential reproduction. Those are loaded words. Say them to your auntie and watch her reaction. Even people who've had one of those new nanobot root canals haven't completely lost their fear of the imagined robotic revolt led by a microscopic Genghis Khan. I'm a science communicator. I know."

"Fair enough, I'll talk to Yoon."

"I was thinking more along the lines of those American naval officers."

Adam shrugged. "I can talk to them too. No secrets here."

It was all any journalist could expect from a scientist. In reality, she wasn't concerned. As he'd said, real nanobots weren't that smart, they were simply useful at performing repetitive tasks in hard-to-reach places. But there was a larger issue. Behind every bot was an intelligent programmer. "Their instructions are coming from somewhere higher up on the tether," she said with quizzical eyes at Adam. It was a guess, nothing she could prove, but new theories had to start somewhere.

Adam took the suggestion without ridicule. He crossed his arms and leaned back in his chair, staring at the screen filled with bots. "I swear, Halie, I keep up with the field. I go to conferences, read the scientific papers. Not one of the nanomaterials labs anywhere in the world has built something this advanced."

"Yet here we are. Two tethers on opposite sides of the planet, likely constructed by self-replicating nanobots."

They sat silently, each one thinking through the implications. "The world needs to know what's up there," Adam finally said. "We have to go, with or without permission."

Halie nodded her agreement. "I'll coordinate with Mash, and I'm not feeling comfortable with text messaging. Who knows what spy tech is being used around here?"

"I'll tell Yoon," Adam said. "His support could make a difference."

Topside, the intense equatorial sun baked every surface of the ship. Adam retrieved his jet pack from the ship's storage locker and strapped it on, helping Halie with the secondary harness. Even from a hundred meters below the platform's deck, Halie could hear shouting.

She turned her back to Adam, and he clipped her in. A minute later, the roar of arm-directed jets lifted them from the ship. Halie was no longer concerned about Adam's flying skills, but she was still anxious about the landing.

They banked toward the sea, avoiding the platform's edge, then turned once they'd gained height. Finally, Halie could see what the fuss was about. A new plane had landed, the largest yet. Broad silver wings swept back in dramatic curves with twin recesses near the trailing edge, just like Yoon's plane. Another STOVL aircraft, no doubt.

The platform's true owner? Halie wondered. She had no idea, but a conventional answer avoided the more imaginative alternatives. A covert mastermind controlling hordes of self-duplicating nanobots was suddenly a top contender.

Peruvian soldiers cheered again as Halie and Adam passed overhead. Halie waved, then remembered to keep her arms crossed. Adam pointed their feet to a spot not far from Yoon's plane. Jet blast blew across the deck, and Halie felt instant relief as they touched down.

Adam stored the equipment next to Yoon's plane, then disappeared inside while Halie scanned the deck for Mash. She didn't see her.

Instead, a tall man with an athletic build swaggered across the deck. He was partially dressed in a see-through mesh t-shirt cropped well above his navel. Sculpted bare abs glistened from oil mixed with sweat. Demi pants hung dangerously low on his hips and finished at the knees with renaissance-style cross-lacing down each side. A sports cap tilted rakishly above his head.

A small entourage followed behind the extravagant superstar who would no doubt be recognized by every human being on the planet.

Marco.

As Yoon had predicted, the Brazilian ex-football star had finally arrived, showy and in-your-face, with an ostentatious plane to match. Halie could almost hear the American naval commander's sigh of dread. The dynamics of this South American squabble had changed.

Marco strutted a beeline straight for Halie. She stood her ground as he approached. Under the hat was a handsome face. Bronze skin, short-cropped hair, a hairless chiseled chin, and slightly offset nose, broken twice over a career dominating Brazilian leagues and the World Cup.

"Sahalie Spark!" he called out. His Brazilian accent added to the overt sex appeal that exuded from this A-list celebrity. The curled sneer on his lips and a knowing wink in his eye were oddly charming, but Halie was well aware of the manipulator beneath. Millions followed this man with cultlike devotion. If he told them to stab baby seals with pitchforks, they would.

"Rumors of infallible greatness precede you, Marco," Halie replied. "I've seen the banners they drape in stadiums. And now, I get to meet the man himself."

He waved one arm in a backhanded Shakespearean style greeting. She tipped her head.

Beads of perspiration dotted his face, shoulders, and muscular arms. The skimpy clothing and physical façade of an athlete stepping off the playing field exactly matched one of Marco's most famous commandments to his mostly male followers, "Wear your sweat."

Marco didn't just speak, he decreed. "Did you know, Miss Sahalie Spark, that your recent broadcast was watched across Brazil—in fact, across all of South America?"

"I didn't. I just stand in front of the camera. The technical folks do the rest. Was it good?"

He lifted the brim of his hat. "In a way, yes. You were the first to reveal this hideous monstrosity and its multiple levels of deceit." Marco waved a hand at the sky where the tapering black shroud met white clouds, leaving only a hint of the twin ribbons that continued higher. "Now we understand what we are up against."

Halie put her hands on her hips. People often made themselves larger when facing an unpredictable wild animal. "So, Marco, what are we up against?"

He flashed perfect white teeth in a practiced grimace. "Immediate and irreparable damage to the purity of our biophotonic radiance."

Halie wasn't about to question him on the specifics of this yet-to-be-measured source of radiation or the pseudoscientific words he had chosen to describe it. Some topics were better left unexplored.

"I tell you what. It's a big platform. Plenty of room for all of us and plenty of mystery to explore. Grab a spot and settle in. Take a few pictures and post to your followers what you think you see. In the meantime, I'll continue to examine the evidence. If it leads me to answers, I'll share them with you and everyone else."

"Your science doesn't interest me, and you'll find there is less mystery than you think. Are you aware, Miss Spark, that there are now three of these profane towers of technology?"

She froze. "Three?" Did he know something she didn't or was he just making up disinformation on the spot? "You sure about that? Last we heard it was two."

"Three," Marco repeated. "The third appeared an hour ago on the slopes of Mount Kenya. Another apparition to foul the spiritual purity of our brothers and sisters in Africa. If I know the techno-zealots—and I do—there will be more of these abominations. When you fight for something, Sahalie Spark, be sure that you are fighting on the right side."

So far, she had come up with a few top-notch retorts to this single-minded man, but this time Halie had nothing to say. In fact, she worried that his criticism might have merit.

14. SIX

A SEARCH OF THE PLATFORM and two unanswered texts left Halie wondering where Mash had disappeared to. The chance of being apprehended by Ecuadoran soldiers seemed remote. More likely was a literal interpretation of Halie's previous message, *we're going stealth.*

Halie returned to Yoon's plane and Jaya waved her in, handing her a bottle of water, which she eagerly accepted. Through the aisle curtains, she spotted Adam speaking with Yoon.

"We're going up again," Halie told Jaya, not wishing to interrupt whatever blessings or cautions Yoon might be conveying upon Adam.

"I overheard," Jaya answered. She pulled a tray of prepared sandwiches from a cabinet and Halie snarfed one down. "Do be careful. Yoon can be impulsive, especially when others are bearing the risk."

Halie tipped her head with a crooked grin. "And just when I was beginning to think of him as a father figure."

"He *is* a businessman."

"I'll try to remember that. Actually, it's not Yoon I'm worried about." Halie tossed her head toward the airplane's open door. "We'll need to hide somewhere until it's dark."

"You're welcome to hide here."

"Thanks, but it needs to be closer to the V-pod. We'll figure something out." Halie excused herself to use the lavatory. When she returned, Adam was munching on his own sandwich.

"Yoon is working the political angles, so he's staying here," Adam said between bites. "But he agrees we should go up, so he's going to run interference for us. Draw attention away from the ribbon by hosting a reconciliation mini-conference among the opposing factions right here in his plane."

"Tough to fit fifty people in here."

"Representatives only. The rest will gather outside, especially when they hear Jaya's providing food and drinks for everyone."

Halie looked to Jaya. "Do you know about these things in advance, or does he just spring them on you?"

Jaya gave her graceful smile. "He's the boss."

Halie's phone beeped. Finally, a response from Mash. *Psst. Meet me*, was all it said. At least she hadn't been thrown overboard.

"It's Mash," she told Adam. "Already hiding, I suspect, since cloak-and-dagger is right up her alley."

"Let's find her, then." Adam grabbed another sandwich to go. "We're underway with Operation…" He struggled to come up with a name for whatever it was they were attempting.

"Don't worry about it, let's go," Halie told him. Mash would have a clever name at the tip of her tongue.

Adam grabbed his duffel, and they started across the platform. Late-afternoon tropical heat meant any hiding place would need to be in the limited shady areas, most likely under the tether's shroud. There was no telling how long they might be gone, but three packs with food and water were still in the V-pod. They'd be fine—as long as they managed to commandeer it.

Halie steered clear of the remaining soldiers. While some had returned to their ships, one particularly argumentative group gathered in the shade along the small buildings that dotted the platform's edge. No one even bothered to look up as they passed, but that didn't mean a run for the tether would be successful.

"You know where Mash is?" Adam asked.

"Not really, but there's a maze under the shroud. That's where I would hide. You could get lost in there."

When they reached the shroud's edge, bright sun gave way to shadows. Halie immediately caught sight of Marco at the top of the boarding gantry, examining the twin ribbons. A group of soldiers and Marco's entourage gathered around.

"Not going to work," Halie said under her breath and made a hard right turn, hoping for the best but expecting the worst. She strolled casually along the shroud's perimeter with Adam not far behind.

Don't mind us, we're catching the next sailing to Peru.

At least the Peruvian ship was in this direction. Once the maze of buildings blocked the view to the tether, Halie ducked beneath the shroud again and randomly selected a narrow passageway, not having the slightest idea where it might lead.

After two intersections, equally narrow and unmarked, Adam grabbed her arm and pulled her to a stop. He leaned in close and whispered, "Your cat burglar technique needs polish."

"Polish?"

"Just a phrase. And I admit the soldiers aren't likely to be in here, but to avoid getting lost shouldn't we be leaving a breadcrumb trail?"

Irritated, Halie searched down each passageway but didn't spot anything that looked familiar. She tossed a coin in her mind. "This way."

After several more turns she didn't recognize, Halie was beginning to wonder if she'd ever find the secret hangar door again. Or Mash. Worse, she'd have to admit to Adam that her cloak-and-dagger skills might indeed need polishing.

Halie turned another corner, flinching as a hand reached out and pulled her into a dark nook.

Thankfully, it was Mash. "Took you long enough," she whispered.

Halie sharply exhaled, keeping her voice low. "Your communications weren't terribly helpful."

"Hey, we're in stealth mode now. Got to keep these morons off our trail. Every one of them has made the pilgrimage to the tether, but that's as far as they get. Marco the Magnificent is the latest."

"Yeah, I saw him. So, no one's found the puzzle?"

"No, and I intend to keep it that way." Mash produced a thick metal bar, a stiffening rod that normally fit into her stabilizing harness.

"You're not planning to whack people, are you?"

"We do what we must." Mash hid her weapon once more.

Halie nodded behind her. "Adam is going with us."

"Up?"

"Yes, up. But not until dark."

"Pajama Llama Ping Pong," Mash declared rather unhelpfully.

"There you go," Adam responded. "Operation *Pajama*. It *will* require an overnight."

Mash beamed. Halie just shrugged. "Whatever."

Mash leaned in close to Adam and fake-whispered to the back of her hand. "She's no fun. She drives *under* the speed limit. In LA. Who does that? If I were you, I'd keep my distance."

Adam took in the advice without comment. Halie ignored it as best she could, given the stakes. Their goal was grand theft, but none of them were equipped to fend off soldiers, even if the V-pod proved impervious to bullets. Their only advantage was that no one had discovered them yet, but that might not last. Nightfall was hours away.

"Hold on… why wait at all?" Halie asked, finally shaking the cobwebs out of her head. "We thought darkness would make it easier to sneak around, but we're already here. No one stopped us. All we need to do now is find the puzzle."

Mash rolled her eyes. "What about Pajama Llama Ping Pong did you not understand?" She slung her camera bag over one shoulder and started down another dark passage. "Follow me."

Halie wasn't any more enlightened, but if Mash knew the way, that was all that mattered. The passageways still didn't look familiar, but she could blame that on afternoon lighting versus morning. After another turn, Mash stopped at a dead end. The hexagon puzzle waited patiently.

No guard, which actually wasn't too surprising. The Ecuadoran soldiers had only seen the V-pod enter the hangar from the opposite side. The puzzle pieces had returned to their original configuration. Halie quickly rearranged them to the solution without any need to consult the recording on Mash's camera. She hovered a hand over the puzzle. One push and all efforts at stealth would end.

"Here's the thing," she told Adam. "When we enter, the hangar door on the other side will open too, with Marco and the guards standing right there. We'll only have a few seconds to reach the V-pod before they start shooting."

"*If* they start shooting," Adam added.

"Shooting?" Mash asked.

"Don't worry, we'll be fine," Halie told her. "I'll go first. You guys store your gear while I climb to the control panel. Once I press the Level 2 button, it's automated from there. I don't see how they can stop us."

"Maybe with their shooting?" Mash asked again.

"You missed that part of the plan. I'll explain when we're inside. Just run."

Halie pushed the button. The door slid open, and she launched herself into the hangar. Lights came on. The outer door on the other side rumbled open.

Halie raced up the mezzanine steps to the V-pod, its hatch open. Mash and Adam were close behind, running faster than Halie thought possible given the bags of gear they were carrying.

Shouts erupted from outside. Halie didn't bother to look up. This part of their hastily prepared plan was an all-or-nothing gambit. She clambered up the V-pod's internal ladder two rungs at a time, freezing momentarily at the top to stare down at Marco, who stood at the slot in the hangar's floor. He locked fierce eyes with Halie, yelling in Portuguese.

She rushed to the control panel and pressed Level 2. Below, the V-pod hatch began to close. Several soldiers ran up the mezzanine steps to reach it. They didn't make it in time.

The pod began its slide along the hangar slot with Marco pounding on its side. The thick glass muffled his words, but Halie caught the gist from his wild-eyed expression alone.

"Sorry, Marco, you're being left behind." He probably couldn't hear her, but she continued anyway. "Don't worry, we'll broadcast to everyone in the world. You too."

Mash joined Halie on the V-pod's second level while Adam took up a position guarding the entryway. It was closed, but with everything automated would it stay that way? Outside, several soldiers pointed automatic weapons. Their commander yelled with fury, though it was impossible to tell what he was saying.

"Uh... guys?" Mash said, scooting close to Halie. "What was that about shooting?"

"Well, they may or may not shoot," Halie answered. "Doesn't matter, Adam and I talked about the material this pod is made from."

"Glass?" Mash asked nervously.

The soldiers aimed their weapons directly at Halie and Mash.

"Can't be glass or we won't make it through the Kill Zone. Adam thinks it might be an aramid compound like Kevlar, but he needs to test it to be sure."

The probably-not-glass ship arrived at the ribbon. The squad leader and several soldiers hurried up the gantry steps. Several pointed their weapons to the V-pod's upper level while others slammed against the lower-level door. It held tight.

Halie remained standing at the window. "Actually, I'd prefer if they did shoot. We may as well test the material now before we reach the high-velocity stuff in the Kill Zone."

The V-pod slipped onto the ribbon. The Ecuadoran squad leader became more animated. The banging on the door increased.

"Should we taunt them?" Mash asked sincerely.

Halie shrugged. "Let's not. At some point we have to return."

They both waved goodbye as the pod gently lifted off the launchpad and rose above confused soldiers and one angry ex-footballer. Guns sagged, mouths hung open. Not a shot was fired. In seconds, the V-pod accelerated through the conical shroud toward its tiny exit overhead.

Halie plopped onto the couch, breathing a sigh of relief. "I can't believe it actually worked."

Adam climbed up from the lower level and sat next to her, grinning. "Cat burglary. Nicely done."

Mash handed out the flight suits they'd left in a pile from their previous ascent. She gave Yoon's suit to Adam. "Get your wings on, people. Climb fast and soar high."

"Yoon's precaution," Halie explained to Adam as she put the pressure suit on. "We didn't need them on the first ascent, but…" She didn't feel the need to bring up the Kill Zone again. The dangers they would face above Level 2 weren't easily forgotten.

At the top of the shroud, they broke into bright daylight. Afternoon sun lit up the surrounding sea at a different angle than their morning trip. The American aircraft carrier now dominated the view below—nearly as wide as the platform and twice as long.

A helicopter flew past, quickly dropping beneath. Perhaps a military jet standing on its tail could climb faster, but their acceleration continued. Even at one-quarter g—the acceleration of a sports car after a traffic light turns green—they would eventually reach speeds no airplane could touch.

Halie relaxed while Adam circled, clearly enjoying the spectacular view. Sea and clouds faded below as they streaked toward deep blue above. Adam called out the altitude displayed on his augmented reality visor—already 20 kilometers. If the visor used the same GPS receiver built into every modern phone, they'd have accurate altitudes at least to 20,000 kilometers where global navigation satellite systems orbited.

Halie grabbed her phone and loaded Google Earth. She scrolled to central Africa and dropped a pin on the north slope of Mount Kenya. As expected, the equator passed through that spot, the first piece of evidence that supported Marco's report of a third platform.

She studied the lines of longitude, looking for 37° 22' 48" east, a coordinate she had precalculated in her head. It wasn't hard to find.

"Marco was right," Halie said to herself.

Adam sat down next to her. "About?"

"A third platform. The latest one is 120 degrees around the Earth from our current position, one-third of the planet's circumference. There's nothing coincidental about that."

Halie elaborated. "Three platforms. One we're climbing. Another that's halfway around the planet, and another that's a third of the way around. If you divide the Earth into six equal segments, each segment is sixty degrees of longitude, and all three platforms fill predefined locations."

"Leaving three empty spots. Or maybe not empty. What if there are six platforms? Where would the others be?"

"Not hard to figure out." She scrolled further east along the equator to just past 97 degrees east, landing near Sumatra. "That's platform number two, already reported." Another sixty-degree scroll brought her to 157 degrees east, a spot in the Pacific Ocean north of the Solomon Islands. Another scroll and a bit of math brought her to 142 degrees west. Still in the Pacific, this time north of French Polynesia.

"The next is where we are now, 82 degrees west." She scrolled one more time. "And finally, in the mid-Atlantic at 22 degrees west."

She thought about the six spots around the globe that she'd just whisked through. "Those three empty spots are all in open ocean, far from land."

Adam picked up the thought. "A platform suddenly appearing overnight in the ocean could go unnoticed. Even if it was near a shipping lane, you'd have to be looking for it."

"Good point. We can."

"We can what? Look for them?"

"Yup." Halie had done it before. The data was there. "All we need is real-time satellite images. Geostationary weather satellites take a new picture every few minutes, and they post that stuff online."

Halie jumped into a browser window. The V-pod had no Wi-Fi, but internet service came with her satellite phone subscription.

She was most familiar with the GOES satellite system that covered North and South America, but the Europeans operated a Meteosat satellite over the Atlantic, and Japanese Himawari satellites covered the Pacific. She picked Himawari, since they provided high-resolution photos every ten minutes, freely available to anyone. The Himiwari-9 satellite at 141 degrees east would match well with the Solomon Islands.

She picked the latest image. The left half was dark, the right half lit by the sun—dawn in that part of the world with the terminator bisecting Australia. Halie zoomed to New Guinea, then scrolled a bit east. The image refreshed as she went. It didn't display lines of latitude or longitude but with some back and forth between Google Earth and the satellite image, she zoomed in on a specific patch of ocean.

An unpopulated atoll named Kapingamarangi was the closest island, still 269 kilometers away, but a quick translation between kilometers on the map and pixels on the satellite image gave her a reasonably good bull's-eye to search.

"What does that look like to you?" she asked Adam, pointing to the only black mark in a sea of blue sprinkled with shades of white.

"Could be a cloud shadow," Adam said, squinting.

"Or one of our theoretical set of six platforms," she said.

"It's possible."

She scrolled the map to a new longitude, this time a point 1,495 kilometers southwest of Monrovia, Liberia. Another website gave her a European Meteosat image. It was already evening in the mid-

Atlantic, but she downloaded an earlier image taken before sunset. After more kilometer-to-pixel calculations, she eventually found the right spot. Another black dot stood out among pixels of blue. It couldn't be a coincidence.

"I think we found them," Halie said with authority. She felt no need to repeat the exercise for the sixth platform in the middle of the Pacific and there probably wasn't enough time anyway before they reached Level 2.

"Six platforms, three that haven't been noticed yet," she said aloud. "Why six? Why am I seeing that number so often? Six dots on the puzzle pieces. Six buttons on the V-pod control panel. Hexagons have six sides, and hexagons have been everywhere."

"Carbon atoms have six protons, six neutrons, and six electrons," Adam added. "And hexagons are a common shape in nature. Columnar basalt formations, dried mud patterns, even beehives."

"Yeah, I know all about bees," Halie said. "Trust me, you'll love the next episode of *Don't Believe It!*"

Mash thrust her phone in Halie's face. "Sorry to interrupt the geography nerd fest, but check out what our friend Marco is doing."

A video showed Marco, still dressed in what the Brazilian fashion industry referred to as a Bare Naked Sports style, but now he'd hung a bullfighter's cape across one shoulder. He stood beneath the tether's conical sheath, gesticulating with angry hands. "Four years ago, the spy satellites that tracked our steps and peered into our personal lives were destroyed by the creator's hand. Then, we rejoiced. Yet the techno-zealots and their shadow politicians learned nothing."

Like a movie star who'd been passed over for a major role, Marco's natural charisma was now tinged with annoyance, masculine and powerful. There was a seething fury in his voice, irritation behind his glare. "Their next plan lies in this monstrous tower and others like it around the world. The shapeshifters will use the sky to rule over us. From this day forward, their tech mind viruses will rain down upon us, injecting transhumanist beliefs into our veins and invading the temple of our bodies with their toxins and microchips.

"My friends, humanity has reached a crisis point. We can obey and lose our spiritual purity forever, or we can fight to regain our supreme self and live the traditions that nature intended. I for one will not cower beneath their spires of techno-idolatry. Will you join me? Men, you are natural born fighters! We will use our strong bodies and minds in opposition. Women, as spirit oracles, apply your inner voice. Warn your neighbors.

"Sadly, one woman—a well-known television personality—does not understand her role. Instead of denouncing this vile structure, she steals its technology for her own glory. Even now, she climbs this tower as an unwitting accomplice of her techno-zealot master. Her dishonest sermons warp our pure thoughts and ask us to bow down to the forces of scientific radicalism."

Mash shut it off. "Fun guy."

Halie sat stunned, pondering the conspiratorial misinformation Marco was unleashing upon millions. "Mind viruses? Injected from the sky? With microchips? It's all so random."

"He just makes stuff up and throws it against the wall to see what sticks," Adam said. "His followers fill in the details, and voila! Gospel."

Halie tilted her head. "Maybe so, but disinformation works because it taps into common fears. Shadows in the dark, loss of freedoms, even the fear of needles. He may sound nutty, but Marco has a *lot* of followers, and he's pretty good at twisting anything unsolved into something to fear."

Halie looked up. Stars were visible now. A glint of sun gave away the path not only of the ribbon but of Level 2's donut-shaped station. They'd be there soon.

"Two can play this game," Halie said. "Mash, get ready for another live shot. Arrival at the Level 2 station."

Halie left Mash to her preparation work and texted Paul. He called back in less than a minute. "The network prefers the evening news slot. More eyeballs," he said breathlessly. "But if you need to go now, we can get you in."

They were offering to go live at the coveted position at 6:35 p.m. Eastern time—the best time slot in the news business. It gave the evening news anchor five minutes to cover an ordinary headline then switch to live breaking news—always a winning format. Right now, it was 5:45 p.m. in New York. Less than an hour to wait, but with Level 2 coming up fast, she had a better idea.

"Get me both slots," she told Paul. "A teaser now and a break into the evening news."

"Jeez, Halie, just ask for the world."

"I'm asking, Paul. Can you deliver?"

There was a pause. "Will there be sparks?"

It was a wordplay on her last name that Paul had always thought funny. "Oh, don't worry, Paul. You'll get sparks. Six of them."

15. LIVE AT LEVEL 2

THE TEASER WAS QUICK AND DIRTY. Mash lay on the floor, pointing her camera straight up to capture the approaching station. Halie stood to one side wearing her full space gear, helmet included. She kept her comments brief.

"I'm minutes away from a three-sixty view that will knock your socks off." She promised breaking news, not just about the South American space elevator but about a larger plan impacting the world. She signed off with a kicker guaranteed to explode the number of viewers for the evening news. "We've now learned how these tethers were made, and we're on the hunt for the instruction manual. I'll explain as soon as we dock at the station."

Mash shut down their transmission as the V-pod slowed. Halie's phone pinged repeatedly as new messages from Paul flooded in. Some were messages he'd forwarded from network execs and directors anxious for more. She had just lit a bonfire under this story.

As before, the ship eased to a stop inside the donut hole at the station's center. Floor and ceiling membranes slid across, pinching against the hull of the V-pod and providing an airtight seal against the vacuum of space. The V-pod's door hissed open. Halie strutted into the lookout like she owned the place. Adam dropped his duffel and made a beeline for one of the windows.

Late afternoon turned out to be a great time to gaze east. The white-topped volcanoes dotting the Ecuadoran Andes stood out against the greens of the Amazon basin beyond. Scattered clouds of the morning had now built into towering cumulonimbi that obscured much of the rainforest but provided their own jaw-dropping examples of Earth's natural beauty.

Like a kid in a treetop, Adam made the complete circle of the donut, pointing and commenting as he went. No one, Halie imagined, could be indifferent to this station's magnificent perspective. Space tourism had a new entry, larger than any suborbital spacecraft, easier to reach, and without the zero-g nausea.

With her prime-time spot coming up fast, Halie answered Paul's messages but blew off the rest to focus on the job at hand. She sent microscopic images of nanotubes and wiggling bots to Mash, then plugged a lapel microphone into a powerpack hooked on her belt. Adam finished ogling the view and headed to the airlock to perform more tests. He'd have easy access to both the ribbon and the ascender—this time without soldiers giving orders.

Minutes ticked down. Mash prepped her camera, video playback, and transmitter. She gave a thumbs-up.

Halie paced alone around the empty lookout, rehearsing what she would say. She stopped once to check makeup using her phone in selfie mode. Ever since they'd removed helmets, she'd felt occasional tickles on her face—probably a loose hair. Either that, or this place had spiders—highly unlikely. The face staring back from the phone was as fresh as any reporter could be while transmitting from space.

Mash called out that she had a connection to the KNS news director. Halie felt her pulse rise. "Tom?" she asked.

This time a woman's voice came over Halie's earbud. "Hi, Sahalie, it's Jamaica Rand."

"Oh, hi, Jamaica. It's been a while."

"It has. How are you?"

"Honestly, a little nervous. How much time do I have?"

"Whatever you need. My guess is that you're going to be the top story from here on out. Feed us whatever you have, whenever you can."

"Good to hear. For now, let's limit to four or five minutes. It's blockbuster material, but staying on point will drive it home."

"You got it, Halie. You have everyone's attention. Not just us in the studio, but around the world. We know about two more platforms, but all we're getting from Sumatra and Kenya are amateur phone clips. You're the only one climbing into space and the only one broadcasting live."

Nothing like a little pressure. Mash pointed her shoulder cam into Halie's face. The director confirmed they had the feed, then started a countdown.

Halie had never met the KNS evening news anchor, Jonah Davidson, but his voice was familiar. "As promised, we're going now to Sahalie Spark for breaking news about the space elevators that everyone is talking about. What do you have for us, Sahalie?"

"A lot, Jonah," Halie said, thankful that the anchor had wasted no time with needless chitchat. "I'm standing inside the station at Level 2. It's an observation deck big enough for thirty or forty people, above the atmosphere but below the Kill Zone with a stunning view to Ecuador and Peru in one direction, and Colombia, Panama, and Central America in another."

Halie passed each window with Mash staying close. "The view is spectacular—I gotta say I feel privileged to be here—but I need to show you the tether we rode up on. We've joined forces with Dr. Adam Estrada from the Universidad Nacional Mayor in Lima, Peru. He's still checking a few things, but we've already learned a lot. Dr. Estrada examined a tether sample under a transmission electron microscope, or TEM, and showed me its structure. I believe we have video."

Halie raised her eyebrows, and Mash gave her a thumbs-up. One of the clips they'd taken from the microscope played over the live feed, showing the rolling-hopping nanobots.

"You're looking at what chemists call an *allotrope of carbon*, and this one may be unique in the world. An allotrope is a molecular structure where atoms come together in repeating patterns. In this case, the pattern is a graphene base with carbon nanotubes layered on top. We still don't fully understand its complexity, but we do know two things. Those little spiky balls you see are nanobots, programmed to create the carbon lattice. The nanobots can also build more nanobots. We even watched one being assembled."

Halie was fully aware the last statement would raise eyebrows. Jonah didn't interrupt, but she could only imagine the alarmist response that would soon come from Marco and others like him. It didn't matter. She wouldn't let the conspiracy nutcases define which discoveries she was allowed to reveal.

"The second thing we learned is that one of those twisted threads on the triple helix is likely to be a communications path—possibly providing instructions to the bots. It suggests that somewhere higher up on the tether is *command central*, if you will, a place where the instructions originate. If we're lucky, we'll find it."

"You'll be going through the Kill Zone?" Jonah asked.

Halie stood in front of the V-pod and leaned one hand against its clear shell. "To get to the next level, yes, we'll need to go through the Kill Zone. But Dr. Estrada will give us a better idea of the risks before we go. I can also tell you that we've discovered three more platforms for a total of six."

Halie explained how they'd located the deep ocean platforms, noting that national security imaging analysts had probably spotted them too. "This is a worldwide phenomenon. We all need to understand what's happening."

Jonah interrupted again. "Sahalie, any further ideas about who is behind this? You reported this morning it was Yoon Ji-ho, but in a BBC phone interview he admitted the space elevators are not his."

Halie was relieved to hear Yoon had come clean in a very public way. It suggested that the dispute down on the platform had been resolved, one way or the other. "Yes, Mr. Yoon told me the same thing. At first, he thought the design was his—and he had good reasons to believe that. But it's now clear someone else is involved."

"Aliens? There are rumors."

Halie hesitated, but she couldn't think of a reason to avoid or deny. "I know. We've talked about it ourselves, and I'm not going to dismiss that idea as nonsense without thinking it through. But we have no evidence and until we do, I'll keep investigating with a clear head and an eye toward answers that make the most sense."

"The Brazilian football player Marco is also on-site in Ecuador. He claims *spiritual vampires* are already invading."

Halie suppressed an eye roll. "Jonah, I'm literally hanging from the tether right now, and I can assure you that no vampires—spiritual, metaphorical, or otherwise—are crawling down it."

"In Kenya, I believe he said."

Halie paused, thinking quickly. As the news director had said, she had everyone's attention. She could continue the on-air banter with Jonah, but when disinformation reared its head, Halie couldn't—and wouldn't—hold back.

"I can't speak to Kenya. I'm not there. But I do know this, and I'm going to draw upon the wisdom of Marie Curie. Most of us have heard her famous quote, 'Nothing in life is to be feared, it is only to be understood.' But you may not have heard the second part of that quote. Marie had just been told by doctors that the radiation exposure from her work was killing her. Her answer? 'Now is the time to understand more so that we may fear less.' Facing imminent death, Marie still placed understanding over fear. That's the strength of science. That's the strength of searching for answers based on evidence. And that's what we all need to do now."

Halie exhaled, staring straight ahead, barely hearing Jonah as he thanked her for the report and offered his best wishes. She didn't respond when Mash said they were off the air, or even when Mash pulled the bud from Halie's ear and handed it to her.

She'd gotten worked up. Gone off script. She'd preached instead of reporting. Nothing she'd said was wrong, and she wouldn't get into trouble over it. In fact, the network was anxious for more, and she would give it.

Only one thing bothered her.

Curie's brave words were true enough, but the strength of evidence-based science was harder to locate when Halie examined her own courage. Soon, she would be climbing higher on the tether. She'd be passing through the Kill Zone, exploring where no one had gone before. She'd be searching for answers, and privately, Halie feared what she might find.

What if aliens really are up there? Not vampires per se, but they wouldn't need to be bloodsuckers to be disturbing. Even the nanobots Adam had discovered looked a little like spiders.

"You okay?" Mash asked.

Halie shook it off, putting a hand on Mash's shoulder. "I'm good. How about you?"

Mash shrugged. "How bad could it get? They call it the Kill Zone, but I bet it's no worse than running across the line of fire at a gun range... in front of guys with shotguns... and bump-stocked AR-15s. Maybe a few hand grenades thrown in there."

Halie huffed out a smile. Mash could do that to her. "Let's check with Adam."

They returned to the airlock, where the pod stood ready to climb further, should they dare. Adam was on hands and knees next to the down ribbon with a variety of tools laid out across the floor.

Halie squatted beside him. "What have you got? Yoon told us the ribbons are taking debris hits."

"Pummeled is the word I think I heard," Mash added. Right or wrong, Halie had no desire to minimize the danger. Adam had better tools than merely placing a hand on the tether.

"The ribbons are taking hits, no question," Adam confirmed without looking away from a handheld device. Its screen displayed a sine wave with a varying amplitude. "But nanobots are crawling all over this thing. Two minutes ago, I simulated a debris hit by lasering a pinhole straight through the ribbon—a hundred micrometers in diameter, which may not sound like much, but down at the nanoscale that's like trying to repair Hoover Dam hit by a Hellfire missile. See for yourself."

He pointed to a red circle he'd drawn on the ribbon. Thankfully, the inside of the circle didn't look any different than outside.

"They're repair bots. They work fast, and they're definitely getting their signal from that third thread. Remember the monitor I clipped on the ribbon at the platform? I just sent a ping down the thread and got a solid return signal. That tells me that the tether isn't just providing strength and electricity. It's also an information conduit, basically a self-contained internet."

"So?" Halie lifted both eyebrows.

"So, we go higher," Adam said. "Figure out where the signal originates."

Halie patted the side of the V-pod. "How about our ride? It's not glass, right?"

"As I suspected, it's an aramid. Transparent Kevlar, essentially. Bullets? No problem. Even pebble-sized space debris will struggle to penetrate the full two centimeters."

"How about a space anvil?" Mash asked.

Adam didn't even crack a smile at Mash's flippant example. "Cataclysmic. Nothing would survive that kind of hit. But chunks of debris with the equivalent mass of an anvil are rare in the Kill Zone. We should be safe." He gave a serious glance to each of them.

Mash seemed satisfied. Halie was too. Risk was forever tied with probability, the Kill Zone being a prime example. Adam had determined that the majority of its debris would be safely absorbed by the V-pod's aramid shield. As long as they didn't linger, their exposure to the larger, deadlier chunks would be limited.

Halie and Mash helped Adam store his tools on the V-pod's lower level, then climbed the ladder. Halie stood in front of the control panel and said to Adam, "Your turn to do the honors."

He twirled a finger in the air and tapped the third button. "Going up."

The V-pod door shut. Floor and ceiling membranes retreated into the airlock cylinder to reveal the Earth below and the blackness of space above. The passengers took their places on the circular couch, each slipping on helmets and zip-on gloves.

"Intercom working?" Halie asked, catching Adam's eye.

"Loud and clear."

To Mash, "Camera rolling?"

"Of course. This could be the best part."

Mash's quips aside, Halie was only slightly surprised to find her confidence building. *We're as prepared as we can be. We'll make it.*

They rose slowly at first, passing through a dozen cables affixed to the outside edges of the ribbons and spreading outward to attachment points around the station's disc. Once clear, acceleration kicked in and the station dropped away, soon becoming an indistinguishable white dot dwarfed by the vast expanse of Earth.

They sat in silence for several minutes, staring out to the eastern horizon. With no atmosphere there could be no wind noise. The only indicator of speed was a hum from unseen mag-lev equipment at the V-pod's notch. The hum increased in pitch.

Adam finally made it formal by tapping his visor and calling out its numbers, "Altitude is 410 kilometers. Vertical speed is 944 meters per second. Faster than the first leg."

"We're out of the atmosphere now, so no friction," Halie offered. "The faster the better. Let's get this done."

She fidgeted with her gloved fingers and kept her stare outside, trying to suss out which side of the ship would likely take the first hit. The bulk of the debris field zipped around the Earth from west to east, but inclinations to the equator ranged wildly, making any fixed location feel like the X-crossing tracks at a demolition derby. After four years of collisions and ricochets, an individual chunk could come from almost anywhere.

Their goal, Level 3, would be somewhere around 2,000 kilometers based on the control panel markings—easily in the clear. But even while flying upward at nearly a kilometer per second, that height felt distant. Every extra minute in the Kill Zone put them at higher risk.

Another precious minute ticked by. Outside, space still looked like space. No clouds of smashed satellite parts, no streaks of light or tiny explosions, only the steady glow of brighter stars competing against the glare of Earth below. Realistically, they'd never see it coming. They'd be hit—or not hit—but nothing they did now would affect their fate either way.

"Did you hear that?" Mash announced. She stood up, pointing her camera in various directions.

"What?"

"A tick. Like a pebble hitting your car windshield."

The next one was obvious, more like the crack of a baseball off a bat. Halie looked around but found no chips in the clear carbon aramid—she still thought of it as glass.

She heard another pop, then several more. Fingernail taps on a table. The loudest, like chopsticks snapping. They came more frequently. Hail on a roof.

Halie stood to inspect the window. No cracks, no marks at all. But that didn't lessen the edgy feeling of being trapped inside a tin can while kids shot it with pellet guns.

After a particularly loud snap, Adam and Mash rushed to the other side with Halie right behind. He pointed a gloved finger to a spot on the glass as Mash's camera zoomed in. A crescent-shaped chip marred the otherwise clear surface. Within seconds, the chip filled in, returning the window to perfection.

Adam grinned behind his helmet glass. "Better than any ordinary aramid—it's self-repairing. Of course, that hit took out a pretty good chunk of material."

"And force is proportional to mass," Halie suggested. "If the next hit has twice the mass, I imagine we could lose twice as much?"

"We could," Adam responded. "But the thickness of any spacecraft hull is set by design. The idea is to protect against a four-sigma event—at least that's the probability we used in Peru's designs. Make sure your ascender can withstand the worst out of sixteen thousand random hits. As long as Mash's anvil doesn't come along, we should be fine."

Their transit was a roll of the dice. From what Halie remembered about probabilities, the chance of rolling a double-six three times in a row was roughly the same as Adam's four-sigma event. Extremely unlikely, but it could still happen. If the Acme anvil came, it would end things quickly; not even pressure suits and helmets would help.

She wondered if that might explain the six space elevators. Redundancy would give humanity a fighting chance to clear the debris field. For good or evil, whoever built these structures would dominate space activities for years to come.

The regular pelting continued—clicks and taps for the most part. But at 900 kilometers, a loud snap directly in front of her made Halie jump. Adrenaline spiking, she rushed to a starburst pattern in the glass. Multiple fractures radiated outward. She covered it with her palm, pressing gently.

"Please heal," she whispered. Lifting her hand, she watched in awe as the cracks filled in like an instant windshield repair job. Her heart took considerably longer to calm.

"You're a miracle worker," Mash deadpanned as Halie dropped back to the couch.

"Hey... millions of bots at my command." They exchanged a more serious glance. "I'll feel better once we're through this."

"Me too."

The clicks and pops continued for several minutes, then slackened. At 1,500 kilometers, they were finally gone. Adam did a walkaround, inspecting every surface of the V-pod and finding nothing to report. They'd survived.

Going up. We still have to get down.

Halie thought of the thirty-four astronauts who hadn't survived, four years before. Their bodies had simply become part of the debris field. Funerals with no caskets. Families with no closure. Space had never been a safe place to work, but the Kessler event had brought danger to a new level. Could a self-repairing space elevator make a difference? Somehow, they'd need to locate and deorbit those anvil-sized chunks still out there. Do that much, and the repair bots might stand a chance.

The system's automation kicked in, slowing their ascent and producing a floating feeling like sitting in a chair partly submerged under water. Halie spied another white disc overhead, significantly larger in diameter than the station at Level 2. Minutes later, the V-pod slipped into another donut hole in the disc's center, and Adam announced 2,024 kilometers.

Halie stood, immediately feeling light on her feet. She didn't need an app to know why. She could almost see the equation floating in the air.

$$g = \frac{GM}{r^2}$$

It was one of several still lodged in her head since high school. Every student of physics learned Newton's equation of gravitational acceleration and its inverse-square relationship with distance, r, from a large mass, M. Until Sir Isaac, the word *gravity* didn't even exist. Aristotle's *natural motion of weight* explained why things fell and also why people believed that heavier objects fell faster, even though Galileo had disproven that notion a century before Newton.

The equation was groundbreaking for scientists and mathematicians. Among the public, not so much—then or now. But it hid big implications that had never truly been explored. Climb to a mountaintop, and the pull of gravity dropped by only a small amount. But *double* the distance from Earth's center, and gravity dropped to *one-quarter* of its surface value. Of course, Newton and every person since—including astronauts—had no way to experience this astonishing aspect of nature.

Until now, Halie realized. *A space elevator changes our relationship with gravity forever.*

Halie jumped. Only a small hop, but enough to instantly prove the point. The hang time in the air felt unnaturally long. The thump on the floor oddly forgiving. Her muscle strength hadn't changed, but she'd just lost more than forty percent of her body weight by climbing two thousand kilometers further above Earth's center.

A distances squared ratio, 6^2 divided by 8^2. Thanks, Sir Isaac!

Halie smiled with pride at her instant calculation and its Age of Enlightenment source, then bounded down the V-pod ladder, out its open door, and into the station airlock at Level 3.

16. BRIDGE TO NOWHERE

STILL IN HER PRESSURE SUIT with helmet on, Halie enjoyed the low-gravity bounce in her step, leaping across the airlock and prancing into the Level 3 station. But once past the entryway, she stopped, mouth open, staring across a grand ballroom.

Donut shaped like Level 2, the station was far larger, and with floor-to-ceiling glass forming its perimeter, giving the empty space an airy feel like an outdoor deck overlooking a million-dollar view. Put a few hundred people in here—plus bartenders and caterers— and you could host a sweet party overlooking the planet.

Halie was instantly drawn to the endless windows. Mash and Adam joined her. From two thousand kilometers, the view was dramatically broader. During the climb, she'd been so focused on debris danger she'd hardly noticed how much higher they were getting.

South America now spread far to the east with the narrow isthmus of Panama its only connection northward. The Caribbean Sea sprawled to a chain of mountainous islands that peeked from behind towering clouds. St. Lucia? Martinique? Beyond the clouds, the horizon's gentle curve reinforced the feeling of extreme altitude. Further north, the distinctive shape of Cuba stood out—khaki on blue—with south Florida and the colorful turquoise waters of the Bahamas beyond. Much of Central America and Mexico was obscured by cloud cover but the curving line of the Gulf of Mexico hinted that a clearer day might provide a view all the way to Texas.

Halie waved a gloved hand through the air, feeling its resistance. Tentatively, she cracked the seal of her helmet. No explosive decompression. She'd been pretty sure it wouldn't happen, but without a pressure gauge it was never a bad idea to be careful. She finished the job, pulling off her helmet and taking a breath. Clean air, fully pressurized just like Level 2. In an odd way, these stations seemed ready for their visit.

"Can you believe this place?" she called out to Adam and Mash. They followed her lead and removed their helmets.

"I love it." Mash gave a thumbs up. "Can I live here?" Even a high-priced Manhattan apartment couldn't match the view.

The three explorers embarked on a slow walk around the donut's full circuit. Part way around, waist-high counters reached out from the tightly curving interior wall. They seemed designed for food service, or perhaps the beginnings of a café or kitchen.

Further along the west side, Adam said, "Look up." The Pacific Ocean stretched unbroken to the horizon, but for the first time, Halie noticed an axle with two huge wheels at either end hooked onto the station's exterior just above the window.

"What is it?"

"What are *they*, is the question." Adam pointed to a second axle with wheels. A third peeked beneath the window further to the east. Each was perhaps twenty meters long with wheels as big as a riverside mill. If there was more to the structure, it was hidden by the station roof.

"Machinery of some kind," Halie guessed, but was at a loss to be any more specific. "I'm sure these weren't at Level 2. This station may be more than an observation deck."

No one had any better ideas. If they were giant winches, they weren't pulling on anything and had no cable to do so.

Halie continued around the station to the south. A rugged tan stripe marked the Andes Mountains, dividing the Pacific from the lush greens of the rest of South America spreading over the horizon.

"Wow, all the way to Chile," Adam declared.

Halie felt sure Adam was right, but without borders, geographic identification depended on colors, coastlines, and a smattering of river valleys, none of which suggested names to Halie. She might do better if Los Angeles came into view, but one drawback of a space elevator was that, unlike an orbiting spacecraft, their position would never change.

"I could hang out here all day," Halie gushed. "So gorgeous. And it feels safer now that we're above the Kill Zone."

"Lake Titicaca." Mash pointed to a splash of blue that stood out well against the browns and tans of the Andes. "Not important, I just like the name."

Adam cozied up to Mash. "Do Dingers make up rhythmic onomatopoeia on the spot? Could you invent something that incorporates Titicaca?" He'd promised they would eventually get around to talking about Mash's oddball language skills.

Mash dropped her gaze to the floor. "Songwriters do it all the time, not that I personally have that talent."

Adam offered, "Like 'Shama Lama Ding Dong,' the Animal House song that spoofed the original 'Rama Lama Ding Dong.'" He seemed to know something about the cult Mash belonged to.

"That, plus 'Hoochy Koochy Sing Song.' A 1970s country singer came up with that one. In the '60s they even had a Maxwell House coffee commercial where a coffee percolator bubbled out the beat... doodle doodle dit dot. A little weird, if you ask me. But the mother lode was John Lennon's song 'I Am the Walrus.' That sucker is swimming with the four-two cadence."

Adam sang several lines, finishing with an amused grin on his face. "Maybe the Beatles were in on it. Unbelievable how deep it goes."

"Yeah, well... I personally stay away from lyrics. My original Dingers are more like Punxsutawney Ground Hog, Oompa Loompa Tick Tock, or maybe Okeechobee Swamp Bog, if I'm in Florida."

"*Geographic* Dingers too. Well done!"

Mash's face turned several shades of pink. She'd probably never had so much attention lavished upon her, and it had her tongue tied. Halie stepped in to help. "Mash throws out some gems. What was the one you came up with last week?"

"Walla Walla Farm Dog?"

"Yeah, that's it. What does that even mean?"

Mash shrugged with her hands. "A dumb hick. No offense to the fine citizens of Walla Walla, Washington, but they probably should have thought of that before they named the city." She directed a stare at Halie. "Don't we have business to do?" She was clearly ready to change the subject.

Adam backed away. "Sorry, I didn't mean to…"

Mash eyed the floor. "No, it's fine. Maybe later." A smile started at one side of her lips. She was enjoying the attention, just not used to it, especially from a handsome guy. Mash had once told Halie she could "go both ways." Men weren't necessarily off-limits.

Halie loved her friend no matter what path she chose in life. But Mash was right. They were here for a reason.

Halie took the lead. "Why build a grand observation deck like this? Don't get me wrong, the view is great, but is space tourism the only purpose? It seems overkill, especially when we start talking about aliens."

"Maybe they're tempting us," Mash suggested. "It's showy, it's empty, it's available. It has outside poles to hang your potted plants. They want us to move in—at a steep price."

It did give off the vibe of a partially completed commercial building waiting for the right tenant to sign a lease. Halie wondered what the contract terms might be.

Every space elevator design was a money-making venture. The owner could launch satellites at far less cost than rockets, could open high-altitude research labs or space-based observatories, and could make ground-based communication towers obsolete by hanging relays at any height. But the owner could also create a space playground unequaled by any mountaintop resort.

"Maybe there's a hotel at Level 4?" Halie asked.

"One way to find out." Adam pointed up. "But before we go…" He reached into a jacket pocket and withdrew what looked like Yoon's magic wire. Adam raised his eyebrows. "I'm told it can do amazing things."

"Yoon let you have it?" Halie asked, incredulous.

"Yoon insisted. Now that we're at Level 3, let's give it a whirl." He held the wire in the air just as Yoon had done at Level 2, then released it. A foggy rectangle stretched in the air, and a new shape formed.

"Looks like a V-pod," Halie said. Without crisp lines, she couldn't be sure, but the shape was right: a winged cylinder with two interior decks and a V-slot in back.

"Why is it flashing?" Mash asked. The image blinked in and out, once every few seconds.

Adam shook his head. "Don't know. But it's not showing the control panel anymore."

"Continuously changing, and still mysterious," Halie said.

There was little point in watching the flashing V-pod. Nothing about the baffling image shed any light on what they should do. With their higher speed, Level 4 was only forty minutes away. Maybe the wire would provide another image there.

Answers remained elusive, but the mere existence of six space elevators positioned around the world compelled Halie to push on. Somewhere above she would find a story that would rock the world.

"Okay." Halie shrugged. "Let's check into the space hotel."

Back onboard, their sleek ascender soared higher, following a vertical track into space and leaving everything resembling home far below. With each passing minute, they climbed another sixty kilometers. The early-evening view across South America, the Caribbean, and the Gulf of Mexico continued to expand. At 3,000 kilometers, Halie spotted the muddy delta of the Mississippi River as it dumped its silt into the green waters of the Gulf. At 3,500, much of the US Atlantic coast was now in view, all the way to Cape Hatteras in North Carolina. Cyclonic storms stretched across the Atlantic, disappearing into the advancing dark of night.

Halie fired off a message to Yoon, attaching a video clip Mash had taken from the Level 3 observation deck. His response was quick: *Keep climbing, you're proving its value, and that gives me leverage. Tempers were high after your V-pod "theft", but between Jaya's snacks and my direct offer to the Ecuadoran president, things are mostly calm. Marco is another story.*

She could only imagine what Yoon's offer might have been. Billionaires had a way of funding the pet projects of political leaders. Marco, though, wouldn't be as easy.

Halie wondered once more about what they might find higher up. LEO, low Earth orbit, lay far below now, yet they were still only ten percent of the way to geostationary height—35,786 kilometers—that special place where orbital speed matched Earth's rotation and a satellite could forever hover at one spot. Some elevator designs went even further. Release a spacecraft at 57,000 kilometers, and the tether's centrifugal force could fling it to Mars—no rocket propulsion required. Release at 119,000 kilometers for a free trip to Jupiter. But those heights required advanced tether engineering, and they didn't match the button spacing on the V-pod's control panel.

Level 6, all agreed, would be at geostationary height. Beyond that, the tether would terminate at what engineers called an apex anchor—a counterweight that might be a collection of machines leftover from the tether deployment or a small asteroid towed into place to fill the role of a dead weight.

But who tows six asteroids into position around the Earth when not a single rocket can survive the Kill Zone? Halie asked herself. She could only think of one answer. *Someone who doesn't come from Earth.*

"Five millirems per hour," Adam announced unexpectedly. He'd gone down the ladder to retrieve another instrument from his duffel.

Halie snapped out of her thoughts. "Huh?"

"That's our radiation exposure from the Van Allen belts we're passing through. Charged particles from the sun get trapped in Earth's magnetic field."

"Is five millirems good or bad?"

"Good. A chest x-ray is ten millirems, a full-body CT scan is a thousand. The pod's shell isn't just protecting us from debris, it may be generating a magnetic field too."

"Notice how everything meets our physical needs? Steps, doors, buttons, air pressure, temperature. A human design, unquestionably. So, if aliens built it, they did a bang-up job for us... well, except for the lack of platform railings... and a tether with a razor-sharp edge... oh, and the lack of warnings before deceleration."

It was a punch list that would send a government safety inspector into a tizzy, but getting worked up about it served no purpose. They were exploring; dangers were part of the deal.

With Adam and Mash both staring, Halie gave up. "Never mind. We'll find out soon enough what's up there."

The ascender began its unannounced deceleration phase. Another off-white station loomed from the darkness above, but unlike both of the circular observation stations, this one was rectangular in shape. It was positioned perpendicular to the ribbons and included the same donut hole in its center, where the ribbons passed through. Narrow planks jutted beyond the ends of the rectangle, each plank stretching a few hundred meters into space before ending abruptly.

At 4,030 kilometers, the V-pod crawled into the station's airlock. This time, no one bothered to put on a helmet. The lower-level door opened with a slight hiss, and since no further air rushed out, another pressurized station was a fair assumption.

Halie stood, immediately noticing the lower gravity. Mash gave a little jump and nearly hit the ceiling. "I always wanted to be a pole vaulter," she said. "Actually not."

"You and sports," Halie said to her friend.

"Not well acquainted," Mash replied.

Halie stepped from the V-pod with Mash following close behind, camera already rolling. The circular airlock was familiar, but a rectangular station wasn't likely to be another observation deck—or a hotel.

"Cars?" Halie stepped inside an enclosed space lit by overhead skylights. Four vehicles were parked against one wall—one large, three smaller. On the opposite wall, shelves were stacked with equipment, parts, and boxes. It looked like a high-tech garage.

The smaller vehicles could easily be stylish minivans, but instead of wheels, the van body straddled a raised monorail. A wraparound window revealed seating inside for eight or ten people. The larger vehicle—essentially a bus—used the same design but with seating for at least twenty.

Halie glanced to the camera and began a narration. "Level 4 seems to be a transportation hub, or maybe a garage for storage and maintenance of vehicles. We saw something similar in the V-pod hangar down at the platform." She picked up a spare part from one shelf, studied it, then returned it.

Each step echoed off of high walls as she continued down the line of vehicles. Each was empty; seats awaiting passengers. No steering wheels or other means of control. They felt like horizontal versions of the V-pod. Maybe there were buttons somewhere inside to push, but Halie didn't see any.

The parked cars ended at two sliding doors ten meters tall that interlocked in a honeycomb pattern at the center. A glass porthole was embedded in one door at eye level. She peered outside to a track with a single raised rail running down its center. "That's cool. It's a stub. A monorail under construction. I wonder where it will go?"

They were climbing higher to find answers, but each level raised more questions. There were no obvious latches to open the garage doors—not that she'd want to without a helmet. The vacuum of space would ensure a quick death.

A second porthole next to the shelves looked into a one-person booth with a sliding door on its far side. "A personal airlock," Adam claimed. "I noticed Level 3 had one too, tucked in a corner. Access to the equipment bay on the V-pod?"

He was probably right. Once stopped at any of the stations, the lower half of the V-pod hung below the main airlock's floor, making for a handy satellite deployment system. Simply step outside and push the satellite overboard.

But there might be other reasons to go outside too. Halie took another look out the east-facing porthole. Brazil spread to the horizon. Somewhere beyond was the Atlantic Ocean and another tether soaring to the same height. A new thought occurred. "Could you build a suspension bridge between tethers?"

"Good point," Adam said. "Maybe a segmented ring that connects all six."

Halie shook her head, partly in disbelief that such a massive project could be contemplated, let alone begun. "You'd still need suspension cables, but the lower gravity up here reduces the load."

Adam pulled out his phone and chose a calculator app. "Pi times diameter. We're roughly four thousand kilometers up, Earth is more than twelve thousand, so…" Adam finished pushing buttons. "Circumference at this height is sixty-five thousand kilometers, which makes the distance to the next tether close to eleven thousand. Hell of a long trip."

"Maybe that's why this level isn't complete. Even when you have nanobots to do the construction, maybe they ran out of material?"

"Could be. It's not clear where all the carbon and metals are coming from. But if the job is ever finished, imagine the result. A ring around the Earth with six elevators to get up and down? Impressive."

Mash climbed to the top of one of the monorail cars in her never-ending attempt to record from every angle. Without a camera in her face, Halie briefly walked past the V-pod to the opposite end of the rectangular station and found much of the same: a stub pointing west with vehicles lined up waiting for a second future bridge. More shelves stockpiled parts and other equipment that might be needed for an eleven-thousand-kilometer journey.

She met Adam and Mash back at the V-pod, ready to move on. Level 4 wasn't the expected hotel, but its engineering scope was larger by an order of magnitude. With more to explore, she was beginning to wonder if each new level was designed to blow away all previous expectations. What could possibly be next?

Halie took a deep breath. "On to Level 5."

17. PACKETS

MARCO GLOWERED AT THE CAMERA like a fire and brimstone preacher before his parishioners. "Seek and destroy the tools of their surveillance, often concealed in everyday devices. Reject their medical poisons. Protect your bodily autonomy. Above all, remember that the technologists and their crisis actors are coming for your freedoms." He held a final pose, eyes to the sky with one eyebrow raised as if to say, "You be the judge."

His assistant, Tonio, switched off a camera, folded a tripod, and followed Marco into the air-conditioned comfort of the private jet. Marco collapsed into his favorite lambskin chair, while Tonio posted the latest video on Flock You, a social media site where millions of Sheeple followed their flock's Top Dog.

"Count trend?" Marco demanded.

"Twenty-five thousand views," Tonio replied. A few seconds later, "Fifty thousand. You'll hit two million by this evening."

Videos always outperformed text on the social media site specifically designed for celebrities. One "bark" could be followed by ten thousand "bleats". But views were the key metric. "I will never understand why it's not two *hundred* million. One out of three followers is not unreasonable."

"Nobody gets that kind of visibility," Tonio answered.

Marco huffed. A flight attendant handed him a fruit drink which he poured down his throat. "I'm not nobody. How many is Sahalie Spark getting?"

"Different media. Not really comparable."

Marco stared, repeating, "How many?"

Tonio's fingers flew across the keyboard on an open laptop. "On the KNS website… about three-hundred thousand. But that doesn't include live streaming which could be five times higher."

Marco settled back into his chair, frustrated. The world should be simpler, and would be, once his message reached to every corner. Always a competitor in sports, business, and life, challenges only energized him.

"We'll focus on core principles," Marco announced. Tonio nodded, faithfully. "My words are true... or true enough. Exaggerations sprinkled here and there arouse the opposition, as intended."

Tonio raised one finger. "Crisis actors. A good twist on a recognized label. You should use it again. I'm less sure about emphasizing freedom. My AI analysis shows it's less relevant to the cause."

Marco tipped his head. "Less relevant, but an effective motivator. If we are to reorganize the nation states of the world into a leader-follower hierarchy, we require nothing less than absolute devotion from every level of the flock. Yet no one wants to lose their personal freedoms. I have their attention and their loyalty—worldwide. But followers easily lose motivation when there are so many glittering temptations in their faces. A new phone, another bio enhancement, a labor-saving device."

"Every worker must know their place."

"Exactly! The global hierarchy of personage will never succeed unless the lust for technology is disrupted." Marco stood and peered out the airplane window. "And here we are at ground zero. A space elevator is the perfect example of their overreach, matched with the perfect spokesperson to pitch their false promises—Sahalie Spark."

He spit out the name. Women had always vexed Marco, but this one would never be satisfied until her religion of science ruled over all others. She was a pest who always seemed to be in his way. They had butted heads before. This time would be the last.

"Tonio, I mean what I say. This platform is *unholy*. It cannot stand. It must be destroyed, and Sahalie Spark with it." The words were harsh, but they felt good. As Machiavelli had declared long ago, when engaged in a holy war, the ends justify the means.

Tonio unfolded a piece of paper and handed it to Marco. "I suspected you'd arrive at this conclusion. It's a note from an Ecuadoran soldier." Scrawled across the paper in poor handwriting was a request to meet with Marco. "Sergeant Alvarez is of the flock. A devout Candomblé guided by the spirits of creation. He asks to be graced by your presence."

Marco examined the message with a wary eye. With millions begging for his attention every day, the vast majority of requests were appeased by AI bots. A personal consultation would be a rare exception.

"What does this man offer?" Marco asked.

"He has experience with high-powered weapons. Perhaps the best way to defeat the forces of technology is to turn their own guns against them."

Marco pondered the option. "Start a war with Peru? Hardly a good plan."

"Not a war. Something more discreet. More local." He glanced out the window toward the black sheath rising into the sky.

Marco read the note again. "Ask him to come."

Twenty minutes later, Tonio escorted a slim man wearing a camouflage uniform down the airplane aisle. Marco remained seated. The man stood at attention, his hat in his hand. He looked nervous, but Marco rarely met a follower who wasn't.

"Your name is Alvarez?"

"Yes," the man coughed out.

"Why did you wish to speak with me?"

"Your arrival was a sign. Marco, you *see*. No one else does. Only you. I have witnessed the dangers myself. My helicopter was thrown into an unnatural void like a wild dog shakes a rag. When I opened my eyes, we had crashed at our base in Guayaquil more than 200 kilometers away. Impossible, but it happened. This tower into space is not a prize for countries to argue over. It is not of this Earth. It is an abomination placed here by the trickster devil Exú himself and must be destroyed."

Marco leaned back in his chair. "Suppose for a moment, my friend, that we agree. Do you have a proposal? I'm told you are a weapons expert."

Alvarez shook his head. "An autocannon can rip holes through steel, but it is difficult to position and impossible to disguise. I have something better." He pulled a plastic package from a jacket pocket. About the size of a man's wallet, it had orange warning symbols stamped on each side.

"The ribbon is not indestructible," Alvarez explained. "Even the scientist from Peru said so. A half kilo of Semtex can cut a steel bridge cable. A wisp such as this ribbon will be no match."

"Resourceful." Marco stood and drew close to Alvarez. "You are also experienced in explosives?"

Alvarez nodded. "The ribbon is under tension. Once cut, the severed end will snap upward, making it impossible for anyone to reattach. Ground will remain ground, heavens will remain heavens, and this unnatural joining of the two will end."

His goal was aligned, though his motivation came from a different place. Candomblés were members of an Afro-Brazilian religion who believed in a variety of spirits, including Exú the trickster. Many had joined Marco's flock.

"The guards stationed under the shroud have doubled since Ms. Spark snatched their climbing machine. You wear the same uniform, but will they let you get close?"

"Tonight, the duty officer will remain on board the ship, and I will be one of only three guards. Our shift begins at midnight. By then, the deck will be clear. If you come by—just to say hello—I assure you, Marco, they will gather around you. Pose for a photo with them. Talk football. But keep their attention away from the ribbon. I will do the rest."

Marco took the plastic packet from Alvarez and turned it over in his hand. Dense like clay, the package had a warning label that made it clear it should be handled with care. But could something so small topple such a giant? Even if successful, other towers would remain. But with 300 million followers around the world, this single act could mark a line in the sand, leading others to follow.

Marco handed the packet to his assistant. "What do you think?"

Tonio examined it, then returned the packet to Alvarez. "It will start a revolution. But it creates dangers."

Tonio positioned himself between Marco and Alvarez, acting almost as a shield. "Sergeant Alvarez, understand that anything you do is of your own will. If Marco chooses to visit your companions tonight, it is only because he cares for everyone. This plan is yours alone. I am witness."

Alvarez nodded vigorously. "I understand. No one will know we have spoken. I am Candomblé. Our word is sacred."

Tonio patted Alvarez on the shoulder, then guided him up the aisle. "Before you go, there is one other question. The platform uses two ribbons, one to climb, another to descend."

Alvarez retrieved a second package from another pocket and grinned.

18. HELL ABOVE

HALIE LEANED AGAINST THE V-pod's glass as they continued their journey, now halfway between Levels 4 and 5. The view outside continued to expand, with the Great Lakes easily visible on the northern horizon while the edge of night progressed westward across North America. Their journey had provided spellbinding, outrageously jaw-dropping sights, but it had also produced questions with no answers.

By now, a spokesperson should have stepped up—either a previously unknown society of very rich space engineers, or aliens beaming down from their starship. With luck, the ultimate plan for this megastructure would be benevolent. So far, there had been little to complain about.

Who doesn't like observation decks in space?

During the climb, Mash transmitted the video they'd taken at the Level 4 bridge stubs to the studio along with a recommendation from Halie that an editor make taped pieces available to the news desk. They'd asked for anything and everything. It didn't have to be live.

A scan of the latest news from the surface had turned up a few comments from presidents and prime ministers, mostly to weigh in on ownership squabbles. They gave dismissive waves when reporters asked about alien rumors. Politicians rarely understood that declining to make a strong statement only created a vacuum that was easily filled by conspiracy nonsense.

She wasn't surprised by Marco's latest. He had regurgitated her statement about nanobots creating nanobots in classic Marco fashion. Viruses, he claimed in a post, were actually nanobots, and had been all along. "It's why vaccinations don't work," he'd declared with a flourish of his sports logo cape. "We cannot fight electronic micro-devils with sharp needles." He hadn't explained what *could* be used to fight these enemies and apparently hadn't grasped that the vaccine inside the syringe was the tool of immunization, not the needle itself.

A new shape came into view overhead. Not a rectangle, but not a disc either. The Level 5 station was roughly spherical, but facets across its surface made it look like the New Year's ball in Times Square, especially given the donut hole in its center.

The ship slowed to a stop at 6,210 kilometers, a number remarkably close to the radius of the Earth. Halie didn't need a calculator to know gravity here would be one-quarter of its surface value, roughly the same as walking on the moon.

"Whoa," Mash exclaimed as she stumbled off the circular couch and sprawled across the floor. When Halie pushed from the couch, she understood why. A slight miscalculation with hands or over-tightened thigh muscles could send the body in a direction not intended. Mass and momentum hadn't changed, but seventy-five percent of the downward pull that every human had experienced from birth was gone. The simple act of standing up required the same level of care as balancing on one foot.

The V-pod ladder produced the opposite experience. In such low gravity, rungs were unneeded. A light grip on its handrails provided sufficient friction to glide down.

Mash pulled a smaller camera from her bag declaring that she'd already captured every possible view of Earth. Her new camera had a lens better suited for the interior lighting of a space hotel—still expected after the conference ballroom of Level 3 and the parking garage of Level 4.

As it turned out, Mash had selected the right camera but for the wrong reason. The airlock door led into a dark passageway that dead ended at a wall of solid rock. At least, it looked like rock. The brownish-gray wall was about four meters tall and twice as wide. Even in the dim light, it sparkled with embedded crystals.

"The hotel is under construction too?" Mash reached out and pounded a fist on the rock. Tiny crystals crumbled away and sprinkled across the floor. From somewhere beneath, a deep rumble shook the floor and reverberated through the air.

Mash backed away. "Aw, now I've done it. Woken the rock trolls."

Cracks appeared. A crystalline spike stabbed outward. Then another. Mash flipped on her camera. Halie stood behind her, holding onto Mash's shoulders. Adam stood firm as more dagger-like crystals spiked outward, some as long as a meter. Curiosity might win out over fear, but the contest would be close.

Some crystals were clear, others translucent purple. Loud snaps and pops shrieked from the rock face as more cracks rendered its center. The whole wall twisted clockwise, its top bulging to the right and its bottom to the left. Rock flakes shattered from its surface, peppering the floor. Dozens of crystals now stabbed through the center, opening a hole that hadn't been there before.

"Oh my…" Halie held a hand over her mouth, feeling like she should run but unable to tear herself away from the impossible spectacle playing out only a few steps away.

The hole enlarged, with dark space beyond. The opening grew wider, deeper, like a monstrous opening to some other world. The rumbling finally stopped. A few more rock chips clattered to the floor. Then silence.

They stared into the yawning entrance of a vast crystalline cavern that angled downward toward indiscernible darkness that could be hundreds of meters deep. Faceted purple crystals with pointy tips extruded from the cavern's floor, walls, and ceiling, making this chasm as impassable as a stairway entangled with razor wire and just as incomprehensible.

Halie's voice quavered. "How is this here?" Echoes returned from the deep hollow before them.

She squatted at the cavern's distinct edge where the station's smooth floor was now impaled by a row of finger-sized purple crystals. Taller prisms stood in a second row, some the size of swords and probably just as sharp. Further back, the available light quickly dimmed. Purples became black with only a few glints beyond.

Halie reached out to one of the less spiky prisms, but it dropped away before her fingers could touch it. "What?" She moved her hand closer to another crystal and it dropped too, forming a flat spot where a spike had once been.

She stood up and waved a foot over the spikes. A group dropped to form a flat spot big enough to step onto. "This is freaky weird."

"Try it," Mash encouraged.

Halie hesitantly placed her shoe into the newly formed step, then put her weight on it. It felt solid enough. She reached out with the other foot. Another patch of crystals flattened. Halie stood on both feet with crystals all around, feeling oddly isolated, even though smooth floor was only a hop away.

Adam tested too, taking four steps with sharp crystals automatically creating the needed openings. "They seem to be sensitive to our movement, almost anticipating where we're going to step."

"Alien crystals are smarter than ours," Mash said.

"You do have a point," Halie admitted.

"I'm always right," Mash said.

"Well… there was that time in San Antonio when—"

Mash cut her off. "We're not in San Antonio. We're not at Carlsbad Caverns either. Look around. This place is alien. Period."

Halie had to admit the station made no sense. If a human had designed it, they were on drugs, and the cavern's depth would have to be an illusion. *But if alien…* Halie took a deep breath. "Well, we knocked. And it opened. And, since we did come to explore…"

Adam held up a hand, "If we're going spelunking, we'll need a flashlight." He was right. The modest light coming through the airlock walkway behind them gave way to total darkness beyond about fifty meters.

"Can do," Mash said, flipping on a floodlight attached to her camera. Its beam split the dark, revealing a rambling descent covered in crystal spikes. "Camera is rolling. Scene: Nasty wild. Level 5 alien cavern… action!"

Halie took several more steps, happy to see the crystals obliging but disturbed when she glanced behind to find her previous steps erased as crystal spikes regrew. She soldiered on, less sure about their decision with each step.

How stupid do you have to be to descend into an alien cavern?

What else could explain it? The crystalline interior of an asteroid? If the builders had towed a counterweight to the tether's apex, maybe they'd dragged along a few extra rocks to be natural wonders for visitors to explore? Unfortunately, that didn't explain the strangely compliant crystals.

A dozen paces turned into a hundred. The opening behind was now only a small oval of light. The relative safety of the V-pod seemed far away.

Halie stopped, listening. Sounds came from somewhere in the cavern's depths, different than any encountered so far. Different than anything she'd ever heard. Humanlike groans, but indistinct. The unholy sounds churned, twisted, and reverberated into an ever-changing chorus of anguish.

Unintelligible voices layered over the groans, as if someone in the far corner of an empty basement was having a conversation—not a speech or an argument, but a quiet chat over nothing without a single recognizable word.

The roiling moans and incoherent voices were interrupted by a single sharp scream that made Halie flinch. Mash swiveled her floodlight to the wall, but it only illuminated more stalactites.

"I should have known there'd be cave ghosts," Mash said.

Halie put a hand on Adam's shoulder and paused to let her heart calm. "What do you think? Turn back, or go on?"

She secretly hoped Adam would invoke his scientist credentials and explain why *toxic concentrations of carbonic gas*—or some other very natural and ordinary danger—merited a return to the top. But he didn't show any signs of being rattled. As a part-time flying daredevil, he no doubt maintained a consistent curl-up-by-the-fire-with-a-good-book sixty-beats-per-minute heart rate.

He spoke with a calm voice too. "I'm less concerned about the sounds than I am about spatial dimensions. I've been estimating in my head how far we've descended, and it's more than fifty meters. This station simply isn't that large."

Halie nodded an acknowledgement. "How does interior space defy its exterior limits?"

"It doesn't."

"Maybe we missed something when we docked. A giant rock attached to the station?"

Adam shrugged, then took a picture with his phone and tapped out a message. "Before we go further, I'm sending a photo to Yoon."

"Good idea, in case we never return," Mash cracked.

As far as Halie knew, Mash wasn't scared of ghosts. But she often made light of difficult circumstances and soldiered on without complaint. Halie double-checked her theory with an inquisitive thumbs-up. As expected, Mash returned a solid thumbs-up.

"Then on we go," Adam said, taking the lead.

Mash bounced her floodlight across every surface. At least they'd see the groaning, fang-toothed monsters when they jumped from the shadows. The voices grew louder, deeper, and—with a morsel of imagination—more dangerous.

"Now is the time to understand more so that we may fear less," Halie said under her breath.

She stumbled but quickly regained her balance. No one had yet tested whether the sharp crystals would go flat if someone fell, though reaching out was enough to lower nearby spikes. They seemed quite responsive, almost alive.

"Did you see *Don't Believe It!* episode four?" Halie asked Adam. She'd do anything right now to keep her mind occupied. "Mash and I had to go inside a river cave in Arkansas. Freezing cold water, knee-deep, flowing from an underground spring. The locals talk about the spring's namesake, John Blanchard, an Arkansas homesteader who died in 1914. They point to a name carved into the back wall of the cave. *John, 1922.* Apparently, the old man carved it himself, a good trick for a dead man, but they say he still lives in the cave even today. His ancient body is somehow kept alive by the miraculous spring waters. Of course, he can't come out or he'll turn to dust, so at night you can still hear him wailing from loneliness."

"Good story. No one else could possibly be named John," Adam sniped. "Or have access to a carving knife."

Mash pointed her light at Adam. "Carving knives and wailing zombies. You two are fun hiking partners."

Mash was just being Mash, but Halie didn't miss a beat. "The point is that fear is story-driven. Our imaginations create a narrative pulled from bits of reality woven together by whole cloth fabrications. The result might be unbelievable, but at an emotional level, we still believe it."

"So true," Adam said.

Where Mash's light passed, the reflections from crystal facets temporarily blinded. Where it was absent, unvarying blackness prevailed. She had locked the camera to her vest to free up both hands—a good move, considering the balance their route required.

Groans, unintelligible babble, and the occasional scream continued unabated. On the plus side, the air remained perfectly breathable. Dry, with a hint of dust or floating lint. Halie found herself continuously brushing odd tickles from her face.

Mash announced, "When we meet these groaning aliens, I'll get a good shot of them. But you do all the greeting stuff. You know, split-fingered salute, mind meld, bend over and take a probe up the rear. With some postproduction blurs, it'll play well, even on KNS."

Halie rolled her eyes in the darkness. "I can't take you anywhere, Mash. You realize you're being recorded."

"Editing."

If cave aliens were ahead, they had better be friendly. The stiffening bar from Mash's vest was their only defensive weapon. Adam might have something more useful in his duffel, but he'd left it at the V-pod. Even running away would be difficult given the sea of crystal spikes they would have to negotiate.

Ahead, another scream punctuated the gibberish voices and echoed off the cavern walls. They stared at each other in silence. Exploring this station might have been a mistake. The first three stations had been easy, even welcoming. But now, ill-equipped and unprepared to defend against anything more than a cave rat, they were venturing into a place not designed for human use. If there were intelligent oversized tarantulas around the next corner, Halie wasn't sure her nerves would hold up.

Mash lifted her floodlight to reveal what looked like an intersection of two tunnels ahead, one to the left and another to the right. Pink and green flashes echoed from around the corners.

"Stop for a minute," Mash said. She turned off the floodlight, plunging them into darkness except for the colored flashes, which bounced a thousand ways through crystal refraction.

"How about we get to the crossroad," Adam said, "and if the trail doesn't improve or we don't learn anything new, we'll turn back?"

Halie voiced the worry that had occupied her mind since they'd begun. "It feels like we're not invited inside this one."

"So, turn back now?" Adam asked as a pink flash illuminated his face.

Halie thought about the easier option, but they'd already descended most of the way. The intersection wasn't much further, and the crystals were still cooperating. "Okay, we'll peek around the corner. But keep the lights on."

Mash flipped the camera light back on. "Funny how in horror movies, the lights always go out at the worst time. Sorry! Now I'm doing it. Erase that last point. Every light since the invention of batteries has been one hundred percent reliable. Dang, I probably just jinxed us."

They tiptoed on, with Mash alternately illuminating the floor and the intersection ahead. They finally reached a flat spot where a smaller tunnel split off to the right. Halie peered around the corner, nervous.

It stretched into the distance, still lined with crystals but none more than ankle high. Alternating flashes of neon pink and green mixed with ghostly murmurs from no discernible source.

Halfway down the tunnel, a pink flash produced an instantaneous image of a flower, then disappeared just as quickly. Halie wondered if she'd only imagined the familiar shape. A second flash formed a green valley with trees on its hillsides. The landscape disappeared but left an indelible image in her mind.

Halie whispered, "The colors seem real, but I'm not sure about the rest. They feel like mental images more than pictures. Are you guys seeing them?"

Adam moved to the center of the intersection. Mash took a few steps down the tunnel and lowered her light to the floor. Another image popped up and disappeared just as quickly. "A snowcapped mountain," Adam described.

Exactly what Halie had seen too. A saguaro cactus was next. Then what might have been a starry sky with a crescent moon, though the details were hard to grasp given only a millisecond view.

Halie turned to Adam. "They're scenes of Earth."

Another pink flash depicted an overhead view of a children's playground with parents sitting on nearby benches. It felt dreamlike. Not quite the same as seeing the scene with eyes but detailed enough to fix it in the mind.

"People too," Adam added.

So far, none seemed to match the uneasy dread of the background noises. Groans and unrecognizable voices continued. Together, the light and sounds felt like a slide show set to random mode with a soundtrack only a shock performance artist could love.

The tunnel continued in the opposite direction too, with the same light and sound show on a perpetual loop.

After a particularly loud screech, Mash turned her camera off and backed up. "This place gives me the jitters. I've got it all captured. Maybe we should move on?"

Halie nodded. "If this is communication, I have no idea what the message is supposed to be. I agree, it's creepy."

Mash pointed her floodlight up the slope, and they started climbing toward the only exit. The V-pod could take them higher still, but Halie couldn't ignore the feeling that their journey had become an inverted descent into hell. Level 5 had taken a sharp turn toward something darker, weirder, and creepier. Level 6 was beginning to feel out of reach and not only because of the greater distance. If they were going to tackle it, Halie would insist on a unanimous vote.

The climb out took less time, and soon they were back on an ordinary flat floor. Halie followed Adam through the open V-pod door and climbed its ladder. He sat on the circular couch and pulled his phone out.

"A message from Yoon," he said, then read from his phone. "*Agitated people here. No luck yet on a solution. Be careful on your way down. A triumphant return would make a statement in our favor!*"

"Triumphant! That's a lark," Halie said. "Our progress seems to have stalled. Finding the source of nanobot instructions seems unlikely. Are we even prepared to reach Level 6?"

Adam raised an eyebrow. "Forty minutes between each of the lower stations, but the final leg is a *lot* further. At our top speed of one kilometer per second, getting to Level 6 will take more than eight hours."

"Plus, ten hours to get down. It's an overnight trip." She rummaged through one of the food packs Jaya had provided. "We won't starve, but we'll be hungry by the time we get back to the platform."

For the first time, the exploration ahead felt daunting. They'd be entering deep space, entirely dependent on a barely tested V-pod. After the creepiness of the cavern and the dead ends of Level 4, she wondered if they'd already gone beyond what was designed for visitors and were now venturing into places best left to security teams and construction crews. At geostationary height, Level 6 might be nothing but a half-completed satellite launchpad.

Halie checked her own messages. Two from Paul, one checking for new material and the other to see if she needed logistical support. KNS had apparently dispatched a second team to South America, but with no billionaire host onboard they'd been diverted to Guayaquil with a demand from the Ecuador government not to go any closer to the platform. Halie was still on her own.

She gave Paul a quick reply: *Level 5 will curl your toes. Mash is sending video. Schedule me for KNS Good Morning? I should be on the summit by then.*

She lifted her head with the odd feeling she was being watched, then jumped when Mash yelled from somewhere outside, "Don't push any buttons!"

Halie twisted around and caught sight of Mash through a V-pod wing window. She was outside, climbing its V-notched backside by pressing hands and feet against opposing wings. In the low gravity, she made it look easy.

"What are you doing?" Halie yelled back. A low-g fall might not break bones, but it would still hurt.

"It'll make a great shot," Mash responded, her voice dampened. She disappeared above the wing window and reappeared at the glass top of the ship, squatting like a rock climber who had reached a lofty pinnacle. She pointed her camera straight down and yelled, "Pretend you're searching for the fabled Level 6 above you."

With so many unanswered questions and hours still ahead of them, Halie was in no mood to feign drama even if Mash had found another unique camera angle. But she'd made an effort to climb to the top, so Halie relented. She stood, managing a stoic expression that would either come across as a determined journalist or an irritated colleague.

Mash lifted the camera. "Okay, got it. You can go about your business."

"Be careful up there," Halie yelled.

"When I was a kid, I used to climb—" But she never finished. One foot slipped. Mash scrambled to regain her balance in the unfamiliar gravity and wildly grabbed for anything around her.

Her hand caught the ribbon's edge, producing a blue electric flash with a loud pop. Smoke curled off Mash's hand, arm, and shoulder. She went limp and plummeted to the airlock floor with a sickening thud.

"Mash!" Halie screamed.

Her heart in her throat, Halie jumped onto the ladder and slid down without touching rungs. Every terrible thought flooded her mind. The knife edge of the ribbon could have cut deeply. An electrical shock as loud as a gunshot and strong enough to produce smoke could be devastating—even fatal.

Nerves jangling, Halie rushed out the pod door and around to its backside with Adam right behind. Mash lay at an unnatural angle, inert, one arm under her body, the other stretched out across the airlock floor. Her eyes were open, her mouth moving but without words.

Halie dropped to her knees and cradled Mash's face in her hands. "Oh no, Mash!" She checked for head injuries, then, with Adam's help, carefully rolled Mash on to her back. "Talk to me!"

Mash's eyes were glassy, her mouth stuck open. A few gasps were followed by a whisper: "That... sucks."

The words provided only a modicum of relief. Halie's mind raced trying to think of what to do next. Adam dashed away. "I have a first aid kit in the duffel."

"Help is coming, Mash. Where does it hurt?" A line of blood crossed her palm. Far worse were the still-smoldering burn marks that started from the slice and followed the sleeve of her shirt up to the neck. Ugly black and blue patches mottled the skin at her jawline.

Mash mumbled, "I hear you."

"Is it your arm? Neck? Can you feel your legs?"

Adam returned with his duffel and searched inside.

Mash stared straight up with bewildered eyes that bypassed Halie like she wasn't there. Her mouth closed, then opened once more. "No... no objections... I understand."

"What is it?" Halie asked, holding her hand. "Mash, you're not making sense." Halie unbuckled the camera harness and pulled Mash's shirt back to reveal bright red marks that fanned out across her skin like tributaries to a river.

Mash's breathing became labored. She forced the words out. "Sure, whatever... better get going." Her lips trembled. She took one more hesitant breath, then closed her eyes. Her hand went limp.

"No!" Halie screamed. She pushed two fingers against Mash's neck, desperate to find a pulse. Nothing.

Adam pushed Halie aside. "I have CPR training." With both hands centered on her chest, he pushed rhythmically several times, then angled Mash's head backward, pinched her nose shut, and blew into her mouth. More pumping, then another breath of air into Mash's lungs.

"Please, please." Tears flooded Halie's eyes. Panic rose in her gut. She gave Adam room but kept a finger on Mash's wrist. Halie's voice quavered. "Any adrenaline shots in your kit?"

Adam shook his head as he pushed on her chest. "No, just the basics—bandages, swabs. That's not going to help." He forced another lungful of air into Mash's unmoving mouth.

Seconds turned into minutes, but Adam never slowed. Sweat beaded on his forehead. His visor slipped off and clattered across the floor, but he kept his focus on resuscitation. He seemed a man possessed. Halie bowed her head, feeling hopeless. "I should have stopped her. I should have remembered the low gravity. She'd stumbled just getting up off the couch."

With tears streaming down her face, Halie finally released Mash's wrist and pulled Adam's arms away from her lifeless body.

She sobbed, hardly recognizing her own weak voice. "It's over. You did your best."

Adam leaned back on his haunches, breathing hard. "I'm really sorry. I can't understand it. I touched that ribbon myself... multiple times."

"I did too," Halie quavered.

They sat in silence. Halie wiped her eyes, but more tears came. Her body shook with sobs. Their mission of exploration wasn't supposed to end this way. Had they been too aggressive? Oblivious to the potential dangers that came with an incomplete structure? Halie recalled standing at the platform's edge and noting its lack of safety railings. The ribbon itself had a razor sharp edge. She should have known they'd encounter more dangers.

She dropped her head into her hands. "I'm so sorry, Mash. It's all my fault."

19. SIGNAL

MIND NUMB AND HANDS SHAKING, Halie positioned Mash's arms across her chest, then backed away, allowing Adam to wrap the body in a mylar survival blanket he pulled from his duffel.

When he was done, he stood and reached out. Halie sagged into his arms. "It was an accident," he told her, his voice caring but firm. "Not anyone's fault. Something changed on the tether. Or maybe the electricity at its edge works differently. We didn't know."

Halie said nothing. She was comforted by his words and his kind embrace, but the pain would be lasting. More than a colleague, Mash was her friend. They'd traveled, worked side by side, shared more meals, drinks, and Griffith Park ice cream cones than she could count. Now Mash was gone, and Halie's quest for answers was over. An overnight climb to Level 6 was out of the question.

"We'll go down," Halie croaked, wiping tears away. "The military will have something… a box or a proper body bag. I'll ask Yoon to fly us back to California. He'll do that much. He's really a pretty decent guy for a billionaire, just wrong about this…"

She looked around. A glass ascender that wasn't really glass. A tether that was equal parts cable, nanobot, and high-voltage powerline. Stations resembling an observation deck or a cavern of terror. "I was wrong too. Unprepared. Too trusting in a strange world."

Adam released her. He didn't counter her self-assessment, but his dark eyes conveyed compassion. His voice was soft. "Take a seat in the pod. I'll bring Mashup inside and meet you in a few minutes."

Halie stumbled around to the front side of the pod and willed her legs to climb the ladder once more. Now began the impossible task of sorting meaning from disaster.

She leaned against the wing window, watching as Adam carefully scooped up the wrapped body of her friend, then returned a minute later to retrieve Mash's vest. A memory drive in one of the pockets would have the video Mash had taken over this long day. Once back in California, Halie would find consolation as she reviewed it. Most of it. She'd skip the last segment.

I should have stopped her. Told her climbing was a dumb idea in unfamiliar gravity. She would have listened to me.

The guilt wouldn't end anytime soon, maybe never. She could tell herself it wasn't her fault, that accidents happen, that nothing in life is guaranteed... but the brain doesn't cooperate.

Paul would say, "Halie, you're only human." Adam too, probably. Scientists always had logical answers. And people—even smart people—routinely ignored them.

What's keeping him? We need to go.

Halie glanced down the ladder. Adam wasn't on the lower level. She peered through the wing window once more and spotted him on his knees next to the ribbon—attaching a wire clip. Her whole body spiked like she'd taken the shock of a million volts. "No!" she screamed.

Halie plunged down the ladder, past Mash's wrapped body, and around the V-pod, screaming. "Whatever you're doing, don't! I couldn't stand to lose two people in one day."

Adam stood and held out both hands to stop her. "It's okay, Halie. I'm being careful. I know how to work around live wires." He *was* wearing gloves.

Halie panted, hyperventilating. Half upset and half angry. "What could possibly be worth the risk? Gloves or not, this is no ordinary wire."

Adam nodded multiple times. "I get it. I promise, I do. But I have to know." He pointed to an electronic box clipped to the tether. "It's a multimeter, and it's already telling me there's no current on the ribbon. Something changed since Mash took that shock. I don't know how or why, but the ribbon is not currently a danger."

"Good, let's get out of here before it changes again."

He pointed to a flickering green light at one side of the meter. "See that? That's a data signal, and even before I sample it, I can tell it's nothing like the data I first measured. It's more repetitive now. There's a new message going out on the ribbon, and I need to know what it is."

His argument might make sense, but it only heightened Halie's concern for his—and her—well-being. If the electricity had been turned off, could they even get down? And even if they could decode the zeros and ones, what would this message say? *Death to trespassers.*

"Give me two minutes to finish." When she didn't reply, he returned to his work.

Halie took a deep breath and brushed back loose hair. She crossed her arms and stood with granite resolve, staring at the tether. *You will not kill again.*

Adam attached a second wire and plugged it into the back of the multimeter. Its LED still flickered green like a network modem. "I have an app that can capture the data stream. We'll examine it on the way down."

"Can we even get down?"

"Things aren't that bad." He pointed to a needle, one of three on the multimeter. "It's measuring current in amperes. It's not a killer current, but not zero either. In fact, it's exactly what you'd expect to see for a multiwalled nanotube carrying current on the inside and wrapped by an insulator. The tether is still active, but it's not dangerous to the touch."

To prove his point, he removed one glove and touched the tether above the metal clip. Halie tensed from fingers to toes, but Adam didn't keel over.

"Okay, I admit you know what you're doing, but how do you know it won't change again?"

He put the glove back on. "You're right, I don't. We've seen it under the microscope. It's not just a wire, it's alive with nanobots. Billions of them, every meter from top to bottom. Send those bots different instructions and they can probably adjust the tether's characteristics pretty quickly. I suspect they've already changed the material, at least its outer layers."

"Which means they could change it again."

"Yes, they could."

"Got your data?"

"I think so. It's repetitive, so I doubt the message itself is very long." He unplugged his laptop, then removed the clip. Halie breathed a sigh of relief. Personally, she'd never touch the ribbon again.

But Adam wasn't being stupid. She understood his goal. Once they were down, others would climb this tether, and they'd need to know how it functioned.

Halie reminded herself of Marie Curie's brave words. Understanding a fearful unknown wasn't a slogan or a catch phrase to toss out lightly in front of the cameras. You had to believe it in your heart.

Adam does. Do you? she asked herself.

Back inside the V-pod, Halie gave a silent nod to Mash's body, then climbed to the seating area. She pressed the control panel's lowest button. The door closed, proof of an electrical connection. The pod detached from one ribbon and pivoted to the other. The airlock floor opened, and they dropped into space.

The instant plunge was just as shocking as their first descent had been, but at least now Halie had the experience to trust it would all work out. Far below, the vast globe of Earth was now mostly dark, with only a bright crescent of sunlight across the western Pacific. City lights along the Venezuelan and Colombian coasts glowed white and orange like phosphorus paint splattered from a brush onto a dark canvas.

The blur of the upbound tether was only a few meters away. Their speed quickly reached something similar to their ascent speed. An engineer could explain the reasons why, but Halie didn't care. Two hours or two minutes, the result would be the same. They'd flash past Levels 4, 3, and 2, then coast to a stop at the platform and Halie's grand adventure riding a space elevator would be over. She'd limp home, lacking success and overflowing with regret.

Adam sat nearby, studying a graph displayed on his laptop. A red line pulsed along the graph's x-axis like a heartbeat on a hospital monitor. "It's only three seconds of data, but the repetition is obvious," he said.

It took effort—rising above self-pity always did—but Halie scooted closer, acknowledging Adam's continuing efforts to figure things out.

The red line rose and fell, but unlike a sine wave, each hilltop looked more like a jagged mountain range—the Italian Alps or the Grand Tetons. A second window displayed thousands of ones and zeros scrolling by in a blur, followed by a break, then thousands more. "How would you begin to decode it?"

"Not sure. But this message is important, don't you think?"

Halie nodded. Her mind began to wander, not to Mash and not to the failure of a mission that had reached five of the six levels but still hadn't found the megastructure's builders or evidence they even existed.

Instead, Halie thought of mountain peaks. And hexagons.

20. MESSAGE

HALIE COUNTED ONCE MORE after Adam enlarged the graph displayed on his laptop. Each heartbeat-like blip topped out with jagged mountain peaks.

Six of them.

A repetitive message was being sent up and down the tether, but these six peaks revealed repetition within the repetition. The zeros and ones of this data were anything but random. Meaning lay deep within this graph.

Halie sat next to Adam on the pod's circular couch, dropping toward Earth. He'd been insistent on documenting—even decoding—this repeating message. Now he had her full attention.

Six.

Six levels on the tether, including the topmost station they hadn't reached and probably never would. Six space elevators positioned in six equal segments. Halie had seen that number pop up often enough that she wasn't going to wave off the graph's six mini-peaks as unimportant.

"Hexagons have six sides," she told Adam. "And hexagons are *everywhere* on this structure, right down to the carbon allotrope at the tether's core."

Adam tilted his head, squinting. "How are hexagons related to this data?"

"I don't know, maybe it's a dumb idea... but what if we grouped those bits into a hexagon shape? We might see it differently than just a stream of ones and zeros."

"Group? How?"

"Map the binary data to a hexagon shape? You know... bit by bit. I honestly don't know where the idea came from... but those six peaks in your graph. It can't be a coincidence."

Adam nodded, thinking. He wasn't dismissing her intuition as nonsense. "Mapping ones and zeros to a hexagon shape is a two-dimensional task, right? You're not just mapping to six sides, it's the interior too."

"Right, so what if you cut a hexagon into six pieces? You get six pizza slices—each one is an equilateral triangle. That's a two-dimensional way to map the data, right?"

Adam nodded thoughtfully, then started a spreadsheet app on his laptop. "Okay, so if you put data bit number one at the tip of the pizza slice, then bits two, three, and four just below it..." He typed:

$$1$$

$$2\ 3\ 4$$

Halie encouraged him, "Yeah, that's it. Just keep going, bit by bit, until you get one pizza slice, then do another until you have all six in the hexagon."

"I get it," Adam said. "What's cool is that we can test in advance if a triangle layout makes sense. We already know how many bits are in the data stream. That number would have to be a multiple of six—six pizza slices—but it would also need to..." His voice trailed off, and he typed more rows in the spreadsheet. "Huh... look at that."

$$1$$

$$2\quad 3\quad 4$$

$$5\quad 6\quad 7\quad 8\quad 9$$

$$10\quad 11\quad 12\quad 13\quad 14\quad 15\quad 16$$

$$17\quad 18\quad 19\quad 20\quad 21\quad 22\quad 23\quad 24\quad 25$$

Adam pointed. "When you lay out an arithmetic sequence in a triangular pattern, the last number in each row is the square of the row number."

Halie saw it too. "Another pretest?" Any mapping plan that could be mathematically tested before investing time was even better. You could tell in advance if there would be any bits left over.

Adam pasted one set of data to a word processor and used a tool to count characters. "A total of 126,150 bits. And..." He picked a calculator app. "That number happens to be divisible by six. You were right."

He smiled, and she smiled back, the first she'd managed since Mash's accident. Adam punched keys, then held up his phone. "Each pizza slice is 21,025 bits. And guess what? The square root of that number is 145, exactly."

Halie's smile grew wider. "No leftover bits. The hex pizza works... in theory."

"Only one thing left to do. Map it." Adam returned his attention to the spreadsheet. "There's a tool that automatically generates a number sequence... ah, here it is."

Adam clicked and dragged, eventually producing a perfect triangle of sequential numbers: 145 rows starting with 1 at the triangle's top and 21,025 at its bottom right corner—every bit in one pizza slice accounted for.

"Now we map these indices to the corresponding message bit." Adam copied the ones and zeros to the spreadsheet, then replaced the number 1 with a table lookup. When he copied his change to the rest of the cells, the triangle flipped from sequential numbers to a complex mix of zeros and ones.

Halie stared at the partial image he'd created. "Zoom out."

He did. The bits formed an equilateral triangle, one-sixth of the whole. Though fuzzy, the partial image wasn't hard to recognize: a human eye.

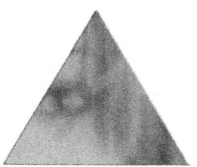

Adam copied and pasted his work into the next row down, then adjusted the starting index to grab the next 21K set of bits. A second triangle appeared below the first, showing hair and one side of a mouth. He placed a third triangle below and left—a chin with piercings on the lower lip. The half hexagon was more than enough.

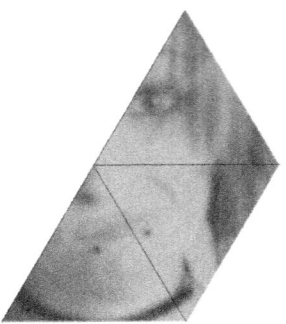

Halie covered her mouth as tears welled up. "It's Mash."

Adam filled in the remaining three pieces of the message hexagon, then leaned back to view the completed image of a dead woman. The slightly blurry black-and-white picture could easily have been taken an hour ago.

Halie's mind raced, trying to come up with a rationale for how and why a hex-coded picture of Mash was being repeatedly transmitted up and down the tether. Had cameras been trained on them from the start?

"There's more," Adam said, catching Halie's attention. His fingers hovered over the keyboard. "I thought the data was repeating, and it is, but the pattern doesn't end with those bits. Each 126K batch is a little different." He scrolled through the stream of ones and zeros, counting blank spaces as he went. "Twenty-four sets, then it loops back to the first."

"Twenty-four frames in a movie?" Halie asked.

"A good guess. I'll write a Python script to map all twenty-four and splice them together in a loop. Might take a few minutes."

Halie peered down through the ladder's hole. No sign yet of the Level 4 station, and there would be two more after that. "We have time. Anything I can do to help?"

"You already did. I wouldn't have come up with the pizza slice hexagon theory if I'd sat here thinking for a hundred years. Hang tight."

Halie got up to stretch her legs, leaving him to his work and still wondering where her idea had come from. The number six, certainly, but the rest seemed to be a flash of insight.

Grief morphing to intuition? She doubted that was a thing.

She wandered into the north-side wing and stared out its window. The Caribbean Sea was now lost in darkness as night fell, but city lights did a surprisingly good job of defining coastlines, especially along Florida further north.

Behind her, Adam typed furiously. His talents extended well beyond microscopes and spectral analyzers. They included jet packs, data manipulation—and, of course, cardiopulmonary resuscitation. The two had forged an unexpected partnership—derailed by tragedy and now changing once again. His diligence in decoding a message that somehow involved Mash felt like a fitting tribute.

Halie hung her head, emotions still roiling.

Why didn't you stay on the floor? What was so important about getting the top-down shot?

Mash had always loved camera shots from a variety of angles, and Halie had to admit the final product had always turned out well. No more. Nothing would be the same again. Poor Mash. Her last few minutes had been lost in a delirium, babbling to herself, probably not even aware Halie was there.

Like she was talking to someone else.

Halie froze. What exactly had Mash said? Something about *no objections*, and *better get going*. Was it delirium? As weird as this place could be, Halie was beginning to wonder.

"It's recorded," Halie said to herself.

"What's recorded?" Adam asked, never looking up from his work.

"Mash's last moments. She never turned off the camera. Whatever she was mumbling, it's recorded."

Halie hurried down the ladder to the lower level. Mash's wrapped body lay on the floor, inert, a testimony to the permanence of death. Her camera bags and stabilizing harness were stuffed on a shelf nearby.

Halie reached for the shoulder cam, then sat on the floor, cradling the camera. She examined its array of buttons—some familiar, others with functions only a professional would understand. She managed to get the power on and selected playback mode for its built-in screen. After a few attempts at rewinding, she found the right spot and pressed Play.

The camera had fallen on its side, pointing to Mash's face with Halie on her knees behind. Mash's final words were breathy. She already looked like death.

I hear you, Mash said.

Her eyes were glassy and unfocused. Her breathing irregular.

No… no objections… I understand.

In the playback, a panicked Halie peeled back Mash's shirt.

Sure, whatever… better get going.

She watched for a few more seconds, then switched it off, staring at the blank screen. "Mash wasn't talking to me."

Something was very wrong. Or right. But the nervous feeling inside communicated to Halie a break with *normal*.

"We are so in over our heads. We always were." Halie looked up to find Adam peering down through the hole between floors.

"You were right," he said. "The data is twenty-four frames in a looping movie clip. You really need to see this."

Halie put the camera away and climbed back up the rungs. They returned to the couch and Adam set his laptop between them. The same hexagonal picture of Mash appeared in a window, but it was now part of a series. As each frame displayed, Mash's expression changed. Her mouth moved.

"Can you speed it up?" Halie asked.

Adam adjusted the frame rate, producing a smooth animation. Though silent, Mash seemed to be saying something.

"Can you read lips?" Adam asked.

"Probably no better than you," Halie answered. She watched the loop play several more times. "A few V or F sounds—upper teeth on the lower lip. *Level*? She might be saying *level five*?"

Adam leaned in close. "But what's that last part?"

Halie let the animation loop run another cycle. "It's not a word… she's blowing a kiss." Halie turned to Adam, their faces close. He seemed just as confused. "Either someone is messing with us or…"

The answer hit her full force. She ran to the pod's control panel. The bottom light blinked—their destination.

"Change of plans," Halie announced, pressing the fourth button. It lit up and began blinking. "We're going back up. That message is for me. It's repeating over and over to get my attention. I don't know how, but the message is coming from Mash."

21. GHOST

THEY STOPPED AT LEVEL 4 only to pivot from one ribbon to the other. A minute later, they were soaring up once more. It wouldn't take long to return to Level 5.

"You remember what's up there," Adam stated. He closed his laptop, turning his full attention to her.

Halie nodded. The crystal cavern filled with groans, screams, and flashing images now seemed an appropriate place for a ghost to haunt. "Mash is there. She's in the cavern."

Adam glanced to the hole leading to the V-pod's lower level where Mash's wrapped body lay. He said nothing.

"I know… it's nuts," Halie continued. "But Mash's last words weren't to me. She was speaking to… whoever built all this. Adam, I don't think she's dead. Not really."

Adam nodded. Still silent.

Halie pressed her hands against the sides of her head, pulling her hair back tight. "God, what a stupid idea." She blew out a breath. "I'm so gullible. Overly trusting. Mash tells me that all the time. This whole thing is probably one giant ruse."

She stared at the floor, thinking and rethinking but never coming to any conclusion that seemed reasonable. "But… what if the message is a call for help? What if Mash is trapped in that cavern?" She looked up, catching his eye.

Adam sighed. "Then I guess we'll have to return to find out."

Halie wondered how far wild guesses would take this increasingly unhinged concept. Returning to a place that now seemed designed to hold ghostly apparitions would be difficult—maybe terrifying—but she'd descend into whatever hell Level 5 represented if Mash was stuck in there.

Halie wiped tears she couldn't seem to prevent. "You don't think I'm crazy?"

Adam scratched the back of his head. "Actually... no. Your *idea* is crazy. But you? I think you're the best friend anyone could have."

She scooted closer to him, letting the built-up anxiety finally release. He wrapped an arm around her. "Thanks, Adam. This is hard."

"It's going to get harder."

Halie nodded.

Halie pressed Send. The text message to Paul only outlined a plan, not her suspicions. Until she found out why Mash's face was being transmitted up and down the tether, she'd only confuse him by reporting Mash's death. Eventually, she'd need to tell him, but for the moment, she wasn't even sure herself.

The pod slowed to a crawl with the faceted sphere of Level 5 directly above. They slid into the donut hole and the airlock sealed shut.

Halie stood, careful of the low gravity. She gathered her emotions and faced Adam. "Sorry for all the drama. We just met and I'm a wreck."

"No explanation needed," he answered. "I feel your loss. Mash was more than a colleague, I could tell right away."

They climbed down, avoiding the body as if ignoring physical reality might increase the odds of a happy ending. Adam pulled a small flashlight from his duffel bag—not the bright floodlight of Mash's camera, but it would do.

At the other side of the airlock, the yawning cavern lined with purple crystals reminded Halie that unanswered questions remained. In fact, they had escalated to new significance.

We asked who built this place, but does it matter? The real questions are why they built it, and what they want from us.

Once more, she gingerly placed a foot onto the field of crystals. Spikes flattened only to regrow a few steps later. Side by side, Halie and Adam descended into darkness. His flashlight beam scanned the right-side wall, where a chorus of clicks erupted like crickets alerted to danger. With each pass of the light, crystals sparkled in multiple colors, but if tiny creatures lived in the crannies, they remained hidden.

Halie froze, hearing the first groan. More followed, deep, rumbling wails calling her to the subterranean world. She closed her eyes, willing her quickening pulse to calm.

They're not ghosts. There's got to be an explanation.

Would a face-to-face alien encounter be any better? What if the tether was a lure to entice Earthlings foolish enough to climb? Halie's imagination, like everyone's, had been shaped by countless stories of nefarious aliens whose sole purpose was to inflict harm, or who would casually trample humans like ants underfoot.

That can't be the answer. Humans created those stories; there's nothing alien about them. Authors simply reflected within their stories a natural human fear of the unknown, an instinct passed down from ancestors over millennia. Fear of the dark and of unfamiliar sounds were evolutionary advantages for anyone living on the African savanna a million years ago. Real dangers lurked there and then.

But Halie's intellectual grasp of her fear didn't mean that face to face contact would be friendly. Incomprehensible and indifferent were perfectly logical options too.

This time, they descended quickly and with more focus. Pink and green lights flashed ahead. They reached the intersection where they had turned back before. Halie chose to go right.

A pink flash displayed a waterfall and was gone in an instant. Another flickered a swamp with moss hanging from trees. Then, a man with face paint carrying a spear that disappeared so quickly it might not have been there at all.

The tunnel narrowed. The crystals spreading across its floor were already smaller and soon became nothing more than gravel.

Adam walked behind, turning his flashlight to the walls, ceiling, and floor but finding nothing moving. Groans came from all around now, with the same distant mumbles they'd heard before, as if a conversation floated in the air without any need to comprehend its meaning.

The tunnel turned and descended further. It already felt like they'd come twice as far as the station's width or depth. The mystery of an interior space that disregarded its exterior boundaries ruined any sense of direction. They could be climbing upward for all Halie knew.

A faint buzz grew into a throbbing hum. Suddenly she was off her feet, floating, not walking. "Whoa." She flailed, unable to grab anything and surprised to find herself being pulled toward a copper-colored wall ahead. The humming grew louder. Halie twisted around. Adam floated too, just as bewildered by the instantaneous loss of gravity.

They thumped against a rectangular indentation, grabbing each other to stop twisting in the unexpected weightlessness. Halie had never been weightless before, and while astronaut videos might prepare the mind, they did little for the body. She suddenly felt lightheaded and nauseous.

The copper surface was surrounded by crystals at its edges. A hazy gray hexagon formed at its center. Halie knew exactly what to do. She took a deep breath and lifted a trembling hand. The hexagon sank at her touch and a door swung open. Air rushed through, pulling them inside.

Halie spun into a vast hollow, dimly lit. She tried to grab Adam but failed. Her cry of alarm echoed in the cavernous chamber. She wasn't panicking yet, but the spinning would need to stop soon, or she would be sick at a minimum and screaming not long after that.

"Uff!" Halie slammed into something hard and grabbed wildly, finally stopping the spin. Adam crashed into her, but she managed to hook one hand on his elbow in time to keep him from flying away. They clawed their way onto a pedestal at the base of a pole.

Halie closed her eyes and held on tight until the involuntary shaking stopped. She took another breath and calmed enough to look around.

They were inside a spherical chamber at least a hundred meters across, maybe more, since size could only be gauged by the copper door they'd blasted through. The curving interior was crisscrossed by rows and columns of tiny lights arranged like lines of longitude and latitude. The dim light made other surface features hard to judge. Etched stone? A weave? Halie sensed enough texture to rule out metal or glass.

The only way in or out was the single copper door, which had now swung closed, unreachable unless they pushed off from their perch and managed to drift in the right direction.

"You okay?" Adam asked.

"I think so. You?"

"Scared," he said.

"And you're the daredevil flying man."

"Some things still scare me. This place, for example. A huge stadium can't possibly exist inside a space station that's no more than thirty meters in diameter, yet here we are." His words produced a tinny echo, different than the cavern. Here there were no crystals. No purples, pinks, or greens. Instead, silver and copper colors, which, along with the lattice of lights, gave it an electronic feel.

Their pedestal formed one end of a silver metal pole about ten meters long. At its opposite end, another disc remained out of reach. The pole had no obvious attachments to the sphere's interior surface, but it felt solid anyway. Vertical or horizontal, it hardly mattered. But Halie couldn't fail to notice the pole was oriented with the lines of longitude lighted around the inside of the sphere, just as the north and south poles are on Earth.

Someone or something had made this aberration of space. Would they be in here? Or was this a place to capture trespassers? She had a feeling they were being watched.

"Mash?" Halie called. "Are you here?" It was worth a try.

The pole vibrated with the same frequency of the throbbing hum they'd heard from the corridor outside. Halie half expected the pedestal to split open and suck them deeper into impossible space. Instead, she heard a voice rise above the vibration.

Distorted and wavering between high and low frequencies, the voice warbled, "Gotcha back, Jack."

"Mash?" It didn't sound like Mash at all, but the words were Mash-like.

"I can barely hear you. Sticky Wicket Dumb Bum."

"*Mash!*" Halie screamed. She nearly lost her grip on the pole.

"Where are you?" the ethereal voice croaked. Vibrations continued, never quite silencing between each buzzing word.

"We're inside a sphere on Level 5. Where are you?" Halie couldn't believe she was talking to Mash. But she had to. Unless…

"I'm in a dark place. Can't see. Can't really hear either. I'm feeling your voice—if that makes sense."

Halie bit her lip as the worry fully formed in her mind. "Are you really Mash?"

"Who else would I be?"

"A simulation. This place and your voice feel very electronic. I can't describe it, but I could be fooled by it."

"Flowers," the electronic voice said.

That caught Halie's attention. "Okay… what about flowers?"

"You know exactly what I mean, Joyce Sahalie Spark," the voice answered. "And you know right this instant that it's really me, don't you?"

Few people knew her full name, and "flowers" wasn't exactly a common greeting. "Maybe. Tell me more."

"What is the one thing in our universe that's perfect?"

Halie's heart lifted as she registered words that could have only come from Mash. The reverberating voice continued. "A flower, that's what. It's beautiful and it's functional. A flower's color and scent attract insects for pollination, which brings genetic variation to the plant... *and* encourages humans to grow it. Perfection, right?"

Tears came to Halie's eyes along with an uncontrollable quavering in her throat. She'd heard Mash tell this story more than once. Several of her colorful tattoos were flowers, and she could explain each one using the same theme of *perfection*. "Dammit, Mash, where are you? You died. I saw with my own eyes!"

"I died? That's bad. All I remember was falling... then feeling pretty messed up. A voice asked me if I wanted to get fixed, but I had to agree to leave my body behind. Of course, I've never been fond of that body, so..."

"You agreed. I heard you. You said, 'better get going.'"

"And now I'm here, wherever *here* is."

Adam had a wide grin on his face. "Have you asked someone where you are?"

"Is that Dinger boy?"

"I'm here with Halie," Adam said. His legs wrapped around the pole with the rest of his body leaning away. "We'll do whatever we can to get you out, but if someone wants you here, we might need their cooperation. I'm wondering if you have a communication path that we don't."

"Kind of. Give me a minute. I'm really not sure how any of this works."

The humming disappeared. Halie exchanged a nervous glance with Adam. She shook her head, not quite comprehending what might be going on, but encouraged. "Her essence?" Halie asked Adam.

"Her consciousness?" Adam answered. "You might be right that this place is electronic. We were looking for the source of the message sent down the tether, and I think we found it. But now we'll need to understand it."

"We should freeze Mash's body." She almost regretted voicing such a dumb idea, but… crazy times. A consciousness maintained in electronic memory seemed like a one-way street, but if they were dealing with advanced technology, anything and everything might be on the table.

Instead of criticizing, Adam ran with it. "The V-pod's cargo bay is exposed to space, so it's cold. We could put on helmets and use the personal airlock on Level 4 to carry the body through."

Before Halie could comment on his plan, the rows and columns of lights around the spherical dome flickered, then in unison changed from all-white to a variety of colors. They formed a pattern, difficult to make out by looking in only one direction. Halie swiveled up and down, left and right, even behind. Taken together, the lights were widely spaced pixels—they formed a picture of Mash.

"It's trying something different now." The voice echoed in the empty sphere, but the humming reverberation was gone, sounding closer to the real person.

"It is you!" Halie said. She cocked her head upward, where Mash's nose and eyes were formed by animated colors. It felt like standing next to a stadium videoboard.

"I can hear you better too," Mash said. "You might feel the filament's touch. Don't worry, that's normal."

Halie brushed away what felt like a spider's silk or a loose hair from her forehead. She'd been feeling the same random tickles at each of the stations, but never more than at Level 5. She'd written it off as dust or her own hair, but now she wondered what electronic tentacles might be floating around them.

"The filament?" Halie asked, not at all sure she wanted to hear the answer.

Mash's oversized face and voice responded from every direction. "Filament is the best word for this thing, but it's complicated. It doesn't have eyes or ears. It senses through microfibers. Millions of them. Too thin to see, but they're all over the place. It can even drop a fiber down to Earth. That's how it stuck the magic wire to Yoon's golf cart."

Halie's mind spun with the barrage of new information. The tickles she'd felt, Yoon's wire, this... *thing*. "The filament is alive?"

"I wouldn't bet against it, but that's complicated too. Maybe not alive like people, but definitely more than plants. It can think. It doesn't have a brain, but it uses bubbles called *prominences* to collect its thoughts and pass them along to other prominences. Kind of a groupthink setup. You're inside a prominence now."

Halie looked around the hollow sphere, feeling like she'd been swallowed by an alien whale.

"How do you know all this?" She struggled to release the nagging feeling: Was it really Mash? Or just a good impostor.

No response. The lights dimmed, then a defeated, "I have no idea. I might be dreaming this stuff. Maybe you're just part of the dream."

"I assure you we're real," Adam answered. He was floating upside down compared to Halie, which didn't matter much since Mash's face was everywhere. "And I don't think you're dreaming."

"You're probably right. Dreams aren't this... Rootie Tootie Back Stab!" Mash yelled each word. Halie felt her pain but quickly realized that if ever there was a time for cursing, this was it. And Mash never cursed.

It sure feels like her.

Her big-screen face tensed with frustration, but the out-of-body version of Mash continued, "No sight, no touch, no smells, nothing. I can't even hear you. Not really. I can *understand* you. The filament is playing some kind of trick. I don't know how."

Halie had no words of encouragement. Platitudes wouldn't do. She'd need to understand what they were up against to have any chance of rescuing Mash from her electronic cage.

She surveyed her surroundings with new insight. "So, there are no aliens to meet?"

"You're looking at them. Him. Her. It."

"How about the tether? Are the nanobots alive too?"

"The filament is everything. The tether, the bots, the ascender, the stations, the platform at the bottom. It's all one thing. People turn their hair into different shapes and colors. The filament changes part of itself into an airlock or a cavern of crystals. Same thing."

"What about the other space elevators?" Adam asked.

"It might be able to break pieces of itself off. Or maybe there's more than one filament. I don't know, I'm not exactly in a classroom."

"Mash, your descriptions are great. Really helpful." Halie sighed. "But I'm worried about your emotional distress."

"Yeah… there's that dead thing. Rama Lama No Joy."

"I'm so sorry, Mash. I should have… there's so many things I should have done."

"Not your fault. Hey, we're still talking, so it's not all bad. But Professor Peru isn't going to make a great camera operator for you."

Adam shook his head. "Definitely not."

Everything about this stored consciousness *was* Mash. How this living filament had done it and whether it could be reversed was something to figure out. For now, Halie needed to deal with her own emotions, strong and mixed. The filament had killed Mash and somehow saved her at the same time.

22. CHANGE OF PLANS

MARCO STEPPED OFF the jet's airstair and strolled alone across a darkened deck. A thousand stars were splayed across a midnight sky. All quiet, except for the sound of waves breaking on the pontoons below.

A laugh came from beneath the shroud at the platform's center. The soldiers of the night watch were the only souls left on deck. Except for one, they would be surprised to see him.

Addressing a small group was always trickier than standing at the center of a stadium filled with thousands of screaming fans. Just last week he had appeared at Mané Garrincha national stadium in Brasilia. But there, he had the benefit of a support team, a warmup speaker, and dozens of banners hung around the stadium to preview his message before the first word reverberated over stadium speakers.

Fighter, Leader, Lover, the banners read and every man in the audience chanted before Marco appeared on stage. *Guardian, Oracle, Receiver* the women echoed back with the same enthusiasm. With the audience primed for a lovefest, Marco's grand entrance always released a frenzy of shouts and cheers. From there it was easy. He had no need for a script, a teleprompter, or an earpiece connected to a stage director. His sermon of traditions, wellness, and spiritual purity came from his heart to theirs.

But a small group lacked a crowd dynamic. Mingling closely with these soldiers would require finesse, especially for this mission. If all went well, Sergeant Alvarez would soon become a heroic fighter for the cause, even if his own military labeled him an insubordinate traitor.

Marco reached the shroud's edge, pausing in the shadows to observe. An electric lantern hung from a hook at the steps leading up to the twin ribbons. Three soldiers sprawled across the steps, one Alvarez, the others with name tags Hernandez and Ruiz. Opposite their makeshift camp, the hangar door remained shut, with no sign of the thieves who had absconded with its ascender.

Each soldier cradled a rifle, but with the ascender gone there was little to protect. The Peruvians had given up. The Americans were gone for the night too, probably watching one of their vulgar movies somewhere inside their soulless mega-ship.

The soldier named Ruiz poked his mate in the leg. "How about Luisa, that little dove in Supply?"

"Eh, I give her a five," his mate, Hernandez, replied. "Not kicking her out of bed, but I move on the older women. Good looking, thirty-five. Already been dumped a few times and looking for young muscle like me."

Ruiz's bulging belly jiggled with a laugh. "Grab that American *rica guapa*. Sahaaalie." He drew out the name.

"*Puta madre, sí!* When they return, you two pin the stupid scientist to the deck, and I will take her into the maze for a party."

Marco had seen their types before. Weak of mind and of body. Their natural masculine instincts had been traded for a steady stream of androgynous-cybernetic indoctrination. Androgynous because nearly every detail in this technology fueled world had been forced into a gender neutral straitjacket. Cybernetic because the message was now generated almost entirely by AI.

In this world, the flood of indoctrination was unrelenting. Internet, television, schools, even churches. Most dupes complied with the decrees from uber-technologists and their shadowy political enablers. Unless something changed, society would continue to spiral into decline.

These men are fools, Marco judged of Alvarez's mates. *But fools are easily manipulated.* He stepped from the shadows into the light cast by the lantern.

Hernandez noticed him immediately, but any soldier's instinct regarding an unexpected intruder was quickly repressed by celebrity status. "Hey, Marco! *Bienvenido, amigo!*"

Alvarez stiffened. Ruiz stood, with a stupid grin spreading across his face.

Remaining calm, Marco reached out, shaking hands with all three. His Spanish was flawless. "Such a beautiful night. I felt I needed a lap or two around the platform before retiring. And to my surprise, I find our guardians still on duty! A pleasure to meet you."

Marco spoke of the beauty of Ecuador and the good people there, as if they'd been friends forever. The soldiers responded as expected, asking about Marco's career, even about specific matches and the opponents he'd faced at the World Cup. Throughout, their gaze never left his face.

For his part, Alvarez nodded and smiled, then slowly backed away toward the ribbons. As planned, Hernandez and Ruiz failed to notice.

Can it be this easy? Marco wondered.

But Alvarez only made it halfway up the steps. A loud thump from somewhere in the darkness interrupted his mission and sent all eyes searching for the source. Rolling wheels squeaked. Not far away, the hangar door was opening.

Marco looked straight up into the shroud. Stars winked through the opening at its top, but there was no sign of the stolen ascender returning to its base. The hangar door continued to lumber open, spilling light across the deck. Hernandez and Ruiz grabbed their rifles and pointed, but if anyone was inside they were well hidden.

"Did you do that?" Marco asked Alvarez.

"Not me."

Marco followed the slot in the deck and stepped across the hangar's threshold with the three soldiers behind. At least thirty meters overhead, the hangar ceiling glowed. The slot ended at the room's center.

The soldiers wandered around the well-lit space. Except for a few shelves with parts and equipment, it was empty. At the opposite side, a smaller door stood open, but no one was there. Marco glanced back to the ribbons. Still no descending pod.

Then why did it open?

He dropped to his knees and peered into the slot, unable to see anything beneath the floor. But a black dot at the slot's edge caught his attention, the only mark on an otherwise smooth off-white floor. As he watched, the dot grew.

The soldiers gathered around. "What is it?" Alvarez asked. The dot inflated to the size of a pea and still grew.

Marco didn't answer. Though small, a plant that could rapidly emerge from a metal slot whispered of danger. He touched the tiny ball with a finger. Not sticky. Not hot or cold. But electric, like the leads of a nine-volt battery.

The pea grew to marble size and gained a marble's glassy shine too. Alvarez stooped and tried to pick it up, but no amount of pulling or twisting could dislodge it. Seconds later, the aberration was the size of a baseball and still growing.

The ball elongated, becoming less spherical and more like a cucumber standing upright—if cucumbers were made of glass. Marco backed away, feeling uneasy. Glass blowers could turn a molten dab into a thin-walled balloon by blowing into a tube, but this object had none of the heat, and no glass blower to make it.

As it enlarged, the cylinder extended two fins on one side that came together in a V. Now as tall as a standing child, it continued to swell. Hernandez shouldered his weapon, but Marco pushed its barrel down. "Wait. I think I see what is happening."

It grew higher and wider, its shape refining and details forming inside its curving glass walls. "It's another ascender," Marco said, now quite sure of himself. How it had grown from a tiny seed he couldn't fathom.

The ship now towered overhead, a full forty meters tall and ten wide. A glass door at its midsection opened as if pulled by an invisible hand. The doorway matched the height of a mezzanine extending from the hangar wall.

Marco led the soldiers up the mezzanine staircase and peered into the open doorway. A lavatory no different than those on commercial airline flights stood on one side. On the other, shelves appeared in a metal frame, forming from nothing.

"This is no machine," Alvarez murmured. "It is nothing created by a Korean businessman or any other person. It is an incarnation of the spirit world."

Hernandez and Ruiz nodded their agreement. All three soldiers lifted weapons with unsteady hands, unsure whether to defend or attack.

"Wait." Marco ran a hand along the smooth glass surface. "Do not the Candomblé speak of spirits whose handiwork can be both evil and divine? This vessel can be no accident. It has arrived precisely when we need it."

Alvarez stared at Marco without speaking.

Marco put an arm around his shoulder and pulled him aside. "Our cause continues, my friend. But not here. Why nip at its ankles when we now have the means to kill the beast at its heart?"

23. FILAMENT

HALIE FLOATED ACROSS the spherical room, no longer feeling the need to hang tight to the pole inexplicably fixed at its center. Adam sat upside down on one of the pole's two discs, his legs wrapped around the pole to keep him in place. Mash's face, including facsimiles of mouth movement and facial expressions, was plastered around the interior of the sphere.

"I have a million questions," Halie said to Mash's stored consciousness.

"I know you do. It knows too," Mash replied.

"Can I speak to it directly?"

Mash's giant image scrunched up her mouth. "Hmm. Maybe. But don't expect to understand it. This thing isn't like us."

"Can I try anyway?"

"Maybe, hang on."

Mash's face disappeared. A minute later, large black hexagons appeared around the inside surface of the sphere. Six of them. White lettering appeared within each hex, formed from a mist that started at the corners and filled in toward the hexagon's center. The mist sharpened into recognizable words.

.sense now.

.prominence 877 local.

.direct contact request accepted.

.subject unrestrained.

.sense complete.

Halie drifted past one apparition. "Yow! Real words! I'm not sure I understand, but *subject unrestrained* sounds promising. You know, like we can ask anything."

She brushed a tickle on her chin, then pulled both hands away from her body. "I guess I shouldn't do that. It's trying to feel me."

"Nothing creepy about that." Adam started to scratch his own face, then stopped.

"We might need to think of the filament as if we were speaking to a deaf and blind person. Touch becomes their main sensory organ, not eyes or ears."

Adam slid a finger along his cheek, no doubt feeling for the invisible silk brushing against him. "If I had to guess, the microfibers are diamond nanothreads. Tetrahedral carbon, somewhat brittle, so they would transmit vibrations well. With enough carbon and nanobots you could make them by the millions and at lengths long enough for remote sensing from space." He shrugged a laugh. "Hell, the filament could have been dragging its threads through our cities for years, and we'd never have known it. Think about every time you've walked into a spider silk hanging in the air. Was it really made by a spider?"

Halie glared at him. "That's a very unnerving thought. Do *not* tell that to my producer. Paul would be all over it." Halie could imagine their next show: "Spiderwebs from Space." The ick factor alone would draw a crowd. But playing on the public's aversion to arachnids was something tabloid journalists did; Halie had a bigger story to tell.

Except that she wasn't ready to tell it—or even frame it. For now, she'd focus on freeing Mash from an electronic jail. The conversation with the jailkeeper had begun and would play out for good, evil, or indifference, but Halie wasn't going to walk away.

She cleared her throat. "Filament, do you feel me?"

Nothing happened.

Halie spoke again. "Go ahead, drape your diamond nanothreads on me. I'm good with that. I only want to communicate." Still nothing. The original six hexagons remained in place, and the writing on them didn't change. "Maybe there's a trigger word I need to say?"

Adam flipped himself over, now right side up compared to Halie. "It does seem procedural. *Sense now, sense complete.* It reads like a programming language." He held up a hand, thinking. "The filament already knows at least a portion of our language, which implies it's been brushing its feelers up against people for a while. Spying on us, or more charitably, preparing to build a tether we can climb."

"Mash says it doesn't think like us, so getting a conversation going might be hard." On a whim, Halie smiled as big as she could manage. Facial expressions might be just as important as vocal cords, and if the microfibers were draped across her mouth, they'd pick it up.

Each hexagon misted over, and new words formed.

.sense refined.

.prominence 877 local.

.human mapped kin identified.

.tolerance to extraction.

.sense complete.

"What did you do?" Adam asked.

"I smiled." Halie shrugged. Whether it had been upturned lips or some other factor, they might never know. Nobody had said communicating with an alien carbon allotrope would be easy.

Halie read the new words, twice. "Obscure, but at least we're on speaking terms."

"*Tolerance to extraction* sounds more like a dental procedure," Adam added.

"Does it think we're kin? Related to Mash?"

"As good a guess as any."

Halie drifted by and reached out. Adam pulled her to the central pole. She spoke quietly to him. "I need to get one question answered, but the filament might get pissed off, so be ready for anything." He gripped the pole tighter. There wasn't much else to do.

Halie took a deep breath and blurted it out. "Why did you kill our kin?"

Adam raised his eyebrows. "You don't mess around with this first contact stuff, do you?"

They waited. Halie smiled again. Nothing happened this time. Communication would apparently be slow. She wondered if they should call for Mash to come back, or even if yelling for Mash would work.

Without warning, all six hexagons blanked out, then redrew words from mist.

.sense now.

.prominence 877 local.

.error microfilament modulation.

.concern supportive repair.

.sense complete.

Halie studied the response, reading twice silently and once out loud. It made even less sense than the first two responses. The only word that stood out was *error*.

"It made a mistake?" Halie asked. "Or did *we* make a mistake?"

Mash's face returned, this time only at one side of the dome. Five of the hexagons disappeared, leaving only one on the opposite side of Mash's avatar. "Me again."

Halie was relieved that Mash seemed to have the power to come and go. Mash was normally an upbeat person, but Halie worried about her ability to cope while being held inside a dark alien dungeon. Even if a person's consciousness was fully functional, sensory deprivation for anything longer than a few hours could be emotionally debilitating. Halie had seen rather cruel experiments, with test subjects entombed in sensory deprivation tanks for long periods. They always ended up screaming to get out.

For now, she could only be supportive. "It's good to hear your voice and see a remarkably good rendition of your face."

"Don't ask how that's happening," Mash said. "I'm surprised I can still think. But I'm getting enough dreamy clues from the filament to help translate."

"Good. So, what does *error microfilament modulation* mean?"

Mash sounded tired. "It means it screwed up. Apparently, the tether has more going on than we thought, with some of its microfilaments carrying electricity and some not. It wasn't expecting anyone to touch where I grabbed. So... zap. The filament has reworked that part of the tether, so it's no longer a problem. But damage done."

"The electrocution wasn't intentional? At least, that's its claim?"

"Right."

Halie had a sinking feeling. "Should we trust it?"

"What choice do we have? Me especially."

Mash had zeroed in on the fundamental issue. The filament, she'd said, was *everything*. Halie and Adam wouldn't get back to the platform without its cooperation. Even the crystal cavern could block their passage if the filament decided to keep its sharp spikes raised. Any plan to rescue Mash was beginning to feel out of reach.

Halie lowered her head. The tears returned. "God, I screwed this up."

"Did not."

"Did. I should have bullied Yoon into his confession *before* we started up the elevator. We shouldn't even be here. Well... *I* shouldn't. This is a job for scientists, linguists, engineers. People who know what they're doing."

Adam held up a hand. "Whoa, wait. You think I know what I'm doing just because I can test materials and deduce how this thing is structured? Nobody on Earth has met an alien intelligence. That's why our imaginations run wild. Invading monsters? Godlike super brains? Cute teddy bears?"

"With razor-sharp fangs," Halie interrupted.

"With fangs," Adam acknowledged. "My point is, when no one knows what we're facing, I'd say a journalist with a scientific mind is the *best* person for the job."

Halie connected eye to eye with Adam and smiled. She could get used to his regular ego boosts. "Thanks. I'm not sure how I feel about being a spokesperson for the nine billion inhabitants of Earth. But… maybe we can help Mash extricate herself."

"Here's the deal," Mash's mind said. "The filament *understands* we place value on our lives. It gets it. It knows it's not like us. It knows it made an error, and it's doing the best it can to correct it."

"You think so, really?"

"Really. It's why I'm still talking to you. It pulled me out of my body. I have no clue how, no idea where I am now, but I'm not dead. *Concern supportive repair*. That's its way of telling you."

Halie closed her eyes and nodded. It felt good to hear it from Mash, not from any interpretation she or Adam had made up on their own.

Halie balled up her fists. "Mash, we'll get you out. We'll go down and bring help. We'll freeze your body, maybe…"

"Yeah, whatever. Go ahead and freeze it. Keeps the smell down. But don't expect my eyelids to flutter open anytime soon. Resurrection isn't really my thing. Especially not in that body."

Halie understood enough about her friend to recognize the gender dysphoria that Mash struggled with. Some people didn't feel like they belonged inside their body. Halie made a mental note not to bring it up again. She'd focus more on freeing Mash from the sightless jail and bringing her consciousness back to Earth.

Store her on a petabyte server? Somebody somewhere would have a better idea.

"We'll bring experts. Psychologists. Neurologists. Computer AI types. Whatever it takes. But... I worry about what we'll face once we get back to the platform."

Halie had no idea where to start. Militaries arguing with each other were only a microcosm of the trouble they'd face. Hopelessly divided, the modern world struggled to agree on the simplest of truths. A complex alien *structure* that was capable of reaching from space to touch the planet in six locations but communicated in obscure handfuls of words would sorely test humanity. Nothing to face off against. No arms, legs, or tentacles. No voice. In an era when people mistrusted anyone not from their self-defined tribe, Halie couldn't imagine very many would trust an alien so utterly foreign.

Or the alien's spokesperson. That's exactly how they'd portray her involvement, especially people like Marco. Halie didn't like it, but she owed Mash her full effort.

"We'll figure something out." Halie looked to the copper doorway they'd used to enter this hollow void. It wouldn't be hard to reach with a good push off the bar. "But before we head down, there are two things I really need to know."

"Whack me."

"First, why does it look so much like Yoon's space elevator designs?"

"It's good at copying."

Halie contemplated how theft of corporate designs might work, imagining invisible feelers sent into labs and workshops to see what the humans were up to. "Okay, that makes sense. Second question, just as easy. Where did the filament come from?"

Mash's image shook her head. "Nah, you don't want to know that. It'll just mess you up."

Halie stared straight ahead. "I do want to know."

"Look, you're the Logical Science Babe. You won't believe the answer because it sounds too corny, like Buck Rogers or some nutcase conspiracy theory."

"I still want to know. Everyone on the platform is going to ask."

"Fine. It's your worldview you're messing with. The filament came from Venus."

24. SENSE NOW

"OH, COME ON. VENUS? We've sent probes there. Recently. They searched for alien life and didn't find it."

Mash's statement that the filament came from Venus fell into the same category as UFO sightings. Decades of eyewitness testimony hadn't convinced Halie the reports of alien visitation were evidence of anything more than the limitations of human perception. It took scientific scrutiny and a willingness to examine alternative hypotheses to break free from conclusions based on anecdotes.

The Venus Life Finder spacecraft, launched in the 2020s, had parachuted an array of scientific instruments into Venus's atmosphere, searching for the chemical traces of airborne life. Its conclusion: Venus was as lifeless as Mars.

"Maybe so," Mash's disembodied voice responded. "But there's lots of carbon at Venus, and the scuttlebutt around here says we missed something."

"Scuttlebutt?" Halie hung on a pole inside a domelike *prominence* with Mash's image projected on its curving surface. The black hexagons, the only direct communication from the filament so far, were gone. "Who exactly are you talking to?"

"It's… complex," Mash proclaimed. "Even weirder than Venus, so maybe I'll keep that little secret to myself."

"Mash," Halie warned.

"You shot down my last revelation, so now you don't get any more."

"Mash, I'm trying to help. I can't do that if you keep secrets. The filament will win, and you'll be stuck… wherever you are."

The big-screen image of Mash disappeared. After a long pause, she returned. "He doesn't want to talk to you. I asked him, or *dreamed* to him, or whatever I'm doing."

"Asked who? The filament?"

"No. His name is Quiso Yupanqui. He says he fought alongside Manco Inca against the Spanish at the battle of Ollantaytambo. That's a big deal for Incans."

"And Quiso is an Inca warrior?"

"One of chief Manco's captains. Died in 1542, he says. Killed by Hernando Pizarro himself. A Spanish lance through the chest, apparently."

Halie dropped her head into her hands. She didn't want to blow off Mash's increasingly weird ramblings for fear the whole conversation might suddenly end. The consciousness on the other side was definitely Mash, but her ability to think clearly may have been compromised by the electronics involved.

Adam scooted closer on the pole they both clung to. "Probe further, let's see where this goes."

They could exit this hollow sphere and probably make it out of the cavern. They'd done it before. Once back on the platform, Halie could locate a qualified physician. American aircraft carriers were floating cities with thousands of sailors. Surely they would have someone on board trained in psychiatric evaluations.

Then again, the current circumstances were unique, and they had Mash's consciousness available to translate. *Okay, I'll bite.* "How does a dead Inca from the 1500s manage to get here?"

"Same as me," Mash answered. "The filament touched him before his body died and asked him if he wanted to live in a different way. He said yes, and he's been here ever since. He seems to have settled in pretty well. Spends his time absorbing stuff the filament senses with its threads—probably where he picked up English. He doesn't seem to be suffering, but I think he misses farming. He talks a lot about potatoes."

"You're telling me that Quiso has been inside this alien machine for five centuries?"

"Alien *filament*. And stop asking questions if you're just going to blow off the answers."

"Sorry, Mash. It's not that I don't believe you, it's just a lot to digest." The same fate might apply to Mash too, not something Halie was willing to suggest, though Mash may have already come to the same conclusion.

Adam asked, "Anybody else in there or is it just you and Quiso?"

"Uh, yeah... there's more. Forty? Fifty? I'm not sure."

"Fifty people?" Adam repeated.

Mash's image around the spherical stadium flashed on and off. "Right... I know... it's jack crack weird. I get it. What I'm telling you shouldn't be happening. Impossible. Stupid. Lame to the nth degree."

"But?" Halie asked carefully.

"But... it's true. Quiso is one of the oldest, but there are a few Chinese from his time. Ming dynasty, I guess. They never learned English, so I doubt I'll ever communicate with them. A few Italians, not sure what century. There are more, but I don't know who they are. Too many languages."

"Are any of these people groaning?" Adam asked. His question showed insight. The groans in the cavern did sound human.

"Could be. If I ever get past all the languages, I'll ask them what they're groaning about. It might be they're tired of the darkness. That's the worst part. There's nothing to see in here. The filament doesn't seem to understand that we're visual."

Halie took a deep breath, believing the situation as Mash described it, but wondering how she could possibly help. The prisoners in this mind jail had been there for centuries. Could anyone get them out? If so, where would they go? Worse, was the filament adding still more consciousnesses? Possibly even now at the other five tethers?

Before Halie reached out to any authorities on the platform, she needed the biggest question answered. "What does it want from us?"

"That might be harder," Mash said. "I'll try to find out but give me a minute."

While Mash was gone, Halie queried Adam, "Does any of this make sense to you?"

He winced. "I think we need to hear the whole story, and I don't think we're there yet."

"Mash says her death was an accident, but if this thing doesn't think like us, isn't it important to clarify its intentions?"

"Agreed. The key to understanding intent—at least as it relates to pulling minds out of dying people—would be to distinguish between premeditation, reckless endangerment, and merely interceding in a compassionate way. Those might be subtle distinctions for the filament. Like I said, I don't think we're there yet."

Mash's face returned to the big screen. "You're not going to like this answer either."

"That's okay," Halie said.

"Don't blame the messenger."

"I won't."

"Quiso says the filament arrived here in 1542, but he doesn't know why. It's sucking up carbon, sure, but Venus is like a fruit stand at the side of the highway. Not the destination, it's just handy."

"Earth is the destination?"

"Probably. The filament does seem curious about us."

"But curious for five centuries?" Halie leaned back, still hanging onto the chamber's central pole with bent knees. "That can't be the whole story, Mash. It must want something from us."

"Maybe, but that question can't be answered at this level. You're in a prominence. The filament uses a prominence for Sense Now—a way of thinking. Kind of like a single neuron in our brains. But there's also Sense Refined, the next step up. That pulls together nearby prominences—like all the neurons in one brain. From the filament's perspective, Venus is nearby, and I get the feeling there are a lot of prominences there. But there's a higher level too, Sense Beyond. That's big-picture stuff. Probably more than our brains can handle. The filament can't answer a Sense Beyond question at a Sense Now level. So, a single prominence is useless for a 'what does it want from us?' question. To get the answer, you need to go higher—like higher on the tether. There's something else up there. Even Quiso doesn't know how it works. You need to climb to Level 6."

"Oh."

"Told you you wouldn't like the answer."

The problem wasn't the greater distance involved, or the hours spent climbing. Mash's consciousness wasn't going anywhere, and returning to the platform involved a cold reception from Marco and Ecuadoran soldiers. But continuing up to Level 6—by far the highest point on the tether—seemed destined to pull them further into a life-form Halie already felt unequipped to face.

She glanced at Adam, who floated within reach. He pinched his brow. "If we go down, that's probably the end of our access."

Halie pondered the caution, but not for long. "We came to figure this out. If Level 6 has the answers, then that's where we go. Mash, it's going to take us a while to get up and down. Will you be okay while we're gone?"

"Don't you kids worry about me. Go have fun. You know where to find me."

"It's definitely Mash," Halie told Adam. "Come on. Push off the bar and we'll sail to the door and back to gravity."

"Which reminds me," Adam said, speaking to Mash's oversized face once more. "Why is there no gravity here?"

"That's easy. The prominence isn't near anything big."

Adam wrinkled his forehead. "We're at Level 5. Six thousand kilometers above Earth. Gravity here should be one-quarter g, not zero."

"Yeah, about that… you're actually not near Earth. Not in any way you can measure. Prominences kind of make their own space."

Panting from their climb out, Halie turned around to face the purple crystal cavern that receded into darkness. "I guess we have the answer for how you fit a giant cavern into a small station. Expand into space beyond three dimensions."

A glow from the Level 5 airlock's floor and ceiling provided all the light they needed. Adam turned off his flashlight. "A half-kilometer hike for us, but the prominence might be a million kilometers away in some non-Cartesian direction. Weird. Very weird."

Halie and Adam stared at each other, wide-eyed, then returned to the waiting V-pod and climbed its ladder. Halie hovered a finger over the control panel's topmost button, Level 6.

She reminded herself of the good advice from a great scientist.

Don't fear the unknown, understand it. Halie shrugged, pressing the button. *How bad could it be?*

The V-pod's door hissed shut. The station's airlock opened without complaint, initiating their journey to the pinnacle of this human-designed but alien-built space elevator.

Halie settled onto the couch, tired. They'd spent an hour in the cavern, and it was now one a.m. down on the platform. A fully darkened Earth below gave only the barest hint of a sunset long past and a sunrise yet to come—a glow not in the west or east but along the northern horizon.

As with gravity, Halie realized a space elevator changed the relationship with sunset. On the ground, sunset was the sun sinking in the west. But from six thousand kilometers, that illusion was shattered. Earth assumed its proper position as a rotating globe against a fixed background that included the sun and every star. The tether was now an extension—a gigantic antenna—rotating along with Earth. They had merely been swept eastward into Earth's shadow.

Halie refocused her attention to her phone, typing a message to Yoon to let him know she was in transit to Level 6. She left out any mention of Mash.

Her next message to Paul was different. She couldn't withhold the terrible news any longer. As producer and studio chief, Paul needed to hear about Mash's death and the extraordinary extension of her consciousness. He'd be obligated to reach out to the emergency contact listed on Mash's employment record—most likely a parent or sibling who Halie had never met.

She got no immediate response from either text. It was only ten p.m. in LA; Paul would surely be awake. Halie imagined him shocked and grieving, just as she was. But soon after, he would take action to extract Halie from the "combat zone," or whatever legal language was in her contract.

Whatever demands Paul or the Kolby security people made, she'd say no. She'd explain that once the button was pushed, a V-pod had no capability of turning around between stations. They'd arrive at Level 6 in the morning, investigate its station for any secrets that could secure Mash's future welfare, then return to the surface. It would be an overnight trip—already committed.

While waiting for responses, Halie checked her news sources, finding dozens of breaking news reports from around the world. Scientists in Indonesia had examined a tether sample under a microscope, confirming its self-repairing mechanism. But their report spread a growing fear that the nanobots had been programmed with more sinister motives. Multiple news stories pointed to aliens, a conclusion impossible to ignore given the six space elevators created simultaneously. The elevator design might resemble human blueprints, but its construction had alien fingerprints everywhere.

Magic wires were in the news too. An Islamic imam from Indonesia had received one and was the first to climb the Telukdalam elevator. Enthralled by the wonderous views from above, he had declared the observation deck at Level 3 open to anyone wishing to see it. The line was getting longer by the hour.

Another wire ended up in the hands of a populist politician in Kenya who was now working his way up each level. A third went to a police chief from Brisbane, Australia. She had no idea why she'd been chosen but was en route to the Solomon Islands platform courtesy of Qantas Airlines.

One wire per platform, distributed to people from all walks of life. The only common denominators were that each recipient was well known and had a personal interest in progress through technology. Yoon was the only billionaire among them and the only one specifically involved in the space elevator business.

Opposition was spreading too, but Halie was surprised to discover that the greatest fear didn't come from alien nanobots. Public anxiety was highest over reports coming from Level 4, including her own recorded clips that Mash had sent to the studio. A ring encircling the Earth—even if incomplete—apparently scared the wits out of people.

Marco himself had spread some of the most frightening scenarios. His latest post declared that the alien ring "will enslave the world." Once complete, the people of Earth would have no defenses against alien invaders who could leisurely walk the ring, dropping "twenty-ton meteors laced with toxins. No city is safe," he'd said, though he hadn't specified how a large rock dropped from a ring over the equator could hit a city far to the north or south, or why toxins were involved.

A notification icon lit on Halie's phone. A response from Yoon.

Alas, Ecuador and Brazil prevail. They demand my departure by morning, with or without my "accomplices." Peru has undocked but their ship will patrol nearby. My best advice is to remain where you are. As long as your food and water hold out, negotiate the terms of surrendering the V-pod. You still have leverage.

Typical of Yoon to see it as a business negotiation. But Halie hadn't told him the whole story. She responded, explaining the filament and its role in absconding with his designs. She added a tip she felt she owed him.

The bridge at Level 4 is wide open. A business opportunity for you? Dust off any monorail plans you might have in your office. The Ecuadorans and others may need you after all.

Inside information, but maybe Yoon could make something of it, plus it could keep his plane and security team on-site for Halie's return.

Her phone rang. Paul. This would be a tough call.

"How?" he asked without any of the standard phone greetings.

"It was an accident, Paul. Electrocution."

His voice quavered. "Then how is she still alive?"

"That I can't tell you. We're in uncharted territory."

Halie relayed the events, praised Adam for his efforts at resuscitation, and made it as clear as she could that the consciousness captured by the filament was unquestionably Mash. Paul took most of it in stride and offered to find experts who might advise. But the call blew up when she told him she was still heading up.

"What the hell are you talking about? You have to come down!"

"I can't, Paul. Even if I could turn around, I wouldn't. We need to reach the top. There's something important up there. It might even save Mash."

For a full minute, Paul nearly screamed into the phone about Halie's own safety, about the number of KNS lawyers that were already knocking down his door, and about the consequences to the company—not to mention his own personal despair—if something should happen to her. In the end, she could only say she'd stay in contact. The final leg on this ascent was a done deal.

When Halie hung up, Adam was at her side. He handed Yoon's magic wire to her. "I didn't want to interrupt your call, but there's something new."

Halie rolled the wire between her fingers, searching for the mechanisms that made it function. Nothing extraordinary jumped out. With a pewter-like finish, it could have been stiff soldering wire. Yet somewhere at its tip was a miniature factory capable of producing diamond nanothreads and ejecting them like Spider-Man's wrist web shooter. Along its length was another nanomachine designed to release shapeable mist.

Halie shook her head. *The world of the very small forever baffles us.*

She held the wire vertically, then let go. If it dropped even a millimeter, she didn't spot it. The rectangle of mist appeared on cue, once more showing the 3-D relief image of a V-pod hovering above the platform steps surrounding the tether.

"It's not quite the same image projected at Level 3. Can you see the differences?" Adam asked.

Halie studied the mist. "It's not flashing on and off anymore."

"Right, but there something else behind the V-pod. Do you see it?"

She closed in on the floating image, trying not to breathe lest she disturb its delicate surface. "Faint, but I do see more lines... parallel to the foreground image... wait... it's another V-pod!"

Adam nodded vigorously. "I wasn't sure myself, but if you see the background pod, then that must be the message."

"It's telling us there's now a second V-pod?"

"It sure looks like it."

25. KILL THE BEAST

MARCO PACED, HIS ANGER RISING with each step. A column of parked cars straddled a monorail on one side of the rectangular station. On the other side were shelves packed with metal components, boxes of tubes and fasteners, gears, pulleys, and larger objects of unknown function. He pulled one box from the shelf, inspected its contents, then flung it across the room. Steel balls clattered across the floor. Alvarez, Hernandez, and Ruiz flinched, but remained silent.

"The builders are not just technologists but *alien* technologists!" Marco shouted. "They tempt us with their observation decks. So beautiful. So... *lucrative*. The landlords will trip over themselves trying to monetize their new view property. And now we arrive at Level 4"—he looked around the room with disdain—"and their ultimate purpose becomes clear. A ring encircling the world. More like a garrote around a neck."

The angry words fueled a growing temper—an internal rage that could be nurtured, shaped, to provide an advantage against opponents both on and off the pitch. It had always been part of his formula for success.

This time, Marco picked on Alvarez. Nose to nose, the trembling soldier tried to make himself small. Marco shouted at full volume, "From a position on their ring, they could kill at will. Imagine! Toxins pouring down, choking whole cities. Boulders the size of Pão de Açucar wreaking destruction. Lasers capable of pinpointing a single hair on your head or wiping out a whole battalion in one pass. When these agents of death complete their ring, our world will be defenseless."

"Yes, Marco," Alvarez squeaked.

Marco reached to the shelf and dragged out a thick metal rod about two meters long. He balanced the weight in his hand, tossing the rod back and forth between strong arms. He gripped it with both hands and swung. The heavy rod smashed a whole row of equipment off the shelf sending it flying across the room. Hernandez and Ruis ducked.

Marco swung again. And again. More parts flew around the room.

"Their plan of domination is aided by traitors within our ranks." The soldiers eyes went wide. They pressed against the wall as Marco swung above their heads. The rod swooshed through the air, missing only by an arm's length. "Sahalie Spark… and others."

Beads of sweat now covered Marco's forehead, giving him the same fierce look that regularly appeared on billboards—a look that terrified players from opposing teams.

Marco swung the rod again, ripping a dish antenna from the roof of one car and sending it clattering across the floor. "This woman takes her orders from the forces of scientific zealotry. She turns the American regulators and their liability prosecutors against me, and when her attack on my products fails, she allies herself with the alien forces behind this profane tower. She charms its monstrous creators with flattery, then claims there is no point in opposing them because their creation is indestructible. Self-repairing!"

Marco hefted the heavy steel bar over his head. With a single thrust, he jammed its point through the window of one car. Thick glass shattered with zigzagging fractures that radiated from the puncture. Bits of glass flew through the air, raining down like hail.

Marco backed away, leaving the car impaled by his spear. "Let their nanobots try to fix that." He returned to the nervous soldiers, looking each of them in the eye. "You see, the beast can be destroyed. And we shall."

A new plan quickly formed in Marco's mind. He spun around with the same flourish he'd use for an overhead bicycle kick and marched back toward the main airlock where their newly created ascender waited.

Alvarez hung close behind. He would need no convincing. But the other two soldiers were needed for the plan too, and they'd been hesitant ever since they'd left the platform. Neither had been informed of the plastic explosives hidden in Alvarez's jacket pockets. Four Semtex packets, not two, plus detonation cord. Enough to turn a military tank into granules of molten metal, according to Alvarez.

"We're going up? Higher still?" Hernandez asked. He lagged several steps behind Marco. "If we destroy it, won't it collapse?"

Of the two, Hernandez had been more nervous about their climb. He'd also complained about departing without telling their captain, a concern easily resolved once Marco offered to speak to each of their commanding officers personally upon return. Simple minds only required simple solutions.

Marco stopped at the open door to the ascender and turned to face Hernandez. His glare alone pushed the man a step backward. "Every man is a fighter. But some require reminders to stiffen their backbone. Do you?"

Hernandez shook. "No, Marco."

"Good. Then follow my orders. When this night is over, you will sleep like a man wrapped in his lover's arms." Marco let the image sink in, then stepped into the ascender.

"No, we shall not go down. Not yet. Have you noticed that Ms. Spark reported on every level except the fifth? She is surely there now, or perhaps even higher, yet she makes no mention of what she found."

Marco climbed the ascender's ladder. "We shall continue to Level 5. Before I kill this beast, I will look it in the eye."

26. MATH AND SCIENCE

ADAM ESTRADA, PROFESSOR of materials science, could recall and discuss any number of scientific papers on exotic materials found in the Earth's crust or created in laboratories. He'd even analyzed the crystalline structure of moon rocks. But he never guessed he'd be studying complex carbon allotropes from Venus.

Venus's surface was typically compared to a pottery kiln. No one expected to find life there. But higher in the planet's thick carbon dioxide atmosphere, temperatures eventually reached Goldilocks perfect. Were microorganisms floating around? Perhaps even airborne insects?

To find out, the Venus Life Finder mission had parachuted an automated lab into the clouds and sampled during its descent. The answer wasn't no, but it wasn't yes either. Instead, mission scientists reported *uncatalogued hydrocarbon chains*. Scientifically ambiguous, but Adam was beginning to understand why.

He had moved to the far side of the V-pod, his laptop connected to the internet via satellite phone. Halie was stretched out on the couch getting much needed rest. It was a long climb to geostationary height. Tired too, Adam knew that sleep would be impossible until a few basic questions were answered. Halie deserved to know. Mashup too. But somewhat selfishly, Adam sought the answers for himself.

Rest can come later.

Alien biology posing as an electromechanical structure formed the first question. What exactly was the filament?

"Life doesn't need oxygen," Adam whispered to himself. "Doesn't even need water, nature's nearly perfect solvent. But what life *does* require is molecular complexity."

At first glance, complexity hardly seemed a prerequisite for life. After all, many perfectly alive organisms on Earth were described as *primitive*. But drop to the molecular scale, and complexity became a key factor that divided the living from the nonliving.

Ordinary quartz (SiO_2), chalk ($CaCO_3$), and even bituminous coal ($C_{137}H_{97}O_9NS$) were found in crystalline and amorphous structures, but they weren't nearly complex enough to be alive. Organic compounds like methane (CH_4) and ethylene (C_2H_4) got a bit more interesting—they could form complex chains called polymers. Polyethylene ($C_2H_4)_n$, a polymer more commonly known as plastic, was a string of ethylene molecules arranged in different ways. Chemists estimated there were 400,000 variations of plastic, many with complex structures comparable to DNA. Yet none were alive.

From a chemistry point of view, life required one step more in complexity: *folding*. Biopolymers—complex molecules such as proteins, carbohydrates, and nucleic acids—differed from their nonliving counterparts by their ability to spontaneously fold into unique shapes beneficial to cellular biology. Hemoglobin was a prime example, a protein that took on specific folds allowing it to pull oxygen from the lungs and trade it for carbon dioxide extracted from living tissues. Biologists had concluded that structural folding was a significant ingredient for life, the difference between an inert polymer and a living biopolymer.

Flash forward to the VLF mission. It found polymers at Venus. Plenty of them. But mission specialists didn't notice—and couldn't have noticed without additional lab work done on Earth—the ability of those polymers to *fold*. Adam hadn't done the lab work either—not yet. But unlike the VLF mission, he had physical samples in his possession. And so far, they looked promising.

"Time to revisit our neighboring planet now that we know what to look for."

He sketched out a plan for how existing Venus orbiters and Earth-based telescopes might collect the needed data, avoiding an expensive sample return mission. Armed with physical samples of the filament, it would be a simple matter of matching observed data with sample data to a statistical significance.

Satisfied with his plan, the results would become an academic paper submitted to the journals. *Nature Nanotechnology* or *Science* would be best. He'd need a good title too. "Spontaneously Folding Allotropes of Carbon at the 300-Millibar Constant Pressure Surface in the Venusian Atmosphere," or some such scientific zinger.

Adam rubbed his tired eyes and quieted his rumbling stomach with a snack from one of the food packs Jaya had given Halie and Mash. Next up in his late-night analysis: where was the filament getting its supply of carbon? Adam felt sure this question would be simpler than how a carbon-based life-form managed to be alive without DNA. Less speculation, more math.

He started a spreadsheet and entered several fixed values for the tether: width, thickness, length. The same for the stations. An estimate of carbon density gave him the first result. Each space elevator could be reduced to about a million tons of carbon, or six million for six elevators.

Next, he looked up the available carbon in the Venusian atmosphere: 400 quadrillion tons. If the material to construct the space elevators came from Venus, the filament had borrowed a minuscule amount. Venus wouldn't notice.

He calculated a similar result for Earth. Removing six million tons from the more than twenty billion tons of carbon emitted from human activities every year wouldn't make a dent. The filament would need to build 3,300 tethers every year to consume the carbon humans dumped into the air.

"That can't be the reason it came," Adam muttered.

But one more thought occurred. He estimated the mass required to complete a transportation ring around the Earth at Level 4—something like 200 billion tons.

"Now we're talking."

The much larger number represented eleven years of carbon emissions. Extract that much carbon from Earth's atmosphere and the calculus for global warming changed significantly, implying a possible motive.

"Handy for us. But what does the filament want in return? And why no contact until now?"

Humans had been pouring carbon dioxide into the air for 150 years, and, according to Mash, the filament had visited multiple times over the past five centuries. When it came to timing, only one answer made sense: the Kessler Syndrome. Humanity had turned low Earth orbit into an unsurvivable Kill Zone. And, while the filament had a repair solution for its tethers, its nanobots would have little chance against larger chunks of debris. Even common lag bolts and steel rivets—which probably numbered in the hundreds of thousands—could hit with enough explosive energy to rip the tether apart, its two tattered ends separating faster than any nanobot could stitch.

Repairing small holes was only a stopgap measure. To continue its multi-century touchy-feely connection to the people of Earth, the filament would need more. "Consuming our excess carbon may be part of it, but it seems to have something else in mind."

The filament had kick-started its conversation with humans by copying human space elevator designs and deploying six of them around the world. Certainly, an in-your-face attention getter. Then it had handed out magic wires to key leaders as an invitation and a head start. Not to everyone. Selected people.

"It picked us. It wants us to climb. To reach Level 6 and discover… whatever is up there."

Adam closed his laptop and stared out to the darkness of space and the blur of the tether flashing by at more than a kilometer per second. They had explored five stations from a base platform to a sentient sphere inside an impossible cavern. But Level 6 had always been the finish line.

They'd be there soon.

27. LEVEL 6

HALIE AWOKE FROM a restless nap not quite sure if she'd slept at all. She glanced at her phone: 5:10 a.m. local Ecuador time, though by now they were nowhere near Ecuador. With each small movement, her body bounced lightly against the tie-down strap at her waist. She peered over the seatback.

Adam waved from the other side of the V-pod. "I'd join you, but the last time I stood up I launched myself to the ceiling. The calculation for apparent gravity is finally making itself known."

He let the mathematical comment hang, but Halie knew what he was talking about. Newton's equation for gravity wasn't enough for anything being slung around in a circle. Space elevator designers included a second term, centrifugal force, the tendency to fly off into space from angular momentum. Close to Earth, gravity dominated the battle. But as height increased, gravity dropped by the square of distance while centrifugal force *increased* linearly, finally winning. The opposing forces gave a calculation for *apparent* gravity, and they exactly balanced at a specific number forever tied to the planet Earth: 35,786 kilometers, geostationary orbit. Put a satellite at that precise height, and it stayed put, never straying from its position over one spot on Earth.

Halie glanced around the well-lit glass capsule. "It's not just gravity that has changed. It's the land of the all-night sun up here." The sun stood out bold and bright to one side of Earth, its glare masking surface features. "How high are we?"

"Thirty-three thousand kilometers," Adam answered. "Getting close. We picked up speed overnight, probably because of the lower gravity. This segment is turning out to be closer to five hours instead of eight."

Halie was thankful for the better-than-expected flight time. The sooner they arrived, the sooner they'd find out what the filament was hiding at Level 6. "Did you get any sleep?"

"Not much. Too many numbers running through my mind. No complaints. All the churning in my head keeps me young." He offered that roguish smile again.

Halie excused herself for a bathroom break. As Adam had noted, the microgravity at this height made ordinary movement clumsy. Each step sent her far too high to create any rhythm. Off-balance, she could easily tip over and sprawl across the floor, though a fall wouldn't hurt.

When she returned, Adam was experimenting with high hops, each one launching him to Olympic medal heights before drifting down to a feather-soft landing.

"Remember, we don't get warnings before deceleration," she told him. Halie strapped into the couch and checked her phone for the latest news from the surface. Two messages from Yoon, both interesting.

"Yoon confirms a second ascender," she told Adam. "He doesn't know where it came from but says Marco took control. Apparently, he's climbing the tether."

"Your reports are better than anything Marco will have to say."

"I'm surprised Marco is even willing to get near this *abomination of techno-idolatry*, or whatever he called it."

"Maybe he's coming around to your inspirational message to seek insight instead of fear. I know I have."

A soft grin opened the corner of Halie's mouth. She looked up to Adam, who was floating down from his latest hop. "That's kind of you to say." His unwavering support through events mysterious and tragic meant a lot. For a natural born daredevil, he could be surprisingly gentle. Calming even. "But don't hold your breath about Marco."

"Forget Marco. He's not worth your time."

Halie sighed. "You're right about that. Yoon also says that somebody discovered clouds in space. Not water clouds, and not space debris either. Particles, they think, pouring out of Venus and heading this way."

In mid-hop, Adam grabbed a couch strap, which only caused him to snap taut with an awkward rebound to the floor. "Cue the ominous music?"

"Yeah, really. You're the materials guy. Could this space cloud be carbon? Maybe the filament is calling for backup?"

Adam twisted his face. "Not sure. Sounds like another 'why are you here?' question. I guess we'll have to ask when we get to the top."

Without warning, the V-pod hit the brakes. Halie lurched upward, held down by the seat straps. Adam went inverted, feet to the ceiling. He clenched the strap like a mountain climber suddenly unsure which way was up.

"Caught!" he said with only a casual level of surprise. The deceleration was strong. He'd have to work hard to get out of his predicament.

"I did warn you," Halie said.

Adam let go and dropped to the ceiling. He stood, managing to stay upright—*upside-down* upright.

Halie craned her neck. "You okay up there?"

"Fine. From here on in, the ceiling is the floor. I may as well stay put."

Through the ladder's hole, Halie could see Mash's wrapped body pinned to the lower-level ceiling. They'd forgotten to tie it down.

"Thirty-five thousand kilometers," Adam announced. Over the next few minutes, the pull of the tie-down straps lessened, increasing the feeling of floating. Above, the sixth station loomed.

"It's not quite spherical, is it?" Halie said as they got closer. "More angular."

"It's a dodecahedron," Adam announced with confidence.

Halie recognized the geometric name, but not much more. "I have a strong suspicion you're going to tell me what that is."

"In the microscopic world, a dodecahedron is a C_{20} fullerene, an allotrope of carbon and the simplest of all fullerenes. It's formed by twelve pentagons connected together in a polyhedron or semispherical shape. Exactly twenty carbon atoms. Unlike the C_{60} fullerenes—buckyballs—the C_{20} is not likely to be found in nature. At the microscopic level, it's unstable."

"Condense, please," Halie requested.

"This station is also a twelve-sided dodecahedron. I have no idea why."

With the upward pull lessening, it was time to abandon the couch. Once deceleration ended they would be in zero-g anyway, and ceilings and floors would be meaningless. Halie released the tie-down straps and "fell" upward. Adam easily caught her just as her feet touched the ceiling.

She stood up, feeling oddly normal, as though the V-pod had turned upside down, not her. The Level 6 station was now beneath her feet and coming up fast. Both ribbons entered through an open pentagon about twenty meters across. The other pentagons were mirrored glass faces—or material that passed for glass.

The pod slid into the station and stopped at 35,786 kilometers, confirmed by Adam's visor.

No longer pressed to the ceiling, Halie pushed off and drifted to the ladder, feeling no ill effects from weightlessness. Perhaps she was getting used to the wide variations of gravity.

On the lower level, Mash's wrapped body floated near the open V-pod door. Adam quickly lashed the bundle to a lower shelf with some twine from his duffel bag. The duffel, camera bags, and their helmets floated too, but minor rearrangements wedged everything tightly enough between shelves to stay put.

Halie drifted to the door, keeping one hand on its edge while she surveyed the unusual surroundings.

A hall of mirrors?

Unlike previous stations, there was no cylindrical airlock. They had simply passed into the dodecahedron's interior. The single open pentagon had closed, sealing them from space and creating an interior large enough to accommodate both ribbons and the V-pod. Twelve mirrored glass pentagons surrounded them, each about twenty meters across and connected to five others at their edges. Every face was paired to an opposing side, which produced an infinity of reflections between them—a hall of mirrors. But with six pairs of mirrors, it was far more confusing than anything a carnival might create.

Even more disturbing, there was no exit. No open door leading to an observatory, monorail, or crystal cavern. Unless there was a Level 7 that wasn't on the control panel, it felt like a dead end. Useless as an observatory since there was no view outside and forever sealed from sunlight. Here, the V-pod's internal glow provided the only light source. Its reflection was everywhere.

Halie unzipped one of Mash's bags and searched until she found the simplest camera to operate—a sports camera, the type snowboarders and skydivers used. She strapped it around her bicep and switched it on. A push sent her drifting toward one pentagonal face, a mirror bigger than a living room wall.

"Funny how it was nothing but hexagons below, and now we've switched to pentagons." Her voice echoed in the enclosed space.

Her slow drift ended with a bump and two handprints left on the mirror. She drifted along its surface like a deep-sea diver who had finally reached the ocean floor.

"What do we do now?" Halie tapped the mirror with a fingertip, somewhat unsettled by the view of a thousand copies of herself disappearing into the distance, all doing the same thing.

"First things first," Adam said. He withdrew Yoon's wire from his jacket and held it up. Already comfortable with the weightlessness, Halie pushed off the mirror and sailed back to the V-pod's doorway.

She watched with anticipation as Adam hung the wire vertically on nothing but air. It did its thing, producing a rectangle of mist. This time, a pentagon button—not a hexagon—formed at the center.

"Consistency! I'll give it that."

"Your turn," Adam offered. Halie reached out and pressed the misty button. As before, it felt like nothing at all.

And nothing happened.

She pushed again, her hand passing straight through the mist.

Adam swiveled, searching in every direction. "I wasn't expecting another cavern, but the button has to do something. Otherwise, we're going nowhere."

"There!" One pentagon on the far side of the V-pod differed from the rest. A translucent fog now roiled in front of its mirrored surface.

She estimated a bank angle to maneuver around the V-pod, then pushed off toward a pentagon that might act as the pool table cushion with herself as the ball. As expected, a gentle bump against its glass deflected her straight to the fogged pentagon. Arriving, she stuck a hand through the fog and felt a sticky resistance.

"It's not glass!" she yelled back to Adam, who was right behind her in the weightless pool game. Halie pulled her hand free of the fog and stared in disbelief at a wrap of crisscrossing white fibers where fingers had been. She tried shaking the cocoon off, then scratched with the other hand to tear it apart. With effort, the fibers ripped, and she flung the shreds across the station.

Halie rubbed her fingers, searching for damage and happily finding smooth skin with no scarring or burns. Adam gently bumped against her, planting his feet on the neighboring pentagon. "You okay?"

"My hand feels fine, but something weird is going on. I never touched anything solid."

"Maybe this pentagon is now open?"

"Open to what?"

They'd seen the dodecahedron from the outside. If reality had anything to say about it, a foggy pentagon-shaped hole could only exit to cold, dark space, though Halie had to admit that ever since their deep dive into the cavern at Level 5, reality seemed to be sleeping on the job.

"Good point," Adam acknowledged. "We need a test." He pushed off and bounced his way back to the V-pod door. A minute later, he returned with both helmets and a tape measure. He handed one helmet to Halie. "Can't be too safe."

They each put on their helmet and zipped on gloves. Halie transferred the sports camera from her arm to the helmet.

Adam slowly extended the tape measure into the fog. One meter. Then two. It hit nothing. "It's definitely an open door." His voice now came over the helmet intercom.

When he reeled the tape in, it quickly stopped, clogged by the same fibrous wrap that had wound around Halie's hand. Adam removed one glove and dug a fingernail through the fibers. "Not frozen. Not even cold. The other side can't be space."

"Same as the cavern?" Halie wondered, even though she had no explanation for how the innards of a station could be vastly larger than its exterior shell.

"I do have a theory forming," Adam said.

"Please share."

"Not enough evidence yet."

"Come on, the tape measure test was successful. What else have you got up your sleeve?"

"Just this." He leaned into the fog face-first. His whole upper body disappeared.

Halie grabbed onto him and tried to pull him back, but getting leverage in zero-g was tough. She tugged at his pressure suit anyway.

Adam curled into a ball, a gymnastic move that extracted his head from the fog. A thick mesh of white fibers covered his helmet and extended down one shoulder. "Well, that was interesting!"

Scowling at him, Halie furiously scraped away the fibers covering his faceplate. "What is wrong with you? What if that stuff had pulled you in?"

The lunatic was smiling. "Best I could think of. Hey, it worked out. Nothing better than eyes to get a feel for weirdness."

"It's weird in there?"

He nodded vigorously. "Out-of-your-mind weird."

"Oh, joy." Halie sighed. "And now you're going to tell me we're going in there?"

"It's the only way forward, Halie. Don't worry, a helmet makes a big difference."

She grimaced. "Adam, you're amazing. Adventurous, talented, thoughtful, full of ideas. But I have to level with you... I'm not excited about letting an alien caterpillar turn me into a human chrysalis. Images of bad horror movies come to mind."

"We'll be fine."

"And you know this how?"

He shrugged. "I saw it. I think I even understand it... maybe."

Halie waited. He finally added, "I'd need to speak with colleagues in Peru, but this could be an entrance to a mathematical variant of spacetime. Extradimensional geometry, if that makes sense."

It made no sense at all. Halie's mind raced. Thoughts of Mash trapped in a sightless electronic jail weren't easy to dismiss, but diving headfirst into paranormal dimensions of alien spew? What if the fibers were toxic? Or tightened around her neck? She could come up with excuses, but somewhere deep in her gut was a counter argument that none of those excuses mattered. They'd come to Level 6 for answers no matter how weird. Turning around and slinking home didn't sit well.

She relented with a sigh. "I guess we're going in."

Halie adjusted her helmet cam and double-checked to make sure it was recording. She spoke to millions of people she'd never met, safe and secure in their homes and workplaces far below. "I'm floating in front of an entrance to a place beyond our world. Alice's looking glass, for lack of a better analogy."

Her audience would hear the words only upon her return. Or never. "We already know we're about to be wrapped in alien goo. An unpleasant thought… but there are compelling reasons to go in, not the least of which is we've made it to the top of the tether and there's nowhere else to go."

She crossed her fingers in front of the camera. "We came to explore. Wish us luck."

Adam forced a grin from behind his still-messy faceplate. "Together, on three."

He counted down. Halie reached into the fog. Sticky threads grabbed her arms and dragged her in. She disappeared beyond light into darkness, beyond the edge of functional reality and into a surreal landscape of endless geometry.

28. SENSE REFINED

THREADS STUCK TO HER ARMS, her shoulders, and head. A hundred thick webs wrapped her body, sticking, overlapping, squeezing—not with rib-crushing pressure, more like a bear hug from a large man. Halie freed one hand from the tangle long enough to wipe her helmet faceplate and, for a moment, had a clear view.

She was floating, perhaps falling, or perhaps pulled by a tangle of threads that coalesced into a single rope in front of her. Any ability to sense motion had vanished along with the three-dimensional reality she'd left behind. Ahead and all around, an absurdly complex grid of geometric shapes glowed against a dark background.

Neon blue lines defined the edges of hexagons, pentagons, and more. By the millions. Billions. Their complex shapes receded into the distance like layers of bricks fronting an enormous building. Yet nothing remained in place. The glowing lines shifted, the edges intersected, crossed, and became parallel once more. A sea of ever-changing polygons, like staring into a rotating kaleidoscope.

"What the…?" Halie started.

Adam grabbed her free hand as the tangled webbing pulled them deeper into a phantasmagoria. "Imagination is required to wrap your mind around extradimensional geometry."

Halie ducked as a polyhedron as big as a truck blew past, tumbling end over end. "The shapes may exist only in our minds," Adam offered with a noticeable reticence in his voice.

"That's your theory?"

He tugged her hand, pulling her closer in their acrobatic flight. Given the tangle of threads, separation wasn't an option, but staying as close as possible felt better. "More of a guess. Still building the theory. What do you know about tessellation?"

As a part-time professor, Adam tended to start his explanations with a question, probably to make it feel more like a conversation than a lecture. Halie was grateful for that, but with an insane mirage of geometry sliding by, she made no pretense. "Something to do with tiles, I think."

"Exactly right. Tessellation is when polygons fit together like tiles on a floor. No gaps or overlaps. A hexagon tessellates across a 2-D plane, creating a honeycomb. Every hexagon fits. Squares and equilateral triangles also tessellate in 2-D. But a circle doesn't."

"Got it." She ducked once more to avoid an iceberg of interconnected shapes crashing by. The white fibers continued to tug, dragging them deeper into this absurdity. On one level, the intricately repeating shapes were fascinating to watch, and Adam's narration gave a feel of intellectual exploration. But this wasn't a video game, and she wasn't sitting on a couch at home. She'd been sucked into an unknown place with no way to turn around. Reality seemed far away.

Don't panic. But be ready for anything.

Adam seemed unperturbed by the chaos all around. "A dodecahedron tessellates in 3-D space."

"Really?"

Halie panned her helmet cam across the complex grid of glowing lines and angles. She studied each brick in the structure, noticing uncountable pentagons connected in the same three-dimensional shape as the Level 6 mirrored station. But here, the shapes were stacked on top of each other. The complexity made it harder to distinguish individual units, but Adam seemed to be right. Most of the 3-D grid surrounding them was formed by a million dodecahedrons, with each pentagonal face shared by a neighbor. Soap bubbles piled together with a slot down the middle where they flew past.

She wondered—and feared—that the stack of blocks might continue without end. "Is your visor giving you any data?"

"Nothing. All zeros, in fact. Which, I suppose, is evidence that this place is imaginary."

Halie scraped off more of the sticky fibers from her faceplate and tossed them at Adam, where they stuck to his shoulder in crisscrossing white lines. "Seems real to me."

He nodded. "Me too. But here's the really weird part."

"Weirder than being dragged by alien dental floss through infinite geometry?"

"Well... your call. But there could be more here than we see. Hexagons tessellate in 2-D, but you can roll the 2-D sheet into a third dimension to make a tube. Strangely, you can do the same thing with a 3-D space filled by dodecahedrons. This place, for example. You could roll it up into a hypertube."

"A hypertube?"

"A geometry we can only imagine because it can't exist in three dimensions. Rolling up a 3-D grid of dodecahedrons requires a fourth spatial dimension. Not sensible in our physical world, but we may be tangled up in a higher-order geometry."

Whatever this place was, they were certainly tangled up. Halie secretly hoped it *was* all in her mind, otherwise they could be on a one-way trip. An empty feeling inside worried her. She'd felt it before, lost on a hike in mountains more rugged than she could handle and with nightfall coming quickly. She couldn't imagine retracing their route to the Level 6 station or even a mechanism for accomplishing it.

She gripped Adam's hand tighter, doing her best to squelch the rising fear. He returned the simple gesture. Wherever they were heading, at least they'd do it together.

A jerk on the towline pulled from a new direction. Halie slammed into Adam, verifying that inertia existed and diminishing the notion that their journey was imaginary.

The view ahead changed radically but in ways hard to comprehend. Her gloved hand grew larger. Closer. At the same time, the infinite grid grew wider. It felt like zooming in and zooming out at the same time, altering scales both up close and far away.

Glowing lines were replaced by sparkling colors, red, blue, yellow, and violet—everywhere, all at once. Textures in the foreground became grainy, with gaps between individual threads.

Halie felt dizzy, confused by the ever-changing geometry now layered with lighting effects both mystifying and beautiful. A deeply resonant voice—certainly not her own and not Adam's either—echoed inside her head.

The words were clear even if their meaning was not:

.sense refined.

.expose spatial cognition.

.await human comprehension.

.alternative psychic crisis.

.sense complete.

Adrenaline spiked. Halie tugged on Adam's hand to be sure he was still there. "Did you hear that?"

Her heart galloped. Colors flashed everywhere. A million polished facets on the finest diamond rotating under a brilliant light could not duplicate the instantaneous spikes of red, orange, yellow, green, and violet. Light itself had fractured, and colors poured out.

Adam answered in a steady voice. "Something about awaiting human comprehension?"

The voice was an intrusion, but more than that—it had felt disembodied. "I'm glad I didn't imagine it."

"Doesn't mean I understood it," he said.

"That's two of us. But the voice must have come from the filament, right? For some reason, I get the feeling these shapes might be part of it, but maybe I'm just remembering your microscope images."

Adam squeezed her hand again. She waited. He finally responded. "Sorry. Getting dizzy."

"Me too. This higher geometry thing has got my bearings twisted around. I can't tell up from down. Worse... I can't tell near from far."

He didn't answer. Halie didn't blame him. Everything around them continued to contradict any rational sense of awareness. Up close, her perception narrowed, focusing on ever-smaller details. Further away, it widened, allowing her to soak in ever-larger expanses. Small and big had almost lost their meanings.

She tried again to parse the words within this bizarre visual context. "Did it say *spatial cognition*?"

No answer from Adam. She was probably depending too much on him anyway. An advanced degree in materials science didn't mean he had the answer to everything. No scientist could claim that. In fact, she might be better qualified in this case. Just last year, she'd researched a show topic on *spatial cognition*, or awareness of scale—essentially, the brain's ability to compare large and small. Kilometers versus micrometers. Some species were better at it than others, and one biologist had claimed that humans had a larger range of spatial cognition than any other species—roughly ten orders of magnitude, from a spider's silk to a mountain range in the distance. Anything smaller couldn't be resolved by our retinas. Anything larger was too hard to internalize without intellectual aids like maps. An ant could identify smaller things, and a dolphin could comprehend larger distances with echolocation. But neither had the range humans did.

Halie held up her gloved hand, a perfect representation of the narrowing close-up view. Her hand hadn't grown, but her ability to distinguish individual fibers in the glove, the sticky web strands wrapped around it, and the tiny gaps between adjacent strands made her feel as though she had magnifying lenses strapped over her eyes.

Glancing up shifted to a faraway view, equally detailed. The grid of sparkling multicolored lights stretched to infinity—and Halie felt like she could see nearly that far.

"Better than binoculars," Halie said. "This is like… superpower weird." Halie struggled to make sense of her newfound abilities. *Await human comprehension*, the voice had said. "The filament must be doing this. But to us? Or for us?"

Adam didn't answer, but another idea occurred to Halie. "It's challenging us. We have to figure out what's going on or go crazy trying. Something like that. What if these are scales the filament can comprehend? It has no eyes, but its sense of touch might be off the charts. And its distributed brain could make distance irrelevant."

Halie squeezed her free hand to get Adam's attention but felt nothing.

"Adam?"

Fibers around her faceplate blocked her peripheral view. She craned her neck. He wasn't there.

"Adam!" Halie screamed. Somehow she'd lost him. She twisted every way the web bindings allowed but couldn't locate him. "Do you hear me? Where did you go?"

No answer came over the helmet intercom. He'd fallen off the fibrous rope—or thrown off. A shiver started from her legs, rising through her nervous system until it consumed her body. Nightmares started this way, and reality wasn't any kinder. People died getting lost.

Halie struggled against the fibers but couldn't free herself from their pull. Adam had been equally bound, strong evidence that something intentional had happened to tear him away.

Please be safe.

Halie's heart beat furiously as the view ahead morphed once more. Flashing colors disappeared like clouds parting after a rain to reveal a dark nighttime sky with a million stars as a background. In the foreground were two crescents, one blue, one gray.

Earth and Venus?

She wasn't moving anymore, or at least she had no sense of falling and felt no further tugs from the fibers that still covered her suit. She squinted. It felt like trying to refocus after looking up from a needlepoint stitching to a grand view.

Both planets were equally detailed, as if Halie's viewpoint had somehow repositioned midway between them with a powerful telescope trained on each. Six thin filaments radiated like barely visible spokes from Earth's equator, turned north and joined together far above the pole. The combined superfilament disappeared into the star field.

Venus showed the same symmetry of six filaments, joining above its north pole and angling onward to the stars. Each thread appeared as clear and sharp as if she'd been floating beside it, yet she could simultaneously comprehend the large distance between the planets.

Halie exhaled sharply, scared that she'd lost Adam and equally frightened of the impossible view: two planets separated by a large distance but intricately detailed. She could make out Australia clearly, even the island of Tasmania to its south. On Venus, masses of white, tan, and orange clouds were stretched into bands and swirls by unseen winds. Yet the thinnest of lines—filaments probably no more than a few meters across—were within her grasp.

Twenty orders of magnitude, at least! How is this possible?

She gazed upward to a complex junction where the thread from Earth mingled with the thread from Venus. A single interplanetary filament continued higher into the brilliant band of the Milky Way stretching overhead, achingly far away.

But, no… it's not far away at all.

Through her stare, the galaxy itself felt oddly within reach. She might be imagining it, but her body seemed to rise, leaving the solar system behind. Fibers were no longer pulling her; she simply drifted alongside the combined thread deeper into space. Uncountable stars across the sky remained fixed in their positions, but each point of light seemed to glow brighter as she rose.

The filament approached closer. It thinned—assuming her super-vision wasn't lying. Within a minute, only a wisp of its former thickness remained. Perhaps it would disappear altogether leaving her drifting, truly alone, toward a cold death.

But am I really in space? She couldn't be sure. Adam had suggested this might be a simulated reality, pumped into her mind no differently than the voice. She worried for Adam. She worried for herself.

Ahead, a microscopic pinprick of light lined up with the filament's narrowing thread. The microdot grew closer, resolving into a circle—more accurately, the tip of a tiny cylinder. What remained of the filament slipped through the microcylinder.

Somehow, Halie slipped through with it.

The stars disappeared, and she found herself in a tunnel. Its microscopic dimension didn't seem to matter, as if the gods of space weren't concerned that a full-sized human had entered a tube smaller than a needle.

Help!

She felt like screaming, but in deep space there could be no aid. Only the filament's wisp of a thread remained by her side. It would take her where it wished. She clearly wasn't in charge.

The improbably narrow tunnel ended within a photon's stride of where it had started. The filament—and Halie—popped back out into space.

Brilliant points of light by the millions now surrounded her— stars colored from white to blue, each a blazing-hot furnace. But their combined radiance was overwhelmed by one furiously burning sphere directly ahead. Tongues of red flame leapt from the surface of a gargantuan star.

She guessed the star's name, or maybe she knew. On this crazy voyage where size and distance didn't matter and voices could appear at will, who could be sure?

"It's Antares," Halie whispered to herself.

29. SENSE BEYOND

HALIE DRIFTED ALONE ACROSS deep space far from home, staring at a blazing titan that filled most of the sky. Her intuition was on overdrive. Where the insight came from, she wasn't sure.

This was Antares, one of the largest stars in Earth's night sky. She'd known about it as a child peering through her father's telescope. The *heart of the scorpion*, he called it, a blood-red star in the constellation Scorpio.

Unlike most stars, this giant was rapidly fusing carbon into oxygen. Other elements—magnesium, silicon, and iron—would soon follow. The predetermined nuclear sequence guaranteed the star would continue to shine only for another thousand years, maybe less. Antares was in its death throes.

Why the filament had taken her here wasn't clear. Why she knew it must be Antares was equally vague. She might be wrong, but she didn't think so.

Not far away, the filament's narrow thread weaved a curving path across black space. It didn't speak. The only sound inside Halie's helmet was from her own heartbeat. She begged for a response, but nothing came.

She continued drifting, away from the enormous star and toward another pinprick. A new microscopic tunnel pulled her inside and sent her across distances that seemed not to matter. She popped out the other side into a much darker place.

In every direction, a dense cloud of hot dust glowed in dim, pulsating reds and browns like the blast zone of a volcano recently quiet after a devastating eruption.

This time, her intuition failed to come up with a name, as if the name itself had been erased in an explosion of unimaginable scale. The remnants were turbulent clouds that roiled with the lingering heat of freshly congealed lava. Something terrible had happened here.

Halie caught a glimpse of the filament snaking its way through the thickest part of the scorching clouds. The thread connected to a spherical globe, the only structure within this chaos of dust and pebbles. Its size was impossible to judge, but facets across its surface and hints of purple crystals within gave it the same look as the station at Level 5.

It's another prominence.

Halie shouted aloud to the node in this creature's distributed brain. "Speak to me! Why have you taken me here?"

Being so close to a prominence, surely she would be heard. Since prominences were interconnected, Mash might even hear. Deep space was starting to feel oppressively lonely.

A faint buzz trembled the air in her helmet, and the deep voice returned.

.sense beyond.

.response to key questions.

.Antares will end as Betelgeuse did.

.as Baade's pulsar before it.

.sense complete.

Halie froze, listening carefully and doing her best to analyze as quickly as the words came. They wouldn't repeat. None of the others had.

Antares. Betelgeuse. Baade's pulsar. Named stars, the first two being red supergiants, she knew that much. She wasn't sure about the third, but it was good to hear she'd been right about Antares.

Everyone knew Betelgeuse, another bright red star relatively close to Earth, though in an entirely different direction than Antares.

Betelgeuse stood at the shoulder of Orion the hunter, its color contrasting with the brilliant blue of Rigel at Orion's foot.

Antares and Betelgeuse had one other thing in common: each star was close to a death by supernova. Astronomers had betting pools on which one would go first.

But the filament had said that Antares would end as Betelgeuse *did*. Not as Betelgeuse *would*. Could this zone of destruction be the remnants of Betelgeuse? Had it already exploded in a supernova?

The scenario was entirely possible. The blinding flash from any supernova could only spread at the speed of light. For all anyone knew, the flash from a Betelgeuse supernova was, right now, speeding its way across the vast distance to Earth.

How far away is Betelgeuse? The answer quickly popped into her head: 556 light-years, astronomy's latest estimate. She'd probably read it somewhere and forgotten until now. Either that or her intuition had become tied to the filament.

Halie shivered as another seemingly random number came to mind: 1542. According to Mash's crazy talk, that was the year an Inca warrior named Quiso was killed by Spanish invaders and his consciousness was extracted and stored by the filament.

Nearly five hundred years ago. The numbers were too close to be a coincidence.

"Could that be it?" Halie whispered, perhaps to herself, perhaps to the filament. "Did you know about the Betelgeuse supernova before coming to Earth?"

No answer came, leaving Halie to piece it together herself in a one-way conversation. "A supernova spews out a *lot* of carbon. Stuff you seem to consume by the megaton. A good source of material for you. Maybe you noticed the flash in the sky. Reacted to it. Pursued the carbon you knew it had produced. I can assure you, when light from this supernova reaches Earth, it will get *our* attention."

No response came, but Halie's nervousness calmed as she spoke. Logical thinking helped to assuage the fact that she'd been flung hundreds of light-years from home. "Is that how you discovered us?

Was it Betelgeuse blowing up that brought you to our neighborhood? You're clearly not from Venus, and maybe not from Betelgeuse either. How far have you come?"

She waited, but instead of an answer, the filament's thread dove into another nanotunnel, dragging Halie with it. The wreckage of Betelgeuse disappeared in a wink. Halie's nervousness returned, along with a frustration that she might never get the answers she wanted.

This wormhole was longer than the first two, with twists that jostled her left and right, once again making an impossible journey feel physically real. After several more tunnel twists, she popped into space amidst an entirely new scene of wonder.

Now a vast tangle of glowing gases—green, pink, orange, and yellow—were interlaced by fingers of darker dust that seemed to extend forever. It was another explosion of matter, but this one was far more organized and intensely colored.

It's a nebula. A stellar nursery.

She'd seen the deep-space photographs of towering dust columns mixed with vast draperies of color, taken by the world's most powerful telescopes. Now she'd been thrown into the middle of one. For a moment, Halie's unease was replaced by awe. The majesty of a single finger of glowing dust dwarfed any landscape she'd ever seen. And here, there were hundreds of these colossal structures angling in various directions, each blushing in their unique color.

Here too, a thin glint of light gave away the presence of the filament, but not just one, many. In every direction, glistening segments scattered like phosphorescent twigs in a forest. This nebula was swarming with filaments.

Halie absorbed the remarkable scene accompanied only by the sound of her own breathing, strong and rapid. Her lips began to tremble. She forced out tentative words. "Is this your home?"

Whether the individual segments were clones, family, or simply fragments detached from the whole, she gazed out across a collection of alien life few on Earth had imagined to exist. Alien life with no planet, no surface, no atmosphere, existing within the vacuum of space yet interconnected across vast distances. She had no idea how far away the last tunnel had taken her, but based on the time spent inside, she might be thousands of light-years from Earth—a home she was increasingly worried she'd never see again.

As she watched, the nearest filament segment coiled into multiple loops, creating a cylinder with both ends pinched to a point. The sticky twine binding her arm and shoulder tugged once more, then dissolved into a fine mist that drifted away. The newly created cylinder yawned open, and Halie fell inside.

She tumbled against curving walls, sliding to a stop at the far end. The cylinder's interior was as large as an oil tank car on a train and had to be rotating because gravity had returned.

Halie stood up, estimating half a g. Not hard to do, given so much recent experience with lower gravities. Overhead, a tightly curving ceiling was only a few meters away. With one hand on the curving wall, she took a few steps, feeling the resistance of air around her and suddenly worried she'd been trapped in a cage only to become a member of the filament's zoo.

"Can you hear me?" she asked, glancing around to curving gray walls that didn't answer.

"You're near, I know you are."

She took a few more tentative steps, then rapped a hand on the slightly reflective surface. It felt like metal, but she'd seen it spun from coils of the filament itself. Carbon, woven in various patterns at the atomic level, could assume almost any form.

A buzz filled the air, easily heard even through her helmet. A sizzling-hot line shot out from one end of the cylinder, heading toward the other. Halie jumped back as the laser bolt zipped past her head. It connected to the cylinder's far end, bisecting its length like a glowing string stretched taut inside a water bottle.

The wire sizzled and popped with energy, radiating in the deep reds and oranges of fire, mere centimeters from her helmet's faceplate. She felt the irrational urge to touch it.

It must be electric, she told the rational side of her brain. But an impulsive craving decreed otherwise. *Touch it*, the urge commanded. *Grasp it with your bare hand.*

Halie raised a shaking hand, wondering what could have possessed her but mesmerized by the sparking wire, so close and so dangerous. She unzipped the glove attached to her pressure suit, quite certain there was air around her, not vacuum.

Sparks can't exist in a vacuum. Perfectly rational, but sparks from a campfire were also red-hot.

With her heart pounding in her chest, Halie reached out barehanded. The wire was no thicker than a pencil. She encircled it, struggling to keep her jittery fingers from accidentally touching it. This act of faith would be done purposefully or not at all.

Things aren't what they seem, she rationalized. *Just do it.*

Halie closed her eyes and squeezed the sizzling wire, anticipating instant pain from charred skin or the electric arc that would stop her heart. She thought of Mash.

Death didn't come, nor pain. Instead, a vibration trembled through her hand and up her arm. It tickled as it crept up her neck and into her head. It formed words not seen or heard, but in a rigid structure that Halie was beginning to understand as the filament's delivery packaging.

.sense beyond.

.close your eyes and ears.

.feel the vibrations in your mind.

.now it is time to learn.

.sense complete.

Please, I'm not a computer!

Plugging into an electrical data line wasn't her idea of a good conversation. She could release the wire, and part of her wanted to.

But deep inside were very human receptors quietly anxious to find out what the filament had to say.

I've come this far...

Halie held tight. The vibration swelled. Individual thoughts and full concepts poured into her.

Light spectra. Frequencies. Wave counts. Electrons. Emission. Absorption.

Like drinking from a fire hose, the torrent of information continued unabated as Halie struggled to comprehend it all.

Supernovae. Atoms. Molecules. Allotropes. Filaments. Wormholes. Tessellation. Hyperbolic geometry.

Places and dates surged through her mind, each moving backwards along a logical path through time.

Earth 1542. Venus 1538. Antares 1530. Betelgeuse 1496. Baade's pulsar 1064.

And finally, a lesson in organic chemistry and its relationship to life.

Filament allotrope. Carbon. Earth life. Carbon. Humans. Carbon. Human allotrope. Carbon.

The vibrations eased. Halie opened her eyes and tried to calm the shakes in her arms and legs. The torrent of information was over, but a final step was required, and she knew exactly what to do.

Halie clenched tighter to the wire and twisted. A segment broke off in her hand, and the rest of the wire melted back into the cylinder.

She held the segment up. About ten centimeters long, the breaks at either end were clean. With no more sparks or sizzles, anyone could be excused for underestimating its power. It was a plain silver wire, but Halie had been given a glimpse into its value. She wouldn't need to memorize the fire hose of information; she held it in her hand.

I understand. I know what to do.

"Sense beyond," Halie whispered in a scratchy voice—still nervous, but for the first time feeling the answers she'd been searching for were falling into place.

A voice that was not a voice replied to her prompt.

.sense beyond.

.prepare yourself to teach.

.use information and its evidence.

.humans trust humans.

.sense complete.

Halie shivered at the personal intrusion, but she'd gotten what she came for—direct communication. "You want me to teach. You've shown me a lot, but I'm not sure I comprehend it all. Maybe, over time, I will." If ever she needed a scientific expert like Adam, it was now.

Halie held up the wire. If she released it, it would remain in place. Of that, she was certain. "You've given me evidence too. That's good. Really good. No one would believe me without evidence, nor should they. But you're mistaken about that last part. Humans *don't* trust humans. I don't think they ever have. Even with evidence, being a teacher is hard. And now you want me to explain your *human allotrope*?"

Bizarre thoughts filled her head. A ring around the Earth would one day be constructed, connecting each of the six space elevators at Level 4. When complete, it would be inhabited by a new kind of human with a body made from complex carbon nanostructures. The result would be a human allotrope, no different than a graphene sheet or a fullerene sphere.

For each incarnation of the allotrope, a human mind would be inserted. People whose bodies had died would live again. If she chose to, Mash would be one of them. The new insight was fantastical, inspiring even. But Halie wasn't sure her human *students* were ready to hear about it.

"I'll need to learn more about the ring before trying to explain it to the world. I understand what you're planning, but even if your intent is benevolent, honestly... breathing new life into dead people could be a bridge too far."

She waited. The filament's silence made her feel uncomfortably alone and a long way from home. *This thing isn't like us*, Mash had said. It was a hard lesson to remember. Halie resolved to remain patient.

The sound, or feeling, or whatever essence of the filament was able to communicate, finally returned.

.sense beyond.

.the fourth ring is reserved.

.allotropes of human consciousness.

.who connect to the beyond.

.sense complete.

She hadn't quite understood before, but now the full picture was clarified. The filament wasn't just planning to resurrect dead humans and place their preserved consciousness into a new body formed from complex carbon nanostructures. These new inhabitants of the Level 4 ring would come with superpowers endowed by the filament.

The new humans will connect to the beyond.

30. TEACHER

HALIE PLUNGED THROUGH a misty barrier and careened into Adam, transferring her momentum and flinging them both across the mirrored dodecahedron station. They twisted together, grabbing for anything that might end their weightless collision. Adam smashed against the V-pod, and Halie grabbed his arm, instantly flipped upside down. The two tangled bodies finally came to an awkward stop when Adam planted his feet against a mirrored pentagon and Halie crushed against him.

Halie gasped, trying to regain her breath. She had no idea how she'd gotten back but was thankful to be in familiar territory with her arms wrapped around the man who had gone missing hours ago.

"I lost you!" she screamed through the helmet intercom. His faceplate was still partly covered with sticky white threads.

He reached out and pulled her close in a tight embrace. "I thought I'd lost you! I got dizzy and noticed the fibers had disconnected. Then something tossed me back here. I was trying to decide if I should go back in, when bam… you came flying through the hole."

Never happier to see anyone, Halie scraped the webs from his helmet, then pushed her faceplate against his, hugging him hard. "Adam, you're a scientist, so this is going to sound crazy, but the filament took me on a journey across the galaxy." He didn't flinch, so she kept going. "Via microscopic wormholes, apparently. Don't ask me how. I saw the star Antares—up close! I floated through the remains of a Betelgeuse supernova." She barely caught her breath. "I swear, it's true. It ended at a stunningly beautiful nebula where the filament spoke to me—no… more than spoke. It *taught* me."

Halie pulled the stiff wire from a pocket on her pressure suit. "There's stuff in here you won't believe."

Adam took the new wire from her and rolled it in his gloved hand. "I won't believe it?"

"Well, actually, you will. There's evidence stored on that thing, and for some of it I'm going to need your help."

He seemed to be weighing his options for exactly how to break it to her that she'd gone crazy. Instead, he handed the wire back and said, "If you've somehow been on a trip across the galaxy in the three minutes that I've been waiting for you, then it's not just me. You need to tell the whole world."

Helmets stored and sticky white threads mostly peeled away from their pressure suits, Halie and Adam spread out on the circular couch as the V-pod plunged downward from Level 6. They'd be in transit for several hours, giving them time to prepare for another broadcast.

Adam volunteered to fill in as camera operator, and Halie connected him via video conferencing to KNS tech support for a crash course in pressing the right buttons at the right time. Some of Mash's equipment was complex, but Adam would manage. He'd have to.

The live broadcast without Mash would feel surreal. Like walking on stage wearing pajamas. Afterwards, they would stop at Level 5, return to the alien cavern, and reengage with what remained of Mash—her consciousness, her spirit. Whatever it was. Halie would tell her about the strange trip into extradimensional geometries and galactic nebulae. Mash wouldn't be surprised, but she'd be anxious to hear what Halie had learned. The details about a human allotrope and a ring at Level 4 might require more thought before springing it on someone unprepared.

With Adam trained in camera operation, he joined Halie as she tested the newest magic wire. As expected, it hovered in the air without falling and displayed a fascinating graph of what scientists called an emissions spectrum. Adam took on the task of examining the spectrum in detail. He even offered to speak about it as a materials expert, once Halie was on air.

But before the camera started rolling, Halie needed to figure out *where* she'd been. Antares and Betelgeuse were already checked off, but the nebula seemed much further away. She had a hunch that pinpointing its location would be a key to understanding the filament's origin and explaining it to the world. The nebula's fingers of dust and colored gas felt familiar, but she'd need to comb through astronomy images to see if her hunch paid off.

Thirty minutes later, with Earth getting larger below, Halie had her answers. She checked the time: 8:20 a.m. in New York. Still predawn in LA but midday in Europe. Workable for an international broadcast. She dialed Paul's number. He might be fast asleep, but a call from her phone number would ring through to him day or night.

"Where are you? Are you okay?" Paul practically yelled into the phone. Not asleep. At least, not anymore.

"I'm fine, Paul. We're on our way down with lots to tell. Get me on the air. I know it's early, but it's always early somewhere. This needs to go global."

"We're way ahead of you. I'm in the control room right now with a room full of people who spent the night here dissecting and replaying everything you've sent so far. KNS has become the tip of the spear—the distribution point to the world. Literally everyone is waiting on your next report."

"Good, because I'm about to blow the doors off this story."

"Music to my ears. Tee me up."

Halie took a deep breath. "Level 6 isn't a station, Paul. It's a passageway to the filament's home nebula which is thousands of light-years away. It took me there—quite literally—and it taught me… everything."

The phone went silent.

"Paul?"

"Stand by. I'm going to get you connected ASAP. Wide distribution."

When Paul said ASAP, he meant it. Halie scrambled to mike up and help Adam with Mash's camera harness. He hoisted the shoulder cam and gave Halie the same thumbs-up he'd seen Mash do. Buttons pressed and a connection made, Halie heard the voice of a news director in New York.

Nothing like being tossed onto stage without a warmup.

Nerves were a natural part of any live broadcast, but this time it felt bigger. She had a sensational story to tell but couldn't claim to have all the answers. Were satisfactory answers even possible given the variation among the nine billion citizens of the world?

The news director counted down in her earphone. In a hundred ways, on-air personalities across the US and on partner networks in dozens of countries in Europe, Asia, and around the world pulled the plug on their regularly scheduled programs to hand the microphone to Halie.

"We're breaking away from…"

"We're interrupting to bring you…"

"I'm told we now have…"

Another voice came in her ear. Benjamin Teller, the KNS morning show anchor. "Sahalie Spark is joining us again with breaking news from the South American space elevator. Where exactly are you, Sahalie? We've heard you are the first to reach the top?"

"Good morning, Ben. I'm descending from Level 6, which is the highest station. And now that I've seen the whole thing, I can tell you that we're dealing with something far bigger than a space elevator with six levels. This structure wasn't *built* by aliens, it *is* the alien."

Halie described most of what she'd learned about the filament, its arrival at Venus and Earth five centuries before, and its ability to form long threads or rigid structures.

Ben interrupted. "So, let me get this straight. The six space elevators are all one thing? And they're alive?"

"They're alive in a different way than we are. And, yes, once you get high enough above the north pole, you see that all six tethers join together. Let me show you." She pointed to Adam.

Adam clicked a button on the uplink module, as tech support had shown him. The sports cam's video would now be streaming to the world, starting at the view she'd witnessed from far above Earth.

"The combined thread eventually disappears into what I'm guessing is a microscopic wormhole. But the filament doesn't stop there. It showed me where it came from, and now I'm going to show you."

Halie pulled the wire from her vest pocket and held it up in front of her face where the camera would pick it up. "Watch this." She let go. "We're not in zero-g. Even in a space elevator, things fall, but this wire is held up by microfilaments that stitch together on the fly."

The wire spread horizontally as expected and displayed a jagged graph that Halie had already seen, and Adam had analyzed. Twenty-six peaks. They'd counted them.

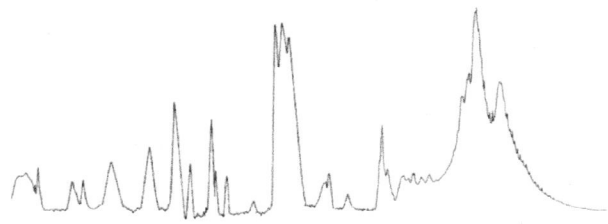

"It's a spectral signature," she explained to any number of millions of people watching, including scientists, she hoped. "It's produced when electrons bound to a molecule change their energy level either by absorbing light or by emitting heat, like when hot metal cools. Different molecules produce different patterns, very much like human signatures. I can't tell you much more about this particular pattern, but luckily I'm with Dr. Adam Estrada, and he's spent some time analyzing it."

She reached out for the camera, and they swapped positions. Halie peered through the camera viewfinder as it autofocused on Adam's somewhat anxious face.

"Uh... hi folks. I'm Adam Estrada."

You've got this, Adam. Just tell them what you learned.

He did. He talked about Raman scattering, electron emissions by wavelength, and how he'd matched the peaks of this spectrum against a collagen molecule, commonly found in humans. His bottom line: these peaks and valleys represented the filament itself. Find this pattern in space using a spectrometer, and you've found the filament. The closest place to look was Venus.

"NASA and ESA, check your Venus Life Finder data again," he said. "Now that you know what to look for, I have a strong feeling you'll see this pattern. As Halie... sorry, Sahalie said, the filament has been at Venus for a while."

With his minor stumble, Adam seemed ready to call it good. Halie handed the camera back to him and resumed her role as spokesperson.

"Thanks, Adam. But we're not done with spectroscopy just yet. Any astronomers out there? Point your telescope at this." She lifted her phone, already showing an astronomy picture she'd found on the internet. "Even non astronomers might recognize this place. It's the Crab Nebula. It's 6,500 light-years away, and in the year 1054 a spectacular supernova occurred here. For several months, it was the brightest light in the sky, documented by Chinese astronomers of the time. The explosion produced dust, gas, and a *lot* of carbon. Today, the remnant of the star is called Baade's pulsar. And guess what—I was just there. I am not kidding."

She pointed to Adam, who started the playback of another clip from Halie's helmet cam. With far more light available, the quality was better. As Halie took in the fantastic scene, the camera captured the towering columns of dust, splashes of orange and green, and one rapidly blinking light.

"That's the pulsar, a neutron star collapsed to only twenty kilometers in diameter. Just like an ice skater pulling in her arms, when a star collapses, it rotates faster. This one is turning at exactly 30.3 times per second. Don't believe me? Look up Baade's pulsar online, then time the pulses in this video. I had to do it to prove to myself I was really there."

Halie pointed to the jagged peaks still hovering in the air. "Astronomers, analyze the Crab Nebula debris field. I'm betting you'll find the filament's spectral signature. This is what scientists call *hard evidence*. No need to take my word. Anyone with the right equipment and knowledge can verify for themselves."

Ben interrupted. "I have a feeling astronomers are getting busy right now."

Halie gave a nod. "I hope they do. Now, I'm going to give one more bit of hard evidence that won't require any special equipment, not even a phone. Simply look up in the sky. There's one catch, though—you'll have to wait a few years. A new supernova is coming. Betelgeuse, the brilliant red star in the constellation of Orion, doesn't exist anymore. From what I've learned, in 1486— about the time Columbus was getting funding from Ferdinand and Isabella to cross the Atlantic—Betelgeuse blew up. But since that star is 556 light-years away, the light from the explosion has been in transit ever since. That light is due to arrive in 2042, by my estimate. Soon, we'll look up and watch as Betelgeuse becomes brighter than the full moon. A few months later, it will be gone forever."

Halie let her astronomical prediction hang. Ben asked several questions and Halie answered as best she could, but she was already thinking about the next topic. The biggest topic. A new kind of human that would soon populate a ring to be built at Level 4. That reveal would blow a few minds.

It's not the right time.

Halie needed to speak to Mash first. Adam too. She'd call Paul and brief him on the details before she attempted a story requiring finesse to deliver. Humanity already struggled with differences in race, gender, and sexual preference. Acceptance of a new type of human with advanced powers to *sense the beyond* would be a struggle.

For now, she decided on a different signoff. "Here's the thing, Ben. The filament isn't going to hang around forever. It roams. It has for hundreds of years—maybe longer. It seems curious about us, and maybe it will stay here long enough to teach us how micro wormholes work or help us clean up the Kill Zone. But after that, it *will* leave, and we'll be on our own."

"Astonishing," Ben replied. "You're describing an inflection point for humanity."

"No question. It's a future none of us expected. How we deal with it is up to us. But here's what I'd tell everyone who's willing to listen. The filament isn't our enemy. It's not waging war against us. Yes, it has an agenda, but it's one that might benefit us in the long run if we're willing to try new ways of thinking. I know it's a lot to unpack. It will take a collective effort from all of us, and we may never be the same again. But let me pose a question to everyone. Once you learn the world is more complex than you thought, are you willing to pull the covers over your eyes and go back to sleep?"

Halie pointed a finger to the camera. "Understand it or fear it. Those are the options. I hope we're not a fearful people."

Hour by hour, the blue-and-white globe beneath grew larger. The line between night and day advanced westward, sweeping sunrise across North America and out into the Pacific. While they descended, Halie disclosed what she knew about the Level 4 ring and human allotropes to Adam. He took it in stride and agreed that a conversation with Mash at the Level 5 prominence would be a good idea. They'd be there soon.

They ate the remaining food Jaya had prepared for them, leaving a half bottle of water to finish their descent. The comfort of Yoon's jet would be welcome after a long night—now stretching into the next day.

The descent to Level 5 finally ended a few minutes past noon, local time. The V-pod slowed into the station and stopped. Airlock floor and ceiling slipped into place and the lower deck door hissed open.

Back in reasonable gravity, Adam stored equipment on the lower deck shelves and followed Halie into the airlock. He'd completed his one-time assignment as Halie's camera operator, and neither of them felt a need to record the crystal cavern again. For this excursion, a single flashlight would be enough.

Halie stepped through the open airlock doorway to the yawning cavern that led into an underworld as creepy as any nighttime graveyard. She felt its darkness even more than their earlier visits to this place.

From the cavern's depths, a human figure emerged. Halie froze, her heart instantly racing, her mind frantically trying to come up with an explanation. "Who's there?" she forced out.

Crystals dropped flat as the figure climbed the cavern's sloping floor. He wore a skin-tight t-shirt with a gold chain around his neck. The beam from Adam's flashlight crossed his face.

Marco.

"How...?" Halie tried to grasp the incongruous encounter thousands of kilometers above the Earth. The second ascender? Then where was it?

"Such a coincidence!" Marco said with a haughty laugh. "Crossing paths with Sahalie Spark and her high-flying male escort."

Adam balled up fists, looking like he might take a swing at Marco. A uniformed soldier appeared from behind Adam and pointed a rifle. *"No se mueva, señor."*

Adam froze, glanced at the weapon, then slowly raised his hands. Reluctantly, Halie did the same.

31. DANGEROUS PLANS

MARCO CIRCLED WHILE the armed Ecuadoran soldier kept his weapon trained on Adam. Halie could only hope Adam wouldn't make any sudden moves. The soldier's firm grip on his weapon and a light touch on its trigger conveyed experience.

Halie had no experience of her own with soldiers but plenty with vain celebrities. She'd engage with Marco, star to star. "Good to see you again, Marco. But this high? I doubt your jet brought you here."

Marco continued circling like a tiger corralling its prey. He pinched fingers together. "It began as a tiny dot. Before our eyes, it grew into a duplicate ascender. That is not technology—that is supernatural. With all the predicting you've been doing, Miss Sahalie Spark, how did you not predict that?"

He'd seen her latest broadcast. Any satellite phone could have tuned in. "Funny, I didn't see your ride parked in the airlock."

"We were dropped off. I knew we wouldn't be waiting long. You really shouldn't announce your plans publicly. I'm surprised a star of your caliber doesn't recognize the risk. It leaves you vulnerable to the riffraff."

"I guess I have more faith in my fellow citizens." Halie glanced at Adam, giving her head a slight shake to try to tell him not to do anything rash. Marco noticed, commanding the soldier in Spanish. The soldier pushed Adam toward the airlock door with the muzzle of his weapon. Adam didn't resist, but several side glances made it clear he was considering it.

Marco grabbed Halie by the arm and pulled her with every bit of the strength she expected from a world-class athlete. "Now that you're here, we'll ride down together."

"Great, that's where we were heading anyway."

She'd lost her chance to speak with Mash, but Halie didn't feel she could press that issue just now. Better to return to the platform and reconnect with the American naval officers to sort things out.

They stepped into the V-pod, passing Mash's wrapped body without comment, then climbed to the seating level, where Marco pressed a control panel button. The V-pod's door shut, and their descent began with a stomach-lifting plunge.

Halie scooted close to Adam on the couch. A few steps away, the soldier braced himself against the glass, holding his weapon across his chest. Halie gave a nervous glance to Adam. Jaw clenched, he looked like he might make a lunge at the soldier any moment.

Halie leaned close. "Don't. We did what we could. We'll be down soon." Adam's stare never faltered.

Marco strolled around the circular couch with a natural athleticism that defied their rapidly increasing speed. He stopped in front of Halie and held out both hands. "Your phones, I think."

Halie looked at Adam, then grudgingly handed over her phone. Adam did too.

Marco slipped the phones into a pocket. He chatted amiably for a man whose fury on the pitch was well known. "I was fascinated by how the up and down ribbons work. The rest of my team is parked at Level 3, but to get there, they had to drop through the Kill Zone to Level 2, then come back up. It was really the only way to leave the down ribbon open for us."

"You're now the Ecuadoran commander?" Halie asked casually.

"Oh, dear woman, no. I am the Brazilian representative. An advisor. But Sergeant Alvarez and I have an understanding. I must say he is showing great restraint. I believe his nature is to shoot at the slightest provocation, so please… remain in your seats."

Their descent reached the V-pod's maximum speed, eliminating the feeling of falling. From Level 5 they would pass through the donut holes of the lower stations, possibly without slowing. But even at high speed, descent to the platform would take two and a half hours. Given the threats, Halie's best approach was to keep the tone as light as possible. "What did you think of the other levels? I assume you stopped on your way up?"

"Two observation areas, a collection of train cars with nowhere to go, and a haunted cave. I have seen enough of this evil."

"It's not evil."

Marco's lip curled in disgust. "So quick to submit. I shouldn't be surprised. Whores will spread their legs for any passerby."

Adam clenched his fists and started to stand, but Halie held him back. Stunned at how fast the conflict had risen, she could only shake her head. "Marco, really... is this about the piece we did on your wellness products? Because if it is, I'm sorry the US government came down on you. But honestly, all you have to do is pull a few items from your sales page and the regulators will go away."

Marco bent down, his face close to hers. Broad shoulders supported a thick neck. "You have no idea what you are up against, do you? You think this beast could be your friend. You tell the world that you speak to it, and when it speaks back, you somehow understand it when no one else does. And still, you refuse to see your deceit or its danger?"

"You're right, Marco, I can't be sure what the filament is. I can't even be sure of its purpose. But I wouldn't be too quick to label it as something to fear. That's where your logic falls apart. You have no evidence of malice."

Marco stood tall. "On the contrary, I believe I do. Where is your camerawoman?" He knew or had guessed what had happened to Mash. Maybe he'd read the despair written on Halie's face.

Halie countered in the simplest way she could. "Your armed abduction prevented us from locating her."

"Your camerawoman has lost her way in the cave? I thought for sure the bag on the lower floor... well, my mistake. If it's only trash, we'll throw it out when we stop."

Halie gritted her teeth. She'd have punched him for his glib disregard if he wasn't backed up by deadly force. The soldier pulled a long knife from his belt, casually passing it back and forth between his hands. He was apparently smart enough to know firing a weapon in a pressurized vessel was never a good idea.

Halie and Adam remained seated while Marco conferred with the soldier. Minutes ticked by. Perhaps Adam was picking up the Spanish, but Halie couldn't. The impromptu conspiracy ended when both nodded in unison.

Marco turned his attention to Adam. "You work with materials, yes? I'm curious… what might be required to cut the ribbon we're riding?"

Halie wondered if she'd heard him right. If Marco wanted to cut the ribbon, their conversation had taken a distinct turn to the dark side.

Adam didn't answer. Marco continued anyway. "Could you do it with a knife? Or would you need explosives? And where would you place explosives to get the best results?"

Adam stared, his brow pinched in a puzzled expression. Halie felt the same way. Was Marco proposing to blow up the tether? The man was a flamboyant manipulator of the masses and wrong about almost everything he said, but could he be that nuts?

Marco reached out, and Alvarez handed him the knife. Marco waved the blade in front of Adam's face. "We do have a very sturdy knife, but my friend says it barely scratches the ribbon. I'm sure you would know why."

Adam remained silent, his eyes darting between Marco and the knife.

"Avoiding a great deal of pain depends upon your cooperation," Marco warned, flipping the knife in the air and easily catching its handle.

Halie pulled on Adam's arm, whispering. "No heroics, please. Tell him."

Adam relented. "The tether's strength comes from a laminate of single-crystal graphene. Your knife won't even leave a mark."

Marco fingered the knife's sharp tip. "How about Semtex? I'm told it has the power to cut a bridge cable."

When Adam delayed, Halie nudged him.

He sighed. "Tethers are designed for tensile strength—which means they resist stretching. A tether is tough, but not indestructible... if some narrow-minded asshole came along."

Halie cringed.

Marco examined the knife like he was trying to decide which side of Adam's chest to plunge it into. "Answer the question. Would the tether break?"

Adam didn't answer. Marco held the knife under his chin. "One last chance."

Adam tipped his head. "A large explosion would break the molecular bonds... enough to shred the tether, or at least to create an amorphous carbon patchwork. Tension would do the rest."

"The rest?"

"Everything above the break would fly into space. Everything below would wrap eastward around the planet, likely snapping in places as it fell, which would send even more of it into space."

Marco nodded, handing the knife back to Alvarez. "See how easy that was?"

"You can't blow it up," Adam said.

"No? You just said we could."

"You could kill people. Any broken pieces will have significant angular momentum eastward. With six elevators along the equator, large pieces from one could hit the next, possibly at high speed. You'd create a falling domino effect, but with no control over where the next tether breaks, how much of it hits the ground, or where it comes down."

Marco nodded thoughtfully. "I see. That is good to know."

Halie was becoming increasingly worried that Marco had the means to pull off his threat. For all she knew, the second ascender parked at Level 3 was already packed with explosives, though how they'd managed to slip past the Americans was hard to fathom.

"They'll know you did it," Halie warned.

Marco waved her off. "Ah, yes, the question of who is responsible. That issue is already covered. If a ribbon breaks anywhere between Level 2 and Level 3, everyone in the world will know exactly why."

Halie sighed, suddenly feeling defeated. "The Kill Zone."

Marco's nasty grin confirmed his plan. And he was right. Most people seemed surprised that the tether was holding at all. A break at Level 3, far from any witnesses, would be her word against his, and the world's most famous footballer had sway no journalist could match. She could point to his provocative posts, but his eccentric nuttiness often left responsible people waving him off as a harmless wacko. She'd have a hard time recharacterizing an outwardly charming man as a devious planner of mayhem. She was surprised to see it herself.

A minute later, the V-pod's deceleration automatically kicked in. Halie looked around, confused. They were still thousands of kilometers above the atmosphere.

We're stopping at Level 4? The station was nothing but a stub waiting for a monorail track and far above the Kill Zone. Setting explosives here would defeat Marco's cover. Besides, he'd already mentioned that the other V-pod was parked at Level 3, not 4.

"Get up," Marco commanded as the V-pod slowed into the Level 4 station. The Ecuadoran soldier dropped down the ladder first and kept his gun trained on them as they each descended.

"Out," Marco said at the open V-pod door.

Still confused, Halie stepped out with Adam right behind. Marco followed, guiding them through the airlock's doorway into the rectangular depot on one side.

Does he want something here?

Midday sunlight streamed in through the windows on the monorail exit door. The place looked messier than the last time she'd been there. Mechanical parts that had been neatly lined up on the shelves were now scattered across the floor. Someone had plunged a metal bar through the window of one of the monorail cars. She swiveled to Marco. "Something about this station you didn't like on your way up?"

"You and I both know this is the beginning of a ring that will surround Earth. Yet you lied by not including it in your report. Why? Could it be that you were told of the coming attack?"

Halie shook her head. "Marco, there's no attack coming. Yes, there are plans to build a ring here, but it's not..." She didn't finish. Would the truth of the ring's purpose be worse than Marco's suspicions? He wasn't the type to tolerate people who didn't fit his notion of traditional roles. A new kind of human body might trigger him further. "It's not what you think."

Marco shoved Halie with both hands, nearly knocking her down. "A traitor to your own people." He shoved her again, slamming her against the wall. Adam tried to intervene, but Marco pulled the metal bar from the fractured window. He swung, barely missing Adam.

"Both of you are traitors," Marco said, gripping the bar between with both hands as he backed toward the V-pod. "It is time for us to part ways."

He's going to leave us here?

From behind Marco, the Ecuadoran soldier walked in, carrying Mash's wrapped body. He tossed it to the ground with the dull thud of bones hitting a hard floor.

Halie screamed. "Leave her alone!" The full scope of Marco's plan became instantly clear. Her anger boiled. She rushed at the soldier, punching wildly as she smashed into him.

Adam jumped into the melee, connecting a solid punch to the man's face. The soldier kept on his feet, struggling to grab the rifle he'd slung over his shoulder or the knife at his belt.

Marco swung the bar, catching the back of Adam's head and sending him sprawling.

"No!" Halie screamed. She untangled herself from the soldier and dropped to the floor next to Adam. He wasn't moving, but shallow breathing gave her hope.

A red welt was already rising along the back of Adam's neck. A spot of blood matted his hair. She pulled the hair apart to reveal split skin and a lump. Not a mortal wound, but he'd need stitches.

She turned to face the culprits, but they'd already left. The door into the airlock automatically closed, followed by the now-familiar sound of the airlock's floor and ceiling opening. Halie rushed to a window. Beneath the station, the V-pod dropped away toward the South American coast far below.

Halie screamed every profanity invented since the dawn of time. She leaned against the wall, panting, weary of the damage caused accidentally by a negligent alien and intentionally by an uncaring human.

Dropping to the floor, she put her face close to Adam's. "Can you hear me?"

His eyes twitched behind closed lids. She checked the head wound. Blood seeped. There was no threat of a bleedout, but he was definitely in need of first aid. She had no bandages. Adam's duffel was on the descending V-pod, but her own shirt might do. She stripped off the upper portion of the pressure suit, then her shirt.

Tearing the shirt turned out to be hard, but she finally got a rip started and tore one sleeve away. For good measure, she tore the other sleeve off too, then carefully wrapped one around Adam's head. It fit, tying snugly at his forehead. Not the greatest of bandages, but that was the least of their worries.

"Best I can do," she told her unconscious patient as she stared at the bull's-eye tattoo on her bare arm. "Actually, no… I do have one more trick up my sleeve."

For the first time in her professional life, Halie tapped one finger against the security tattoo in a simply coded message: *dit dit dit…*

dah dah dah… dit dit dit. A slight chill ran up to her bare shoulder in response.

Always connected—even in space—the microchip under her fake tattoo had already completed its job, sending her SOS signal to headquarters in LA. Someone might already be on the phone, notifying key people and reporting her geolocation. They'd find the nearest private security organization already under contract for emergency response services. Minutes later, a base in Ecuador or Peru would dispatch an armed search-and-rescue team with Halie's photograph and her location—down to the meter. They'd need a helicopter to get to the platform, but for the sum of money the insurance company would pay for a successful rescue, they could afford to send several. Arrive within an hour, and their pay would double.

There was only one flaw. Geolocations were horizontal positions, and Halie wasn't anywhere near the surface. Without a third ascender, climbing the tether might not be possible. But Yoon would notice the security team's arrival. He might have ideas.

A distinct chill in the air—not to mention what Adam would think of a bare-chested nurse when he roused—made her put the tattered remains of her shirt back on, then the pressure suit over it.

Help will come. But in time?

Halie couldn't be sure. She sat cross-legged next to her patient, pondering their predicament. They were stranded at Level 4 with a maniac heading down the tether, intent on destroying it. No phone. No medications for Adam's pain when he came to. No water for his thirst. No promises she could offer him that they'd ever see Earth's surface again.

Instead, she did what she could. She gently stroked his cheek. And pondered their predicament.

Fifteen minutes later, Adam groaned.

He lifted up on one elbow, reaching to the back of his head. "Ow."

"Careful," Halie said. "Marco smacked you pretty good." The metal bar lay on the floor.

He crawled to a seated position, inspecting the cloth tied around his head with tentative fingers. "I'm bleeding?"

"Some. A shirtsleeve was the best I could do." She lifted the spare sleeve.

"Thanks." He winced, then recovered with a deep breath. "Did I do any damage to Marco's buddy?"

"I sure hope so. They're gone."

"Where?"

"Down. They left us here. Mash too." She glanced to Mash's wrapped body. "The best I can figure, Marco wants to eliminate all traces of us. Our bodies, our V-pod, your duffel bag, Mash's cameras. When he gets to Level 3, he'll transfer the bags to the parked ascender, set a timer for the explosives they've probably already packed inside, then continue down. He arrives at the platform, but two thousand kilometers above there's a big boom and the tether breaks at Level 3. Everything above that point goes flying off into space. He simply tells everyone he made it as high as Level 5 but never saw us."

"Bastard."

"I've already notified my company's security office that I need assistance." Halie tapped the inside of her elbow. "Built-in tech— long story—but it guarantees a private security team will show up. They'll know I'm in trouble—still, Marco might get away with the lie. He'll claim I called for help because I saw the tether tearing apart or felt its shudders."

"What a mess we're in." Adam got to his feet with Halie's help. She wished she could offer more but was feeling pretty hopeless about their chances. "How much time do you think we have?" He took a few steps. Not bad for a man who'd nearly had his head taken off.

"I've been calculating that too," Halie said. "They'll need forty minutes to get down to Level 3. Maybe ten minutes to set a timer, then another hour to descend to the surface. They left about twenty minutes ago, so I'm estimating we have an hour and a half, plus whatever buffer they build into their scheme."

Adam huffed. "Damn. What do you do with the last hour and a half of your life?"

"I'd call my brother. Maybe my dad, though we haven't spoken in a few years. But... no phone. And don't bother checking Mash's body. I put her phone in a camera bag... which, of course, is in the V-pod."

"The Americans might not buy Marco's story, especially if the tether goes slack minutes after he gets to the platform."

"True," Halie agreed, "but I doubt he'd delay his timer by hours. Someone else would surely take the V-pod and head up. No, he'll want the evidence gone as quickly as possible. He arrives at the base, then..." She drew her index finger across her throat.

"Which sends us into deep space."

Halie nodded. "I wonder how long our air will hold out?"

Adam paused, then replied, "The cavern at Level 5 might offer some shelter, but how do we get up there?"

"How do we get anywhere?"

Halie glanced around the train car depot—horizontal transportation only, no extra V-pods. The large garage door led to the beginnings of a ring around the Earth, currently a dead-end. Another sealed door led to the main airlock. A third smaller door led to the personal airlock they'd discovered on their first stop here. Three exits, all leading directly into the vacuum of space.

Halie raised her head as an idea struck. She was surprised she hadn't thought of it before. "That's it."

"What's it?" Adam asked.

She turned to face him. "We'll jump."

"Jump from here to the surface? That's four thousand kilometers. Are you out of your mind?"

Halie quickly sorted through the obvious reasons why Adam was entirely correct, then settled on one key fact.

"Yeah… I am out of my mind. But in an hour and a half, you and I will be dead. What do we have to lose?"

32. HOPELESS

"SURE, IT'S A VACUUM OUT THERE, but we're both wearing pressure suits, and we have oxygen bottles." Halie held Adam by the arm, in part because she wasn't sure he was steady enough to remain standing. The swelling at the back of his head was worse but he showed no signs of shock or delirium.

"Our helmets are on the shelf in the V-pod, which by now is a thousand kilometers below us," he pointed out.

Halie nodded, hands raised. "Yeah, I admit that's our biggest problem, but we have an hour and a half to solve it. No, I take that back. We only have an hour. We need the other thirty minutes for a free fall to Level 3."

"You want to jump from Level 4 to Level 3?" His expression mirrored a parent trying to explain to their child why skateboarding on the roof would be a bad idea. Halie couldn't blame him. The idea scared the wits out of her.

"I don't *want* to do anything. But something tells me Marco is setting explosives at Level 3 right now. Somebody has to stop him. If I had a parachute, I'd jump all the way to the platform and get help, but…"

Adam stared at the floor, shaking his head in bewilderment. "A parachute wouldn't do you any good. From four thousand kilometers, you'd be going so fast when you hit the atmosphere you'd need a heat shield. Which begs the question… how do you stop at Level 3?"

Halie nervously tapped her fingers together. "We grab the tether. Not with our hands, of course. We'll need brakes or at least something to jam against the tether. We do have a chance…" She opened a hand to the collection of sheet metal, train components, and miscellaneous junk on shelves and scattered across the floor.

"This is nuts." Adam turned away.

"You're not helping, Adam. We only have an hour, and we've already wasted two minutes. I thought you were the high-flying rocket man. I thought nothing scares you."

Adam paced, then pivoted to face her. "I'll let you in on a personal secret. I'm not a hotheaded daredevil, I'm an adventurer. There's a difference, and it's all about controlling risk. The odds of crashing in my jet suit are less than getting hit crossing a street in New York. To get those odds, I train in emergency procedures, and I rely on tested, certified hardware. But this…" He waved his hands around the room cluttered with junk. "Even MacGyver couldn't MacGyver his way out with this."

Halie moved closer, tensing. "Adam. We… will… soon… be… dead." She meant it. She had every reason to believe it.

He moved closer still. "So, the TV star who is altitude-challenged is going to step to the edge of a two-thousand-kilometer cliff and jump?"

Nostrils flared. Halie closed her eyes, trying to think of a way to counter, but she couldn't. He was right. Even standing at the edge of the platform without a railing had been terrifying. Adam's thirty-second jet pack flight had put her on edge. The truth was, she'd always been anxious about heights—mainly because any climb up required a way to get down. She'd never considered the fear debilitating. Just cautiously smart about avoiding dangerous cliffs, rock overhangs, or anything higher than…

Halie lowered her head, grasping for something that might make sense. "You're right, Adam. I *am* terrified. Even if we figure out how to survive the vacuum, I'll be sweating bullets when I put my toes to the edge. But I don't see any other way. I have no phone, no radio, no spaceship, and no time left. It's either act now… or curl up in a fetal position and wait to die."

He lowered his head next to hers. "Look, Halie… I'm sorry. I shouldn't have said that. You're being brave, and… it's not a completely stupid idea."

Halie lifted her face. "Only a partly stupid idea?"

He tipped his head. "Actually, it's deranged. There are a dozen critical issues to solve and a low probability of success even if we solve them. But…"

"You'll help?"

Adam looked to the ceiling for inspiration. "Set aside the helmet issue for now. To pull this off, we have to calculate velocities for an accelerating free fall in a gravitational field that gets stronger as we drop. We'd need a way to hang onto the tether the whole way down, otherwise angular momentum sends us on a curving trajectory that completely misses our target. We'd also need accurate calcs for a braking deceleration that stops exactly at Level 3. Ridiculously hard to get it right. Then we'd still need to get inside the station, find the explosives, and disable a timer we've never seen."

"Yeah, that's pretty much it."

"So how do we do all that?"

Halie pointed to the personal airlock at the side of the depot. The only reason it existed was likely because it appeared in one of Yoon's designs as a way to access external portions of the station used for satellite deployment.

"Start with the airlock. That's how we get out. There's another one like it at the Level 3 station, right? You said you saw one. That's how we get back in. Finding explosives can't be that hard, and there's bound to be a timer. We turn it off, climb into the V-pod Marco left at Level 3, and go home."

Adam nodded. "Okay, I buy that much."

"That's a lot."

"You're right, it is."

The gears were starting to turn in his head. Halie's too. It was the first time she allowed herself to think this insane idea had a chance.

Adam glanced around. "Where's my visor?"

Since the fight with Marco, she hadn't noticed that his wraparound transparent visor was missing. "There." She pointed to the glasses lying a few meters away. "I don't suppose it can send text messages?"

He hurried over and picked up the visor. "Not without a connection to my phone. But…" He held up the visor, badly cracked from the blow he'd taken. He slipped it on and tapped the less damaged side. "Damn. The app OS is dead, which means no calculator. But the clock is still working, that's something. Braking needs split-second timing, or we could easily overshoot."

"Can you set an alarm for about fifty-five minutes?"

"Good thinking. We certainly don't want to be late to the party." He slid one finger against the visor rim, then tapped. "Alarm set for fifty-five minutes. I'll need all of that time to figure out the velocity numbers."

It was a worrisome factor in this crazy scheme. Halie would never be able to compute the velocity numbers herself. "How well do you know the math and physics?"

"Well enough. There's a meme on social media… a speeding car slams into a brick wall, and the tagline is, it's not the $v_f = v_i + at$ that kills you, it's the $F = m\ dv/dt$. An acceleration that avoids a smash at the end is exactly what we're doing, just vertically. It's velocity calculus, but the derivatives boil down to a few hundred incremental computations—which, unfortunately, will have to be done in my head." He lifted the makeshift bandage. "How does it look back there?"

Halie inspected. "I think you're past the worst of it. How's the headache?"

"Truly awful. But kiss me."

"Kiss you?"

"Yeah, that will help."

She did. On the lips. "How's that?"

He waited, then nodded. "Better, actually. You'd be surprised how the male body works. A tiny bit of dopamine released in the brain can mask most any pain."

As difficult as their circumstances were, Halie couldn't suppress a smile. "Not sure I'm buying your pretext, but I'll kiss you every five minutes if it gives us the numbers we need."

Adam adjusted the torn sleeve bandage. "No way. You'll be too busy. You have to come up with a braking system—something that will squeeze tight to the ribbon, won't melt from friction, and is strong enough to hold our weight. Plus, there's that little matter of helmets."

Halie grimaced at the challenge. "The good news is we're surrounded by..." She looked around. "I don't know what all this stuff is, but I'll salvage whatever I can."

"The clock is ticking," Adam said.

He mentally disappeared into his computations, while Halie headed for the shelves to search for anything that would slow a fast-moving projectile.

The jump idea was only feasible because they were back in gravity. Like a skydiver exiting an airplane, they *would* fall. But with no air resistance, the terminal velocity that skydivers encountered didn't apply. Their speed would increase until they either grabbed the tether or splatted onto the roof of Level 3. Adam's calculation for when to start braking *had* to be right.

Halie had no ideas yet on how to stay alive for thirty minutes in space without a helmet. But she decided solving the braking issue would be a better use of limited time.

How do you grab a tether speeding past you at a kilometer per second? Or will it be faster? Again, Adam's numbers would tell them.

She rummaged through the shelves, looking for anything resembling a spring-loaded clamp. Even a giant set of tweezers cinched together by rope might do. Grabbing the tether with their hands definitely would *not* work. Even if their hands weren't sliced off by the ribbon's razor edge, they'd need a viselike grip capable of holding their weight.

She found a box full of powdered chalk. It might be useful to produce smooth braking. It might also be useful for Adam. She dropped the box where he sat and sprinkled a dusting of chalk on the floor. "Need a chalkboard?"

She squatted and wrote *2 + 2 = 4* in the dust, then erased it with a gentle blow. She lifted eyebrows to Adam.

"Thanks," he answered. "That does help. I won't have to keep everything in my head."

She left the box for him and kept searching. With plenty to worry about, Halie steeled herself to the job. Panic would only make things worse.

"Tension... tension... I need a spring." She didn't see anything that looked like a coiled spring, but even a bent piece of metal was a spring of sorts. An idea occurred. "How do mag-lev cars brake?"

She dropped beneath one of the monorail train cars to check its undercarriage. As expected, it had no wheels. Mag-lev technology used magnets to levitate the vehicle above an electrified track, and this alien machine seemed to be a copy of a human design, just as the V-pod was.

"They probably reverse the current in electromagnets to slow down." She had little chance of adapting a complicated system to a hand-operated brake. But while lying on her back, she wondered what the car was resting on. "There must be a parking system. Wouldn't it have a brake?"

Halie crawled deeper into the underbelly of the machine, wedging her body into a tight space between the monorail track and the train car body. She reached a point where she could lift her head above the top edge of the track. "Well, what do you know? A wheel." It wasn't large, and most of it was tucked into a cubby in the undercarriage, but the lower portion stuck out enough to keep the car raised while parked. She could see a second wheel further down the track.

Does it have a brake?

She reached into the cubby and felt around. A smooth metal disc protruded a few centimeters from the wheel itself. In the tight confines, she couldn't reach further and certainly had no way to remove the wheel without a hydraulic lift. But now that she'd verified how it worked, she had a better idea what to look for.

But first, she'd need to squeeze her way back out, a task that turned out to be almost impossible. With minutes ticking by, she finally gave up. "A little help!" she yelled.

A minute later, a hand grasped one ankle and pulled. Scraping and twisting, Adam dragged her out. Halie inspected her wounds, mostly scratches on her hands and knees. "Thanks. I got stuck in there."

"Find anything useful?"

"Maybe. Sorry to take you away from your calculations."

"Actually, it's going better than expected. Our max velocity works out to 3.8 kilometers per second. Ridiculously fast, but it gets us down to a height of 2,387 kilometers in fifteen minutes. Then we brake for four minutes... I think. Still some details to work out."

"So only nineteen minutes total?"

"Give or take. Faster than the V-pod—which makes sense when you think about it. Our V-pod descents were never in free fall, or we would have been floating."

"Good work. You just gave us eleven minutes I didn't think we had." She kissed him again. "More dopamine for the final stretch."

Adam grinned. "Damn, we make a great team."

"So far it's all your half. I'm trying to find a spare part that may not even exist."

With only thirty-seven minutes left, according to Adam's visor, Halie searched the equipment shelves, sifting through dozens of components that didn't resemble anything like what she'd felt beneath the car. She was about to give up when she noticed a semicircular hunk of metal lying on the floor. Someone—Marco, maybe—had flung it there. It certainly looked like what she'd felt.

She scooped it up and turned it over in her hands. U-shaped like a hardcover book with its pages ripped out, the slot down its middle was wide enough to slip over the disc she'd felt with fingertips. Two holes at the opposing ends looked ready for bolts. A raised lever protruded above smooth metal on one side. She pulled the lever. Something inside the component rung with a distinct hammer-to-concrete sound. She peered into the slot and pulled again. *Clack.*

Excited, but not ready to declare victory, Halie ran back to the shelves and scrounged until she located a flat piece of sheet metal and slipped it into the device's slot. When she pulled the lever, the sheet metal locked into place. She couldn't move it. "It's a parking brake!"

Adam called out from the other side of the depot. "You found something?"

Halie raced to him. "Yeah, try this." She repeated her experiment. "Tug on it." He did. Nothing happened. He pulled harder. When she flipped the lever back to its original position, the sheet metal fell away from the slot.

Adam peered into the slot. "Outstanding. On or off, which for our use is a good thing. But we'll need two of them."

"Why?"

"Center of gravity. If we clamp this doohickey onto one edge of the ribbon and run a harness through the bolt holes, we'll be off-center. We'd get slammed against a knife edge sharper than a barber's razor. Not good. But rig a harness between both edges, and our center of gravity will keep us on the flat side during braking."

Halie recalled seeing a second support wheel on the undercarriage. "Hang tight."

Would there be a second spare part? She couldn't find anything on the shelves, but the first parking brake hadn't been there anyway. Some jerk, likely named Marco, had scattered parts everywhere. But now that she knew what to look for, a second U-shaped component wouldn't be hard to spot.

Nothing jumped out.

Halie crouched down next to a bus-sized vehicle and peered underneath. "Ah, there you are!" She reached in and pulled out the twin component and raced back to Adam. She held it out with a broad smile.

"Sweet," Adam said. "I can work with that." He peered into the slot and triggered the lever to produce another clack. "I wonder if those are brake pads snapping together? We're going to produce a *lot* of friction."

"Hey, I found the brakes. Calculating the friction is your gig. I still need to come up with helmets."

She said it like she'd find a helmet substitute lying on the shelf, but she'd already searched and had found nothing useful. At this point, she'd be happy with an inverted fish bowl and duct tape.

Without a helmet there'd be no jump. Marco would win, possibly destroying all six tethers and taking out Mash's consciousness too. And how would the filament react to having one or more of its limbs blown off?

Adam called out twenty-two minutes. Their deadline felt impossibly close. While he was busy untangling a bundle of wire, Halie wandered, mentally sorting through every possible substitute for a helmet. Break the car windshields and piece together the glass? With what glue? Melt the glass into a mold? No heat source. No mold either. The ideas came, but none panned out. To make an airtight seal, a makeshift helmet would need to snap into the indented slot around the neck of her pressure suit—essentially an oversized ziplock bag. The requirements were very specific. Only an actual helmet would meet them.

Halie sat cross-legged on the floor next to Mash's body. It wasn't really Mash anymore, but that didn't stop her from giving a gentle pat. "Sorry, my friend. We're trying, but I'm not sure we'll be able to save you. We could sure use the filament's help on this."

Nothing happened. No replacement helmets grew from a tiny dot to full size. No answer from Mash either. They weren't inside the

Level 5 prominence, and according to Mash, that was the only place communication could occur.

Halie lifted the edge of the emergency blanket that Adam had wrapped around the body. Mash's purple hair was visible beneath, driving home the reality of her physical death.

She lifted the mylar blanket higher, noticing a hint of transparency. She held her hand behind the mylar. Though dull and colorless, her fingers were visible.

Could it work?

Excited, Halie ran to the car window that Marco had smashed. Shards of glass lay across the floor. She picked up the sharpest piece she could find and returned to Mash's body and gently unwrapped the mylar. Pushing the glass fragment against its crinkly surface, she sliced a jagged line.

Slowly, she continued cutting until completing a full circle about a meter in diameter. She pulled the mylar circle over her head, squeezed it tight around her neck, and forced out a breath. The mylar bag inflated, with small leaks where her finger pressure was uneven.

"Close. So close."

She pivoted in a three-sixty turn, only able to make out vague outlines through the dull mylar—not enough detail to distinguish a garden hose from a snake. But when shapes were lit by direct sunlight, they were easier to identify. One was Adam. He stood by the window, bending a thin wire back and forth.

"That's it!" Halie jerked the mylar off her head and dashed to him just as the wire snapped into two pieces. Halie snatched one segment. "That'll do." She unzipped the front of her pressure suit and slipped the wire through the open top while Adam watched.

She pushed the mylar against the ziplock ring, then fitted the wire over it and pressed. It took a few tries, but the wire finally snapped into the indented slot. She continued around the ring, finishing with her hand reaching through the open zipper.

Satisfied, Halie zipped up and turned on the small oxygen bottle still secured in a side pocket. The flexible mylar helmet crinkled, inflating slightly.

"What do you think?" She turned to Adam, though all she saw was a dark form. Crinkling sounds gave away the locations of his touch.

"Can you see out?" His voice was muffled.

She walked him backward until his face was lit by the sun. It wasn't any worse than looking through a piece of smoked glass. "Lighting makes all the difference, and we'll be in full sun the whole way down."

"And you can breathe in there?"

"Feels fine so far. Check around the rim for leaks."

He held her shoulders and rotated her in a circle. "Nothing noticeable, but then we're not in a vacuum. The real test will be outside."

"True." Halie unzipped and turned off the oxygen. If she lifted the collar just right, she could slip her head out of the pressure suit through the chest zipper while leaving the makeshift helmet ziplocked into place.

Now the upper part of her suit hung at her waist. Her torn, sleeveless shirt looked like a rag, with her breasts bulging at the sides.

Adam noticed. "Dressed for a hot summer day."

"Stare all you want, but at this point proper clothing is optional."

His face flushed. "Honestly, I was thinking more about staying warm. Your helmet solution just made this crazy idea very real. So, if we're really going to step out into the cold of space..."

A nervousness showed in the squint of his eyes that Halie hadn't seen before. He'd been so composed and sure of himself during their jet pack flight and had shown the same steadiness when examining the electrified tether that had killed Mash. Even when Marco had held a knife to his throat he hadn't flinched. But now his whole demeanor had changed. He looked like a boy wishing he hadn't jumped the fence into a cow pasture only to discover an angry bull.

Halie placed one hand on his cheek. "Yes, Adam, we're really going to jump. We have to."

He looked to the floor and nodded. "Twelve minutes. I'll finish the harness."

"I'll make another mylar helmet for you."

She left him to his work, feeling less sure than ever about their prospects. If Adam was having second thoughts, his uncertainty would make it that much harder for Halie to take the first step.

Pushing that thought aside, she went to work on a second circle of mylar. When she finished, there wasn't much left to cover Mash's body. Halie sat next to her friend and tucked the last shreds around her shoulders.

"Sorry, Mash. We have to leave your body here. If we pull this off, I promise I'll come back. I'll bring a body bag and people who know how to properly handle these things. We'll do all we can."

She was about to get up, but something kept her talking. "When Adam was knocked out, I made a decision. All the uneducated foot-dragging laggards of the world get too much attention. They have an oversized voice—Marco's a perfect example. But you can't divide people into binary categories. It's not the luddites versus the enlightened, there are groups in the middle too. People who are just trying to understand what's true and what's false and are being misled by all the chaos. If I want to reach those people, I need to go high, not low. So, when I get back to LA—*if* I get back—I'm going to change the show. Refocus on the amazing stuff that's all around us. Investigate what we don't fully understand. Highlight things that are real, but most people don't know about. And celebrate our successes too—like space elevators. The filament didn't make this place. Not really. Humans did. Like you said, the filament is just good at copying."

Halie caressed Mash's pale hand. "It doesn't look like you'll get a chance to be part of the new show, and that makes me sad. Anyway…"

Halie couldn't think of anything else to say. She stood and brought the second mylar swath to Adam.

"I heard what you told Mash," he said. He was braiding multiple wires into a flexible wire rope. It looked sturdy, if uncomfortable as a harness. "I want you to know that I'm committed to this."

Halie let him talk. It felt like he had something to get off his chest.

"I tend to think about failure modes, always trying to minimize the chance of disaster. Pilots do that. This time, the odds are against us." He held up a hand. "Don't get me wrong, your mylar helmet was a stroke of genius. And finding working brakes… well, nobody does stuff like that except the incredible Sahalie Spark."

Halie reached for his hand. "I get it. You're a numbers guy and these numbers are scary. I'm scared too."

He squeezed. "Actually, you're surprisingly courageous. It seems to come naturally to you."

"Believe me, it doesn't."

Adam nodded. "Well… you're helping me to find my courage… even against the odds."

She pulled his face close and kissed him once more. "Adam, we have to do this. I don't see any other way."

"You're right, we do." He hung the wire rope he'd been working on across a metal frame that seemed to be part of his plan to secure them to the tether. He unzipped his pressure suit. "Help me with my new head gear?"

Halie placed mylar over his head, making sure the wire snapped tightly into the slot on his pressure suit. Then she slipped her own crinkly helmet back over her head, leaving the chest zipper open for breathing.

"We'll call them Flex Helmets," Adam said through the muffling mylar. "It'll become a new thing at NASA." He zipped up and hugged her. "Screw the odds. I'll go through the airlock first and knock three times when I'm outside."

With oxygen on, they fumbled their way half blind to the personal airlock door. Halie imagined they both looked like walking birthday party balloons. Adam gathered the components of his harness system, including the steel bar that Marco had used to smack him, and entered the airlock. He closed its door with a quiet thud. There was a cranking sound, then a whoosh of air. Nervous for him, she thought she heard a creak from the outer door opening, followed by another cranking sound.

Three knocks came from outside. Her turn.

33. FALLING FREE

WITH A SINGLE BUTTON PRESS, the personal airlock evacuated its life-sustaining contents. The mylar cutout that was wrapped around Halie's head ballooned outward—her Flex Helmet, as Adam had named it. Nervous, she ran through an impromptu checklist before stepping out.

Oxygen? Check.

She listened for leaks. Sound waves can't travel in a vacuum, but any escaping air should produce an audible whistle inside the suit. Halie didn't notice anything, though a small leak might actually be useful to keep the pressure from building as the oxygen bottle discharged.

Gloves and suit fully zipped? Check.

The zippers seemed sturdy and airtight. Rubbery booties covered her shoes. So far, Yoon's suit was performing as expected.

Radio working? I wish.

Flex Helmets didn't come with built-in radios. Like deep-sea divers in a dark ocean, they'd have to communicate by touch. Adam would watch his visor's timer and push the braking tab after fifteen minutes and forty-seven seconds of free fall, according to his final calculation. Braking would take another four minutes. They'd either stop at the Level 3 station or smash into it if Adam's calculations were off.

Halie felt for the outer door handle and pulled down. It hissed open as the last remaining molecules of air rushed out. She stepped through, feeling with her foot for whatever outside deck might be hiding in the shadows. She tapped a toe across a hard metal grating, narrow, with no safety railing.

Why am I not surprised?

Adam stood nearby, his silver balloon head and upper torso backlit by sunlight. She shuffled closer, sliding one hand along the exterior wall of the station. When she stepped into sunlight, details sharpened. Each fold in her own mylar helmet produced reflections and distortions, but if she tilted her head just right, she gained a clearer view.

She could make out Adam's smiling face behind his layer of plastic film. He tugged her arm.

Halie followed, shuffling across the metal grating like a first-time skier venturing outside the safety of the ski lodge. The afternoon sun felt warm on her back but nonexistent on her shaded face. With only a single layer of mylar between her and the vacuum of space, her nose and cheeks were already getting cold.

Twenty minutes. That's all we need.

She rolled her shoulders, hoping the body heat below would rise into the balloon covering her head. The air itself was breathable, though she had no idea how long the oxygen bottle would last. They'd already used a lot, especially at Level 6, and had no replacement bottles.

Adam started down steps. Halie carefully tapped for the first step with her toe, then placed her foot flat. Sturdy enough, but a railing would help. After ten steps, the grating flattened to a wide deck that curved around two brilliantly lit pillars—the twin ribbons in their mirrored glory.

Adam stopped near the closest ribbon, sliding his hand up her wrist and gripping hard. She gripped his wrist in the same way. He tapped with his other hand as if to say, "Hold on tight." Halie braced her feet. Adam leaned away from her, toward the ribbon.

Well lit, his movements were easy to follow. He slipped their makeshift braking devices over both edges of the ribbon, securing them to each other with braided wire rope that ran across the flat side of the ribbon. The metal box frame then hooked onto the braided rope. The front side of the frame was covered by sheet metal, making it look like a kid's sled ready for a snowy hill. Two human-sized slings already hung from the sled, one longer than the other. They'd be riding down in tandem.

While he worked, Halie allowed herself a glance down. From 4,000 kilometers, the vast disc of Earth dominated the view. Through the mylar, its curving horizon was easy enough to distinguish, but with muted colors, clouds, land, and water were intermingled shapes. She could be skydiving wearing welding goggles.

This is insane. We're really going to jump.

One step was all it would take, such a simple action leading to profound consequences. A four-thousand-kilometer plunge awaited, with a hard requirement to stop halfway down. There was no room for error.

Halie held a gloved hand to her half-frozen nose and cheeks, but when the thin sheet of mylar touched her skin, the cold was worse. She let go and the balloon around her head puffed up again.

This might be a huge mistake. Halie had to consciously will the tension away from her jaw, neck, and shoulders.

Apparently satisfied with the braking rig, Adam slipped one of the braided wire slings over his head and turned his back to the tether. He lifted the second sling over Halie's head and secured it under her arms. They'd be facing each other with the tether behind him and the sled acting as a buffer.

Good planning. Only the rails of the sled will touch the ribbon.

Adam pressed his Flex Helmet against hers and yelled. A faint vibration passed from his mylar to hers. "We'll hold ar— and j— together, okay?" Incomplete and faint, the technique worked well enough to add a communication path beyond impromptu hand signals they hadn't had time to rehearse.

Halie yelled back, making sure their balloon heads touched, "Ready. I think. What's the bar for?"

He held up the metal bar, probably still bloody on one end. "Got to flip both brakes simul—." He held the bar up against the ribbon. Its ends touched the brake levers on each side. He was certainly thinking ahead. Halie was glad to have such a smart partner. It improved their chances, however low.

"Don't t— the edge of the rib—," he yelled again. Halie nodded, understanding most of his warning. Her lips were getting numb. A light frost was forming on the inside of the mylar where she exhaled.

She pushed her face toward his. "I'm cold."

"Me too. Let's go. Feel the edge w— toes. J— straight down, don't push off. On three."

Halie tapped one foot, finding the deck's edge. She inched closer, still hanging on to Adam with the wire sling at her armpits. Her heart pounded.

Adam tapped her arm. One. Two. Three.

Without a second thought, she stepped off the edge.

Instantly weightless, the stomach-in-your-throat feeling certainly matched a leap off a tall cliff. But this jump came with no rush of wind. No flapping clothes. No hair flying around her face. Just an eerie quiet. It felt unnatural.

Halie looked up. The rectangular shape of the Level 4 station silently disappeared into darkness above. The ribbon's bright reflection remained close enough behind Adam to touch. She didn't dare, imagining herself next to an operating bandsaw at a lumber mill. As Adam had warned, touching the ribbon's edge could be fatal.

With the wire slings, sled, and braking clamps all falling at the same speed, there was no tension at her armpits. She could rotate in place without compromising Adam's handiwork—at least until it was time to trigger the brakes. Halie twisted enough to allow the sunlight to hit her face. If visible light was getting through the mylar, then infrared might too. Her face warmed, only incrementally, but enough to keep skin from freezing.

A jolt in the braided wire warned her to stop twisting. The sled behind Adam had likely glanced off the ribbon's surface. She'd need to be careful not to disturb his complicated—and very smart— design, lest she cause a wreck before they even got a chance to use it.

Adam raised one finger. One minute, according to the clock on his visor.

Trembles, either from the cold or from nervousness, couldn't be stopped no matter how hard she tried to will herself to be calm. Even with the dose of sunlight, she couldn't feel her nose, lips or chin. There wasn't anything to do about it. Even a so-called *space blanket* had its thermal limits when the temperature in the shade was probably colder than Antarctica in the winter.

Adam held up two fingers.

With only the featureless ribbon to compare against, their fall had no feel of speed. The sun remained fixed at one angle. The disc of Earth below didn't grow any larger. But Halie imagined they were already plunging at hundreds of meters per second. Bullet speeds, increasing rapidly.

Adam held up three fingers and pushed his mylar helmet against hers. "You okay?"

"Good. Except for the cold."

He pointed up. "Some damage."

Halie lifted her head. One of the braided strands he'd strung across the ribbon to keep the twin brakes attached had been sliced and was now dangling, bouncing against the ribbon's flat face like a flat stone skipping across water. It wasn't clear how it had happened, but she'd refrain from any more twisting to face the sun.

The braking unit itself hadn't fallen off. Like the loose wire, it wiggled as glancing blows from the high-speed ribbon knocked it this way and that, but the random nature of the blows seemed to keep it heading straight down. Rig dynamics would all change when Adam pulled the brake levers. Halie wasn't looking forward to what would surely be a traumatizing jolt from an unpadded wire rope.

Four minutes turned into ten with no change. Halie's face was getting enough time in the sun to stay on the healthy side of frozen, but her hands and feet were getting cold too. A look down still revealed two shiny ribbons dropping into darkness, but for the first time she noticed a slight increase in the size of the Earth. Suggestions of towering cumulus clouds dotted the eastern horizon, though detail was difficult to discern through the mylar. There was no hint of the Level 3 station, though by now they'd be well over halfway there.

Adam held up ten fingers, then added one more. His regular status reports gave her confidence they would avoid a splat. Still, a lot depended on the brakes. By now, they were hurtling downward at 2,000 meters per second or more, a speed usually associated with missiles.

Four minutes later, Adam reached over his head with one arm and hovered the bar over the twin brake levers about a meter apart. Shivering, Halie forced herself to take another trembling breath. Nerves jangled for what felt like an hour but had to be less than thirty seconds.

Finally, Adam tugged on the bar, flipping both brake levers simultaneously.

The rope snapped taut in a jolt that knocked the wind out of her. The sling dug into her armpits and back. Pain flashed across her body. She screamed into the mylar balloon feeling like she'd been cut in half.

Now she was being dragged upward, or so it felt. Adam's own sling had pushed higher on the side where he'd reached up, forcing his arm over his head into what looked to be a painful position. He'd dropped the bar, turning it into a high-speed javelin streaking toward the Earth below. Above, tiny red globules of molten metal sprayed into the darkness above. With the spring-loaded clamp now locked into place, Halie could imagine the shriek the brakes were making, kept silent only because there was no air.

She tried to pull Adam's sling down to free his extended arm, but the forces generated by their terrific speed were too great. A dislocated shoulder was likely. Torn ligaments were possible.

She pressed her face against his and yelled, "Your arm?"

He winced. They should have thought of another way to trigger the brake, but they'd run out of time. They might still be out of time. If Marco's threatened explosion happened now, Halie was sure they'd see it beneath their feet. Within microseconds, the ribbon's tension would snap, sending an explosive whiplash up its length that would either send them flying or crush their bodies like an empty aluminum can hit by a baseball bat.

Adam's timer no longer mattered. Four minutes of braking or five, their fate was set. The calculated drag would either be enough to arrest the plunge before they hit the station, or things would end quickly.

Halie dared a glance down, relieved to see a tiny white disc on the ribbon—still distant. A hundred kilometers away? Two hundred? It was impossible to estimate, but its size grew as she watched. They were still moving at a frightening speed.

Above, molten sparks continued to spew in their wake. She expected two deep gouges marking their braking path, but the ribbon above looked no different than below. Definitely sturdy, but would it hold up against explosives?

"Almost there," she yelled to Adam. He looked weak and was likely in pain. Her own pain centered on her back and underarms. Irregular jolts sent stings down her arms. Her legs dangled uselessly below.

She was beginning to feel dizzy along with a faster heart rate, signs the oxygen bottle might have finally given out. There was nothing to do but continue on.

Frostbite, back pain, and dizziness she could deal with. But Adam's arm worried her. It still stuck straight up, wedged in place by an unforgiving force that neither of them could diminish.

Molten sparks above reduced to a glowing splatter of fine droplets, a sure sign they were slowing down. The station below loomed larger. This was going to be close.

As designed.

She reached down and shook the oxygen bottle on her hip. Before, it had felt partially full. Now it felt empty, though if a red flag had popped up, she couldn't see it. The station now filled the view, blotting out most of the Earth. Braking became jerky, sending ripples of pain across her back.

With one last jolt, they stopped, bouncing and swaying until the slings and sled finally settled against the flat side of the ribbon. Halie reached over Adam's shoulder to touch the ribbon. They weren't moving. She looked down. Her feet still dangled high above the station's roof.

So close. A hundred meters?

If she slipped out of the sling, the remaining fall could be fatal—bone-breaking at least. With no extra length of rope, she quickly formed the only remaining plan available. She yelled through the mylar, "Adam, we're here, but we're high. I'll help you out of the sling, and we'll slide down the ribbon together. Can you use your feet to help us brake?"

He nodded with a weak reply: "The edge — sharp."

She hadn't forgotten, but she had nothing to use as padding or protection against the ribbon's razor-sharp edge. With their braking clamps now melted to the ribbon, they would have to continue under human power alone. There was no other choice. Not far below, a bomb was surely ticking.

Halie slipped out of her sling, feeling the higher gravity at this lower level. With one hand on the sling, she swung her leg to the other side of the paper-thin ribbon and pressed both feet together.

Adam struggled out of his sling, keeping his injured arm against his chest and grabbing his sling with his good arm. Halie put a shoulder against him, surprised he'd managed to get into position at all.

Now came the hard part. They'd have to let go of the slings and slap gloved hands on either side of the ribbon. She could. But with a dislocated shoulder, he probably couldn't. She'd need to hold at least some of his weight.

Halie went first, slapping her hands together in the praying position with the ribbon between. She slid down just enough to tuck her head beneath his bottom. Her face was now centimeters from a razor-sharp edge with arm and leg muscles already shaking from the effort.

She shoved her head upward, hoping he got the signal, then squeezed her hands and feet even tighter. Adam let go of the sling, and they both started sliding. Halie pressed harder, but it was no use. Their combined weight was too much for her, even with his feet pressing into the ribbon.

They slid faster. Halie's muscles burned as she pressed ever harder. The ribbon's blade rushed past her chest and face. She felt like a cherry tomato against the kitchen's sharpest knife.

Faster and faster.

Adam's leg bumped against her head, jamming her chin against the ribbon's edge. A stab of pain was followed by a trickle of blood down her neck. She'd been cut to the bone. Worse, it meant her mylar helmet had been compromised.

Do or die trying.

If air was leaking, she might have less than a minute before passing out. Halie let go and pushed off with her feet, plunging the remaining distance to the station's roof. She crashed on her side and tumbled down its sloping surface. Adam hit next to her.

Frantically grabbing for anything available, Halie finally caught one hand on an indentation that stopped her roll. Adam slid past. She grabbed his good arm and held tight, stopping him at the roof's edge.

No time to waste, she scooted onto her stomach, keeping as much contact with the sloping roof as possible. She peered over the edge to a sheer drop. Ten meters below was another metal deck grating. No ladder, they'd have to jump.

Halie put a glove to her chin. It came back wet, most likely red, though colors were impossible through the mylar. But no air bubbles. Perhaps the blood was keeping the slit partially sealed?

Dizziness was getting worse, but her own blood might have given her another minute of consciousness. Halie patted three times on Adam's back, then swung her legs over the edge. He'd either jump along with her or stay put. Either way, she needed to help herself first, him later. She let go and plunged once more, thankful when her feet hit grating but wincing as her left side crumpled and her head hit hard.

Dazed, but alive, she pulled herself to her feet. A ten-meter fall on Earth might have killed her. In two-thirds gravity it only hurt like hell.

She stumbled across the deck, searching for an airlock entry into the station. Adam had sworn he'd seen one, but Halie had missed it when they'd stopped here, probably too dazzled by the view of Earth. Halfway around the huge circular station, she found stairs and climbed up. At the top, she reached a door, pulled its handle, and lurched inside. She felt loopy and weak at the knees.

There was only one button to press. The door snapped shut. A second later, sound returned—rushing air—a sound Halie had never thought much about before but would treasure for the remainder of her life.

The inner door of the airlock opened, and Halie collapsed into the station. Her strength fading, she unzipped her pressure suit and ripped the mylar helmet off, sucking air into starved lungs.

She lay on the floor, panting. Her frozen face warmed. Blood trickled down her neck. She'd deal with that later.

Find the explosives!

She peeled herself from the floor and ran. Now back inside the ballroom-sized observation deck, she realized that placing explosives anywhere within its expansive floor space made no sense. Marco's goal was to destroy the tether. The explosives would have to be there.

The doorway to the V-pod airlock stood wide open. She raced through. Inside, a V-pod was attached to the up ribbon. Nothing on the down ribbon. No soldiers, no Marco. By now, they were probably on the platform 2,000 kilometers below.

She scanned the empty ribbon looking for anything stuck onto it. Nothing.

She raced to the V-pod. Inside its lower level, Mash's camera bags were piled up on one side. Three precious helmets too. Nothing among the pile looked remotely like explosives. Had the bomb threat been a hoax? Or had they abandoned their plans after an argument among the conspirators? Unlikely. Marco had been in complete control.

Halie climbed the V-pod's ladder, a painful process with aches across her back where the sling had dug in. With every step up, several drops of blood fell from her chin.

Keep going.

At the top, her worst fears became reality. Next to the control panel, a tangle of rope, wire, and what looked like blocks of cheddar cheese were secured to the V-pod's wall by several crisscrossing strips of tape. A skull and crossbones was stamped in black ink on each orange block.

Halie approached cautiously and stopped in front of the tangle at eye level. An explosion now would take her head off. A sudden burst. A bright flash. It would be over quickly.

Halie swallowed hard, feeling overwhelmed. This setup wasn't what she'd expected. Braided copper wire fed through the middle of a white nylon rope decorated with black stripes. The words "Detonator Cord" were written repeatedly along the rope's length. The cord wrapped around each of four cheese blocks with knotted loops.

Plastic explosives.

That much wasn't hard to diagnose, but she could only guess from there. The wires suggested electricity. The detonator cord would likely trigger a much larger explosion. She imagined the four cheese blocks were enough to bring down a building.

Unsure how sensitive any of it might be, she carefully lifted the braided copper wire, searching down its length for an energy source. Hidden under the tape, the wire fed into a white metal box about the size of a sunglasses case.

Heart pounding, Halie peeled back the tape around the box. A digital readout showed 2:49, counting down by the second. Halie took a shaky breath, not sure what to do but terrified that she had less than three minutes to figure it out.

She pulled the box away from the coils of wire. Three buttons were arranged horizontally across its top: an up arrow, down arrow, and one marked Set.

Halie pressed the up arrow. The digital readout flickered to Locked, then returned to the countdown: 2:27. She pressed each of the other two keys, getting the same result. Once set, this countdown seemed destined to reach zero.

Hands trembling, she flipped the box over. The wire ran beneath a metal plate secured by two screws. Without a screwdriver, she had little chance of taking it apart. She pulled on the wire but couldn't separate it from the box. The other end of the braided wire joined the detonator cord. She pulled on that too. It wouldn't budge. Bending the wire back and forth had no effect either—the braids were flexible enough to avoid breaking. She even bit it, rubbing the wire across her front teeth until they ached. Not a dent.

Stomp on the box? Would it break the circuitry inside? Or would that set the bomb off?

She could wish for a second opinion, but Adam was still on the roof and military experts were 2,000 kilometers away, straight down.

What to do? Come on, think!

Halie tried to calm rapid breaths. Hyperventilating would only make things worse. This thing was going to blow, and there didn't seem to be any way to stop it. The display now showed 1:54.

Halie focused on the bare essentials. *I can't stop it. It's going to detonate… but it doesn't have to bring the house down.*

She stripped the remaining tape from the bundle and delicately laid the collection of wires, cord, and explosive packs on the floor. Working carefully but quickly, she began untying the detonator cord, loosening its loops and knots tied around one of the orange blocks. It wasn't any different than handling nylon rope found in any hardware store, but the cord's flexibility also made the knots tight. She finally got it loose enough to slip one block out. The display read: 1:31.

The second block was more difficult, but two broken nails later, she freed it as the display clicked to 0:57.

Hurry!

The last two blocks went faster once she realized every knot didn't need to be untied, just loosened. The blocks dropped to the floor.

Go, go, go!

She left all four explosive packs where they were and gathered the detonator cord and timer in her arms.

Separate as far as possible!

She had no idea how powerful detonation cord might be, but it seemed a reasonable guess that its purpose was only to trigger a main explosive nearby.

Racing down the V-pod ladder, Halie dashed into the station and heard a door unlatch. Adam.

He limped through the personal airlock and fell to his knees, reaching for the zipper on his pressure suit.

The countdown ticked to 0:17.

"Hang tight!" Halie raced across the open floor space to the far side of the donut-shaped room and tossed the bundle behind a counter. She hurried back to Adam and dropped to her knees. Inside the open zipper on his chest, she found the ziplock ring. With one pull, she stripped the mylar away from Adam's head.

He sucked in gulps of air, his eyes blinking furiously.

"Hurry," she said, dragging Adam onto his feet. They only made it two steps when the explosion hit.

BANG!

A flash of fire erupted at the far side of the room with a shock wave that sent them both sprawling. The floor shook. A flaming ball of fire roiled in the air. Shredded chunks of the counter rained down, along with bits of hot wire that scorched everything they touched.

Halie lifted her head from the floor. Her ears were ringing, but the observation deck remained intact. Even the windows near what was left of the counter showed no signs of cracking. The detonator cord had done its job to initiate a blast, but no more.

Color returned to Adam's face. He blinked. "You found it."

Halie pulled herself to her knees. "Plastic explosive blocks. They're still in the V-pod. I'm no demolition expert, but I have a feeling they're no longer a concern."

Adam sat up too, cradling his arm. He had to be in pain, but he kept a brave face. "The V-pod is functional?"

"Bags, helmets, and everything—just waiting for us to descend."

He reached out. "You're bleeding. Bad."

The upper part of her pressure suit was splattered with blood. "Could have been far worse. That ribbon could have split my whole head down the middle, bones and all. It stings like hell, and stitches are in my near future. Not a great look for a television personality."

"Is my duffel bag in the V-pod?" he asked.

"Should be. Everything else was."

"Good. We have a first aid kit, plus I can help with the stitches. Let's get out of here." He pushed himself up to a standing position with surprising agility for having only one working hand.

"Just a sec." Halie stepped through shredded debris to a strand of battered wire and picked it up. The remains of a white metal box hung at one end. "Evidence. We're going to nail this guy."

34. FINDING ANSWERS

FOUR PACKETS OF HIGH EXPLOSIVES remained on the floor below the V-pod's control panel. Halie left them untouched—critical evidence for when they reached the platform. She pressed the bottom button. The V-pod door hissed shut, and they dropped through the Level 3 station's donut hole. Two thousand kilometers below, cumulonimbus cloud shadows pointing east told the story of late afternoon in South America.

She hadn't found her phone anywhere. Not in Mash's camera bag. Not in Adam's duffel. Not anywhere in the Level 3 station. What Marco had done with it, she didn't know, but he wasn't stupid enough to carry it with him. His alibi would surely be that he'd climbed the tether but never saw anyone.

"Still an hour to get down," Halie told Adam, her anger barely in check. The man who had nearly killed them both would pay. She'd report the crime in person to the Americans, the Ecuadorans, or anyone who would listen.

Adam pulled a medical kit from his duffel along with a curious tool that looked like a combination paper binder clip and garage door opener. "Time for surgery."

"You sure you know what you're doing?" Halie asked. Drips of blood still fell from her chin to her chest. The wound needed attention.

"You won't believe how easy this is," he said, holding up his surgical device. When he pinched, the clip opened to show two serrated rows.

Halie closed her eyes. "I've learned to trust you, but that doesn't mean I want to watch."

He swabbed her chin with an alcohol wipe. One minute and a painful pinch later, he claimed he was done. Halie opened her eyes.

"All stitched up," Adam said with pride. "It's basically a microscopic sewing machine for delicate materials, but every hospital emergency room should have one. The suture is thinner than a hair, but stronger. It'll dissolve on its own in the next week or two. Won't leave a scar."

Halie wiggled her chin. It felt better already. "Thank you. It's amazing what materials science can do these days. How's your head and arm?"

He sat on the couch next to her, and she inspected his wounds. The lump on his head wasn't bad and if his shoulder had been dislocated, it had snapped back into place on its own. Keeping his arm supported was all anyone could do until they reached the platform and sought medical care.

A loud pop jerked their heads toward the V-pod window. More pops and ticks followed. They were in the Kill Zone. Halie locked eyes with Adam, unable to suppress a smile that quickly turned into a grim laugh. "Still more danger? I'm sorry, it's just that after all we've been through…"

He started to chuckle himself, giving Halie a dismissive wave. "Eh, what's a few hundred bullets firing at your head when the windows are made of self-repairing aramid? We'll be fine. Now… try jumping off a two-thousand kilometer cliff. That takes a special kind of stupid."

He reached out with his good arm. She gladly fell against his chest in a warm embrace. The pops from outside continued, but Halie easily set that detail aside, preferring instead to listen to his heart as it thumped in a steady rhythm. She melted further into his arms, content to feel secure once more.

Neither spoke for minutes. Finally, he whispered, "That first step. I couldn't have done it without you there."

Halie nodded against his chin. "Yeah, same for me. Crazy stuff. I can almost hear my mother's scold… if someone told you to jump off a cliff, would you do it?"

"Peer pressure. Necessary in this case."

"So true. We hear about survival instinct, but that's not really how it works. It's too easy to curl up in a ball and close your eyes. Giving up is the default instinct. We're good at self-pity. Survival doesn't happen without someone else beside you—"

Without a sound, an enormous building flashed by outside, shaking the V-pod and startling both of them. Halie pulled away from Adam. Not far above, the Level 2 station rapidly disappeared into a star-filled sky. They'd blasted through its donut hole without so much as a seat belt light coming on.

"I gotta say, the filament did a fantastic job copying Yoon's space elevator designs, but it seems to have missed the appendix on safety procedures. How hard is it to get a warning here or there?"

Halie rose to look out the windows. They were nearing the top of the atmosphere. Earth had lost its globe feel, becoming a flat horizon in every direction. Orange and pink clouds hung across the eastern rainforest of Brazil. They'd be arriving at sunset.

A second V-pod shot past on the up ribbon, missing a head-on collision by only a few meters. Reflexively, Halie jumped backward, then crept back to the window and peered up. The unexpected V-pod was already far above, making it impossible to see who might be inside. Halie doubted it was Marco. Surely the man wouldn't venture up a tether he'd rigged to explode.

"Army?" Adam asked.

"Or my rescue team. If it was, they must have seen us."

With no phone to coordinate, there was nothing to do. Her security tattoo only had a cancel code—something she wasn't ready to enter until she was safely back down. That first step onto the platform would be most welcome.

The Pacific Ocean sparkled in late-afternoon light. Stars above winked out as the atmosphere of Earth welcomed them home. Soon, the square black platform was visible, then the funnel-shaped shroud. The American aircraft carrier was still nearby, along with two smaller ships.

The V-pod dropped through the shroud's hole, slowing. A small crowd gathered around the tether steps. Halie spotted Yoon, Quong, and Jaya standing together, a sure sign that the Ecuador-Brazil alliance hadn't turned the platform into a no-entry zone.

Halie grabbed the remains of the detonator wire and made her way down the ladder, standing at the V-pod door as they came to a stop. She stepped out with Adam right behind. Yoon was the first to rush forward, helping her down the steps.

"You're injured," he said. Splattered blood across her partly open pressure suit and the shirt beneath no doubt looked horrific.

"A bad cut," Halie told him. There would be time later to fill in the details. "Where's Marco?"

"Still holed up, I believe. The second V-pod returned not long ago, and Marco went straight to his jet. The pilots started the engines—"

"We have to stop him from leaving!" Halie started for the platform's corner, but Yoon held up a hand.

"Don't worry, Marco is not going anywhere. A remarkable turn of events prevented his departure. You will need to see it for yourself."

"Fine, but you're sure he's still here?"

Another man stepped forward dressed in a green uniform. "Marco is still here, ma'am." Not military, his nametag read, *Servicios de Seguridad*. KNS had sent him.

"Were those your guys going up to find me?" Halie asked him.

He nodded. "I just notified them that you're down."

Jaya held out three bottles of water. "You've been gone longer than expected. Where is your camera operator?"

Halie lowered her head. "She didn't make it." Ashen faces, eyes wide, Jaya and Yoon both fumbled for words. Halie waved a hand. "It's complicated. We'll talk. But right now, we need justice."

Two US Naval officers parted the crowd, the same officers Halie had spoken to before. She handed the detonator wire to Commander Stevens who examined it with interest. "Marco tried to blow up the tether. There are four packages of explosives in this V-pod and more evidence at the Level 3 observation station. Any chance you can arrest him?"

Commander Stevens squinted. "Tricky business in international waters. But we can help preserve this evidence and inform authorities in Ecuador and Brazil."

Behind him, Stevens's partner, Lieutenant Commander Gutierrez, spoke into a handheld radio. "Charlie, I need a bomb disposal team up here ASAP—with security. And a medical unit too. Two injured. Doesn't appear to be life threatening but get 'em up here quick as you can."

After a radio reply, Gutierrez turned her attention to Halie and Adam. "We'll have medics here in a few minutes. Do either of you need to sit? You look like you've lost some blood, Ms. Spark."

"I'll live," Halie told her. "But Adam may have a dislocated shoulder."

"I'll live too," he said, cradling his arm.

Halie spotted another face in the crowd she recognized. He wore the uniform of the Ecuadoran Army and was doing his best to hide behind his mates. She whispered to the lieutenant commander. "When your security people get here, have them talk to that soldier." She pointed with her eyes. The soldier lowered his head, trying to make himself smaller. "Take his fingerprints. I bet they're all over the explosive packs."

Gutierrez spoke again into the radio. "Charlie, add the on-duty master at arms to that security detail and tell him to bring his cuffs. Plus an NCIS officer if we have one on board. We might be looking at a full-on terrorism investigation."

For the first time, Halie felt confident that Marco wouldn't slip away. The rich and powerful had a way of avoiding justice. Medics soon arrived, providing proper bandages and a sling for Adam's arm. Bed rest, they recommended, offering spots in the ship's hospital.

But Yoon's offer was better. First class reclining seats on a short flight to Guayaquil where a seaside villa and a private nurse awaited. They headed to Yoon's plane but only made it halfway across the deck before stopping to gape at Marco's jet.

A tangle of white fibers grew from a root system beneath the plane. Sticky strings by the thousands sealed the plane's landing gear to the deck. Still more tangled threads climbed over its wings, intertwined around its ailerons and flaps, and obscured the view out the pilot's windshield.

Halie stared, mouth agape at the now-familiar fibers. She still had a few clinging to her bloodied pressure suit. "The filament? But how did it know?"

Adam examined one bundle that had been sliced with a knife, only to be overwhelmed by more threads. "The filament couldn't have known about the explosives. Its communications pathway is only at Level 5."

Halie shook her head in amazement as the answer finally came to mind. "Mash!"

ONE WEEK LATER...

Adam Estrada stood at the heart of the Sunset Boulevard television studio, soaking up its high-tech ambiance. An elevated control room overlooked the stage. Racks of lights hung overhead. A lone anchor desk was backed by green screens and surrounded by futuristic cameras that seemed to float across the floor. To one side, empty seats waited for an audience.

He hardly believed he was here, invited by the woman who had shared a vertical adventure ending in a death-defying leap through space. It hadn't been a dream or mistaken identity, she really *was* Sahalie Spark, television megastar. He had hugged her, comforted her as she cried over a lost friend, stitched up a nasty cut on her chin, and gripped her hand as they'd ventured into a bizarre world never before seen by humans.

He'd even kissed her—three times.

But today, he felt less the bold daredevil of space adventures and more the obscure professor of materials science who'd somehow gotten lucky enough to be on the home turf of one of the most recognizable faces in the world.

How ridiculously unlikely.

As unlikely as surviving a two-thousand-kilometer plummet through space with cobbled-together brakes. As unlikely as six working space elevators that hadn't existed two weeks ago. As unlikely as an allotrope of carbon—alive, intelligent, and capable of spanning vast stretches of space. Adam had news for Halie on that front and couldn't wait to tell her.

On his first day back at the university in Lima, he had reached out to a professor of mathematics and described the bizarre grid of dodecahedrons that he and Halie had witnessed. The professor pinpointed the structure immediately, telling Adam, "Tessellation, yes, but not necessarily involving extra dimensions. More likely a form of hyperbolic geometry."

Adam hadn't heard the term before, but a few online searches provided images that matched the Level 6 infinities. Moreover, a structure like this had been modeled way back in the nineteenth century by Henri Poincaré, the same French mathematician who addressed the so-called "three-body problem" of orbital mechanics. A Poincaré disc was a way to map infinite tessellations onto a hyperbolic plane. Dutch artist M. C. Escher was famous for drawing these discs using intertwined patterns of fish or birds that became smaller toward the edge.

When Adam asked how hyperbolic geometry might relate to the filament, his colleague had shrugged. "It could, I suppose, provide a mathematical basis for instantly transporting an army helicopter hundreds of kilometers away."

Finally, a rational answer, Adam thought with a wide smile. Hyperbolic projection might also explain how an entire cavern could be wedged into 3-D space no larger than a hotel ballroom, though that particular mathematical abstraction would require more study.

Halie would be happy to hear there was already a name for the craziness they'd encountered. She'd be even more interested in what Adam had learned about the Crab Nebula.

The woman herself was only steps away in her all-glass office a half level above the stage, explaining something to her producer. Adam watched their interaction. Halie's confidence and poise. A warm smile. A more forceful expression as she argued a point. A congenial pat on Paul's arm, and the obvious relief on his face that his television star was back home safe and sound.

She's at the peak of her game. Somehow even more impressive when the cameras aren't rolling.

Her email invite was quickly accepted and prompted his own invitation to dinner for this evening. Declined, unfortunately. Too busy, she'd explained, both before and after the show. But she'd take a rain check.

It kept Adam's hopes alive. He'd ask her again tomorrow. And the day after that. Eventually, he'd find out if those kisses had meant anything, or if the celebrity—now back in her element—was out of his league.

The office door opened, and Halie bounded down the half flight of stairs with her producer right behind. Her eyes sparkled with excitement. She hopped onto the stage and grabbed Adam's good arm, the other still in a sling.

"You're not going to believe it. Paul just signed a deal with SASEA for journalist access to any level, anytime."

She pronounced the acronym *sassy*, but it stood for South American Space Elevator Alliance, a new agreement among Central and South American nations to share access to the platform off their Pacific shore. The mid-Atlantic elevator would likely be operated by European countries since Africa had their own in Kenya, leaving the

United States and Canada to scramble for a more complicated arrangement at the mid-Pacific elevator located between Tahiti and Hawaii. It was a rare case of the most powerful countries of the world potentially receiving a smaller share of the pie.

There hadn't been any announcements regarding the remaining two space elevators on the Asian side of the world, but China had sent warships to Sumatra, giving India, Malaysia, and Indonesia a strong incentive to band together.

"So, you'll be returning to Ecuador?" Adam asked.

Halie orbited the empty stage, her energy seemingly boundless. "Absolutely. I could gather more for the show, plus access to Level 5 means I can stay in touch with Mash. Maybe the filament too. After all, I'm one of only three designated teachers."

According to reports, seven more explorers had made it to Level 6 on other tethers around the world. Four of them had been selected by the filament for a journey across the galaxy, but only two of the four had been bold enough to touch the electrified wire that Halie had grabbed. She hadn't yet met her counterparts, she'd explained to Adam in an email, a man named Reth who lived in Nairobi and a woman named Sariyah who lived in Kuala Lumpur.

"You could come with me," Halie offered Adam.

"I'm hardly a journalist."

"You could be my personal guest." She said it like she meant it.

Adam shrugged. "Okay then, I'm in. I don't suppose Marco is involved?"

"Well... he hasn't been arrested, but Brazil dropped him as their rep. I'm not going to lose sleep over Marco. Karma will catch up with him sooner or later. Did you hear? Every platform now has six V-pods standing by in the hangar, ready to climb. Apparently, the filament has opened the doors wide open."

Adam chuckled. "It had to be six. No other number could work. Guess what?" He held up his new phone, his previous model very likely being at the bottom of the ocean.

He scrolled to an image showing clouds of interstellar gas. "An astronomer operating the Giant Magellan Telescope in Chile sent this to me. He did exactly what you told astronomers to do. He pointed to the Crab Nebula. See all those pink lines? They're false-colored for easier identification, but each one is a filament thread. They match the spectral signature your magic wire showed us. The guy told me it was like finding buried clams on a seashore—easy, once you knew what signs to look for."

Halie studied the photo sprinkled with pink lines, then looked up. "There are so many."

Adam nodded. "The filament probably isn't one continuous thread but a whole bunch of interrelated threads. As long as the prominences are close together, they can communicate as though they're a single organism."

"Sense Local and Sense Refined," Halie said.

"Exactly, with Sense Beyond requiring a communications passageway through at least one wormhole. I read up on this. Some cosmologists think microscopic wormholes are a routine part of the fabric of space-time, so it's possible the filament didn't create them... it may have discovered them. Which means we may be able to use them too."

Halie shook her head. "Still so much to learn."

"You're telling me. Materials science alone has years of studies and technical papers to write. Mathematicians, astrophysicists, biologists, neuroscientists... lots of people are going to be busy trying to understand this thing. A door has opened. We're getting a glimpse into an entirely new form of life and maybe some new astrophysics too. My astronomer friend says this photo explains what he called the *missing mass* problem of the Crab Nebula. Apparently, the ejecta from its supernova in 1054 doesn't match the light output of the neutron star at the nebula's center. Until now, no one knew why. Their supernovae theory wasn't wrong, the filament was just gobbling up that mass."

"I love it! That's a whole show in itself. By the way, Paul and I decided to rebrand. *Don't Believe It!* is becoming *Reason to Believe.* Gives the show an investigator vibe with room to focus on the amazing-but-real stuff."

"And I get to watch you in action?"

"You do. Front row." She leaned in close. "But no distractions, I have to focus. Paul and I are putting together a lot of material fast."

Adam took a step back and held up both hands. "Just consider me a friendly neighbor who asked for tickets."

Halie rolled her eyes. "Oh, come on, Adam. I *wave* at my neighbors." She grabbed his hand and pulled him around the corner to an empty hallway lined with photographs. Moving in close, her lips brushed against his—briefly, cautiously, but with a hint of purpose. Her voice was soft. "You're in a different category, mister. You know that, right?"

Adam brushed his nose against a lock of her hair, inhaling heavenly scents of lavender and jasmine. "A guy can always hope he's on a woman's mind."

"Oh, yeah. I've been thinking about you a lot. I wouldn't have made it through all that stress without you. I..." She waved her hands to cancel whatever she was about to say. "How's this... if your offer for dinner is still on the table, can we make it Friday?"

"Done." He'd have to extend his return flight, but he wasn't about to miss out on what might be the best date of his life.

Halie stepped back. "Deal. Make yourself at home. Check with Jen in the lobby if you need anything. The show starts in two hours, and I'm not nearly ready so you won't see me for a while." With the brush of a soft hand against his cheek, she left.

The time passed quickly. Employees hustled around the studio. A stage manager began seating the audience and told Adam to take whichever front-row seat he wanted. Stage lights came on. Cameras swung into position. A disembodied voice from the control room called for everyone's attention.

And then... there she was. Sahalie Spark, television star, walking briskly onto the stage with a smile as big as life. Adam applauded along with everyone else. Halie introduced herself without a hint of panic even though everything had been pulled together at the last minute.

She's a pro. No doubt about it.

After answering a few questions from the audience, she made eye contact with Adam and waved him up to the stage. Suddenly nervous, Adam stood, taking a rather awkward position next to Halie. She introduced him, telling the crowd, "We are so lucky to have such a prominent materials scientist in the studio. Today's show is on a different topic, but maybe we could coax Dr. Estrada to come back another time to tell us more about these amazing self-repairing tethers?" The audience encouraged the idea with applause.

Face flushed, Adam was thankful to sit down again.

How does she do this every week?

Halie took a seat at the anchor desk. The studio quieted, and the stage manager pointed a finger. Cameras were rolling, and the audience had instantly increased by several million.

"Big week," Halie started with a knowing smile to the nearest camera. "So big our show has a new name. I'm still Sahalie Spark, but from now on you're watching *Reason to Believe*. And trust me, by the end of the show you'll see why. Tonight, we'll begin to answer one of the most profound questions humanity has ever faced. What is the filament and what does it want from us?"

The studio burst into spontaneous applause. Adam joined in, laughing. In all their interactions with the filament, Adam couldn't honestly say he knew the answer.

What a show. She has the eye and the heart for drama.

Halie laid out the story, framed as a developing theory that might be true but could be mistaken. The audience would decide, picking from a range of choices starting with That's Amazing to Not Buying It.

She connected live to a professional psychologist who had noticed the filament was exhibiting many of the same symptoms as people with obsessive-compulsive personality disorder. The filament, the psychologist declared, had an obsession with order and a compulsive need to create order from chaos. He offered as evidence the filament's tendency to produce ordered geometric shapes: hexagons, pentagons, squares, and dodecahedrons. Each of these shapes tessellated in 2-D, 3-D, or 4-D.

The filament was also obsessed with the numbers three and six. It used three ways to communicate: Sense Now, Sense Refined, and Sense Beyond. Its tether relied upon a microscopic triple helix. It created six equally spaced elevators with six stations and six ascenders mostly from carbon, element six, with six protons, six neutrons, and six electrons.

He claimed the filament abhorred both chaos and entropy—things like a supernova or death. It created order by consuming carbon and other elements ejected by a supernova to create a finely organized structure—the filament itself. And, since it perceived of life as order within an otherwise disordered universe, it sought out life, protected it, even recreated it.

In his summary, the psychologist suggested that while obsessive-compulsive behavior in humans was considered a personality disorder, the same traits might be central to the filament's way of thinking.

In the end, the audience voted for the middle ground: Promising, But I Need to Hear More. Adam voted for it himself. Many questions about the filament didn't have answers, at least not yet. Evidence obtained from the natural world often pointed only in a general direction, without ruling out alternatives. In this case, it was simply too soon to know if a truly alien life-form would become a helpful partner or an outsider with a philosophy so foreign we might eventually label it our nemesis.

Science was like that. Trying to comprehend a complex reality that didn't easily hand over its secrets couldn't be any other way.

The show wrapped, and Friday night's dinner date finally arrived. Halie picked an Italian restaurant with a sea view and red checkerboard tablecloths. Adam ordered their best bottle of Montepulciano, and they talked of their separate travels to Italian hill towns in Tuscany and Umbria. Adam dared to ask if she'd like to meet him there sometime.

Halie rested both hands on the table and leaned close. She lifted dark round eyes to Adam. "Travel is a great way to get to know someone, but it comes with a key question. One room or two?"

For Adam, the answer was obvious, but he took a moment to think about it from her perspective. Every woman—especially a female television personality—had to be careful with relationships. Guys needed to be vetted—a sad reality, but absolutely true. "Two rooms, I think… unless this rather sensitive question has been settled before the trip begins."

Halie nodded thoughtfully. She finished her last sip of wine and glanced up with a sizzling side-eye. "Then let's settle it. Spend the weekend at my house?"

Wide-eyed, Adam searched for the right words. "Remember seven days ago when we met on the platform, and you said you couldn't wait to see my lab?"

"I do. I loved it."

He pointed. "You had me then."

She laughed. "Remember yesterday when I dragged you onto the stage in front of all those people?"

He offered a cautious, "Yeah?"

"Your reaction was priceless. And that's when I decided to invite you over for the weekend."

He stared into her eyes, unable to break away even for a millisecond. "The things we learn when we're being honest."

She stared back, waiting. "So, that's a yes?"

Adam nodded. "That's a yes. I'd love to spend the weekend with you. When, exactly, do weekends start?"

Halie laughed again. "You are so precise!" She stood, checking her phone. "Almost ten p.m. on a Friday night. I'd say the weekend starts... um, right about now." She beckoned him with a curled finger.

Heart triggered, Adam stood. He felt lighter on his feet, as if he was back in one-quarter gravity. He wondered if he'd ever feel heavy again. It wasn't just their shared experience climbing to space—she had inspired him. Pushed him beyond the daredevil with scientific credentials to someone with greater awareness. Alongside Halie, he'd glimpsed grandeur hidden in an unexplored corner of the universe and had no doubt that by staying near to her, his sense of awe would only grow.

Adam helped Halie with her jacket, and they walked out arm in arm beneath a night sky sprinkled with stars, life, and much more.

EPILOGUE

SIX MONTHS LATER...

HALIE HOPPED FROM THE V-POD and through the Level 3 airlock. It wasn't any different than the Ecuador tether, but her first step into the station itself made it clear she was exactly sixty degrees of longitude further west.

A banner hung from the ceiling: "Welcome to Nuku Hiva!" Party balloons decorated with the coordinates 0° N 142° 37' 12" W formed an arched entryway. Beyond the arch were tables set with food and drink. Several hundred well-dressed people gathered in small groups or along the windows, enjoying the view from two thousand kilometers up.

She picked up a glass of champagne and headed to the windows, waving to guests who recognized her along the way. Halie stopped at the floor-to-ceiling glass and marveled at the grandeur of Earth spread before her, sighing.

This view will never get old.

The immense blue-and-white globe stretched to a curving horizon fully lit by a midday sun. This tether's mid-Pacific location made it the only one completely surrounded by water. No browns, tans, or greens of any continent. The nearest island was Nuku Hiva, French Polynesia, a thousand kilometers to the south.

"Stunning, isn't it?" the man nearest to her said, his eyes fixed outside. When he turned, he slapped his forehead. "Oh my God, you're Sahalie Spark! My apologies, you saw this view before any of us!"

Halie shook his hand. "Well, I haven't seen it from this tether. Lucky for us, we have six locations where we can gaze down on our beautiful planet. Wouldn't it be fun to climb them all?"

"Actually, I'm content with this one. I can see my house from here." He pointed.

Halie scrunched her brow, having a hard time imagining a house in the Pacific Ocean.

"See it? Just under those clouds."

Halie followed his pointing finger as best she could, finally noticing the only colors not blue or white. A faint green shoreline was capped by black. "Is that Hawaii?"

The man nodded. "The Big Island. I live in Kailua. I work with Yoon Ji-ho, so when I got the invitation I couldn't miss the chance of a lifetime."

"It's a wonderful opportunity, I agree. I hope more people will get the chance as time goes by. By the way, where is our party host?" Halie glanced around the crowd.

"Yoon took a group up to see the new ring segment at Level 4, but he should be back anytime."

The planned ring connecting all six tethers was the whole reason for the celebration. Yoon's company had been contracted to build three of its segments—with the filament's help, of course. Hauling up the required carbon, metals, and minerals by V-pod would have taken many years, but the filament had another method of transporting mass, a technique involving billions of microfibers that reached to the surface. Details were still not fully understood.

The first Level 4 ring segment was now open for business, stretching from the Nuku Hiva tether to the Ecuador tether, a distance of nearly eleven thousand kilometers. Halie couldn't wait to see it. She'd be spending the next several nights along this high altitude route as a guest.

She peered straight down, as much as the window allowed. "I heard they deployed debris screens?"

The man looked down too. "Yeah, they're hard to see, but follow the attachment cables and you'll notice a shimmer. That's the collection gel."

An axle about twenty meters long was positioned at the top of the window. Adam had noticed it on the Ecuador tether, but at the time it hadn't been functional, and they'd had no guesses what it was for.

Now, cables were attached at either end of the axle, disappearing from view as they dropped toward the ocean below. The cables could be raised or lowered depending on the desired collection elevation. A thin sheet of a flexible polymer gel was stretched between them, with a dozen more identical assemblies forming a hanging curtain beneath the station. As space debris hit the gel it would either be absorbed like a bug hitting flypaper or deflected to a slower trajectory that would send it spiraling into the atmosphere. Over time, debris was either collected or it disintegrated on reentry. With all six Level 3 stations in operation, space scientists calculated they would clear the Kill Zone within four years.

Halie thanked the man for his well-trained eye, posed for a selfie with him, then headed back to the crowd. She caught a glimpse of Yoon surrounded by reporters, cameras, and well-wishers. When she neared, he looked up and waved her over.

"The man of the hour," Halie said, easily parting the crowd and giving Yoon a hug.

"The woman of the year," he replied.

She pointed. "You know you're quite good at elevating a compliment. Is that a billionaire thing?"

Yoon smiled. "It is a Korean thing."

"Ah, I guess I need to spend more time in Seoul."

"My dear Sahalie Spark, you are better equipped than most when it comes to foreign cultures. I watch your show each week, usually while on my way to Level 4. You surprise me every time."

Halie hung on Yoon's arm while the surrounding crowd pretended not to listen in. "Surprise you in a good way?"

"Yes, of course. You have a commitment to your cause that most others cannot fathom."

"My *cause* is only to tell the truth—backed up by evidence, of course. It's not complicated."

"Yet few others do it. They spin, they cherry-pick, they promote misinformation and outright fantasies designed to make it hard for people to distinguish what's real. But you cut through the nonsense. You, Halie, are one of a kind."

"Thanks, Yoon. It's good to see you again. And thanks for hosting the party."

"Stay as long as you wish, my dear. When you are ready to continue up, the V-pod security staff are aware of our plans."

Halie kissed him on the cheek. Probably not what Koreans did on parting—more of an LA thing. She lingered at the party, chatted with people she'd never met, posed for pictures, and signed a few autographs.

When she'd had her fill of party-going, she made a beeline for the airlock. A V-pod waited on the up ribbon with a security officer standing at its door. "Going up, Ms. Spark?" he asked.

"Level 4, please." Her overnight bag was already stowed on the lower deck shelves.

He followed her inside and up the ladder to the seating area. She could have pressed the button herself, but she got the feeling that access was far more controlled now. She didn't mind. An elevator operator gave it a nostalgic feel, like walking into the lobby of the Empire State Building in an old 1940s movie.

Forty minutes and a chat about television productions later, they arrived at Level 4. Halie pulled her overnight bag from the luggage rack, and the operator guided her into the monorail train depot, instantly bringing back memories of an insane leap that had happened one-sixth of a world away. Her chin had completely healed, leaving hardly a mark. Her fear of falling was tamed too. Only last week, she'd stood with Adam on a narrow wall at the top of Lima's sea cliff, both of them giddy while taunting its fifty-meter drop—until a groundskeeper asked them to step down.

A monorail car waited on a single track pointing east. Halie peered through the exit door window. No longer a stub, the track extended indefinitely into space, looking much like a lonely desert highway that vanishes at the horizon.

She'd been told the track was a little like the causeway connecting the Florida Keys—long stretches of roadway with nothing on either side, eventually widening to isolated islands of enclosed land. In places, Yoon's construction crews had built whole villages. Someday, a full ring would encircle the planet with room for millions to live and work. But for now, this first segment was a refuge for a select group: people who had lost their bodies to death but whose minds had been stored in electronic holding pens, in some cases for centuries.

Human allotropes.

Not robots, but flesh and blood—just different. Today, she would be a guest among them. They'd constructed their own town at the halfway point between Nuku Hiva and Ecuador. If the rumors were true, more than a hundred people lived there. They'd named their town Sahalie.

After a quick explanation of monorail operation—which wasn't any more complicated than a V-pod—Halie said goodbye. The V-pod operator promised to return to pick her up in three days' time.

She climbed into a train car with seating space for six and pushed a single button. Automation took care of the rest. The airlock door closed behind. The exit door opened ahead, and the monorail car started forward. It gained speed without a sound and only minimal vibration. Above was a scattering of stars and a daytime moon in its third-quarter phase. Below, the blue Pacific stretched to the eastern horizon. It felt like a high-flying jet on cruise.

Minutes became an hour, and the vast expanse of the Pacific continued. Halie had crossed on commercial flights, but now she was hundreds of times higher and still couldn't find the boundaries of this grandest of oceans.

Earth truly is a water planet.

Halie closed her eyes. When she opened them, the car was slowing, and land was now in sight—the coastline of Mexico, Baja, and the conspicuous intermountain depression of the central valley of California.

The car shot into a tunnel, past several bank-vault-style doors, and into an enclosed space that widened rapidly. The tunnel's ceiling lifted higher overhead—clear glass that allowed the sun to shine in. To the left and right, farmland mixed with carefully organized groves of trees. She could easily be riding a bullet train crossing rural Japan except for a distinct edge to the land, visible at either side. Beyond the artificial landscape's edges, Earth made its presence known, lest visitors forget they were traveling along a vast ring at the planet's waistline.

After a minute, the car slowed into a station and stopped alongside a platform no different than a metro or subway system. Halie stepped out, roller bag in tow.

Fresh air filled her lungs, as clean as any countryside. It had an earthy smell that complemented the rustle of leaves on trees and the chirps of birds. In the distance, Halie could swear she heard a cow moo.

A sign on the platform read:

Welcome to Sahalie
Elevation: 4,029,824 meters
Gravity: 37%
Population: growing

Halie took a selfie, then started down the only pathway leading away from the station. Ahead, a classic angled-roof barn stood next to a small pond surrounded by modest hills. Houses of various sizes, designs, and colors dotted the hillsides. The path led up the first hill, easy enough to climb in low gravity.

"Anyone home?" Halie called out. Only the chirping birds replied. She watched as several flew over the house, their wings flapping no differently than on Earth, though these birds probably enjoyed the ease of movement as much as humans.

At the crest of the hill, she had a better view to farmlands beyond, alive with activity. A tractor drove slowly along a gravel road. A hay bailer worked one field and a cultivator on another. The higher vantage point also gave a stunning view beyond the ring's edge. The coastline of California stood out clearly, perhaps why the human allotropes had chosen this place. Los Angeles, the home Mash could never return to, was a glance away.

"Hey!" a voice yelled. Halie turned to see two black figures running along a path bordering one of the fields. Humanlike, but not human.

She watched with nervous anticipation as the two-legged figures bounded up the hill with long strides and an African impala spring in their step. Knees and ankles moved in ways no human could. A slim waist broadened to shoulders wide enough and arms long enough to wrap around a ponderosa pine. As the two came closer, Halie was charmed by a very human face framed by collar-length hair. Pink hair.

"Smack-a-doodle whack jack! It's great to see you again!"

Smooth facial skin was colored in glossy tones of dark brown. Silver accents on the nose line and eyebrow ridges gracefully swirled as if they'd been drawn by a calligrapher with a sure hand. Eyes sparkled in a rainbow of colors. Her irises might literally be inset diamonds.

"It's the new me. What do you think?"

Halie opened her mouth, but only a breezy "Uhh" came out.

"That bad?" A rust-red shirt inscribed with "Aloha Maui" covered her torso. Dark blue spandex served as shorts with flip-flops to match. She extended impressively long arms straight out. Black hands had an extra digit. She didn't look at all like the original Mash, but she sounded like her.

"Sorry, Mash," Halie said. "It's all great. It's just that I wasn't expecting—"

"Such polish?" Mash finished. Her grin showed teeth. She drew fingers across a handsome chin. "No pores. No zits. Smooth as a baby's bottom."

Halie laughed and rushed into the new Mash's waiting oversized arms. Her back felt warm. Her hair smelled of bubble gum and baker's yeast. "It's great to see you too, Mash."

Mash ushered forward her slightly taller companion who lagged a few paces behind. "This is Quiso Yupanqui, my Incan friend."

Halie attempted an awkward shake with his larger hand. "Nice to meet you, Quiso. Mash says you're originally from the sixteenth century?"

"Indeed I was." His voice was deep and resonant. Instead of silver, green accents adorned his dark face. Curly hair tumbled over black ears. He wore the same spandex shorts as Mash, but without a top. Muscular ripples across his chest, shoulders, and upper arms seemed functional but bore little resemblance to familiar male anatomy. "Over the years, I have found time to educate myself to modern standards. My long period of bonding with the filament had its advantages."

"So, what do you think of the twenty-first century?"

"Busy," Quiso said, a tight smile forming on his narrow lips. "I prefer potato farming. In five centuries, soil has not changed."

"He's teaching me how to farm," Mash said. "You should see me hoeing weeds. It's surprisingly meditative—once I set my arms to automatic mode. I was always an earthy type, I just needed to put the camera down long enough to see the world with my own eyes. Well... not my *original* eyes."

She rapidly beat silvery eyelids, creating a mystical effect of sparkling colors projected outward in a vibration of effervescent light. Halie watched, dumbfounded by the radiant spectacle. "Do that again." Mash did. A Disney animation of a gentle forest creature in love couldn't produce such a delightful visual effect.

"Hell of a body you have now. Got any other tricks in there?"

"You have no idea," Mash offered, straight-faced. She gave a knowing glance to Quiso. "But on certain matters, my lips are sealed."

Halie pulled back, hands up in surrender. "None of my business."

"It could be, if you get your own Gazelle Shell," Mash offered.

"Is that what they're calling these bodies?"

"Eh, we make this stuff up as we go. Gazelle Shell, Super-Vision, Zappy Tips."

"Zappy Tips?"

"Kind of a lightning-bolt-out-of-the-fingertips thing that he does." Mash motioned to Quiso. "I'm still in training on that one."

"Wow. So, these new bodies have some… extra features?"

"They do. When you're an old lady with creaks and pains, you should join us," Mash said with silver brows raised.

Halie sighed. "I'd have to think about that. I'm happy for you, but it's a new world, and we all need time to navigate it."

News reports had identified three people so far who had voluntarily opted to switch bodies. All were physically disabled in some way. Each had been excited about their new option, even if it meant never returning to Earth's surface again. Unlike human bodies, the Gazelle Shells, as Mash called them, weren't fully independent. The ring provided essential support to keep a consciousness tied to a physical form. No one yet knew the details, but the filament had made it clear it would not hold secrets for long. Education was the key to understanding. But like so many complex scientific topics, inserting a mind into a constructed body wasn't something that could be explained in a social media post.

Halie glanced back and forth between the exotic faces. "I'm trying to use my show to explore some of the concepts the filament showed me, but I can't claim to be a qualified teacher just yet. I have a feeling you two are way ahead on things like wormholes and hyperbolic geometries."

Mash pointed an extra thumb to Quiso. "This guy. Not me. That stuff is jack crack weird."

"You are doing fine, my love," Quiso reassured. "Fifty years from now you'll be surprised how much more you know." He turned his attention to Halie. "Do you understand how gears on a bicycle work?"

It was an odd question, but Halie answered, "I suppose. Maybe not as well as a mechanical engineer."

"But if that engineer explained sprocket teeth ratios and the leverage gained via a linked chain pulley, you *could* understand?"

"I'm sure I could."

"Wormholes are no different, once you have mastered the basics."

"Ah, yes." Halie mocked a whisper to Mash. "Hang on to this guy. He's good. Zappy Tips and all."

"I have learned from Sense Beyond," Quiso said. "The filament seeks order over chaos wherever it goes. It seeks life over death. It attempts to turn a Kill Zone of debris into useful space. But it does not pretend it can create widespread order without help. And so, it teaches when it finds receptive students."

"That's us?"

"For this moment in time, yes, that is us."

"I'd love to hear more," Halie said.

"Then you shall," Quiso replied. "You are here for three days?"

"I am. Can you put me up?"

Mash pointed to a house with a grass roof near the top of one hill. "That's ours. Warning, it's rustic. Closer to the remodeled shacks in Topanga Canyon than Beverly Hills posh."

"But I'm guessing you have a view of California?" Halie asked.

"A great view. We have a telescope too. We watch the fog rolling into LA and make bets how far it will get before sunset. Quiso wins every time. He's like an ancient Incan meteorologist. Amazing what this guy knows."

Quiso put an arm around Mash. Halie glanced to both of them, feeling comfortable that Mash had found a good, if unlikely, partner. Their age difference was more than five hundred years, but their bodies were exactly the same—brand-new.

"Have they nailed Marco yet?" Mash asked as they climbed the hill.

"Still in progress. Justice is slow, but thanks for your testimony. Sounds like you were a star witness."

"A dead witness! First time ever! I told the prosecutors we overheard Marco and his mobsters crowing about their plan in the Level 5 cavern before you and Adam got back from Level 6. No mention of explosives, but Quiso and I knew something bad was going down."

"Bad indeed. It could have been awful."

"That guy is such an Oompa Loompa Sick Prick. I hope he rots in a Brazilian jail cell."

"Yeah, who knows. I've learned to compartmentalize my thoughts of Marco to a few neurons. He's not worth anything more."

Halie reached into her overnight bag and handed Mash a small box. She had planned to wait until she got settled, but something about the unexpected beauty of farmland backed up by an ocean planet made it feel an appropriate setting. "I brought something special for you."

With four dexterous fingers and two thumbs on each hand, Mash opened the box and withdrew a golden trophy—a statuette of a winged woman thrusting six intertwined golden rings to the sky. Only recently had Halie realized the award given by the National Academy of Television Arts and Sciences represented a model of a carbon atom orbited by six electrons—a coincidence she didn't take lightly.

"We won an Emmy for our Ecuador story," Halie explained. "You, me, and Paul. I was never prouder when I walked on to that stage. I only wish you could have been there."

Mash's diamond eyes sparkled. She put a hand over her heart, assuming she had one somewhere inside. "Aw, that's fantastic. Really, this means a lot to me." She ran a finger across the engraved name on the statuette's pedestal: *Mashup*. "A reminder of who I used to be."

"Seems to me that Mashup is still who you are."

Mash dragged her pink hair back with her flexible black hand. "More of a physical mashup these days, but, yeah, I'm still me inside."

Halie pulled her friend close. "Inside is where it counts."

Arm in arm, they walked to the house. In the coming months, Halie would need to explain to the world the incredible story of human allotropes and their ability to learn from Sense Beyond—superpowers included. No doubt, some topics would be met with accusations and fear. Halie had her own concerns. But she would tell the story truthfully, as best she could, with an eye out for the intrigue embedded within the mysterious, the awe existing beside the unsettling.

The human adventure had always been this way. Curiosity balanced by fear or mistrust. Challenging quests that led to grand discoveries. Successes and failures. Halie had no complaints. In fact, it put a smile on her face.

For one lifetime, I get to be part of this amazing universe. Lucky me!

THE END

AFTERWORD

I hope you enjoyed this story. I had a lot of fun writing it. Funny how writing can sometimes be even more enjoyable than reading. As I edited this book and finished its illustrations, a dozen new story ideas came to mind, each worth exploring. Of course, a single book can't include every spinoff, so I imagine a new series has begun.

If you enjoyed this story, please leave a review on Amazon. Good reviews convince others to join in, and that makes a sequel far more likely. I also do my best to read those reviews because it helps me shape the next story. But enough of next stories. Let's talk about the science in this story.

Gravity

Some readers may not believe me when I say gravity exists in space. We're so used to seeing astronauts floating both inside and outside their spacecraft. We've read or watched science fiction featuring interplanetary spacecraft that employ a rotating cylinder for centrifugal acceleration or use *gravity generators* that function in some unknown way. In fact, any science fiction that *doesn't* mention how crew members manage to walk around their spaceship runs the risk of being labeled fantasy! Oh, the shame!

But gravity exists in space. There's nothing inaccurate about prior sci-fi. Occupants on a ship bound for Jupiter would in fact be weightless once the engines shut off. Their ship is then falling toward Jupiter, and falling is weightlessness. Interplanetary voyages use what astronautical engineers call the Hohmann transfer, which is an elliptical path around the sun that is precisely calculated to intersect the targeted planet.

Solar gravity reaches out across all of interplanetary space. It's what keeps the planets together as a solar system. A spacecraft's momentum can act against the downward pull (like a basketball arcing upward), but unless additional rocket thrust pushes it beyond escape velocity, any spacecraft will eventually reach the apogee of its elliptical arc and fall back.

A space elevator is different. Stations like those depicted in this story are fixed to the tether, which is fixed to Earth's surface. Nothing is coasting or arcing or orbiting. Climb to a station, drop a basketball from waist height, and it will fall straight down just as it would on Earth—with one slight difference. At the surface, the basketball hits the floor in 0.45 seconds. At the Level 2 observatory (300 kilometers up), it takes slightly longer to hit the floor, 0.47 seconds. Climb higher to the Level 3 observatory (2,024 kilometers up), and now it takes 0.60 seconds. Gravity decreases as you climb, but it's always there.

So, why did Halie and Adam become weightless at Level 6? To explain that we need to include Earth's rotation. Our planet is like a merry-go-round. As it spins, it's trying to throw us off! The word spin might be too aggressive, since our 24-hour cycle is more like a lazy turn against the fixed background of stars. But it's fast enough to measure a difference in our body weight. Stand at the equator and you'll weigh about a half-kilogram less than you would at the north or south poles. Earth really is trying to throw you off, it's just not succeeding.

But climb higher and the centrifugal acceleration from Earth's rotation gets stronger. Think of it as being slung around in a circle at the end of a rope. The longer the rope, the faster you move.

I didn't include it in Chapter 27, but here's the complete equation for Apparent Gravity, which combines Earth's gravitational pull (the first term) and centrifugal acceleration (the second term which acts in the opposite direction, so it's subtracted).

$$g_{app} = \frac{GM}{r^2} - \omega^2 r$$

As distance (r) increases, Earth's gravity decreases by a factor of r^2. At the same time, centrifugal acceleration increases by a factor of

r. The math tells us that gravity decreases more rapidly than centrifugal acceleration increases. And, while gravity overwhelms us at the surface, eventually these opposing forces balance. That balance occurs at a specific height forever tied to our planet: 35,786 kilometers above the surface. Geostationary height.

I love this number. I love that we've learned how to calculate it. It tells us that nature isn't capricious or vague. Nature is mathematical, exacting, and unchanging. Nature can be understood.

Space Elevators

For much of 2024, I had the opportunity and privilege to work with the fine people at the International Space Elevator Consortium—top level scientists, engineers, and proponents of a positive future. They took me in as one of their own. Some had read my previous books and told me how much they enjoyed them. If a "Key to the Elevator" existed, they would have awarded it to me. They were very kind.

I had already consumed every word in Bradley C. Edwards' 2002 book, *The Space Elevator*, but I learned much more from people who are dedicating their talents to make this pie in the sky dream a reality. I can tell you without a shred of exaggeration that many of you reading this will live to see a working space elevator in your lifetime. It won't be the colossal tower of past science fiction... you know, the bazillion-story megastructure that's basically an elongated, futuristic skyscraper.

No, a real space elevator will be more modest: a plain, thin ribbon and industrial-grade climbers that dutifully drag satellites and other cargo into space for $1/100^{th}$ the price of a rocket launch. Simplicity and efficiency, that's the plan. Once they've proven cargo transport, I'm sure the designers will add a climber capable of carrying people too.

For this book, I decided to start close to the reality planned by ISEC. The tether described in this story is close to what we will see someday: a ribbon thinner than cellophane but as firm as steel—so thin, its edge could slice you in half, and with a polished surface like a mirror. Its tensile strength will be higher than any material ever produced. They're already close to manufacturing such a ribbon in short lengths. Making it longer is mostly a matter of scaling.

A real space elevator will certainly have an apex anchor station at its top (100,000 kilometers or higher) and a geosynchronous station at 35,786 kilometers. These will be places where satellites and spacecraft to other planets are launched, but they could also serve as hotels for space tourism.

When someone builds the first space elevator, I vote for adding at least one low-Earth station. A station at 2,000 kilometers would provide a stunning view of our beautiful planet, far better than at geostationary height (which is just too far away). Want to see for yourself? Fire up Google Earth and use the zoom slider to set the distance to 35,786 kilometers. The Earth becomes a small ball in the distance. But drop down to 2,000 kilometers then look up to the horizon. Dramatic, right?

A space elevator with publicly accessible low-Earth observation stations would quickly become the most popular structure ever built. It would inspire the world, provide access for more of us to witness the beauty of our planet from above, and encourage generations to protect our thin and fragile atmosphere. A space elevator will cost billions but will be worth trillions.

Kill Zone

Tragically, we're as close to a debris catastrophe as we are to building a space elevator, which is why it occurred to me to combine them into one story. Whatever you think about billionaires in space, know that each one of them has their own plan to launch tens of thousands of private satellites. As of 2024, Starlink already had 6,400 satellites in low Earth orbit with plans to increase that number to 34,400. These are *proprietary* satellites. Only one company, Starlink, can use them. Every other communications company must launch their own satellite array, and that's exactly what is happening.

No one knows how many satellites can be managed safely without crashing into each other in a chain reaction disaster called the Kessler Syndrome (yes, it's a real thing). But we do know we're already skirting the edges of orbital capacity. Near misses and lack of coordination among the players are already occurring today. And while satellite arrays are designed to be deorbited on command, once a satellite is turned into shredded metal it becomes an uncontrollable swarm of high-speed projectiles impossible to track. It won't take much to turn managed spaceflight into deadly chaos.

To this day, no space agency or government is proposing the obvious alternative: treating space like any other precious resource and establishing strict regulations and high fees for anyone consuming an orbit. Use the funds to clean up existing space debris. Today, we are truly in the wild west days of spaceflight where anything goes.

Rhythmic Onomatopoeia

Mash often speaks in a four-beat two-beat cadence, essentially *doodle-doodle dit dot.* She belongs to a cultish group called Dingers who came into existence from the 1950s song Rama Lama Ding Dong and went from there. Surprisingly, Dingers find the same cadence in many songs, but especially in John Lennon's "I Am the Walrus". Because of copyright laws, I'm not allowed to print those lyrics, but you can easily find them online.

Are Dingers real? No. I made them up. Is the cadence real? It is now. Go ahead and search, I bet you'll find it all over the place, sometimes in the most unlikely places. For example, in the word *onomatopoeia* itself. Or in this Maxwell House coffee commercial from the 1960s:

https://www.youtube.com/watch?v=BWEYjEQ75ZM

My editor, Eliza Dee, is one of the smartest people I know. Here's what she had to say about the Dinger beat and Mash's use of it:

In poetic terms, the four beats would consist of two trochees (long-short or stressed-unstressed) plus one spondee (long-long or stressed-stressed). I mention this because 1) I'm a nerd; 2) it's something the character would probably know and find interesting; 3) this format yields "trochee trochee spondee"—itself an example of the practice (or at least it could be depending how you intoned it), which Mash would definitely enjoy, I think.

Indeed, Mash would enjoy this absurd deep dive into cultish behavior and circular references. All I can say is, trochee trochee spondee to everyone!

Carbon Life

When I was a kid, most aliens were depicted as bulbous-headed humanoids wearing Greek robes. Sure, they were more intelligent than us, but their bodies were laughable, limited either by what the television and movie people could imagine or by their makeup budget. Writers like Isaac Asimov and Larry Niven did considerably better. And in 1977, *Star Wars* moved the needle toward exotic.

Today, most scientists and fans of sci-fi believe that life beyond Earth almost certainly exists. And while our opinions of what we'll someday discover diverge, the scientific consensus is that alien life will be unlike anything on Earth.

This is where things get fun. I love it when people with good imaginations push the boundaries. What could an alien look like? How would it think? How would it interact with its environment?

I tried to answer some of these questions. I wanted to create a carbon lifeform that was difficult to distinguish from a machine, wasn't confined to a compact shape, and thought using a layered structure unlike any Earth organism.

But why is such an exotic lifeform still based on carbon? Because no other atom has its range of chemistry. With four valence electrons just aching to attach to another atom, carbon will bond with almost anything, but especially with itself, hydrogen, oxygen, nitrogen, boron, phosphorus, silicon, fluorine, and lithium. The molecular recipes are endless, and many are useful to life. Carbon is so aggressively combinatorial it has its own branch of chemistry, organic chemistry. And because carbon can be found everywhere, there's no question in my mind that when we finally discover life elsewhere, it will be carbon based. In a word, carbon is amazing.

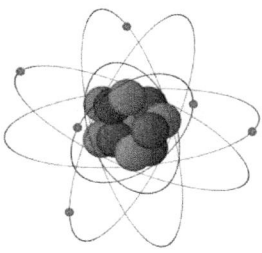

Thanks for reading!

Douglas Phillips

Want to stay in touch? Add your name to my email list and I'll keep you informed about new books I'm writing and upcoming events.

http://douglasphillipsbooks.com

If you enjoyed this book, please consider writing a short review (in addition to your star rating). It only takes only a minute, and your review helps future readers as well as the author. Books and book series really do live or die on reader reviews. For more information on how to leave a review, go to http://douglasphillipsbooks.com/contact.

ACKNOWLEDGMENTS

Thanks to my wife, Marlene, and my son, Bryant, both excellent writers themselves. Your brilliant ideas, feedback, and support along the way were invaluable.

Many thanks to my author friends at Critique Circle, especially Kathryn Hoff, Darren Cook, and Michael Shoemaker. Portions of this story went through significant rewrites based on your early and insightful critiques.

Thank you to my new friends at the International Space Elevator Consortium. Dennis Wright, Adrian Nixon, Larry Bartoszek, Peter Swan, Sandee Schaeffer, Michael Schaeffer, Charlie Krone, and many others who I had the opportunity to meet in person. Your expertise and enthusiasm not only made this a better story but left me without any doubt that space elevators will one day rise into the sky, and the vision of Konstantin Tsiolkovsky and Bradley Edwards will become real.

Beta readers, what can I say? You're the best! I was so lucky to have friends Cindy and Ron Vandor to give me the inside scoop on television journalism, provide guidance on how breaking news is covered, and teach me a thing or two about Emmys. There's part of both of you in Sahalie Spark! I was also blown away by the incredibly detailed feedback I got from professionals in science and law: Greg Mendell, Robert Rubinstayn, and Laura Leigh Blackston. Your help greatly improved the science and the characters! I was also fortunate to work with a motivated group of people, many who know the English language better than me, or science fiction, or both: David Ryzman, Terri Crotti, Juliana Greco, Trevor Davenport, Jay Moskowitz, Georganna Hancock, Patti Struck, and John Stephens. Thank you all!

Thanks to Dane Low at ebooklaunch.com for another great cover. Thanks also to Stewart McElhannon who created the 3D model for the V-pod based on nothing more than my imagined description! It turned out great!

And finally, thanks to my proof reader, Michelle Coxall, for spotting the glitches that any edited manuscript has before it's committed to paper, e-book pixels, and audio recording. Great job!

FROM THE AUTHOR

Ascending Carbon Series

First Ascent —Book 1

Quantum Series

Quantum Incident —Prologue

Quantum Space —Book 1

Quantum Void —Book 2

Quantum Time —Book 3

Quantum Entangled —Book 4

Quantum Chaos —Book 5

And more…

Phenomena

Lost at L3

For these and other works by Douglas Phillips, please visit
http://douglasphillipsbooks.com. While you're there, sign up to the
mailing list to stay informed on new books in the works and
upcoming events.

Printed in Great Britain
by Amazon

61862580R00211